"Beloved auth... ...new heights
in this wise and beautiful novel.... The timeless wisdom
in these pages will stay with you long after the book is
closed."
—Susan Wiggs, #1 *New York Times* bestselling author, on
A Girl's Guide to Moving On

"Macomber fans will leave the Rose Harbor Inn with
warm memories of healing, hope, and enduring love."
—*Kirkus Reviews*

"*A Girl's Guide to Moving On* is Debbie Macomber's finest
novel.... I absolutely loved it!"
—Dorothea Benton Frank,
New York Times bestselling author

"Debbie dazzles! A wonderful sto... ...
forgiveness and the power of love... ...
page!"

...an Mallery,
#1 *New York* ... ...es bestselling author

Praise for *New York Times* bes... ...hor
Linda Good...

"The second of Goodnight's Hon... Ridge no... ...
Sparrow] is an aching, absorbing ...yet ... ...ad."

..Booklist

"*The Memory House* is a beautiful... ...
story filled with tenderness and ...
—*New Yor*... ...

"Goodnight's prose is elegant."

Also available from Debbie Macomber

Blossom Street

The Shop on Blossom Street
A Good Yarn
Susannah's Garden
Back on Blossom Street
Twenty Wishes
Summer on Blossom Street
Hannah's List
The Knitting Diaries
   "The Twenty-First Wish"
A Turn in the Road

Cedar Cove

16 Lighthouse Road
204 Rosewood Lane
311 Pelican Court
44 Cranberry Point
50 Harbor Street
6 Rainier Drive
74 Seaside Avenue
8 Sandpiper Way
92 Pacific Boulevard
1022 Evergreen Place
Christmas in Cedar Cove
   (*5-B Poppy Lane* and
   A Cedar Cove Christmas)
1105 Yakima Street
1225 Christmas Tree Lane

The Dakota Series

Dakota Born
Dakota Home
Always Dakota
Buffalo Valley

For a complete list of books by Debbie Macomber, please visit www.debbiemacomber.com.

And from Linda Goodnight

The Memory House
The Rain Sparrow

and don't miss
The Innkeeper's Sister,
coming soon!

DEBBIE MACOMBER

LINDA GOODNIGHT

The Road to Love

HQN™

ISBN-13: 978-0-373-79929-9

The Road to Love

Copyright © 2017 by Harlequin Books S.A.

The publisher acknowledges the copyright holders
of the additional works as follows:

Love by Degree
Copyright © 1987 by Debbie Macomber

The Rain Sparrow
Copyright © 2016 by Linda Goodnight

Recycling programs
for this product may
not exist in your area.

CONTENTS

LOVE BY DEGREE

Debbie Macomber

To all my friends at the Vero Beach Book Center—
Chad, Cynthia, Sheila, Debbie, Jamie and Rose Marie.
Thank you for all you do to support my books.

CHAPTER ONE

THE MELODIOUS SOUNDS of a love ballad drifted through the huge three-storey house in Seattle's Capitol Hill. Ellen Cunningham hummed along as she rubbed her wet curls with a thick towel. These late-afternoon hours before her housemates returned were the only time she had the place to herself, so she'd taken advantage of the peaceful interlude to wash her hair. Privacy was at a premium with three men in the house, and she couldn't always count on the upstairs bathroom being available later in the evening.

Twisting the fire-engine-red towel around her head, turban style, Ellen walked barefoot across the hallway toward her bedroom to retrieve her blouse. Halfway there, she heard the faint ding of the oven timer, signalling that her apple pie was ready to come out.

She altered her course and bounded down the wide stairway. Her classes that day had gone exceptionally well. She couldn't remember ever being happier, even though she still missed Yakima, the small apple-growing community in central Washington, where she'd been raised. But she was adjusting well to life in the big city. She'd waited impatiently for the right time—and enough money—to complete her education, and she'd been gratified by the way everything had fallen into place during the past summer. Her older sis-

ter had married, and her "baby" brother had entered the
military. For a while, Ellen was worried that her wid-
owed mother might suffer from empty nest syndrome,
so she'd decided to delay her education another year.
But her worries had been groundless, as it turned out.
James Simonson, a widower friend of her mother's, had
started dropping by the house often enough for Ellen
to recognize a romance brewing between them. The
time had finally come for Ellen to make the break, and
she did it without guilt or self-reproach.

Clutching a pot holder in one hand, she opened the
oven door and lifted out the steaming pie. The fragrance of spicy apples spread through the kitchen, mingling with the savory aroma of the stew that simmered
on top of the stove. Carefully, Ellen set the pie on a wire
rack. Her housemates appreciated her culinary efforts
and she enjoyed doing little things to please them. As
the oldest, Ellen fit easily into this household of young
men; in fact, she felt that the arrangement was ideal. In
exchange for cooking, a little mothering on the side and
a share of the cleaning, Ellen paid only a nominal rent.

The unexpected sound of the back door opening
made her swivel around.

"What's going on?" Standing in the doorway was a
man with the most piercing green eyes Ellen had ever
seen. She noticed immediately that the rest of his features were strongly defined and perfectly balanced. His
cheekbones were high and wide, yet his face was lean
and appealing. He frowned, and his mouth twisted in
an unspoken question.

In one clenched hand he held a small leather suitcase, which he slowly lowered to the kitchen floor.
"Who are you?" He spoke sharply, but it wasn't anger

or disdain that edged his voice; it was genuine bewilderment.

Ellen was too shocked to move. When she'd whirled around, the towel had slipped from her head and covered one eye, blocking her vision. But even a one-eyed view of this stranger was enough to intimidate her. She had to admit that his impeccable business suit didn't look very threatening—but then she glanced at his glowering face again.

With as much poise as possible, she raised a hand to straighten the turban and realized that she was standing in the kitchen wearing washed-out jeans and a white bra. Grabbing the towel from her head, she clasped it to her chest for protection. "Who are *you?*" she snapped back.

She must have made a laughable sight, holding a red bath towel in front of her like a matador before a charging bull. This man reminded her of a bull. He was tall, muscular and solidly built. And she somehow knew that when he moved, it would be with effortless power and sudden speed. Not exactly the type of man she'd want to meet in a dark alley. Or a deserted house, for that matter. Already Ellen could see the headlines: Small-Town Girl Assaulted in Capitol Hill Kitchen.

"What are you doing here?" she asked in her sternest voice.

"This is my home!" The words vibrated against the walls like claps of thunder.

"Your home?" Ellen choked out. "But… I live here."

"Not anymore, you don't."

"Who are you?" she demanded a second time.

"Reed Morgan."

Ellen relaxed. "Derek's brother?"

"Half-brother."

No wonder they didn't look anything alike. Derek was a lanky, easy-going nineteen-year-old, with dark hair and equally dark eyes. Ellen would certainly never have expected Derek to have a brother—even a half-brother—like this.

"I—I didn't know you were coming," she hedged, feeling utterly foolish.

"Apparently." He cocked one eyebrow ever so slightly as he stared at her bare shoulders. He shoved his bag out of the doorway, then sighed deeply and ran his hands through his hair. Ellen couldn't help making the irrelevant observation that it was a dark auburn, thick and lustrous with health.

He looked tired and irritable, and he obviously wasn't in the best frame of mind for any explanation as to why she was running around his kitchen half-naked. "Would you like a cup of coffee?" she offered congenially, hoping to ease the shock of her presence.

"What I'd like is for you to put some clothes on."

"Yes, of course." Forcing a smile, Ellen turned abruptly and left the kitchen, feeling humiliated that she could stand there discussing coffee with a stranger when she was practically naked. Running up the stairs, she entered her room and removed her shirt from the end of the bed. Her fingers were trembling as she fastened the buttons.

Her thoughts spun in confusion. If this house was indeed Reed Morgan's, then he had every right to ask her to leave. She sincerely hoped he'd made some mistake. Or that she'd misunderstood. It would be difficult to find another place to share this far into the school term. And her meager savings would be quickly wiped out if she had to live somewhere on her own. Ellen's brow wrinkled with worry as she dragged a brush through her short, bouncy curls, still slightly damp. Being forced to move wouldn't be a tragedy, but definitely a problem, and she was understandably apprehensive. The role of housemother came naturally to Ellen. The boys could hardly boil water without her. She'd only recently broken them in to using the vacuum cleaner and the washing machine without her assistance.

When she returned to the kitchen, she found Reed leaning against the counter, holding a mug of coffee.

"How long has this cozy set-up with you and Derek been going on?"

"About two months now," she answered, pouring herself a cup of coffee. Although she rarely drank it she felt she needed something to occupy her hands. "But it's not what you're implying. Derek and I are nothing more than friends."

"I'll just bet."

Ellen could deal with almost anything except sarcasm. Gritting her teeth until her jaws ached, she replied in an even, controlled voice. "I'm not going to stand here and argue with you. Derek advertised for a housemate and I answered the ad. I came to live here with him and the others and—"

"The *others?*" Reed choked on his mouthful of coffee. "You mean there's more of you around?"

Expelling her breath slowly, Ellen met his scowl. "There's Derek, Pat and—"

"Is Pat male or female?" The sheer strength of his personality seemed to fill the kitchen. But Ellen refused to be intimidated.

"Pat is a male friend who attends classes at the university with Derek and me."

"So you're all students?"

"Yes."

"All freshmen?"

"Yes."

He eyed her curiously. "Aren't you a bit old for that?"

"I'm twenty-five." She wasn't about to explain her circumstances to this man.

The sound of the front door opening and closing drew their attention to the opposite end of the house. Carrying an armload of books, Derek Morgan sauntered into the kitchen and stopped cold when he caught sight of his older brother.

"Hi, Reed." Uncertain eyes flew to Ellen as if seeking reassurance. A worried look pinched the boyishly handsome face. Slowly, he placed his books on the counter.

"Derek."

"I see you've met Ellen." Derek's welcoming smile was decidedly forced.

"We more or less stumbled into each other." Derek's stiff shoulders relaxed as Reed straightened and set the mug aside.

"I didn't expect you back so soon."

Momentarily, Reed's gaze slid to Ellen. "That much is obvious. Do you want to tell me what's going on here, little brother?"

"It's not as bad is it looks."

"Right now it doesn't look particularly good."

"I can explain everything."

"I hope so."

Nervously swinging her arms, Ellen stepped forward. "If you two will excuse me, I'll be up in my room." The last thing she wanted was to find herself stuck between the two brothers while they settled their differences.

"No, don't go," Derek said quickly. His dark eyes pleaded with her to stay.

Almost involuntarily Ellen glanced at Reed for guidance.

"By all means, stay." But his expression wasn't encouraging.

A growing sense of resentment made her arch her back and thrust out her chin defiantly. Who was this... this *man* to burst into their tranquil lives and raise havoc? The four of them lived congenially together, all doing their parts in the smooth running of the household.

"Are you charging rent?" Reed asked.

Briefly Derek's eyes met Ellen's. "It makes sense, doesn't it? This big old house has practically as many bedrooms as a dorm. I didn't think it would hurt." He swallowed. "I mean, with you being in the Middle East and all. The house was...so empty."

"How much are you paying?" Reed directed the question at Ellen. That sarcastic look was back and Ellen hesitated.

"How much?" Reed repeated.

Ellen knew from the way Derek's eyes widened that they were entering into dangerous territory.

"It's different with Ellen," Derek hurried to explain. "She does all the shopping and the cooking, so the rest of us—"

"Are you sure that's all she provides?" Reed interrupted harshly.

Ellen's gaze didn't waver. "I pay thirty dollars a week, but believe me, I earn my keep." The second the words slipped out, Ellen wanted to take them back.

"I'm sure you do."

Ellen was too furious and outraged to speak. How dared he barge into this house and immediately assume the worst? All right, she'd been walking around half-naked, but she hadn't exactly been expecting company.

Angrily Derek stepped forward. "It's not like that, Reed."

"I discovered her prancing around the kitchen in her bra. What else am I supposed to think?"

Derek groaned and cast an accusing look at Ellen. "I just ran down to get the pie out of the oven," she said in her own defence.

"Let me assure you," Derek said, his voice quavering with righteousness. "You've got this all wrong." He glared indignantly at his older brother. "Ellen isn't that kind of woman. I resent the implication. You owe us both an apology."

From the stunned look on Reed's face, Ellen surmised that this could well be the first time Derek had stood up to his domineering brother. Her impulse was to clap her hands and shout: "Attaboy!" With immense effort she restrained herself.

Reed wiped a hand over his face and pinched the bridge of his nose. "Perhaps I do."

The front door opened and closed again. "Anyone here?" Monte's eager voice rang from the living room. The slam of his books hitting the stairs echoed through the hallway that led to the kitchen. "Something smells good." Skidding to an abrupt halt just inside the room, the tall student looked around at the somber faces. "What's up? You three look like you're about to attend a funeral."

"Are you Pat?" Reed asked.

"No, Monte."

Reed closed his eyes and wearily rubbed the back of his neck. "Just how many bedrooms have you rented out?"

Derek lowered his gaze to his hands. "Three."

"My room?" Reed asked.

"Yes, well, Ellen needed a place and it seemed logical to give her that one. You were supposed to be gone for a year. What happened?"

"I came home early."

Stepping forward, her fingers nervously laced together, Ellen broke into the tense interchange. "I'll move up a floor. I don't mind." No one was using the third floor of the house, which had at one time been reserved for the servants. The rooms were small and airless, but sleeping there was preferable to suffering the wrath of Derek's brother. Or worse, having to find somewhere else to live.

Reed responded with a dismissive gesture of his hand. "Don't worry about it. Until things are straightened out, I'll sleep up there. Once I've taken a long, hot shower and gotten some rest I might be able to make sense out of this mess."

"No, please," Ellen persisted. "If I'm in your room, then I should move."

"No," Reed grumbled on his way out the door, waving aside her offer. "It's only my house. I'll sleep in the servants' quarters."

Before Ellen could argue further, Reed was out of the kitchen and halfway up the stairs.

"Is there a problem?" Monte asked, opening the refrigerator. He didn't seem very concerned, but then he rarely worried about anything unless it directly affected his stomach. Ellen didn't know how any one person could eat so much. He never seemed to gain weight, but if it were up to him he'd feed himself exclusively on pizza and french fries.

"Do you want to tell me what's going on?" Ellen pressed Derek, feeling guilty but not quite knowing why. "I assumed your family owned the house."

"Well...sort of." He sank slowly into one of the kitchen chairs.

"It's the *sort of* that worries me." She pulled out the chair across from Derek and looked at him sternly.

"Reed *is* family."

"But he didn't know you were renting out the bedrooms?"

"He told me this job would last nine months to a year. I couldn't see any harm in it. Everywhere I looked there were ads for students wanting rooms to rent. It didn't seem right to live alone in this house with all these bedrooms."

"Maybe I should try to find someplace else to live," Ellen said reluctantly. The more she thought about it, the harder it was to see any other solution now that Reed had returned.

"Not before dinner," Monte protested, bringing a loaf of bread and assorted sandwich makings to the table.

"There's no need for anyone to leave," Derek said with defiant bravado. "Reed will probably only be around for a couple of weeks before he goes away on another assignment."

"Assignment?" Ellen asked, her curiosity piqued.

"Yeah. He travels all over the place—we hardly ever see him. And from what I hear, I don't think Danielle likes him being gone so much, either."

"Danielle?"

"They've been practically engaged for ages and... I don't know the whole story, but apparently Reed's put off tying the knot because he does so much traveling."

"Danielle must really love him if she's willing to wait." Ellen watched as Monte spread several layers of smoked ham over the inch-thick slice of Swiss cheese. She knew better than to warn her housemate that he'd ruin his dinner. After his triple-decker sandwich, Monte could sit down to a five-course meal—and then ask about dessert.

"I guess," Derek answered nonchalantly. "Reed's perfect for her. You'd have to meet Danielle to understand." Reaching into the teddy-bear-shaped cookie jar and helping himself to a handful, Derek continued. "Reed didn't mean to snap at everyone. Usually, he's a great brother. And Danielle's all right," he added without enthusiasm.

"It takes a special kind of woman to stick by a man that long without a commitment."

Derek shrugged. "I suppose. Danielle's got her own reasons, if you know what I mean."

Ellen didn't, but she let it go. "What does Reed do?"

"He's an aeronautical engineer for Boeing. He travels around the world working on different projects. This last one was somewhere in Saudi Arabia."

"What about the house?"

"Well, that's his, an inheritance from his mother's family, but he's gone so much of the time that he asked me if I'd live here and look after the place."

"What about us?" Monte asked. "Will big brother want us to move out?"

"I don't think so. Tomorrow morning I'll ask him. I can't see me all alone in this huge old place. It's not like I'm trying to make a fortune by collecting a lot of rent."

"If Reed wants us to leave, I'm sure something can be arranged." Already Ellen was considering different options. She didn't want her fate to be determined by a whim of Derek's brother.

"Let's not do anything drastic. I doubt he'll mind once he has a chance to think it through," Derek murmured with a thoughtful frown. "At least, I hope he won't."

Later that night as Ellen slipped between the crisply laundered sheets, she wondered about the man whose bed she occupied. Tucking the thick quilt around her shoulders, she fought back a wave of anxiety. Everything had worked out so perfectly that she should've expected *something* to go wrong. If anyone voiced objections to her being in Reed's house, it would probably be his almost-fiancée. Ellen sighed apprehensively. She had to admit that if the positions were reversed, she wouldn't want the man she loved sharing his house with another woman. Tomorrow she'd check around to see if she could find a new place to live.

ELLEN WAS SCRAMBLING EGGS the next morning when Reed appeared, coming down the narrow stairs that led from the third floor to the kitchen. He'd shaved, which emphasized the chiseled look of his jaw. His handsome face was weathered and everything about him spoke of health and vitality. Ellen paused, her fork suspended with raw egg dripping from the tines. She wouldn't call Reed Morgan handsome so much as striking. He had an unmistakable masculine appeal. Apparently the duties of an aeronautical engineer were more physically demanding than she'd suspected. Strength showed in the wide muscular shoulders and lean, hard build. He looked even more formidable this morning.

"Good morning," she greeted him cheerfully, as she continued to beat the eggs. "I hope you slept well."

Reed poured coffee into the same mug he'd used the day before. A creature of habit, Ellen mused. "Morning," he responded somewhat gruffly.

"Can I fix you some eggs?"

"Derek and I have already talked. You can all stay."

"Is that a yes or a no to the eggs?"

"I'm trying to tell you that you don't need to worry about impressing me with your cooking."

With a grunt of impatience, Ellen set the bowl aside and leaned forward, slapping her open palms on the countertop. "I'm scrambling eggs here. Whether you want some or not is entirely up to you. Believe me, if I was concerned about impressing you, I wouldn't do it with eggs."

For the first time, Ellen saw a hint of amusement touch those brilliant green eyes. "No, I don't suppose you would."

"Now that we've got that settled, would you like breakfast or not?"

"All right."

His eyes boldly searched hers and for an instant Ellen found herself regretting that there was a Danielle. With an effort, she turned away and brought her concentration back to preparing breakfast.

"Do you do all the cooking?" Just the way he asked made it sound as though he was already criticizing their household arrangements. Ellen bit back a sarcastic reply and busied herself melting butter and putting bread in the toaster. She'd bide her time. If Derek was right, his brother would soon be away on another assignment.

"Most of it," Ellen answered, pouring the eggs into the hot skillet.

"Who pays for the groceries?"

Ellen shrugged, hoping to give the appearance of nonchalance. "We all chip in." She did the shopping and most of the cooking. In return, the boys did their share of the housework—now that she'd taught them how.

The bread popped up from the toaster and Ellen reached for the butter knife, doing her best to ignore the overpowering presence of Reed Morgan.

"What about the shopping?"

"I enjoy it," she said simply, putting two more slices of bread in the toaster.

"I thought women all over America were fighting to get out of the kitchen."

"When a replacement is found, I'll be happy to step aside." She wasn't comfortable with the direction this conversation seemed to be taking. Reed was looking at her as though she was some kind of 1950s throwback.

Ellen liked to cook and as it turned out, the boys needed someone who knew her way around a kitchen, and she needed an inexpensive place to live. Everything had worked out perfectly....

She spooned the cooked eggs onto one plate and piled the toast on another, then carried it to the table, which gave her enough time to control her indignation. She was temporarily playing the role of surrogate mother to a bunch of college-age boys. All right, maybe that made her a little unusual these days, but she enjoyed living with Derek and the others. It helped her feel at home, and for now she needed that.

"Aren't you going to eat?" Reed stopped her on her way out of the kitchen.

"I'll have something later. The only time I can count on the bathroom being free in the mornings is when the boys are having breakfast. That is, unless you were planning to use it?"

Reed's eyes narrowed fractionally. "No."

"What's the matter? You've got that look on your face again."

"What look?"

"The one where you pinch your lips together as if you aren't pleased about something and you're wondering just how much you should say."

His tight expression relaxed into a slow, sensual grin. "Do you always read people this well?"

Ellen shook her head. "Not always. I just want to know what I've done this time."

"Aren't you concerned about living with three men?"

"No. Should I be?" She crossed her arms and leaned against the doorjamb, almost enjoying their conversation. The earlier antagonism had disappeared. She'd agree that her living arrangements were a bit unconventional, but they suited her. The situation was advantageous for her *and* the boys.

"Any one of them could fall in love with you."

With difficulty, Ellen restrained her laughter. "That's unlikely. They see me as their mother."

The corners of his mouth formed deep grooves as he tried—and failed—to suppress a grin. Raising one brow, he did a thorough inspection of her curves.

Hot color flooded her pale cheeks. "All right—a sister. I'm too old for them."

Monte sauntered into the kitchen, followed closely by Pat who muttered, "I thought I smelled breakfast."

"I was just about to call you," she told them and hurried from the room, wanting to avoid a head-on collision with Reed. And that was where this conversation was going.

Fifteen minutes later, Ellen returned to the kitchen. She was dressed in cords and an Irish cable-knit sweater; soft dark curls framed her small oval face. Ellen had no illusions about her looks. Men on the street weren't going to stop and stare, but she knew she was reasonably attractive. With her short, dark hair and deep brown eyes, she considered herself average. Ordinary. Far too ordinary for a man like Reed Morgan. One look at Ellen, and Danielle would feel completely reassured. Angry at the self-pitying thought, she grabbed a pen and tore out a sheet of notebook paper.

Intent on making the shopping list, Ellen was halfway into the kitchen before she noticed Reed standing at the sink, wiping the frying pan dry. The table had been cleared and the dishes were stacked on the counter, ready for the dishwasher.

"Oh," she said, a little startled. "I would've done that."

"While I'm here, I'll do my share." He said it without looking at her, his eyes avoiding hers.

"But this is your home. I certainly don't mind—"

"I wouldn't be comfortable otherwise. Haven't you got a class this morning?" He sounded anxious to be rid of her.

"Not until eleven."

"What's your major?" He'd turned around, leaning against the sink and crossing his arms. He was the picture of nonchalance, but Ellen wasn't fooled. She knew very well that he wasn't pleased about her living in his home, and she felt he'd given his permission reluctantly. She suspected he was even looking for ways to dislike her. Ellen understood that. Reed was bound to face some awkward questions once Danielle discovered there was a woman living in his house. Especially a woman who slept in his bed and took charge of his kitchen. But that would change this afternoon—at least the sleeping in his bed part.

"I'm majoring in education."

"That's the mother in you coming out again."

Ellen hadn't thought of it that way. Reed simply felt more comfortable seeing her in that light—as a maternal, even matronly figure—she decided. She'd let him, if it meant he'd be willing to accept her arrangement with Derek and the others.

"I suppose you're right," she murmured as she began opening and closing cupboard doors, checking the contents on each shelf, and scribbling down several items she'd need the following week.

"What are you doing now?"

Mentally, Ellen counted to ten before answering. She resented his overbearing tone, and despite her earlier resolve to humor him, she snapped, "I'm making a grocery list. Do you have a problem with that?"

"No," he answered gruffly.

"I'll be out of here in just a minute," she said, trying hard to maintain her patience.

"You aren't in my way."

"And while we're on the subject of being in someone's way, I want you to know I plan to move my things out of your room this afternoon."

"Don't. I won't be here long enough to make it worth your while."

CHAPTER TWO

So REED WAS LEAVING. Ellen felt guilty and relieved at the same time. Derek had told her Reed would probably be sent on another job soon, but she hadn't expected it to be quite *this* soon.

"There's a project Boeing is sending me on. California this time—the Monterey area."

Resuming her task, Ellen added several more items to the grocery list. "I've heard that's a lovely part of the state."

"It is beautiful." But his voice held no enthusiasm.

Ellen couldn't help feeling a twinge of disappointment for Reed. One look convinced her that he didn't want to leave again. After all, he'd just returned from several months in the Middle East and already he had another assignment in California. If he was dreading this latest job, Ellen could well imagine how Danielle must feel.

"Nonetheless, I think it's important to give you back your room. I'll move my things this afternoon." She'd ask the boys to help and it wouldn't take long.

With his arms crossed, Reed lounged against the doorjamb, watching her.

"And if you feel that my being here is a problem," she went on, thinking of Danielle, "I'll look for another place. The only thing I ask is that you give me a couple of weeks to find something."

He hesitated as though he was considering the offer, then shook his head, grinning slightly. "I don't think that'll be necessary."

"I don't mind telling you I'm relieved to hear it, but I'm prepared to move if necessary."

His left brow rose a fraction of an inch as the grin spread across his face. "Having you here does have certain advantages."

"Such as?"

"You're an excellent cook, the house hasn't been this clean in months and Derek's mother says you're a good influence on these boys."

Ellen had briefly met Mary Morgan, Derek's mother, a few weeks before. "Thank you."

He sauntered over to the coffeepot and poured himself a cup. "And for that matter, Derek's right. This house is too big to sit empty. I'm often out of town, but there's no reason others shouldn't use it. Especially with someone as…domestically inclined as you around to keep things running smoothly."

So he viewed her as little more than a live-in housekeeper and cook! Ellen felt a flush of anger. Before she could say something she'd regret, she turned quickly and fled out the back door on her way to the local grocery store. Actually, Reed Morgan had interpreted the situation correctly, but it somehow bothered her that he saw her in such an unflattering light.

ELLEN DIDN'T SEE Reed again until late that night. Friday evenings were lazy ones for her. She'd dated Charlie Hanson, a fellow student, a couple of times but usually preferred the company of a good book. With her heavy class schedule, most of Ellen's free time was devoted to her studies. Particularly algebra. This one class was getting her down. It didn't matter how hard she hit the books, she couldn't seem to grasp the theory.

Dressed in her housecoat and a pair of bright purple knee socks, she sat at the kitchen table, her legs propped on the chair across from her. Holding a paperback novel open with one hand, she dipped chocolate-chip cookies in a tall glass of milk with the other. At the unexpected sound of the back door opening, she looked curiously up from her book.

Reed seemed surprised to see her. He frowned as his eyes darted past her to the clock above the stove. "You're up late."

"On weekends my mommy doesn't make me go to bed until midnight," she said sarcastically, doing her best to ignore him. Reed managed to look fantastic without even trying. He didn't need her gawking at him to tell him that. If his expensive sports jacket was anything to judge by, he'd spent the evening with Danielle.

"You've got that look," he grumbled.

"What look?"

"The same one you said I have—wanting to say something and unsure if you should."

"Oh." She couldn't very well deny it.

"And what did you want to tell me?"

"Only that you look good." She paused, wondering how much she should say. "You even smell expensive."

His gaze slid over her. "From the way you're dressed, you look to me as though you'd smell of cotton candy."

"Thank you, but actually it's chocolate chip." She

pushed the package of cookies in his direction. "Here. Save me from myself."

"No, thanks," Reed murmured and headed toward the living room.

"Don't go in there," Ellen cried, swinging her legs off the chair and coming abruptly to her feet.

Reed's hand was on the kitchen door, ready to open it. "Don't go into the living room?"

"Derek's got a girl in there."

Reed continued to stare at her blankly. "So?"

"So. He's with Michelle Tanner. *The* Michelle Tanner. The girl he's been crazy about for the last six weeks. She finally agreed to a date with him. They rented a movie."

"That doesn't explain why I can't go in there."

"Yes, it does," Ellen whispered. "The last time I peeked, Derek was getting ready to make his move. You'll ruin everything if you barge in there now."

"His move?" Reed didn't seem to like the sound of this. "What do you mean, 'his move'? The kid's barely nineteen."

Ellen smiled. "Honestly, Reed, you must've been young once. Don't you remember what it's like to have a crush on a girl? All Derek's doing is plotting that first kiss."

Reed dropped his hand as he stared at Ellen. He seemed to focus on her mouth. Then the glittering green eyes skimmed hers, and Ellen's breath caught somewhere between her throat and her lungs as she struggled to pull her gaze away from his. Reed had no business giving her that kind of look. Not when he'd so recently left Danielle's arms. And not when Ellen reacted so profoundly to a mere glance.

"I haven't forgotten," he said. "And as for that re-mark about being young *once,* I'm not exactly over the hill."

This was ridiculous! With a sigh of annoyance, Ellen sat down again, swinging her feet onto the opposite chair. She picked up her book and forced her eyes—if not her attention—back to the page in front of her. "I'm glad to hear that." If she could get a grip on her-self for the next few days everything would be fine. Reed would leave and her life with the boys would settle back into its routine.

She heard the refrigerator opening and watched Reed pour himself a glass of milk, then reach for a handful of chocolate-chip cookies. When he pulled out the chair across from her, Ellen reluctantly low-ered her legs.

"What are you reading?"

Feeling irritable and angry for allowing him to af-fect her, she deliberately waited until she'd finished the page before answering. "A book," she muttered.

"My, my, you're a regular Mary Sunshine. What's wrong—did your boyfriend stand you up tonight?"

With exaggerated patience she slowly lowered the paperback to the table and marked her place. "Listen. I'm twenty-five years old and well beyond the age of *boyfriends.*"

Reed shrugged. "All right. Your lover."

She hadn't meant to imply that at all! And Reed knew it. He'd wanted to fluster her and he'd succeeded.

"Women these days have this habit of letting their mouths hang open," he said pointedly. "I suppose they think it looks sexy, but actually, they resemble beached trout." With that, he deposited his empty glass in the sink and marched briskly up the back stairs.

Ellen closed her eyes and groaned in embarrassment. He must think she was an idiot, and with good reason. She'd done a remarkable job of imitating one. She groaned again, infuriated by the fact that she found Reed Morgan so attractive.

Ellen didn't climb the stairs to her new bedroom on the third floor for another hour. And then it was only after Derek had paid her a quick visit in the kitchen and given her a thumbs-up. At least his night had gone well.

Twenty minutes after she'd turned off her reading light, Ellen lay staring into the silent, shadow-filled room. She wasn't sleepy, and the mystery novel no longer held her interest. Her thoughts were troubled by that brief incident in the kitchen with Reed. Burying her head in her pillow, Ellen yawned and closed her eyes. But sleep still wouldn't come. A half-hour later, she threw back the covers and grabbed her housecoat from the end of the bed. Perhaps another glass of milk would help.

Not bothering to turn on any lights, she took a clean glass from the dishwasher and pulled the carton of milk from the refrigerator. Drink in hand, she stood at the kitchen window, looking out at the huge oak tree in the backyard. Its bare limbs stretched upward like skeletal hands, silhouetted against the full moon.

"I've heard that a woman's work is never done, but this is ridiculous."

She nearly spilled her milk at the sudden sound of Reed's voice behind her. She whirled around and glared at him. "I see there's a full moon tonight. I wonder if it's safe to be alone with you. And wouldn't you know it, I left my silver bullet upstairs."

"No woman's ever accused me of being a were-wolf. A number of other things," he murmured, "but never that."

"Maybe that's because you hadn't frightened them half out of their wits."

"I couldn't resist. Sorry," he said, reaching for the milk carton.

"You know, if we'd stop snapping at each other, it might make life a lot easier around here."

"Perhaps," he agreed. "I will admit it's a whole lot easier to talk to you when you're dressed."

Ellen slammed down her empty glass. "I'm getting a little tired of hearing about that."

But Reed went on, clearly unperturbed. "Unfortunately, ever since that first time when I found you in your bra, you've insisted on overdressing. From one extreme to another—too few clothes to too many." He paused. "Do you always wear socks to bed?"

"Usually."

"I pity the man you sleep with."

"Well, you needn't worry—" She expelled a lung-ful of oxygen. "We're doing it again."

"So, you're suggesting we stop trading insults for the sake of the children."

"I hadn't thought of it that way," she said with an involuntary smile, "but you're right. No one's going to be comfortable if the two of us are constantly snip-ing at each other. I'm willing to try if you are. Okay?"

"Okay." A smile softened Reed's features, angular and shadowed in the moonlight.

"And I'm not a threat to your relationship with Danielle, am I? In fact, if you'd rather, she need never even know I'm here," Ellen said casually.

"Maybe that would've been best," he conceded, setting aside his empty glass. "But I doubt it. Besides, she already knows. I told her tonight." He muttered something else she didn't catch.

"And?"

"And," he went on, "she says she doesn't mind, but she'd like to meet you."

This was one encounter Ellen wasn't going to enjoy.

THE NEXT MORNING, Ellen brought down her laundry and was using the washing machine and the dryer before Reed and the others were even awake.

She sighed as she tested the iron with the wet tip of her index finger and found that it still wasn't hot, although she'd turned it on at least five minutes earlier. This house was owned by a wealthy engineer, so why were there only two electrical outlets in the kitchen? It meant that she couldn't use the washer, the dryer and the iron at the same time without causing a blow-out.

"Darn it," she groaned, setting the iron upright on the padded board.

"What's the matter?" Reed asked from the doorway leading into the kitchen. He got himself a cup of coffee.

"This iron."

"Hey, Ellen, if you're doing some ironing, would you press a few things for me?" Monte asked, walking barefoot into the kitchen. He peered into the refrigerator and took out a slice of cold pizza.

"I was afraid this would happen," she grumbled, still upset by the house's electrical problems.

"Ellen's not your personal maid," Reed said sharply.

"If you've got something you want pressed, do it yourself."

A hand on her hip, Ellen turned to Reed, defiantly meeting his glare. "If you don't mind, I can answer for myself."

"Fine," he snorted and took a sip of his coffee.

She directed her next words to Monte, who stood looking at her expectantly. "I am not your personal maid. If you want something pressed, do it yourself."

Monte glanced from Reed to Ellen and back to Reed again. "Sorry I asked," he mumbled on his way out of the kitchen. The door was left swinging in his wake.

"You said that well," Reed commented with a soft chuckle.

"Believe me, I was conned into enough schemes by my sister and brother to know how to handle Monte and the others."

Reed's gaze was admiring. "If your brother's anything like mine, I don't doubt it."

"All brothers are alike," she said. Unable to hold back a grin, Ellen tested the iron a second time and noticed that it was only slightly warmer. "Have you ever thought about putting another outlet in this kitchen?"

Reed looked at her in surprise. "No. Do you need one?"

"Need one?" she echoed. "There are only two in here. It's ridiculous."

Reed scanned the kitchen. "I hadn't thought about it." Setting his coffee mug aside, he shook his head. "Your mood's not much better today than it was last night." With that remark, he hurried out of the room, following in Monte's footsteps.

Frustrated, Ellen tightened her grip on the iron.

Reed was right. She was being unreasonable and she really didn't understand why. But she was honest enough to admit, at least to herself, that she was attracted to this man whose house she occupied. She realized she'd have to erect a wall of reserve between them to protect them both from embarrassment.

"Morning, Ellen," Derek said as he entered the kitchen and threw himself into a chair. As he emptied a box of cornflakes into a huge bowl, he said, "I've got some shirts that need pressing."

"If you want anything pressed, do it yourself," she almost shouted.

Stunned, Derek blinked. "Okay."

Setting the iron upright again, Ellen released a lengthy sigh. "I didn't mean to scream at you."

"That's all right."

Turning off the iron, she joined Derek at the table and reached for the cornflakes.

"Are you still worried about that math paper you're supposed to do?" he asked.

"I'm working my way to an early grave over it."

"I would've thought you'd do well in math."

Ellen snickered. "Hardly."

"Have you come up with a topic?"

"Not yet. I'm going to the library later, where I pray some form of inspiration will strike me."

"Have you asked the other people in your class what they're writing about?" Derek asked as he refilled his bowl, this time with rice puffs.

Ellen nodded. "That's what worries me most. The brain who sits beside me is doing hers on the probability of solving Goldbach's conjecture in our lifetime."

Derek's eyes widened. "That's a tough act to follow."

"Let me tell you about the guy who sits behind me. He's doing his paper on mathematics during World War II."

"You're in the big leagues now," Derek said with a sympathetic shake of his head.

"I know," Ellen lamented. She was taking this course only because it was compulsory; all she wanted out of it was a passing grade. The quadratic formula certainly wasn't going to have any lasting influence on *her* life.

"Good luck," Derek said.

"Thanks. I'm going to need it."

After straightening up the kitchen, Ellen changed into old jeans and a faded sweatshirt. The jeans had been washed so many times they were nearly white. They fit her hips so snugly she could hardly slide her fingers into the pockets, but she hated the idea of throwing them out.

She tied an old red scarf around her hair and headed for the garage. While rooting around for a ladder a few days earlier, she'd discovered some pruning shears. She'd noticed several overgrown bushes in the backyard and decided to tackle those first, before cleaning the drainpipes.

After an hour, she had a pile of underbrush large enough to be worth a haul to the dump. She'd have one of the boys do that later. For now, the drainpipes demanded her attention.

"Derek!" she called as she pushed open the back door. She knew her face was flushed and damp from exertion.

"Yeah?" His voice drifted toward her from the living room.

Ellen wandered in to discover him on the phone. "I'm ready for you now."

"Now?" His eyes pleaded with her as his palm covered the mouthpiece. "It's Michelle."

"All right, I'll ask Monte."

"Thanks." He gave her a smile of appreciation.

But Monte was nowhere to be found, and Pat was at the Y shooting baskets with some friends. When she stuck her head into the living room again, she saw Derek still draped over the sofa, deep in conversation. Unwilling to interfere with the course of young love, she decided she could probably manage to climb onto the roof unaided.

Dragging the aluminum ladder from the garage, she thought she might not need Derek's help anyway. She'd mentioned her plan earlier in the week, and he hadn't looked particularly enthusiastic.

With the extension ladder braced against the side of the house, she climbed onto the roof of the back porch. Very carefully, she reached for the ladder and extended it to the very top of the house.

She maneuvered herself back onto the ladder and climbed slowly and cautiously up.

Once she'd managed to position herself on the slanting roof, she was fine. She even took a moment to enjoy the spectacular view. She could see Lake Washington, with its deep-green water, and the spacious grounds of the university campus.

Using the brush she'd tucked—with some struggle—into her back pocket, Ellen began clearing away the leaves and other debris that clogged the gutters and drainpipes.

She was about half finished when she heard raised

voices below. Pausing, she sat down, drawing her knees against her chest, and watched the scene unfolding on the front lawn. Reed and his brother were embroiled in a heated discussion—with Reed doing most of the talking. Derek was raking leaves and didn't seem at all pleased about devoting his Saturday morning to chores. Ellen guessed that Reed had summarily interrupted the telephone conversation between Derek and Michelle.

With a lackadaisical swish of the rake, Derek flung the multicolored leaves skyward. Ellen restrained a laugh. Reed had obviously pulled rank and felt no hesitation about giving him orders.

To her further amusement, Reed then motioned toward his black Porsche, apparently suggesting that his brother wash the car when he'd finished with the leaves. Still chuckling, Ellen grabbed for the brush, but she missed and accidentally sent it tumbling down the side of the roof. It hit the green shingles over the front porch with a loud thump before flying onto the grass only a few feet from where Derek and Reed were standing.

Two pairs of astonished eyes turned swiftly in her direction. "Hi," she called down and waved. "I don't suppose I could talk one of you into bringing that up to me?" She braced her feet and pulled herself into a standing position as she waited for a reply.

Reed pointed his finger at her and yelled, "What do you think you're doing up there?"

"Playing tiddlywinks," she shouted back. "What do *you* think I'm doing?"

"I don't know, but I want you down."

"In a minute."

"Now."

"Yes, *sir.*" She gave him a mocking salute and would have bowed if she hadn't been afraid she might lose her footing.

Derek burst out laughing but was quickly silenced by a scathing glance from his older brother.

"Tell Derek to bring me the broom," Ellen called, moving closer to the edge.

Ellen couldn't decipher Reed's response, but from the way he stormed around the back of the house, she figured it was best to come down before he had a heart attack. She had the ladder lowered to the back-porch roof before she saw him.

"You idiot!" he shouted. He was standing in the driveway, hands on his hips, glaring at her in fury. "I can't believe anyone would do anything so stupid."

"What do you mean?" The calmness of her words belied the way the blood pulsed through her veins. Alarm rang in his voice and that surprised her. She certainly hadn't expected Reed, of all people, to be concerned about her safety. He held the ladder steady until she'd climbed down and was standing squarely in front of him. Then he started pacing. For a minute Ellen didn't know what to think.

"What's wrong?" she asked. "You look as pale as a sheet."

"What's wrong?" he sputtered. "You were on the *roof* and—"

"I wasn't in any danger."

He shook his head, clearly upset. "There are people who specialize in that sort of thing. I don't want you up there again. Understand?"

"Yes, but—"

"No buts. You do anything that stupid again and you're out of here. Have you got that?"

"Yes," she said with forced calm. "I understand."

"Good."

Before she could think of anything else to say, Reed was gone.

"You all right?" Derek asked a minute later. Shocked by Reed's outburst, Ellen hadn't moved. Rarely had anyone been that angry with her. Heavens, she'd cleaned out drainpipes lots of times. Her father had died when Ellen was fourteen, and over the years she'd assumed most of the maintenance duties around the house. She'd learned that, with the help of a good book and a well-stocked hardware store, there wasn't anything she couldn't fix. She'd repaired the plumbing, built bookshelves and done a multitude of household projects. It was just part of her life. Reed had acted as though she'd done something hazardous, as though she'd taken some extraordinary risk, and that seemed totally ridiculous to her. She knew what she was doing. Besides, heights didn't frighten her; they never had.

"Ellen?" Derek prompted.

"I'm fine."

"I've never seen Reed act like that. He didn't mean anything."

"I know," she whispered, brushing the dirt from her knees. Derek drifted off, leaving her to return the ladder to the garage single-handed.

Reed found her an hour later folding laundry in her bedroom. He knocked on the open door.

"Yes?" She looked up expectantly.

"I owe you an apology."

She continued folding towels at the foot of her bed. "Oh?"

"I didn't mean to come at you like Attila the Hun."

Hugging a University of Washington T-shirt to her stomach, she lowered her gaze to the bedspread and nodded. "Apology accepted and I'll offer one of my own. I didn't mean to come back at you like a spoiled brat."

"Accepted." They smiled at each other and she caught her breath as those incredible green eyes gazed into hers. It was a repeat of the scene in the kitchen the night before. For a long, silent moment they did nothing but stare, and she realized that a welter of conflicting emotions must have registered on her face. A similar turmoil raged on his.

"If it'll make you feel any better, I won't go up on the roof again," she said at last.

"I'd appreciate it." His lips barely moved. The words were more of a sigh than a sentence.

She managed a slight nod in response.

At the sound of footsteps, they guiltily looked away.

"Say, Ellen." Pat stopped in the doorway, a basketball under his left arm. "Got time to shoot a few baskets with me?"

"Sure," she whispered, stepping around Reed. At that moment, she would've agreed to just about anything to escape his company. There was something happening between them and she felt frightened and confused and excited, all at the same time.

The basketball hoop was positioned above the garage door at the end of the long driveway. Pat was attending the University of Washington with the express hope of making the Husky basketball team. His whole life revolved around the game. He was rarely seen without a ball tucked under his arm and sometimes Ellen wondered if he showered with it. She was well aware that the invitation to practice a few free throws with him was not meant to be taken literally. The only slam dunk Ellen had ever accomplished was with a doughnut in her hot chocolate. Her main job was to stand on the sidelines and be awed by Pat's talent.

They hadn't been in the driveway fifteen minutes when the back door opened and Derek strolled out. "Say, Ellen, have you got a minute?" he asked, frowning.

"What's the problem?"

"It's Michelle."

Sitting on the concrete porch step, Derek looked at Ellen with those wide pleading eyes of his.

Ellen sat beside him and wrapped her arms around her bent knees. "What's wrong with Michelle?"

"Nothing. She's beautiful and I think she might even fall in love with me, given the chance." He paused to sigh expressively. "I asked her out to dinner tonight."

"She agreed. Right?" If Michelle was anywhere near as taken with Derek as he was with her, she wasn't likely to refuse.

The boyishly thin shoulders heaved in a gesture of despair. "She can't."

"Why not?" Ellen watched as Pat bounced the basketball across the driveway, pivoted, jumped high in the air and sent the ball through the net.

"Michelle promised her older sister that she'd babysit tonight."

"That's too bad." Ellen gave him a sympathetic look.

"The thing is, she'd probably go out with me if there

was someone who could watch her niece and nephew for her."

"Uh-huh." Pat made another skillful play and Ellen applauded vigorously. He rewarded her with a triumphant smile.

"Then you will?"

Ellen switched her attention from Pat's antics at the basketball hoop back to Derek. "Will I what?"

"Babysit Michelle's niece and nephew?"

"What?" she exploded. "Not me. I've got to do research for a term paper."

"Ellen, please, please, please."

"No. No. No." She sliced the air forcefully with her hand and got to her feet.

Derek rose with her. "I sense some resistance to this idea."

"The boy's a genius," she mumbled under her breath as she hurried into the kitchen. "I've got to write my term paper. You know that."

Derek followed her inside. "Ellen, please? I promise I'll never ask anything of you again."

"I've heard that before." She tried to ignore him as he trailed her to the refrigerator and watched her take out sandwich makings for lunch.

"It's a matter of the utmost importance," Derek pleaded anew.

"What is?" Reed spoke from behind the paper he was reading at the kitchen table.

"My date with Michelle. Listen, Ellen, I bet Reed would help you. You're not doing anything tonight, are you?"

Reed lowered the newspaper. "Help Ellen with what?"

"Babysitting."

Reed glanced from the intent expression on his younger brother's face to the stubborn look on Ellen's. "You two leave me out of this."

"Ellen. Dear, *sweet* Ellen, you've got to understand that it could be weeks—weeks," he repeated dramatically, "before Michelle will be able to go out with me again."

Ellen put down an armload of cheese, ham and assorted jars of mustard and pickles. "*No!* Can I make it any plainer than that? I'm sorry, Derek, honest. But I can't."

"Reed," Derek pleaded with his brother. "Say something that'll convince her."

"Like I said, I'm out of this one."

He raised the paper again, but Ellen could sense a smile hidden behind it. Still, she doubted that Reed would be foolish enough to involve himself in this situation.

"Ellen, puleease."

"No." Ellen realized that if she wanted any peace, she'd have to forget about lunch and make an immediate escape. She whirled around and headed out of the kitchen, the door swinging in her wake.

"I think she's weakening," she heard Derek say as he followed her.

She was on her way up the stairs when she caught sight of Derek in the dining room, coming toward her on his knees, hands folded in supplication. "Won't you please reconsider?"

Ellen groaned. "What do I need to say to convince you? I've got to get to the library. That paper is due Monday morning."

"I'll write it for you."

"No, thanks."

At just that moment Reed came through the door. "It shouldn't be too difficult to find a reliable sitter. There are a few families with teenagers in the neighbourhood, as I recall."

"I...don't know," Derek hedged.

"If we can't find anyone, then Danielle and I'll manage. It'll be good practice for us. Besides, just how much trouble can two kids be?"

When she heard that, Ellen had to swallow a burst of laughter. Reed obviously hadn't spent much time around children, she thought with a mischievous grin.

"How old did you say these kids are?" she couldn't resist asking.

"Nine and four." Derek's dark eyes brightened as he leaped to his feet and gave his brother a grateful smile. "So I can tell Michelle everything's taken care of?"

"I suppose." Reed turned to Ellen. "I was young once myself," he said pointedly, reminding her of the comment she'd made the night before.

"I really appreciate this, Reed," Derek was saying. "I'll be your slave for life. I'd even lend you money if I had some. By the way, can I borrow your car tonight?"

"Don't press your luck."

"Right." Derek chuckled, bounding up the stairs. He paused for a moment. "Oh, I forgot to tell you. Michelle's bringing the kids over here, okay?"

He didn't wait for a response.

THE DOORBELL CHIMED close to six o'clock, just as Ellen was gathering up her books and preparing to leave for the library.

"That'll be Michelle," Derek called excitedly. "Can you get it, Ellen?"

"No problem."

Coloring books and crayons were arranged on the coffee table, along with some building blocks Reed must have purchased that afternoon. From bits and pieces of information she'd picked up, she concluded that Reed had discovered it wasn't quite as easy to find a baby-sitter as he'd assumed. And with no other recourse, he and Danielle were apparently taking over the task. Ellen wished him luck, but she really did need to concentrate on this stupid term paper. Reed hadn't suggested that Ellen wait around to meet Danielle. But she had to admit she'd been wondering about the woman from the time Derek had first mentioned her.

"Hello, Ellen." Blonde Michelle greeted Ellen with a warm, eager smile. They'd met briefly the other night, when she'd come over to watch the movie. "This sure is great of Derek's brother and his girlfriend, isn't it?"

"It sure is."

The four-year-old boy was clinging to Michelle's trouser leg so that her gait was stiff-kneed as she limped into the house with the child attached.

"Jimmy, this is Ellen. You'll be staying in her house tonight while Auntie Michelle goes out to dinner with Derek."

"I want my mommy."

"He won't be a problem," Michelle told Ellen confidently.

"I thought there were two children."

"Yeah, the baby's in the car. I'll be right back."

"Baby?" Ellen swallowed down a laugh. "What baby?"

"Jenny's nine months."

"Nine *months?*" A small uncontrollable giggle slid from her throat. This would be marvelous. Reed with a nine-month-old was almost too good to miss.

"Jimmy, you stay here." Somehow Michelle was able to pry the four-year-old's fingers from her leg and pass the struggling child to Ellen.

Kicking and thrashing, Jimmy broke into loud sobs as Ellen carried him into the living room. "Here's a coloring book. Do you like to color, Jimmy?"

But he refused to talk to Ellen or even look at her as he buried his face in the sofa cushions. "I want my mommy," he wailed again.

By the time Michelle had returned with a baby carrier and a fussing nine-month-old, Derek sauntered out from the kitchen. "Hey, Michelle, you're lookin' good."

Reed, who was following closely behind, came to a shocked standstill when he saw the baby. "I thought you said they were nine and four."

"I did," Derek explained patiently, his eyes devouring the blonde at his side.

"They won't be any trouble," Michelle cooed as Derek placed an arm around her shoulders and led her toward the open door.

"Derek, we need to talk," Reed insisted.

"Haven't got time now. Our reservations are for seven." His hand slid from Michelle's shoulders to her waist. "I'm taking my lady out for a night on the town."

"Derek," Reed demanded.

"Oh." Michelle tore her gaze from Derek's. "The diaper bag is in the entry. Jenny should be dry, but you might want to check her later. She'll probably cry for a few minutes once she sees I'm gone, but that'll stop almost immediately."

Reed's face was grim as he cast a speculative glance at Jimmy, who was still howling for his mother. The happily gurgling Jenny stared up at the unfamiliar dark-haired man and noticed for the first time that she was at the mercy of a stranger. She immediately burst into heart-wrenching tears.

"I want my mommy," Jimmy wailed yet again.

"I can see you've got everything under control," Ellen said, reaching for her coat. "I'm sure Danielle will be here any minute."

"Ellen…"

"Don't expect me back soon. I've got hours of research ahead of me."

"You aren't really going to leave, are you?" Reed gave her a horrified look.

"I wish I could stay," she lied breezily. "Another time." With that, she was out the door, smiling as she bounded down the steps.

CHAPTER THREE

AN UNEASY FEELING struck Ellen as she stood waiting at the bus stop. But she resolutely hardened herself against the impulse to rush back to Reed and his disconsolate charges. Danielle would show up any minute and Ellen really was obliged to do the research for her yet-to-be-determined math paper. Besides, she reminded herself, Reed had volunteered to babysit and she wasn't responsible for rescuing him. But his eyes had pleaded with her so earnestly. Ellen felt herself beginning to weaken. *No!* she mumbled under her breath. Reed had Danielle, and as far as Ellen was concerned, they were on their own.

However, by the time she arrived at the undergraduate library, Ellen discovered that she couldn't get Reed's pleading look out of her mind. From everything she'd heard about Danielle, Ellen figured the woman probably didn't know the first thing about babies. As for the term paper, she supposed she could put it off until Sunday. After all, she'd found excuses all day to avoid working on it. She'd done the laundry, trimmed the shrubs, cleaned the drainpipes and washed the upstairs walls in an effort to escape that paper. One more night wasn't going to make much difference.

Hurriedly, she signed out some books and journals that looked as though they might be helpful and headed

for the bus stop. Ellen had to admit that she was curious
enough to want to meet Danielle. Reed's girlfriend had
to be someone very special to put up with his frequent
absences—or else a schemer, as Derek had implied.
But Ellen couldn't see Reed being duped by a woman,
no matter how clever or sophisticated she might be.

Her speculations came to an end as the bus arrived,
and she quickly jumped on for the short ride home.

Reed was kneeling on the carpet changing the still-
tearful Jenny's diaper when Ellen walked in the front
door. He seemed to have aged ten years in the past
hour. The long sleeves of his wool shirt were rolled up
to the elbows as he struggled with the tape on Jenny's
disposable diaper.

Reed shook his head and sagged with relief. "Good
thing you're here. She hasn't stopped crying from the
minute you left."

"You look like you're doing a good job without me.
Where's Danielle?" She glanced around, smiling at
Jimmy; the little boy hadn't moved from the sofa, his
face still hidden in the cushions.

Reed muttered a few words under his breath. "She
couldn't stay." He finally finished with the diaper.
"That wasn't so difficult after all," he said, glancing
proudly at Ellen as he stood Jenny up on the floor, holding the baby upright by her small arms.

Ellen swallowed a laugh. The diaper hung crook-
edly, bunched up in front. She was trying to think of a
tactful way of pointing it out to Reed when the whole
thing began to slide down Jenny's pudgy legs, settling
at her ankles.

"Maybe you should try," Reed conceded, handing
her the baby. Within minutes, Ellen had successfully

secured the diaper. Unfortunately, she didn't manage to soothe the baby any more than Reed had.

Cradling Jenny in her arms, Ellen paced the area in front of the fireplace, at a loss to comfort the sobbing child. "I doubt I'll do any better. It's been a long while since my brother was this size."

"Women are always better at this kind of stuff," Reed argued, rubbing a hand over his face. "Most women," he amended, with such a look of frustration that Ellen smiled.

"I'll bet Jimmy knows what to do," she suggested next, pleased with her inspiration. The little boy might actually come up with something helpful, and involving him in their attempts to comfort Jenny might distract him from his own unhappiness. Or so Ellen hoped. "Jimmy's a good big brother. Isn't that right, honey?"

The child lifted his face from the cushion. "I want my mommy."

"Let's pretend Ellen is your mommy," Reed coaxed.

"No! She's like that other lady who said bad words."

Meanwhile, Jenny wailed all the louder. Digging around in the bag, Reed found a stuffed teddy bear and pressed it into her arms. But Jenny angrily tossed the toy aside, the tears flowing unabated down her face.

"Come on, Jimmy," Reed said desperately. "We need a little help here. Your sister's crying."

Holding his hands over his eyes, Jimmy straightened and peeked through two fingers. The distraught Jenny continued to cry at full volume in spite of Ellen's best efforts.

"Mommy bounces her."

Ellen had been gently doing that from the beginning. "What else?" she asked.

"She likes her boo-loo."

"What's that?"

"Her teddy bear."

"I've already tried that," Reed said. "What else does your mommy do when she cries like this?"

Jimmy was thoughtful for a moment. "Oh." The four-year-old's eyes sparkled. "Mommy nurses her."

Reed and Ellen glanced at each other and dissolved into giggles. The laughter faded from his eyes and was replaced with a roguish grin. "That could be interesting."

Hiding a smile, Ellen decided to ignore Reed's comment. "Sorry, Jenny," she said softly to the baby girl.

"But maybe he's got an idea," Reed suggested. "Could she be hungry?"

"It's worth a try. At this point, anything is."

Jenny's bellowing had finally dwindled into a few hiccuping sobs. And for some reason, Jimmy suddenly straightened and stared at Reed's craggy face, at his deep auburn hair and brilliant green eyes. Then he pointed to the plaid wool shirt, its long sleeves rolled up to the elbow. "Are you a lumberjack?"

"A lumberjack?" Reed repeated, looking puzzled. He broke into a full laugh. "No, but I imagine I must look like one to you."

Rummaging through the diaper bag, Ellen found a plastic bottle filled with what was presumably formula. Jenny eyed it skeptically, but no sooner had Ellen removed the cap than Jenny grabbed it from her hands and began sucking eagerly at the nipple.

Sighing, Ellen sank into the rocking chair and swayed back and forth with the baby tucked in her arms. "I guess that settles that."

The silence was so blissful that she wanted to wrap it around herself. She felt the tension drain from her muscles as she relaxed in the rocking chair. From what Jimmy had dropped, she surmised that Danielle hadn't been much help. Everything she'd learned about the other woman told Ellen that Danielle would probably find young children frustrating—and apparently she had.

Jimmy had crawled into Reed's lap with a book and demanded the lumberjack read to him. Together the two leafed through the storybook. Several times during the peaceful interlude, Ellen's eyes met Reed's across the room and they exchanged a contented smile.

Jenny sucked tranquilly at the bottle, and her eyes slowly drooped shut. At peace with her world, the baby was satisfied to be held and rocked to sleep. Ellen gazed down at the angelic face and brushed fine wisps of hair from the untroubled forehead. Releasing her breath in a slow, drawn-out sigh, she glanced up to discover Reed watching her, the little boy still sitting quietly on his lap.

"Ellen?" Reed spoke in a low voice. "Did you finish your math paper?"

"Finish it?" She groaned. "Are you kidding? I haven't even started it."

"What's a math paper?" Jimmy asked.

Rocking the baby, Ellen looked solemnly over at the boy. "Well, it's something I have to write for a math class. And if I don't write a paper, I haven't got a hope of passing the course." She didn't think he'd understand any algebraic terms. For that matter, neither did she.

"What's math?"

"Numbers," Reed told the boy.

"And, in this case, sometimes letters—like x and y."

"I like numbers," Jimmy declared. "I like three and nine and seven."

"Well, Jimmy, my boy, how would you like to write my paper for me?"

"Can I?"

Ellen grinned at him. "You bet."

Reed got out pencil and paper and set the four-year-old to work.

Glancing up, she gave Reed a smile. "See how easy this is? You're good with kids." Reed smiled in answer as he carefully drew numbers for Jimmy to copy.

After several minutes of this activity, Jimmy decided it was time to put on his pajamas. Seeing him yawn, Reed brought down a pillow and blanket and tucked him into a hastily made bed on the sofa. Then he read a bedtime story until the four-year-old again yawned loudly and fell almost instantly asleep.

Ellen still hadn't moved, fearing that the slightest jolt would rouse the baby.

"Why don't we set her down in the baby seat?" Reed said.

"I'm afraid she'll wake up."

"If she does, you can rock her again."

His suggestion made sense and besides, her arms were beginning to ache. "Okay." He moved to her side and took the sleeping child. Ellen held her breath momentarily when Jenny stirred. But the little girl simply rolled her head against the cushion and returned to sleep.

Ellen rose to her feet and turned the lamp down to its dimmest setting, surrounding them with a warm circle of light.

"I couldn't have done it without you," Reed whispered, coming to stand beside her. He rested his hand at the back of her neck.

An unfamiliar warmth seeped through Ellen, and she began to talk quickly, hoping to conceal her sudden nervousness. "Sure you could have. It looked to me as if you had everything under control."

Reed snorted. "I was ten minutes away from calling the crisis clinic. Thanks for coming to the rescue." He casually withdrew his hand, and Ellen felt both relieved and disappointed.

"You're welcome." She was dying to know what had happened with Danielle, but she didn't want to ask. Apparently, the other woman hadn't stayed around for long.

"Have you eaten?"

Ellen had been so busy that she'd forgotten about dinner, but once Reed mentioned it, she realized how hungry she was. "No, and I'm starved."

"Do you like Chinese food?"

"Love it."

"Good. There's enough for an army out in the kitchen. I ordered it earlier."

Ellen didn't need to be told that he'd made dinner plans with Danielle in mind. He'd expected to share an intimate evening with her. "Listen," she began awkwardly, clasping her hands. "I really have to get going on this term paper. Why don't you call Danielle and invite her back? Now that the kids are asleep, I'm sure everything will be better. I—"

"Children make Danielle nervous. She warned me about it, but I refused to listen. She's home now and has probably taken some aspirin and gone to sleep. I can't see letting good food go to waste. Besides, this gives me an opportunity to thank you."

"Oh." It was the longest speech that Reed had made. "All right," she agreed with a slight nod.

While Reed warmed the food in the microwave, Ellen set out plates and forks and prepared a large pot of green tea, placing it in the middle of the table. The swinging door that connected the kitchen with the living room was left open in case either child woke.

"What do we need plates for?" Reed asked with a questioning arch of his brow.

"Plates are the customary eating device."

"Not tonight."

"Not tonight?" Something amusing glinted in Reed's eyes as he set out several white boxes and brandished two pairs of chopsticks. "Since it's only the two of us, we can eat right out of the boxes."

"I'm not very adept with chopsticks." The smell drifting from the open boxes was tangy and enticing.

"You'll learn if you're hungry."

"I'm famished."

"Good." Deftly he took the first pair of chopsticks and showed her how to work them with her thumb and index finger.

Imitating his movements Ellen discovered that her fingers weren't nearly as agile as his. Two or three tries at picking up small pieces of spicy diced chicken succeeded only in frustrating her.

"Here." Reed fed her a bite from the end of his chopsticks. "Be a little more patient with yourself."

"That's easy for you to say while you're eating your fill and I'm starving to death."

"It'll come."

Ellen grumbled under her breath, but a few tries later she managed to deliver a portion of the hot food to her eager mouth.

"See, I told you you'd pick this up fast enough."

"Do you always tell someone 'I told you so'?" she asked with pretended annoyance. The mood was too congenial for any real discontent. Ellen felt that they'd shared a special time together looking after the two small children. More than special—astonishing. They hadn't clashed once or found a single thing to squabble over.

"I enjoy teasing you. Your eyes have an irresistible way of lighting up when you're angry."

"If you continue to insist that I eat with these absurd pieces of wood, you'll see my eyes brighten the entire room."

"I'm looking forward to that," he murmured with a laugh. "No forks. You can't properly enjoy Chinese food unless you use chopsticks."

"I can't properly *taste* it without a fork."

"Here, I'll feed you." Again he brought a spicy morsel to her mouth.

A drop of the sauce fell onto her chin and Ellen wiped it off. "You aren't any better at this than me." She dipped the chopsticks into the chicken mixture and attempted to transport a tidbit to Reed's mouth. It balanced precariously on the end of her chopsticks, and Reed lowered his mouth to catch it before it could land in his lap.

"You're improving," he told her, his voice low and slightly husky.

Their eyes met. Unable to face the caressing look in his warm gaze, Ellen bent her head and pretended to be engrossed in her dinner. But her appetite was instantly gone—vanished.

A tense silence filled the room. The air between them was so charged that she felt breathless and weak, as though she'd lost the energy to move or speak. Ellen didn't dare raise her eyes for fear of what she'd see in his.

"Ellen."

She took a deep breath and scrambled to her feet. "I think I hear Jimmy," she whispered.

"Maybe it was Jenny," Reed added hurriedly.

Ellen paused in the doorway between the two rooms. They were both overwhelmingly aware that neither child had made a sound. "I guess they're still asleep."

"That's good." The scraping sound of his chair against the floor told her that Reed, too, had risen from the table. When she turned, she found him depositing the leftovers in the refrigerator. His preoccupation with the task gave her a moment to reflect on what had just happened. There were too many problems involved in pursuing this attraction; the best thing was to ignore it and hope the craziness passed. They were mature adults, not adolescents, and besides, this would complicate her life, which was something she didn't need right now. Neither, she was sure, did he. Especially with Danielle in the picture...

"If you don't mind, I'm going to head upstairs," she began awkwardly, taking a step in retreat.

"Okay, then. And thanks. I appreciated the help."

"I appreciated the dinner," she returned.

"See you in the morning."

"Right." Neither seemed eager to bring the evening to an end.

"Good night, Ellen."

"Night, Reed. Call if you need me."

"I will."

Turning decisively, she took the stairs and was panting by the time she'd climbed up the second narrow flight. Since the third floor had originally been built to accommodate servants, the five bedrooms were small and opened onto a large central room, which was where Ellen had placed her bed. She'd chosen the largest of the bedrooms as her study.

She sat resolutely down at her desk and leafed through several books, hoping to come across an idea she could use for her term paper. But her thoughts were dominated by the man two floors below. Clutching a study on the origins of algebra to her chest, she sighed deeply and wondered whether Danielle truly valued Reed. She must, Ellen decided, or she wouldn't be so willing to sit at home waiting, while her fiancé traipsed around the world directing a variety of projects.

Reed had been so patient and good-natured with Jimmy and Jenny. When the little boy had climbed into his lap, Reed had read to him and held him with a tenderness that stirred her heart. And Reed was generous to a fault. Another man might have told Pat, Monte and Ellen to pack their bags. This was his home, after all, and Derek had been wrong to rent out the rooms without Reed's knowledge. But Reed had let them stay.

Disgruntled with the trend her thoughts were taking, Ellen forced her mind back to the books in front of her. But it wasn't long before her concentration started to drift again. Reed had Danielle, and she had... Charlie Hanson. First thing in the morning, she'd call dependable old Charlie and suggest they get together; he'd probably be as surprised as he was pleased to hear from her. Feeling relieved and a little light-headed, Ellen turned off the light and went to bed.

"WHAT ARE YOU DOING?" Reed arrived in the kitchen early the next afternoon, looking as though he'd just finished eighteen holes of golf or a vigorous game of tennis. He'd already left by the time she'd wandered down to the kitchen that morning.

"Ellen?" he repeated impatiently.

She'd taken the wall plates off the electrical outlets and pulled the receptacle out of its box, from which two thin colored wires now protruded. "I'm trying to figure out why this outlet won't heat the iron," she answered without looking in his direction.

"You're what!" he bellowed.

She wiped her face to remove a layer of dust before she straightened. "Don't yell at me."

"Good grief, woman. You run around on the roof like a trapeze artist, cook like a dream and do electrical work on the side. Is there anything you *can't* do?"

"Algebra," she muttered.

Reed closed the instruction manual Ellen had propped against the sugar bowl in the middle of the table. He took her by the shoulders and pushed her gently aside, then reattached the electrical wires and fastened the whole thing back in place.

As he finished securing the wall plate, Ellen burst out, "What did you do that for? I've almost got the problem traced."

"No doubt, but if you don't mind, I'd rather have a real electrician look at this."

"What can I say? It's your house."

"Right. Now sit down." He nudged her into a chair. "How much longer are you going to delay writing that term paper?"

"It's written," she snapped. She wasn't particularly pleased with it, but at least the assignment was done. Her subject matter might impress four-year-old Jimmy, but she wasn't too confident that her professor would feel the same way.

"Do you want me to look it over?"

The offer surprised her. "No, thanks." She stuck the screwdriver in the pocket of her gray-striped coveralls.

"Well, that wasn't so hard, was it?"

"I just don't think I've got a snowball's chance of getting a decent grade on it. Anyway, I have to go and iron a dress. I've got a date."

A dark brow lifted over inscrutable green eyes and he seemed about to say something.

"Reed." Unexpectedly, the kitchen door swung open and a soft, feminine voice purred his name. "What's taking you so long?"

"Danielle, I'd like you to meet Ellen."

"Hello." Ellen resisted the urge to kick Reed. If he was going to introduce her to his friend, the least he could have done was waited until she looked a little more presentable. Just as she'd figured, Danielle was beautiful. No, the word was *gorgeous*. She wore a cute pale blue tennis outfit with a short, pleated skirt. A dark blue silk scarf held back the curly cascade of long blond hair—Ellen should have known the other woman would be blonde. Naturally, Danielle possessed a trim waist, perfect legs and blue eyes to match the heavens. She'd apparently just finished playing golf or tennis with Reed, but she still looked cool and elegant.

"I feel as though I already know you," Danielle was saying with a pleasant smile. "Reed told me how much help you were with the children."

"It was nothing, really." Embarrassed by her ridiculous outfit, Ellen tried to conceal as much of it as possible by grabbing the electrical repair book and clasping it to her stomach.

"Not according to Reed." Danielle slipped her arm around his and smiled adoringly up at him. "Unfortunately, I came down with a terrible headache."

"Danielle doesn't have your knack with young children," Reed said.

"If we decide to have our own, things will be different," Danielle continued sweetly. "But I'm not convinced I'm the maternal type."

Ellen sent the couple a wan smile. "If you'll excuse me, I've got to go change my clothes."

"Of course. It was nice meeting you, Elaine."

"Ellen," Reed and Ellen corrected simultaneously.

"You, too." Gallantly, Ellen stifled the childish impulse to call the other woman Diane. As she turned and hurried up the stairs leading from the kitchen, she heard Danielle whisper that she didn't mind at all if Ellen lived in Reed's home. Of course not, Ellen muttered to herself. How could Danielle possibly be jealous?

Winded by the time she'd marched up both flights, Ellen walked into the tiny bedroom where she stored her clothes. She threw down the electrical manual and slammed the door shut. Then she sighed with despair as she saw her reflection in the full-length mirror on the back of the door; it revealed baggy coveralls, a faded white T-shirt and smudges of dirt across her cheekbone. She struck a seductive pose with her hand on her hip and vampishly puffed up her hair. "Of course I don't mind if sweet little Elaine lives here, darling," she mimicked in a high-pitched falsely sweet voice.

Dropping her coveralls to the ground, Ellen gruffly kicked them aside. Hands on her hips, she glared at her reflection. Her figure was no less attractive than Danielle's, and her face was pretty enough—even if she did say so herself. But Danielle had barely looked at Ellen and certainly hadn't seen her as a potential rival.

As she brushed her hair away from her face, Ellen's shoulders suddenly dropped. She was losing her mind! She liked living with the boys. Their arrangement was ideal, yet here she was, complaining bitterly because her presence hadn't been challenged.

Carefully choosing a light pink blouse and denim skirt, Ellen told herself that Charlie, at least, would appreciate her. And for now, Ellen needed that. Her self-confidence had been shaken by Danielle's casual acceptance of her role in Reed's house. She didn't like Danielle. But then, she hadn't expected to.

"ELLEN." HER NAME was followed by a loud pounding on the bedroom door. "Wake up! There's a phone call for you."

"Okay," she mumbled into her pillow, still caught in the dregs of sleep. It felt so warm and cozy under the blankets that she didn't want to stir. Charlie had taken her to dinner and a movie and they'd returned a little after ten. The boys had stayed in that evening, but Reed was out and Ellen didn't need to ask with whom. She hadn't heard him come home.

"Ellen!"

"I'm awake, I'm awake," she grumbled, slipping one leg free of the covers and dangling it over the edge of the bed. The sudden cold that assailed her bare foot made her eyes flutter open in momentary shock.

"It's long distance."

Her eyes did open then. She knew only one person who could be calling. Her mother!

Hurriedly tossing the covers aside, she grabbed her housecoat and scurried out of the room. "Why didn't you tell me it was long distance?"

"I tried," Pat said. "But you were more interested in sleeping."

A glance at her clock radio told her it was barely seven.

Taking a deep, calming breath, Ellen walked quickly down one flight of stairs and picked up the phone at the end of the hallway.

"Good morning, Mom."

"How'd you know it was me?"

Although they emailed each other regularly, this was the first time her mother had actually phoned since she'd left home. "Lucky guess."

"Who was that young man who answered the phone?"

"Patrick."

"The basketball kid."

Her mother had read every word of her emails. "That's him."

"Has Monte eaten you out of house and home yet?"

"Just about."

"And has this Derek kid finally summoned up enough nerve to ask out…what was her name again?"

"Michelle."

"Right. That's the one."

"They saw each other twice this weekend," Ellen told her, feeling a sharp pang of homesickness.

"And what about you, Ellen? Are you dating?" It wasn't an idle question. Through the years, Ellen's mother had often fretted that her oldest child was giving up her youth in order to care for the family. Ellen didn't deny that she'd made sacrifices, but they'd been willing ones.

Her emails had been chatty, but she hadn't mentioned Charlie, and Ellen wasn't sure she wanted her mother to know about him. Her relationship with him was based on friendship and nothing more, although Ellen suspected that Charlie would've liked it to develop into something romantic.

"Mom, you didn't phone me long distance on a Monday morning to discuss my social life."

"You're right. I called to discuss mine."

"And?" Ellen's heart hammered against her ribs. She already knew what was coming. She'd known it months ago, even before she'd moved to Seattle. Her mother was going to remarry. After ten years of widowhood, Barbara Cunningham had found another man to love.

"And—" her mother faltered "—James has asked me to be his wife."

"And?" It seemed to Ellen that her vocabulary had suddenly been reduced to one word.

"And I've said yes."

Ellen closed her eyes, expecting to feel a rush of bittersweet nostalgia for the father she remembered so well and had loved so much. Instead, she felt only gladness that her mother had discovered this new happiness.

"Congratulations, Mom."

"Do you mean that?"

"With all my heart. When's the wedding?"

"Well, actually…" Her mother hedged again. "Honey, don't be angry."

"Angry?"

"We're already married. I'm calling from Reno."

"Oh."

"Are you mad?"

"Of course not."

"James has a winter home in Arizona and we're going to stay there until April."

"April," Ellen repeated, feeling a little dazed.

"If you object, honey, I'll come back to Yakima for Christmas."

"No… I don't object. It's just kind of sudden."

"Dad's been gone ten years."

"I know, Mom. Don't worry, okay?"

"I'll email you soon."

"Do that. And much happiness, Mom. You and James deserve it."

"Thank you, love."

They spoke for a few more minutes before saying goodbye. Ellen walked down the stairs in a state of stunned disbelief, absentmindedly tightening the belt of her housecoat. In a matter of months, her entire family had disintegrated. Her sister and mother had married and Bud had joined the military.

"Good morning," she cautiously greeted Reed, who was sitting at the kitchen table dressed and reading the paper.

"Morning," he responded dryly, as he lowered his paper.

Her hands trembling, Ellen reached for a mug, but it slipped out of her fingers and hit the counter, luckily without breaking.

Reed carefully folded the newspaper and studied her face. "What's wrong? You look like you've just seen a ghost."

"My mom's married," she murmured in a subdued voice. Tears burned in her eyes. She was no longer sure just what she was feeling. Happiness for her mother, yes, but also sadness as she remembered her father and his untimely death.

"Remarried?" he asked.

"Yes." She sat down across from him, holding the mug in both hands and staring into its depths. "It's not like this is sudden. Dad's been gone a lot of years. What surprises me is all the emotion I'm feeling."

"That's only natural. I remember how I felt when my dad remarried. I'd known about Mary and Dad for months. But the day of the wedding I couldn't help feeling, somehow, that my father had betrayed my mother's memory. Those were heavy thoughts for a ten-year-old boy." His hand reached for hers. "As I recall, that was the last time I cried."

Ellen nodded. It was the only way she could thank him, because speaking was impossible just then. She knew instinctively that Reed didn't often share the hurts of his youth.

Just when her throat had relaxed and she felt she could speak, Derek threw open the back door and dashed in, tossing his older brother a set of keys.

"I had them add a quart of oil," Derek said. "Are you sure you can't stay longer?"

The sip of coffee sank to the pit of Ellen's stomach

and sat there. "You're leaving?" It seemed as though someone had jerked her chair out from under her.

He released her hand and gave it a gentle pat. "You'll be fine."

Ellen forced her concentration back to her coffee. For days she'd been telling herself that she'd be relieved and delighted when Reed left. Now she dreaded it. More than anything, she wanted him to stay.

CHAPTER FOUR

"ELLEN," DEREK SHOUTED as he burst in the front door, his hands full of mail. "Can I invite Michelle to dinner on Friday night?"

Casually, Ellen looked up from the textbook she was studying. By mutual agreement, they all went their separate ways on Friday evenings and Ellen didn't cook. If one of the boys happened to be in the house, he heated up soup or put together a sandwich or made do with leftovers. In Monte's case, he did all three.

"What are you planning to fix?" Ellen responded cagily.

"Cook? Me?" Derek slapped his hand against his chest and looked utterly shocked. "I can't cook. You know that."

"But you're inviting company."

His gaze dropped and he restlessly shuffled his feet. "I was hoping that maybe this one Friday you could…" He paused and his head jerked up. "You don't have a date, do you?" He sounded as if that was the worst possible thing that could happen.

"Not this Friday."

"Oh, good. For a minute there, I thought we might have a problem."

"We?" She rolled her eyes. "I don't have a problem,

but it sounds like you do." She wasn't going to let him con her into his schemes quite so easily.

"But you'll be here."

"I was planning on soaking in the tub, giving my hair a hot-oil treatment and hibernating with a good book."

"But you could still make dinner, couldn't you? Something simple like seafood jambalaya with shrimp, stuffed eggplant and pecan pie for dessert."

"Are you planning to rob a bank, as well?" At his blank stare, she elaborated. "Honestly, Derek, have you checked out the price of seafood lately?"

"No, but you cooked that Cajun meal not long ago and—"

"Shrimp was on sale," she broke in.

He continued undaunted. "And it was probably the most delicious meal I've ever tasted in my whole life. I was kicking myself because Reed wasn't here and he would have loved it as much as everyone else."

At the mention of Reed's name, Ellen's lashes fell, hiding the confusion and longing in her eyes. The house had been full of college boys, yet it had seemed astonishingly empty without Reed. He'd been with them barely a week and Ellen couldn't believe how much his presence had affected her. The morning he'd left, she'd walked him out to his truck, trying to think of a way to say goodbye and to thank him for understanding the emotions that raged through her at the news of her mother's remarriage. But nothing had turned out quite as she'd expected. Reed had seemed just as reluctant to say goodbye as she was, and before climbing into the truck, he'd leaned forward and lightly brushed his lips over hers. The kiss had been so spontaneous that Ellen wasn't sure if he'd really meant to do it. But intentional or not, he *had,* and the memory of that kiss stayed with her. Now hardly a day passed that he didn't enter her thoughts.

A couple of times when she was on the second floor she'd wandered into her old bedroom, forgetting that it now belonged to Reed. Both times, she'd lingered there, enjoying the sensation of remembering Reed and their verbal battles.

Repeatedly Ellen told herself that it was because Derek's brother was over twenty-one and she could therefore carry on an adult conversation with him. Although she was genuinely fond of the boys, she'd discovered that a constant diet of their antics and their adolescent preoccupations—Pat's basketball, Monte's appetite and Derek's Michelle—didn't exactly make for stimulating conversation.

"You really are a fantastic cook," Derek went on. "Even better than my mother. You know, only the other day Monte was saying—"

"Don't you think you're putting it on a little thick, Derek?"

He blinked. "I just wanted to tell you how much I'd appreciate it if you decided to do me this tiny favor."

"You'll buy the ingredients yourself?"

"The grocery budget couldn't manage it?"

"Not unless everyone else is willing to eat oatmeal three times a week for the remainder of the month."

"I don't suppose they would be," he muttered. "All right, make me a list and I'll buy what you need."

Ellen was half hoping that once he saw the price of

fresh shrimp, he'd realize it might be cheaper to take Michelle to a seafood restaurant.

"Oh, by the way," Derek said, examining one of the envelopes in his hand. "You got a letter. Looks like it's from Reed."

"Reed?" Her lungs slowly contracted as she said his name, and it was all she could do not to snatch the envelope out of Derek's hand. The instant he gave it to her, she tore it open.

"What does he say?" Derek asked, sorting through the rest of the mail. "He didn't write me."

Ellen quickly scanned the contents. "He's asking if the electrician has showed up yet. That's all."

"Oh? Then why didn't he just call? Or send an email?"

She didn't respond, but made a show of putting the letter back inside the envelope. "I'll go into the kitchen and make that grocery list before I forget."

"I'm really grateful, Ellen, honest."

"Sure," she grumbled.

As soon as the kitchen door swung shut, Ellen took out Reed's letter again, intent on savoring every word.

Dear Ellen,

I realized I don't have your email address, so I thought I'd do this the old-fashioned way—by mail. There's something so leisurely and personal about writing a letter, isn't there?

You're right, the Monterey area is beautiful. I wish I could say that everything else is as peaceful as the scenery here. Unfortunately it's not. Things have been hectic. But if all goes well, I should be back at the house by Saturday, which is earlier than I expected.

Have you become accustomed to the idea that your mother's remarried? I know it was a shock. Like I said, I remember how I felt, and that was many years ago. I've been thinking about it all— and wondering about you. If I'd known what was happening, I might have been able to postpone this trip. You looked like you needed someone. And knowing you, it isn't often that you're willing to lean on anyone. Not the independent, self-sufficient woman I discovered walking around my kitchen half-naked. I can almost see your face getting red when you read that. I shouldn't tease you, but I can't help it.

By the way, I contacted a friend of mine who owns an electrical business and told him about the problem with the kitchen outlet. He said he'd try to stop by soon. He'll call first.

I wanted you to know that I was thinking about you—and the boys, but mostly you. Actually, I'm pleased you're there to keep those kids in line.

Take care and I'll see you late Saturday.

Say hi to the boys for me. I'm trusting that they aren't giving you any problems.
Reed

Ellen folded the letter and slipped it into her pocket. She crossed her arms, smiling to herself, feeling incredibly good. So Reed had been thinking about her. And she sensed that it was more than the troublesome kitchen outlet that had prompted his letter. Although she knew it would be dangerous for her to read too much into Reed's message, Ellen couldn't help feeling encouraged.

She propped open her cookbook, compiling the list of items Derek would need for his fancy dinner with Michelle. A few minutes later, her spirits soared still higher when the electrical contractor phoned and arranged a date and a time to check the faulty outlet. Somehow, that seemed like a good omen to her—a kind of proof that she really was in Reed's thoughts.

"Was the phone for me?" Derek called from halfway down the stairs.

Ellen finished writing the information on the pad by the phone before answering. "It was the electrician."

"Oh. I'm expecting a call from Michelle."

"Speaking of your true love, here's your grocery list."

Derek took it and slowly ran his finger down the items she'd need for his dinner with Michelle. "Is this going to cost more than twenty-five dollars?" He glanced up, his face doubtful.

"The pecans alone will be that much," she exaggerated.

With only a hint of disappointment, Derek shook his head. "I think maybe Michelle and I should find a nice, cozy, *inexpensive* restaurant."

Satisfied that her plan had worked so well, Ellen hid a smile. "Good idea. By the way," she added, "Reed says he'll be home Saturday."

"So soon? He's just been gone two weeks."

"Apparently it's a short job."

"Apparently," Derek grumbled. "I don't have to be here, do I? Michelle wanted me to help her and her sister paint."

"Derek," Ellen said. "I didn't even know you could wield a brush. The upstairs hallway—"

"Forget it," he told her sharply. "I'm only doing this to help Michelle."

"Right, but I'm sure Michelle would be willing to help you in exchange."

"Hey, we're students, not slaves."

The following afternoon, the electrician arrived and was in and out of the house within thirty minutes. Ellen felt proud that she'd correctly traced the problem. She could probably have fixed it if Reed hadn't become so frantic at the thought of her fumbling around with the wiring. Still, recalling his reaction made her smile.

THAT EVENING, ELLEN had finished loading the dishwasher and had just settled down at the kitchen table to study when the phone rang. Pat, who happened to be walking past it, answered.

"It's Reed," he told Ellen. "He wants to talk to you."

With reflexes that surprised even her, Ellen bounded out of her chair.

"Reed," she said into the receiver, holding it tightly against her ear. "Hello, how are you?"

"Fine. Did the electrician come?"

"He was here this afternoon."

"Any problems?"

"No," she breathed. He sounded wonderfully close, his voice warm and vibrant. "In fact, I was on the right track. I probably could've handled it myself."

"I don't want you to even think about fixing anything like that. You could end up killing yourself or someone else. I absolutely forbid it."

"Aye, aye, sir." His words had the immediate effect of igniting her temper, sending the hot blood roaring through her veins. She hadn't been able to stop thinking about Reed since he'd left, but two minutes after picking up the phone, she was ready to argue with him again.

There was a long, awkward silence. Reed was the first to speak, expelling his breath sharply. "I didn't mean to snap your head off," he said. "I'm sorry."

"Thank you," she responded, instantly soothed.

"How's everything else going?"

"Fine."

"Have the boys talked you into any more of their schemes?"

"They keep trying."

"They wouldn't be college kids if they didn't."

"I know." It piqued her a little that Reed assumed she could be manipulated by three teenagers. "Don't worry about me. I can hold my own with these guys."

His low sensuous chuckle did funny things to her pulse. "It's not you I'm concerned about."

"Just what are you implying?" she asked with mock seriousness.

"I'm going to play this one smart and leave that last comment open-ended."

"Clever of you, my friend, very clever."

"I thought as much."

After a short pause, Ellen quickly asked, "How's everything with you?" She knew there really wasn't anything more to say, but she didn't want the conversation to end. Talking to Reed was almost as good as having him there.

"Much better, thanks. I shouldn't have any problem getting home by Saturday."

"Good."

Another short silence followed.

"Well, I guess that's all I've got to say. If I'm going to be any later than Saturday, I'll give you a call."

"Drive carefully."

"I will. Bye, Ellen."

"Goodbye, Reed." Smiling, she replaced the receiver. When she glanced up, all three boys were staring at her, their arms crossed dramatically over their chests.

"I think something's going on here." Pat spoke first. "I answered the phone and Reed asked for Ellen. He didn't even ask for Derek—his own brother."

"Right." Derek nodded vigorously.

"I'm wondering," Monte said, rubbing his chin. "Could we have the makings of a romance on our hands?"

"I think we do," Pat concurred.

"Stop it." Ellen did her best to join in the banter, although she felt the color flooding her cheeks. "It makes sense that Reed would want to talk to me. I'm the oldest."

"But I'm his brother," Derek countered.

"I refuse to listen to any of this," she said with a small laugh and turned back to the kitchen. "You three are being ridiculous. Reed's dating Danielle."

All three followed her. "He could have married Danielle months ago if he was really interested," Derek informed the small gathering.

"Be still, my beating heart," Monte joked, melodramatically folding both hands over his chest and pretending to swoon.

Not to be outdone, Pat rested the back of his hand against his forehead and rolled his eyes. "Ah, love."

"I'm out of here." Before anyone could argue, Ellen ran up the back stairs to her room, laughing as she went. She had to admit she'd found the boys' little performances quite funny. But if they pulled any of their pranks around Reed, it would be extremely embarrassing. Ellen resolved to say something to them when the time seemed appropriate.

FRIDAY AFTERNOON, ELLEN walked into the kitchen, her book bag clutched tightly to her chest.

"What's the matter? You're as pale as a ghost," Monte remarked, cramming a chocolate-chip cookie in his mouth.

Derek and Pat turned toward her, their faces revealing concern.

"I got my algebra paper back today."

"And?" Derek prompted.

"I don't know. I haven't looked."

"Why not?"

"Because I know how tough Engstrom was on the others. The girl who wrote about solving that oddball conjecture got a C-minus and the guy who was so enthusiastic about Mathematics in World War II got a D. With impressive subjects like that getting low grades, I'm doomed."

"But you worked hard on that paper." Loyally, Derek defended her and placed a consoling arm around her shoulders. "You found out a whole bunch of interesting facts about the number nine."

"You did your paper on that?" Pat asked, his smooth brow wrinkling with amusement.

"Don't laugh." She already felt enough of a fool.

"It isn't going to do any good to worry," Monte insisted, pulling the folded assignment from between her fingers.

Ellen watched his expression intently as he looked at the paper, then handed it to Derek who raised his brows and gave it to Pat.

"Well?"

"You got a B-minus," Pat said in obvious surprise. "I don't believe it."

"Me neither." Ellen reveled in the delicious feeling of relief. She sank luxuriously into a chair. "I'm calling Charlie." Almost immediately she jumped up again and dashed to the phone. "This is too exciting! I'm celebrating."

The other three had drifted into the living room and two minutes later, she joined them there. "Charlie's out, but his roommate said he'd give him the message." Too happy to contain her excitement, she added, "But I'm not sitting home alone. How about if we go out for pizza tonight? My treat."

"Sorry, Ellen." Derek looked up with a frown. "I've already made plans with Michelle."

"I'm getting together with a bunch of guys at the gym," Pat informed her. "Throw a few baskets."

"And I told my mom I'd be home for dinner."

Some of the excitement drained from her, but she put on a brave front. "No problem. We'll do it another night."

"I'll go."

The small group whirled around, shocked to discover Reed standing there, framed in the living-room doorway.

CHAPTER FIVE

"REED," ELLEN BURST OUT, ASTONISHED. "When did you get here?" The instant she'd finished speaking, she realized how stupid the question was. He'd just walked in the back door.

With a grin, he checked his wristwatch. "About fifteen seconds ago."

"How was the trip?" Derek asked.

"Did you drive straight through?" Pat asked, then said, "I don't suppose you had a chance to see the Lakers play, did you?"

"You must be exhausted," Ellen murmured, noting how tired his eyes looked.

As his smiling gaze met hers, the fine laugh lines that fanned out from his eyes became more pronounced. "I'm hungry *and* tired. Didn't I just hear you offer to buy me pizza?"

"Ellen got a B-minus on her crazy algebra paper," Monte said with pride.

Rolling her eyes playfully toward the ceiling, Ellen laughed. "Who would have guessed it—I'm a mathematical genius!"

"So that's the reason for this dinner. I thought you might have won the lottery."

He was more deeply tanned than Ellen remembered. Handsome. Vital. And incredibly male. He seemed glad to be home, she thought. Not a hint of hostility showed in the eyes that smiled back at her.

"No such luck."

Derek made a show of glancing at his watch. "I gotta go or I'll be late picking up Michelle. It's good to see you, Reed."

"Yeah, welcome home," Pat said, reaching for his basketball. "I'll see you later."

Reed raised his right hand in salute and picked up his suitcase, then headed up the wide stairs. "Give me fifteen minutes to shower and I'll meet you down here."

The minute Reed's back was turned, Monte placed his hand over his heart and batted his lashes wildly as he mouthed something about love, true love. Ellen practically threw him out of the house, slamming the door after him.

At the top of the stairs, Reed turned and glanced down at her. "What was that all about?"

Ellen leaned against the closed door, one hand covering her mouth to smother her giggles. But the laughter drained from her as she looked at his puzzled face, and she slowly straightened. She cleared her throat. "Nothing. Did you want me to order pizza? Or do you want to go out?"

"Whatever you prefer."

"If you leave it up to me, my choice would be to get away from these four walls."

"I'll be ready in a few minutes."

Ellen suppressed a shudder at the thought of what would've happened had Reed caught a glimpse of Monte's antics. She herself handled the boys' teasing with good-natured indulgence, but she was fairly sure that Reed would take offense at their nonsense. And heaven forbid that Danielle should ever catch a hint of what was going on—not that anything *was* going on.

With her thoughts becoming more muddled every minute, Ellen made her way to the third floor to change into a pair of gray tailored pants and a frilly pale blue silk blouse. One glance in the mirror and she sadly shook her head. They were only going out for pizza— there was no need to wear anything so elaborate. Hurriedly, she changed into dark brown cords and a turtleneck sweater the color of summer wheat. Then she ran a brush through her short curls and freshened her lipstick.

When Ellen returned to the living room, Reed was already waiting for her. "You're sure you don't mind going out?" she asked again.

"Are you dodging your pizza offer?"

He was so serious that Ellen couldn't help laughing. "Not at all."

"Good. I hope you like spicy sausage with lots of olives."

"Love it."

His hand rested on her shoulder. "And a cold beer."

"This is sounding better all the time." Ellen would have guessed that Reed was the type of man who drank martinis or expensive cocktails. In some ways, he was completely down-to-earth and in others, surprisingly complex. Perceptive, unpretentious and unpredictable— she knew that much about him, but she didn't expect to understand him anytime soon.

Reed helped her into his pickup, which was parked in the driveway. The evening sky was already dark and Ellen regretted not having brought her coat.

"Cold?" Reed asked her when they stopped at a red light.

"Only a little."

He adjusted the switches for the heater and soon a rush of warm air filled the cab. Reed chatted easily, telling her about his project in California and explaining why his work demanded so much travel. "That's changing now."

"Oh?" She couldn't restrain a little shiver of gladness at his announcement. "Will you be coming home more often?"

"Not for another three or four months. I'm up for promotion and then I'll be able to pick and choose my assignments more carefully. Over the past four years, I've traveled enough to last me a lifetime."

"Then it's true that there's no place like home."

"Be it ever so humble," he added with a chuckle.

"I don't exactly consider a three-storey, twenty-room turn-of-the-century mansion all that humble."

"Throw in four college students and you'll quickly discover how unassuming it can become."

"Oh?"

"You like that word, don't you?"

"Yes," she agreed, her mouth curving into a lazy smile. "It's amazing how much you can say with that one little sound."

Reed exited the freeway close to the Seattle Center and continued north. At her questioning glance, he explained, "The best pizza in Seattle is made at a small place near the Center. You don't mind coming this far, do you?"

"Of course not. I'll travel a whole lot farther than this for a good pizza." Suddenly slouching forward, she dropped her forehead into her hand. "Oh, no. It's happening."

"What is?"

"I'm beginning to sound like Monte."

They both laughed. It felt so good to be sitting there with Reed, sharing an easy, relaxed companionship, that Ellen could almost forget about Danielle. Almost, but not quite.

Although Ellen had said she'd pay for the pizza, Reed insisted on picking up the tab. They sat across from each other at a narrow booth in the corner of the semidarkened room. A lighted red candle in a glass bowl flickered on the table between them and Ellen decided this was the perfect atmosphere. The old-fashioned jukebox blared out the latest country hits, drowning out the possibility of any audible conversation, but that seemed just as well since she was feeling strangely tongue-tied.

When their number was called, Reed slid from the booth and returned a minute later with two frothy beers in ice-cold mugs and a huge steaming pizza.

"I hope you don't expect us to eat all this?" Ellen said, shouting above the music. The pizza certainly smelled enticing, but Ellen doubted she'd manage to eat more than two or three pieces.

"We'll put a dent in it, anyway," Reed said, resuming his seat. "I bought the largest, figuring the boys would enjoy the leftovers."

"You're a terrific older brother."

The song on the jukebox was fading into silence at last.

"There are times I'd like to shake some sense into Derek, though," Reed said.

Ellen looked down at the spicy pizza and put a small slice on her plate. Strings of melted cheese still linked the piece to the rest of the pie. She pulled them loose and licked her fingers. "I can imagine how you felt when you discovered that Derek had accidentally-on-purpose forgotten to tell you about renting out rooms."

Reed shrugged noncommittally. "I was thinking more about the time he let you climb on top of the roof," he muttered.

"He didn't *let* me, I went all by myself."

"But you won't do it again. Right?"

"Right." Ellen nodded reluctantly. Behind Reed's slow smiles and easy banter, she recognized his unrelenting male pride. "You still haven't forgiven me for that, have you?"

"Not you. Derek."

"I think this is one of those subjects on which we should agree to disagree."

"Have you heard from your mother?" Reed asked, apparently just as willing to change the subject.

"Yes. She's emailed me several times. She seems very happy and after a day or two, I discovered I couldn't be more pleased for her. She deserves a lot of contentment."

"I knew you'd realize that." Warmth briefly showed in his green eyes.

"I felt a lot better after talking to you. I was surprised when Mom announced her marriage, but I shouldn't have been. The signs were there all along. I suppose once the three of us kids were gone, she felt free to remarry. And I suppose she thought that presenting it to the family as a fait accompli would make it easier for all of us."

There was a comfortable silence as they finished eating. The pizza was thick with sausage and cheese, and Ellen placed her hands on her stomach after leisurely eating two narrow pieces. "I'm stuffed," she declared, leaning back. "But you're right, this has got to be the best pizza in town."

"I thought you'd like it."

Reed brought over a carry-out box and Ellen carefully put the leftovers inside.

"How about a movie?" he asked once they were in the car park.

Astounded, Ellen darted him a sideways glance, but his features were unreadable. "You're kidding, aren't you?"

"I wouldn't have asked you if I was."

"But you must be exhausted." Ellen guessed he'd probably spent most of the day driving.

"A little," he admitted.

Her frown deepened. Suddenly, it no longer seemed right for them to be together—because of Danielle. The problem was that Ellen had been so pleased to see him that she hadn't stopped to think about the consequences of their going out together. "Thanks anyway, but it's been a long week. I think I'll call it a night."

When they reached the house, Reed parked on the street rather than the driveway. The light from the stars and the silvery moon penetrated the branches that hung overhead and created shadows on his face. Neither of them seemed eager to leave the warm cab of the pickup truck. The mood was intimate and Ellen didn't want to disturb this moment of tranquillity. Lowering her gaze, she admitted to herself how attracted she was to

Reed and how much she liked him. She admitted, too, that it was wrong for her to feel this way about him.

"You're quiet all of a sudden."

Ellen's smile was decidedly forced. She turned toward him to apologise for putting a damper on their evening, but the words never left her lips. Instead, her eyes met his. Paralyzed, she stared at Reed, fighting to disguise the intense attraction she felt for him. It seemed the most natural thing in the world to lean toward him and brush her lips against his. She could smell the woodsy scent of his aftershave and could almost taste his mouth on hers. With determination, she pulled her gaze away and reached for the door, like a drowning person grasping a life preserver.

She was on the front porch by the time Reed joined her. Her fingers shook as she inserted the key in the lock.

"Ellen." He spoke her name softly and placed his hand on her shoulder.

"I don't know why we went out tonight." Her voice was high and strained as she drew free of his touch. "We shouldn't have been together."

In response, Reed mockingly lifted one eyebrow. "I believe it was you who asked me."

"Be serious, will you," she snapped irritably and shoved open the door.

Reed slammed it shut behind him and followed her into the kitchen. He set the pizza on the counter, then turned to face her. "What the hell do you mean? I *was* being serious."

"You shouldn't have been with me tonight."

"Why not?"

"Where's Danielle? I'm not the one who's been pa-

tiently waiting around for you. *She* is. You had no business taking me out to dinner and then suggesting a
movie. You're my landlord, not my boyfriend."

"Let's get two things straight here. First, what's between Danielle and me is none of *your* business. And
second, you invited *me* out. Remember?"

"But…it wasn't like that and you know it."

"Besides, I thought you said you were far too old
for *boyfriends*." She detected an undertone of amusement in his voice.

Confused, Ellen marched into the living room and
immediately busied herself straightening magazines.
Reed charged in after her, leaving the kitchen door
swinging in his wake. Clutching a sofa pillow, she
searched for some witty retort. Naturally, whenever she
needed a clever comeback, her mind was a total blank.

"You're making a joke out of everything," she told
him, angry that her voice was shaking. "And I don't
like that. If you want to play games, do it with someone other than me."

"Ellen, listen—"

The phone rang and she jerked her attention to the
hallway.

"I didn't mean—" Reed paused and raked his fingers through his hair. The phone pealed a second time.
"Go ahead and answer that."

She hurried away, relieved to interrupt this disturbing conversation. "Hello." Her voice sounded breathless, as though she'd raced down the stairs.

"Ellen? This is Charlie. I got a message that you
phoned."

For one crazy instant, Ellen forgot why she'd wanted
to talk to Charlie. "I phoned? Oh, right. Remember

that algebra paper I was struggling with? Well, I got it back today."

"How'd you do?"

A little of the surprised pleasure returned. "I still can't believe it. I got a B-minus. My simple paper about the wonders of the number nine received one of the highest marks in the class. I'm still in shock."

Charlie's delighted chuckle came over the wire. "This calls for a celebration. How about if we go out tomorrow night? Dinner, drinks, the works."

Ellen almost regretted the impulse to contact Charlie. She sincerely liked him, and she hated the thought of stringing him along or taking advantage of his attraction to her. "Nothing so elaborate. Chinese food and a movie would be great."

"You let me worry about that. Just be ready by seven."

"Charlie."

"No arguing. I'll see you at seven."

By the time Ellen got off the phone, Reed was nowhere to be seen. Nor was he around the following afternoon. The boys didn't comment and she couldn't very well ask about him without arousing their suspicions. As it was, the less she mentioned Reed around them, the better. The boys had obviously read more into the letter, phone call and dinner than Reed had intended. But she couldn't blame them; she'd read enough into it herself to be frightened by what was happening between them. He'd almost kissed her when he'd parked in front of the house. And she'd wanted him to—that was what disturbed her most. But if she allowed her emotions to get involved, she knew that someone would probably end up being hurt. And the most likely *someone* was Ellen herself.

Besides, if Reed was attracted to Danielle's sleek elegance, then he would hardly be interested in her own more homespun qualities.

A few minutes before seven, Ellen was ready for her evening with Charlie. She stood before the downstairs hallway mirror to put the finishing touches on her appearance, fastening her gold earrings and straightening the single chain necklace.

"Where's Reed been today?" Pat inquired of no one in particular.

"His sports car is gone," Monte said, munching on a chocolate bar. "I noticed it wasn't in the garage when I took out the garbage."

Slowly Ellen sauntered into the living room. She didn't want to appear too curious, but at the same time, she was definitely interested in the conversation.

She had flopped into a chair and picked up a two-month-old magazine before she noticed all three boys staring at her.

"What are you looking at me for?"

"We thought you might know something."

"About what?" she asked, playing dumb.

"Reed," all three said simultaneously.

"Why should I know anything?" Her gaze flittered from them to the magazine and back again.

"You went out with him last night."

"We didn't *go out* the way you're implying."

Pat pointed an accusing finger at her. "The two of you were alone together, and both of you have been acting weird ever since."

"And I say the three of you have overactive imaginations."

"All I know is that Reed was like a wounded bear this morning," Derek volunteered.

"Everyone's entitled to an off day." Hoping to give a casual impression, she leafed through the magazine, idly fanning the pages with her thumb.

"That might explain Reed. But what about you?"

"Me?"

"For the first time since you moved in, you weren't downstairs until after ten."

"I slept in. Is that a crime?"

"It just might be. You and Reed are both acting really strange. It's like the two of you are avoiding each other and we want to know why."

"It's your imagination. Believe me, if there was anything to tell you, I would."

"Sure, you would," Derek mocked.

From the corner of her eye, Ellen saw Charlie's car pull up in front of the house. Releasing a sigh of relief, she quickly stood and gave the boys a falsely bright smile. "If you'll excuse me, my date has arrived."

"Should we tell Reed you're out with Charlie if he wants to know where you are?" Monte looked uncomfortable asking the question.

"Of course. Besides, he probably already knows. He's free to see anyone he wants and so am I. For that matter, so are you." She whirled around and made her way to the front door, pulling it open before Charlie even got a chance to ring the doorbell.

The evening didn't go well. Charlie took her out for a steak dinner and spent more money than Ellen knew he could afford. She regretted having phoned him. Charlie had obviously interpreted her call as a sign that she was interested in becoming romantically involved. She wasn't, and didn't know how to make it clear without offending him.

"Did you have a good time?" he asked as they drove back toward Capitol Hill.

"Lovely, thank you, Charlie."

His hand reached for hers and squeezed it reassuringly. "We don't go out enough."

"Neither of us can afford it too often."

"We don't need to go to a fancy restaurant to be together," he said lightly. "Just being with you is a joy."

"Thank you." If only Charlie weren't so nice. She hated the idea of hurting him. But she couldn't allow him to go on hoping that she would ever return his feelings. As much as she dreaded it, she knew she had to disillusion him. Anything else would be cruel and dishonest.

"I don't think I've made a secret of how I feel about you, Ellen. You're wonderful."

"Come on, Charlie, I'm not that different from a thousand other girls on campus." She tried to swallow the tightness in her throat. "In fact, I saw the way that girl in our sociology class—what's her name—Lisa, has been looking at you lately."

"I hadn't noticed."

"I believe you've got yourself an admirer."

"But I'm only interested in you."

"Charlie, listen. I think you're a very special person. I—"

"Shh," he demanded softly as he parked in front of Ellen's house and turned off the engine. He slid his arm along the back of the seat and caressed her shoulder. "I don't want you to say anything."

"But I feel I may have—"

"Ellen," he whispered seductively. "Be quiet and just let me kiss you."

Before she could utter another word, Charlie claimed her mouth in a short but surprisingly ardent kiss. Charlie had kissed her on several occasions, but that was as far as things had ever gone.

When his arms tightened around her, Ellen resisted.

"Invite me in for coffee," he whispered urgently in her ear.

She pressed her forehead against his shirt collar. "Not tonight."

He tensed. "Can I see you again soon?"

"I don't know. We see each other every day. Why don't we just meet after class for coffee one day next week?"

"But I want more than that," he protested.

"I know," she answered, dropping her eyes. She felt confused and miserable.

Ellen could tell he was disappointed from the way he climbed out of the car and trudged around to her side. There was tense silence between them as he walked her up to the front door and kissed her a second time. Again, Ellen had to break away from him by pushing her hands against his chest.

"Thank you for everything," she whispered.

"Right. Thanks, but no thanks."

"Oh, Charlie, don't start that. Not now."

Eyes downcast, he wearily rubbed a hand along the side of his face. "I guess I'll see you Monday," he said with a sigh.

"Thanks for the lovely evening." She didn't let herself inside until Charlie had climbed into his car and driven away.

Releasing a jagged breath, Ellen had just started to unbutton her coat when she glanced up to find Reed standing in the living room, glowering at her.

"Is something wrong?" The undisguised anger that twisted his mouth and hardened his gaze was a shock.

"Do you always linger outside with your boyfriends?"

"We didn't linger."

"Right." He dragged one hand roughly through his hair and marched a few paces toward her, only to do an abrupt about-face. "I saw the two of you necking."

"Necking?" Ellen was so startled by his unreasonable anger that she didn't know whether to laugh or argue. "Be serious, will you? Two chaste kisses hardly constitute necking."

"What kind of influence are you on Derek and the others?" He couldn't seem to stand still and paced back and forth in agitation.

He was obviously furious, but Ellen didn't understand why. He couldn't possibly believe these absurd insinuations. Perhaps he was upset about something else and merely taking it out on her. "Reed, what's wrong?" she finally asked.

"I saw you out there."

"You were spying on me?"

"I wasn't spying," he snapped.

"Charlie and I were in his car. You must've been staring out the window to have seen us."

He didn't answer her, but instead hurled another accusation in her direction. "You're corrupting the boys."

"I'm *what?*" She couldn't believe what she was hearing. "What year do you think this is?" She shook her head, bewildered. "They're nineteen. Trust me, they've kissed girls before."

"You can kiss anyone you like. Just don't do it in front of the boys."

From the way this conversation was going, Ellen could see that Reed was in no mood to listen to reason. "I think we should discuss this some other time," she said quietly.

"We'll talk about it right now."

Ignoring his domineering tone as much as possible, Ellen forced a smile. "Good night, Reed. I'll see you in the morning."

She was halfway to the stairs when he called her, his voice calm. "Ellen."

She turned around, holding herself tense, watching him stride quickly across the short distance that separated them. With his thumb and forefinger, he caught her chin, tilting it slightly so he could study her face. He rubbed his thumb across her lips. "Funny, you don't look kissed."

In one breath he was accusing her of necking and in the next, claiming she was unkissed. Not knowing how to respond, Ellen didn't. She merely gazed at him, her eyes wide and questioning.

"If you're going to engage in that sort of activity, the least you can do—" He paused. With each word his mouth drew closer and closer to hers until his lips hovered over her own and their breath mingled. "The least you can do is look kissed." His hand located the vein pounding wildly in her throat as his mouth settled over hers.

Slowly, patiently, his mouth moved over hers with an exquisite tenderness that left her quivering with anticipation and delight. Timidly, her hands crept across his chest to link behind his neck. Again his lips descended on hers, more hungrily now, as he groaned and pulled her even closer.

Ellen felt her face grow hot as she surrendered to the sensations that stole through her. Yet all the while, her mind was telling her she had no right to feel this contentment, this warmth. Reed belonged to another woman. Not to her...to someone else.

Color seeped into her face. When she'd understood that he intended to kiss her, her first thought had been to resist. But once she'd felt his mouth on hers, all her resolve had drained away. Embarrassed now, she realized she'd pliantly wrapped her arms around his neck. And worse, she'd responded with enough enthusiasm for him to know exactly what she was feeling.

He pressed his mouth to her forehead as though he couldn't bear to release her.

Ellen struggled to breathe normally. She let her arms slip from his neck to his chest and through the palm of her hand she could feel the rapid beating of his heart. She closed her eyes, knowing that her own pulse was pounding no less wildly.

She could feel his mouth move against her temple. "I've been wanting to do that for days." The grudging admission came in a voice that was low and taut.

The words to tell him that she'd wanted it just as much were quickly silenced by the sound of someone walking into the room.

Guiltily Reed and Ellen jerked apart. Her face

turned a deep shade of red as Derek stopped in his tracks, staring at them.

"Hi."

"Hi," Reed and Ellen said together.

"Hey, I'm not interrupting anything, am I? If you like, I could turn around and pretend I didn't see a thing."

"Do it," Reed ordered.

"No," Ellen said in the same moment.

Derek's eyes sparkled with boyish delight. "You know," he said, "I had a feeling about the two of you." While he spoke, he was taking small steps backward until he stood pressed against the polished kitchen door. He gave his brother a thumbs-up as he nudged open the door with one foot and hurriedly backed out of the room.

"Now look what you've done," Ellen wailed.

"Me? As I recall you were just as eager for this as I was."

"It was a mistake," she blurted out. A ridiculous, illogical mistake. He'd accused her of being a bad influence on the boys and then proceeded to kiss her senseless.

"You're telling me." A distinct coolness entered his eyes. "It's probably a good thing I'm leaving."

There was no hiding her stricken look. "Again? So soon?"

"After what's just happened, I'd say it wasn't soon enough."

"But…where to this time?"

"Denver. I'll be back before Thanksgiving."

Mentally, Ellen calculated that he'd be away another two weeks.

When he spoke again, his voice was gentle. "It's just as well, don't you think?"

CHAPTER SIX

"LOOKS LIKE RAIN." Pat stood in front of the window above the kitchen sink and frowned at the thick black clouds that darkened the late-afternoon sky. "Why does it have to rain?"

Ellen glanced up at him. "Are you seeking a scientific response or will a simple 'I don't know' suffice?"

The kitchen door swung open and Derek sauntered in. "Has anyone seen Reed?"

Instantly, Ellen's gaze dropped to her textbook. Reed had returned to Seattle two days earlier and so far, they'd done an admirable job of avoiding each other. Both mornings, he'd left for his office before she was up. Each evening, he'd come home, showered, changed and then gone off again. It didn't require much detective work to figure out that he was with Danielle. Ellen had attempted—unsuccessfully—not to think of Reed at all. And especially not of him and Danielle together.

She secretly wished she'd had the nerve to arrange an opportunity to talk to Reed. So much remained unclear in her mind. Reed had kissed her and it had been wonderful, yet that was something neither seemed willing to admit. It was as if they'd tacitly agreed that the kiss had been a terrible mistake and should be forgotten. The problem was, Ellen *couldn't* forget it.

"Reed hasn't been around the house much," Pat answered.

"I know." Derek sounded slightly disgruntled and cast an accusing look in Ellen's direction. "It's almost like he doesn't live here anymore."

"He doesn't. Not really." Pat stepped away from the window and gently set his basketball on a chair. "It's sort of like he's a guest who stops in now and then."

Ellen preferred not to be drawn into this conversation. She hastily closed her book and stood up to leave.

"Hey, Ellen." Pat stopped her.

She sighed and met his questioning gaze with a nervous smile. "Yes?"

"I'll be leaving in a few minutes. Have a nice Thanksgiving."

Relieved that the subject of Reed had been dropped, she threw him a brilliant smile. "You, too."

"Where are you having dinner tomorrow?" Derek asked, as if the thought had unexpectedly occurred to him.

Her mother was still in Arizona, her sister had gone to visit her in-laws and Bud couldn't get leave, so Ellen had decided to stay in Seattle. "Here."

"In this house?" Derek's eyes widened with concern. "But why? Shouldn't you be with your family?"

"My family is going in different directions this year. It's no problem. In fact, I'm looking forward to having the whole house to myself."

"There's no reason to spend the day alone," Derek argued. "My parents wouldn't mind putting out an extra plate. There's always plenty of food."

Her heart was touched by the sincerity of his invitation. "Thank you, but honestly, I prefer it this way."

"It's because of Reed, isn't it?" Both boys studied her with inquisitive eyes.

"Nonsense."

"But, Ellen, he isn't going to be there."

"Reed isn't the reason," she assured him. Undoubtedly, Reed would be spending the holiday with Danielle. She made an effort to ignore the flash of pain that accompanied the thought; she knew she had no right to feel hurt if Reed chose to spend Thanksgiving with his "almost" fiancée.

"You're sure?" Derek didn't look convinced.

"You could come and spend the day with my family," Pat offered next.

"Will you two quit acting like it's such a terrible tragedy? I'm going to *enjoy* an entire day alone. Look at these nails." She fanned her fingers and held them up for their inspection. "For once, I'll have an uninterrupted block of time to do all the things I've delayed for weeks."

"All right, but if you change your mind, give me a call."

"I asked her first," Derek argued. "You'll call me. Right?"

"Right to you both."

THANKSGIVING MORNING, ELLEN woke to a torrential downpour. Rain pelted against the window and the day seemed destined to be a melancholy one. She lounged in her room and read, enjoying the luxury of not having to rush around, preparing breakfast for the whole household.

She wandered down to the kitchen, where she was greeted by a heavy silence. The house was definitely empty. Apparently, Reed, too, had started his day early. Ellen couldn't decide whether she was pleased or annoyed that she had seen so little of him since his return from Denver. He'd been the one to avoid her, and she'd concluded that two could play his silly game. So she'd purposely stayed out of his way. She smiled sadly as she reflected on the past few days. She and Reed had been acting like a couple of adolescents.

She ate a bowl of cornflakes and spent the next hour wiping down the cupboards, with the radio tuned to the soft-rock music station. Whenever a particularly romantic ballad aired, she danced around the kitchen with an imaginary partner. Not so imaginary, really. In her mind, she was in Reed's arms.

The silence became more oppressive during the afternoon, while Ellen busied herself fussing over her nails. When the final layer of polish had dried, she decided to turn on the television to drown out the quiet. An hour into the football game, Ellen noticed that it was nearly dinnertime, and she suddenly felt hungry.

She made popcorn in the microwave and splurged by dripping melted butter over the top. She carried the bowl into the living room and got back on the sofa, tucking her legs beneath her. She'd just found a comfortable position when she heard a noise in the kitchen.

Frowning, she twisted around, wondering who it could be.

The door into the living room swung open and Ellen's heart rate soared into double time.

"Reed?" She blinked to make sure he wasn't an apparition.

"Hello."

He didn't vanish. Instead he took several steps in her direction. "That popcorn smells great."

Without considering the wisdom of her offer, she held out the bowl to him. "Help yourself."

"Thanks." He took off his jacket and tossed it over the back of a chair before joining her on the sofa. He leaned forward, studying the TV. "Who's winning?"

Ellen was momentarily confused, until she realized he was asking about the football game. "I don't know. I haven't paid that much attention."

Reed reached for another handful of popcorn and Ellen set the bowl on the coffee table. Her emotions were muddled. She couldn't imagine what Reed was doing here when he was supposed to be at Danielle's. Although the question burned in her mind, she couldn't bring herself to ask. She glanced at him covertly, but Reed was staring at the TV as though he was alone in the room.

"I'll get us something to drink," she volunteered.

"Great."

Even while she was speaking, Reed hadn't looked in her direction. Slightly piqued by his attitude, she stalked into the kitchen and took two Pepsis out of the refrigerator.

When she returned with the soft drinks and two glasses filled with ice, Reed took one set from her. "Thanks," he murmured, popping open the can. He carefully poured his soda over the ice and set the can aside before taking a sip.

"You're welcome." She flopped down again, pretending to watch television. But her mind was spinning in a hundred different directions. When she couldn't tolerate it any longer, she blurted out the question that dominated her thoughts.

"Reed, what are you doing here?"

He took a long swallow before answering her. "I happen to live here."

"You know what I mean. You should be with Danielle."

"I was earlier, but I decided I preferred your company."

"I don't need your sympathy," she snapped, then swallowed painfully and averted her gaze. Her fingers tightened around the cold glass until the chill extended up her arm. "I'm perfectly content to spend the day alone. I just wish everyone would quit saving me from myself."

His low chuckle was unexpected. "That wasn't my intention."

"Then why are you here?"

"I already told you."

"I can't accept that," she said shakily. He was toying with her emotions, and the thought made her all the more furious.

"All right." Determinedly, he set down his drink and turned toward her. "I felt this was the perfect opportunity for us to talk."

"You haven't said more than ten words to me in three days. What makes this one day so special?"

"We're alone, aren't we, and that's more than we can usually say." His voice was strained. He hesitated a moment, his lips pressed together in a thin, hard line. "I don't know what's happening with us."

"Nothing's happening," she said wildly. "You kissed

me, and we both admitted it was a mistake. Can't we leave it at that?"

"No," he answered dryly. "I don't believe it was such a major tragedy, and neither do you."

If it had really been a mistake, Ellen wouldn't have remembered it with such vivid clarity. Nor would she yearn for the taste of him again and again, or hurt so much when she knew he was with Danielle.

Swiftly she turned her eyes away from the disturbing intensity of his, unwilling to reveal the depth of her feelings.

"It wasn't a mistake, was it, Ellen?" he prompted in a husky voice.

She squeezed her eyes shut and shook her head. "No," she whispered, but the word was barely audible.

He gathered her close and she felt his deep shudder of satisfaction as he buried his face in her hair. Long moments passed before he spoke. "Nothing that felt so right could have been a mistake."

Tenderly he kissed her, his lips touching hers with a gentleness she hadn't expected. As if he feared she was somehow fragile; as if he found her highly precious. Without conscious decision, she slipped her arms around him.

"The whole time Danielle and I were together this afternoon, I was wishing it was you. Today, of all days, it seemed important to be with you."

Ellen gazed up into his eyes and saw not only his gentleness, but his confusion. Her fingers slid into the thick hair around his lean, rugged face. "Danielle couldn't have been pleased when you left."

"She wasn't. I didn't even know how to explain it to her. I don't know how to explain it to myself."

Ellen swallowed the dryness that constricted her throat. "Do you want me to move out of the house?"

"No," he said forcefully, then added more quietly, "I think I'd go crazy if you did. Are you a witch who's cast some spell over me?"

She tried unsuccessfully to answer him, but no words of denial came. The knowledge that he was experiencing these strange whirling emotions was enough to overwhelm her.

"If so, the spell is working," he murmured, although he didn't sound particularly happy about the idea.

"I'm confused, too," she admitted and leaned her forehead against his chest. She could feel his heart pounding beneath her open hand.

His long fingers stroked her hair. "I know." He leaned down and kissed the top of her head. "The night you went out with Charlie, I was completely unreasonable. I need to apologize for the things I said. To put it simply, I was jealous. I've acknowledged that, these last weeks in Denver." Some of the tightness left his voice, as though the events of that night had weighed heavily on his mind. "I didn't like the idea of another man holding you, and when I saw the two of you kissing, I think I went a little berserk."

"I...we don't date often."

"I won't ask you not to see him again," he said reluctantly. "I can't ask anything of you."

"Nor can I ask anything of you."

His grip around her tightened. "Let's give this time."

"It's the only thing we can do."

Reed straightened and draped his arm around Ellen's shoulders, drawing her close to his side. Her head nestled against his chest. "I'd like us to start going out together," he said, his chin resting on the crown of her head. "Will that cause a problem for you?"

"Cause a problem?" she repeated uncertainly.

"I'm thinking about the boys."

Remembering their earlier buffoonery and the way they'd taken such delight in teasing her, Ellen shrugged. If those three had any evidence of a romance between her and Reed, they could make everyone's lives miserable. "I don't know."

"Then let's play it cool for a while. We'll move into this gradually until they become accustomed to seeing us together. That way it won't be any big deal."

"I think you might be right." She didn't like pretence or deceit, but she'd be the one subjected to their heckling. They wouldn't dare try it with Reed.

"Can I take you to dinner tomorrow night?"

"I'd like that."

"Not as much as I will. But how are we going to do this? It'll be obvious that we're going out," he mused aloud.

"Not if we leave the house at different times," she said.

She could feel his frown. "Is that really necessary?"

"I'm afraid so...."

Ellen and Reed spent the rest of the evening doing nothing more exciting than watching television. His arm remained securely around her shoulders and she felt a sense of deep contentment that was new to her. It was a peaceful interlude during a time that had become increasingly wrought with stress.

Derek got back to the house close to nine-thirty. They both heard him lope in through the kitchen and

Reed gave Ellen a quick kiss before withdrawing his arm.

"Hi." Derek entered the room and stood beside the sofa, shuffling his feet. "Dad wondered where you were." His gaze flitted from Ellen to his brother.

"I told them I wouldn't be there for dinner."

"I know. But Danielle called looking for you."

"She knew where I was."

"Apparently not." Reed's younger brother gestured with one hand. "Are you two friends again?"

Reed's eyes found Ellen's and he smiled. "You could say that."

"Good. You haven't been the easiest people to be around lately." Without giving them a chance to respond, he whirled around and marched upstairs.

Ellen placed a hand over her mouth to smother her giggles. "Well, he certainly told us."

Amusement flared in Reed's eyes, and he chuckled softly. "I guess he did, at that." His arm slid around Ellen's shoulders once again. "Have you been difficult lately?"

"I'm never difficult," she said.

"Me neither."

They exchanged smiles and went back to watching their movie.

As much as Ellen tried to concentrate on the television, her mind unwillingly returned to Derek's announcement. "Do you think you should call Danielle?" She cast her eyes down, disguising her discomfort. Spending these past few hours with Reed had been like an unexpected Christmas gift, granted early. But she felt guilty that it had been at the other woman's expense.

Impatience tightened Reed's mouth. "Maybe I'd better. I didn't mean to offend her or her family by leaving early." He paused a moment, then added, "Danielle's kind of high-strung."

Ellen had noticed that, but she had no intention of mentioning it. And she had no intention of listening in on their conversation, either. "While you're doing that, I'll wash up the popcorn dishes, then go to bed."

Reed's eyes widened slightly in a mock reprimand. "It's a little early, isn't it?"

"Perhaps," she said, faking a yawn, "but I've got this hot date tomorrow night and I want to be well rested for it."

The front door opened and Pat sauntered in, carrying his duffel bag. "Hi." He stopped and studied them curiously. "Hi," he repeated.

"I thought you were staying at your parents' for the weekend." Ellen remembered that he'd said something about being gone for the entire four-day holiday.

"Mom gave my bedroom to one of my aunts. I can't see any reason to sleep on the floor when I've got a bed here."

"Makes sense," Reed said with a grin.

"Are you two getting along again?"

"We never fought."

"Yeah, sure," Pat mumbled sarcastically. "And a basket isn't worth two points."

Ellen had been unaware how much her disagreement with Reed had affected the boys. Apparently, Reed's reaction was the same as hers; their eyes met briefly in silent communication.

"I'll go up with you," she told Pat. "See you in the morning, Reed."

"Sure thing."

She left Pat on the second floor to trudge up to the third.

It shouldn't have been a surprise that she slept so well. Her mind was at ease and she awoke feeling contented and hopeful. Neither she nor Reed had made any commitments yet. They didn't know if what they felt would last a day or a lifetime. They were explorers, discovering the uncharted territory of a new relationship.

She hurried down the stairs early the next morning. Reed was already up, sitting at the kitchen table drinking coffee and reading the paper.

"Morning," she said, pouring water into the tea kettle and setting it on the burner.

"Morning." His eyes didn't leave the paper.

Ellen got a mug from the cupboard and walked past Reed on her way to get the canister of tea. His hand reached out and clasped her around the waist, pulling her down into his lap.

Before she could protest, his mouth firmly covered hers. When the kiss was over, Ellen straightened, resting her hands on his shoulders. "What was that for?" she asked to disguise how flustered he made her feel.

"Just to say good morning," he said in a warm, husky voice. "I don't imagine I'll have too many opportunities to do it in such a pleasant manner."

"No," she said and cleared her throat. "Probably not."

Ellen was sitting at the table, with a section of the paper propped up in front of her, when the boys came into the kitchen.

"Morning," Monte murmured vaguely as he opened

the refrigerator. He was barefoot, his hair was un-combed and his shirt was still unbuttoned. "What's for breakfast?"

"Whatever your little heart desires," she told him, neatly folding over a page of the paper.

"Does this mean you're not cooking?"

"That's right."

"But—"

Reed lowered the sports page and glared openly at Monte.

"Cold cereal will be fine," Monte grumbled and took down a large serving bowl, emptying half the contents of a box of rice crisps inside.

"Hey, save some for me," Pat hollered from the doorway. "That's my favorite."

"I was here first."

Derek strolled into the kitchen. "Does everyone have to argue?"

"Everyone?" Reed cocked a brow in his brother's direction.

"First it was you and Ellen, and now it's Pat and Monte."

"Hey, that's right," Monte cried. "You two aren't fighting. That's great." He set his serving bowl of rice crisps on the table. "Does this mean…you're…you know?"

Lowering the paper, Ellen eyed him sardonically. "No, I don't know."

"Are you…seeing each other?" A deep flush dark-ened Monte's face.

"We see each other every day."

"That's not what I'm asking."

"But that's all I'm answering." From the corner of her eye, she caught sight of Pat pantomiming a fiddler, and she groaned inwardly. The boys were going to make it difficult to maintain any kind of romantic relationship with Reed. She cast him a speculative glance. But if Reed had noticed the activity around him, he wasn't letting on, and Ellen was grateful.

"I've got a practice game tonight," Pat told Ellen as he buttered a piece of toast. "Do you want to come?"

Flustered, she automatically sought out Reed. "Sorry... I'd like to come, but I've got a date."

"Bring him along."

"I...don't know if he likes basketball."

"Yeah, he does," Derek supplied. "Charlie and I were talking about it recently and he said it's one of his favorite games."

She didn't want to tell an outright lie. But she would save herself a lot of aggravation if she simply let Derek and the others assume it was Charlie she'd be seeing.

"What about you, Reed?" Derek asked.

His gaze didn't flicker from the paper and Ellen marveled at his ability to appear so dispassionate. "Not tonight. Thanks anyway."

"Have you got a date, too?" Derek pressed.

It seemed as though everyone in the kitchen was watching Reed, waiting for his response. "I generally go out on Friday nights."

"Well," Ellen said, coming to her feet. "I think I'll get moving. I want to take advantage of the holiday to do some errands. Does anybody need anything picked up at the cleaners?"

"I do," Monte said, raising his hand. "If you'll wait a minute, I'll get the slip."

"Sure."

By some miracle, Ellen was able to avoid any more questions for the remainder of the day. She went about her errands and didn't see Reed until late in the afternoon, when their paths happened to cross in the kitchen. He quickly whispered a time and meeting place and explained that he'd leave first. Ellen didn't have a chance to do more than agree before the boys were upon them.

At precisely seven, Ellen met Reed at the grocery store parking lot two blocks from the house. He'd left ten minutes earlier to wait for her there. As soon as he spotted her, he leaned across the cab of the pickup and opened the door on her side. Ellen found it slightly amusing that when he was with her he drove the pickup, and when he was with Danielle he took the sports car. She wondered whether or not this was a conscious decision. In any event, it told her quite a bit about the way Reed viewed the two women in his life.

"Did you get away unscathed?" he asked, chuckling softly.

She slid into the seat beside him in the cab and shook her head. "Not entirely. All three of them were curious about why Charlie wasn't coming to the house to pick me up. I didn't want to lie, so I told them they'd have to ask him."

"Will they?"

"I certainly hope not."

Reed's hand reached for hers and his eyes grew serious. "I'm not convinced that keeping this a secret is the right thing to do."

"I don't like it, either, but it's better than their constant teasing."

"I'll put a stop to that." His voice dropped ominously and Ellen didn't doubt that he'd quickly handle the situation.

"But, Reed, they don't mean any harm. I was hoping we could lead them gradually into accepting us as a couple. Let them get used to seeing us together before we spring it on them that we're…dating."

"Ellen, I don't know."

"Trust me on this," she pleaded, her eyes imploring him. This arrangement, with its furtiveness and deception, was far from ideal, but for now it seemed necessary. She hoped the secrecy could end soon.

His kiss was brief and ardent. "I don't think I could deny you anything." But he didn't sound happy about it.

The restaurant he took her to was located in the south end of Seattle, thirty minutes from Capitol Hill. At first, Ellen was surprised that he'd chosen one so far from home but the food was fantastic and the view from the Des Moines Marina alone would have been worth the drive.

Reed ordered a bottle of an award-winning wine, a sauvignon blanc from a local winery. It was satisfyingly clear and crisp.

"I spoke to Danielle," Reed began.

"Reed." She stopped him, placing her hand over his. "What goes on between you and Danielle has nothing to do with me. We've made no promises and no commitments." In fact, of course, she was dying to know about the other woman Reed had dated for so long. She hoped that if she pretended no interest in his relationship with Danielle, she'd seem more mature and sophisticated than she really was. She didn't want Reid to think she was threatened by Danielle or that she expected anything from him. Hoped, yes. Expected, no.

He looked a little stunned. "But—"

Swiftly she lowered her gaze. "I don't want to know." Naturally, she was longing to hear every detail. As it was, she felt guilty about the other woman. Danielle might have had her faults, but she loved Reed. She must love him to be so patient with his traveling all these months. And when Derek had first mentioned her, he'd spoken as though Reed and Danielle's relationship was a permanent one.

Danielle and Ellen couldn't have been more different. Ellen was practical and down-to-earth. She'd had to be. After her father's death, she'd become the cornerstone that held the family together.

Danielle, on the other hand, had obviously been pampered and indulged all her life. Ellen guessed that she'd been destined from birth to be a wealthy socialite, someone who might, in time, turn to charitable works to occupy herself. They were obviously women with completely dissimilar backgrounds, she and Danielle.

"I'll be in Atlanta the latter part of next week," Reed was saying.

"You're full of good news, aren't you?"

"It's my work, Ellen."

"I wasn't complaining. It just seems that five minutes after you get home, you're off again."

"I won't be long this time. A couple of days. I'll fly in for the meeting and be back soon afterward."

"You'll be here for Christmas?" Her thoughts flew to her family and how much she wished they could meet Reed. Bud, especially. He'd be in Yakima over the holidays and Ellen was planning to take the bus home to spend some time with him. But first she had to get through her exams.

"I'll be here."

"Good." But it was too soon to ask Reed to join her for the trip. He might misinterpret her invitation, see something that wasn't there. She had no desire to pressure him into the sort of commitment that meeting her family might imply.

After their meal, they walked along the pier, holding hands. The evening air was chilly and when Ellen shivered, Reed wrapped his arm around her shoulders.

"I enjoyed tonight," he murmured.

"I did, too." She bent her arm so that her fingers linked with his.

"Tomorrow night—"

"No." She stopped him, turning so that her arm slid around his middle. Tilting her head back, she stared into the troubled green eyes. "Let's not talk about tomorrow. For right now, let's take one day at a time."

His mouth met hers before she could finish speaking. A gentle brushing of lips. Then he deepened the kiss, and his arms tightened around her, and her whole body hummed with joy.

Ellen was lost, irretrievably lost, in the taste and scent of this man. She felt frightened by her response to him—it would be so easy to fall in love with Reed.

Completely in love. But she couldn't allow that to happen. Not yet. It was too soon.

HER WORDS ABOUT taking each day as it came were forcefully brought to Ellen's mind the following evening. She'd gone to the store and noticed Reed's Porsche parked in the driveway. When she returned, both Reed and the sports car had disappeared.

He was with Danielle.

CHAPTER SEVEN

"WHY COULDN'T I see that?" Ellen moaned, looking over the algebraic equation Reed had worked out. "If I can fix a stopped-up sink, tune a car engine and manage a budget, why can't I understand something this simple?" She was quickly losing a grip on the more advanced theories they were now studying.

"Here, let me show it to you again."

Her hand lifted the curls off her forehead. "Do you think it'll do any good?"

"Yes, I do." Reed obviously had more faith in her powers of comprehension than she did. Step by step, he led her through another problem. When he explained the textbook examples, the whole process seemed so logical. Yet when she set out to solve a similar equation on her own, nothing went right.

"I give up." Throwing her hands over her head, she leaned back in the kitchen chair and groaned. "I should've realized that algebra would be too much for me. I had difficulty memorizing the multiplication tables, for heaven's sake."

"What you need is a break."

"I couldn't agree more. Twenty years?" She stood up and brought the cookie jar to the table. "Here, this will help ease the suffering." She offered him a chocolate-chip cookie and took one herself.

"Be more patient with yourself," Reed urged.

"There's only two weeks left in this term—and then exams. I need to understand this stuff and I need to understand it now."

He laid his hands on her shoulders, massaging gently. "No, you don't. Come on, I'm taking you to a movie."

"I've got to study," she protested, but not too strenuously. Escaping for an hour or two sounded infinitely more appealing than struggling with these impossible equations.

"There's a wonderful foreign film showing at the Moore Egyptian Theatre and we're going. We can worry about that assignment once we get back."

"But, Reed—"

"No buts. We're going." He took her firmly by the hand and led her into the front hall. Derek and Monte were watching TV and the staccato sounds of machine guns firing could be heard in the background. Neither boy noticed them until Reed opened the hall closet.

"Where are you two headed?" Derek asked, peering around the living-room door as Reed handed Ellen her jacket.

"A movie."

Instantly Derek muted the television. "The two of you alone? Together?"

"I imagine there'll be one or two others at the cinema," Reed responded dryly.

"Can I come?" Monte had joined Derek in the doorway.

Instantly Derek's elbow shoved the other boy in the ribs. "On second thought, just bring me back some popcorn, okay?"

"Sure."

Ellen pulled a knit cap over her ears. "Do either of you want anything else? I'd buy out the concession stand if one of you felt inclined to do my algebra assignment."

"No way."

"Bribing them won't help," Reed commented.

"I know, but I was hoping…."

It was a cold, blustery night. An icy north wind whipped against them as they hurried to Reed's truck. He opened the door for her before running around to the driver's side.

"Brr." Ellen shoved her hands inside her pockets. "If I doubted it was winter before, now I know."

"Come here and I'll warm you." He patted the seat beside him, indicating that she should slide closer.

Willingly she complied, until she sat so near him that her thigh pressed against his. Neither of them moved. It had been several days since they'd been completely alone together and longer still since he'd held or kissed her without interruption. The past week had been filled with frustration. Often she'd noticed Reed's gaze on her, studying her face and her movements, but it seemed that every time he touched her one of the boys would unexpectedly appear.

Reed turned to her. Their thoughts seemed to echo each other's; their eyes locked hungrily. Ellen required no invitation. She'd been longing for his touch. With a tiny cry she reached for him just as his arms came out to encircle her, drawing her even closer.

"This is crazy," he whispered fervently into her hair.

"I know."

As though he couldn't deny himself any longer, he

cradled her face with both hands and he slowly lowered his mouth to hers.

Their lips clung and Reed's hand went around her ribs as he held her tight. The kiss was long and thoroughly satisfying.

Panting, he tore his mouth from hers and buried his face in her neck. "We'd better get to that movie."

It was all Ellen could do to nod her head in agreement.

They moved apart and fastened their seat belts, both of them silent.

When Reed started the truck, she saw that his hand was trembling. She was shaking too, but no longer from the cold. Reed had promised to warm her and he had, but not quite in the way she'd expected.

They were silent as Reed pulled onto the street. After days of carefully avoiding any kind of touch, any lingering glances, they'd sat in the driveway kissing in direct view of curious eyes. She realized the boys could easily have been watching them.

Ellen felt caught up in a tide that tossed her closer and closer to a long stretch of rocky beach. Powerless to alter the course of her emotions, she feared for her heart, afraid of being caught in the undertow.

"The engineering department is having a Christmas party this weekend at the Space Needle," Reed murmured.

Ellen nodded. Twice in the past week he'd left the house wearing formal evening clothes. He hadn't told her where he was going, but she knew. He'd driven the Porsche and he'd come back smelling of expensive perfume. For a Christmas party with his peers,

Reed would escort Danielle. She understood that and tried to accept it.

"I want you to come with me."

"Reed," she breathed, uncertain. "Are you sure?"

"Yes." His hand reached for hers. "I want you with me."

"The boys—"

"Forget the boys. I'm tired of playing games with them."

Her smile came from her heart. "I am, too," she whispered.

"I'm going to have a talk with them."

"Don't," she pleaded. "It's not necessary to say anything."

"They'll start in with their teasing," he warned. "I thought you hated that."

"I don't care as much anymore. And if they do, we can say something then."

He frowned briefly. "All right."

The Moore Egyptian was located in the heart of downtown Seattle, so parking was limited. They finally found a spot on the street three blocks away. They left the truck and hurried through the cold, arm in arm, not talking. The French film was a popular one; by the time they got to the cinema, a long line had already formed outside.

A blast of wind sliced through Ellen's jacket and she buried her hands in her pockets. Reed leaned close to ask her something, then paused, slowly straightening.

"Morgan." A tall, brusque-looking man approached Reed.

"Dailey," Reed said, quickly stepping away from Ellen.

"I wouldn't have expected to see you out on a night like this," the man Reed had called Dailey was saying.

"I'm surprised to see you, too."

"This film is supposed to be good," Dailey said.

"Yeah. It's got great reviews."

Dailey's eyes returned to the line and rested on Ellen, seeking an introduction. Reed didn't give him one. Reed was obviously pretending he wasn't with Ellen.

She offered the man a feeble smile, wondering why Reed would move away from her, why he wouldn't introduce her to his acquaintance. The line moved slowly toward the ticket booth and Ellen went with it, leaving Reed talking to Dailey on the pavement. She felt a flare of resentment when he rejoined her a few minutes later.

"That was a friend of a friend."

Ellen didn't respond. Somehow she didn't believe him. And she resented the fact that he'd ignored the most basic of courtesies and left her standing on the sidewalk alone, while he spoke with a friend. The way he'd acted, anyone would assume Reed didn't want the man to know Ellen was with him. That hurt. Fifteen minutes earlier she'd been soaring with happiness at his unexpected invitation to the Christmas party, and now she was consumed with doubt and bitterness. Perhaps this Dailey was a friend of Danielle's and Reed didn't want the other woman to know he was out with Ellen. But that didn't really sound like Reed.

Once inside the cinema, Reed bought a huge bucket of buttered popcorn. They located good seats, despite the crowd, and sat down, neither of them speaking. As the lights went down, Reed placed his hand on the back of her neck.

Ellen stiffened. "Are you sure you want to do that?"

"What?"

"Touch me. Someone you know might recognize you."

"Ellen, listen…"

The credits started to roll on the huge screen and she shook her head, not wanting to hear any of his excuses.

But maintaining her bad mood was impossible with the comedy that played out before them. Unable to stop herself, Ellen laughed until tears formed in her eyes; she was clutching her stomach because it hurt from laughing. Reed seemed just as amused as she was, and a couple of times during the film, their smiling gazes met. Before she knew it, Reed was holding her hand and she didn't resist when he draped his arm over her shoulders.

Afterward, as they strolled outside, he tucked her hand in the crook of his elbow. "I told you a movie would make you feel better."

It had and it hadn't. Yes, she'd needed the break, but Reed's behavior outside the cinema earlier had revived the insecurities she was trying so hard to suppress. She knew she wasn't nearly as beautiful or sophisticated as Danielle.

"You *do* feel better?" His finger lifted her chin to study her eyes.

There was no denying that the film had been wonderful. "I haven't laughed so hard in ages," she told him, smiling.

"Good."

FRIDAY NIGHT, ELLEN wore her most elaborate outfit— slim black velvet pants and a silver lamé top. She'd spent hours debating whether an evening gown would have been more appropriate, but had finally decided on the pants. Examining herself from every direction in the full-length mirror that hung from her closet door, Ellen released a pent-up breath and closed her eyes. This one night, she wanted everything to be perfect. Her heels felt a little uncomfortable, but she'd get used to them. She rarely had any reason to wear heels. She'd chosen them now because Reed had said there'd be dancing and she wanted to adjust her height to his.

By the time she reached the foot of the stairs, Reed was waiting for her. His eyes softened as he looked at her. "You're lovely."

"Oh, Reed, are you sure? I don't mind changing if you'd rather I wear something else."

His eyes held hers for a long moment. "I don't want you to change a thing."

"Hey, Ellen." Derek burst out of the kitchen, and stopped abruptly. "Wow." For an instant he looked as though he'd lost his breath. "Hey, guys," he called eagerly. "Come and see Ellen."

The other two joined Derek. "You look like a movie star," Pat breathed.

Monte closed his mouth and opened it again. "You're *pretty.*"

"Don't sound so shocked."

"It's just that we've never seen you dressed…like this," Pat mumbled.

"Are you going out with Charlie?"

Ellen glanced at Reed, suddenly unsure. She hadn't dated Charlie in weeks. She hadn't wanted to.

"She's going out with me," Reed explained in an even voice that didn't invite comment.

"With you? Where?" Derek's eyes got that mischievous twinkle Ellen recognized immediately.

"A party."

"What about—" He stopped suddenly, swallowing several times.

"You had a comment?" Reed lifted his eyebrows.

"I thought I was going to say something," Derek muttered, clearly embarrassed, "but then I realized I wasn't."

Hiding a smile, Reed held Ellen's coat for her.

She slipped her arms into the satin-lined sleeves and reached for her beaded bag. "Good night, guys, and don't wait up."

"Right." Monte raised his index finger. "We won't wait up."

Derek took a step forward. "Should I say anything to someone…anyone…in case either of you gets a phone call?"

"Try *hello,*" Reed answered, shaking his head.

"Right." Derek stuck his hand in his jeans pocket. "Have a good time."

"We intend to."

Ellen managed to hold back her laughter until they were on the front porch. But when the door clicked shut the giggles escaped and she pressed a hand to her mouth. "Derek *thought* he was going to say something."

"Then he realized he wasn't," Reed finished for her, chuckling. His hand at her elbow guided her down the steps. "They're right about one thing. You do look gorgeous."

"Thank you, but I hadn't expected it to be such a shock."

"The problem is, the boys are used to seeing you

as a substitute mother. It's suddenly dawned on them what an attractive woman you are."

"And how was it *you* noticed?"

"The day I arrived and found you in my kitchen wearing only a bra, I knew."

"I was wearing more than that," she argued.

"Maybe, but at the time that was all I saw." He stroked her cheek with the tip of his finger, then tucked her arm in his.

Ellen felt a warm contentment as Reed led her to the sports car. This was the first time she'd been inside, and the significance of that seemed unmistakable. She sensed that somewhere in the past two weeks Reed had made an unconscious decision about their relationship. Maybe she was being silly in judging the strength of their bond by what car he chose to drive. And maybe not. Reed was escorting her to this party in his Porsche because he viewed her in a new light. He saw her now as a beautiful, alluring woman—no longer as the college student who seemed capable of mastering everything but algebra.

The Space Needle came into view as Reed pulled onto Denny Street. The world-famous Needle, which had been built for the 1962 World's Fair, rose 605 feet above the Seattle skyline. Ellen had taken the trip up to the observation deck only once and she'd been thrilled at the unobstructed view of the Olympic and Cascade mountain ranges. Looking out at the unspoiled beauty of Puget Sound, she'd understood immediately why Seattle was described as one of the world's most livable cities.

For this evening, Reed explained, his office had booked the convention rooms on the hundred-foot level of the Needle. The banquet facilities had been an addition, and Ellen wondered what sort of view would be available.

As Reed stopped in front of the Needle, a valet appeared, opening Ellen's door and offering her his gloved hand. She climbed as gracefully as she could from the low-built vehicle. Her smile felt a little strained, and she took a deep breath to dispel the gathering tension. She wanted everything about the evening to be perfect; she longed for Reed to be proud of her, to feel that she belonged in his life—and in his world.

Her curiosity about the view was answered as soon as they stepped from the elevator into the large room. She glanced at the darkened sky that resembled folds of black velvet, sprinkled with glittering gems. When she had a chance she'd walk over toward the windows. For now, she was more concerned with fitting into Reed's circle and being accepted by his friends and colleagues.

Bracing herself for the inevitable round of introductions, she scanned the crowd for the man she'd seen outside the cinema. He didn't seem to be at the party and Ellen breathed easier. If Dailey was there, he would surely make a comment about seeing her with Reed that night, and she wouldn't know how to respond.

As they made their way through the large room, several people called out to Reed. When he introduced Ellen, two or three of them appeared to have trouble concealing their surprise that he wasn't with Danielle. But no one mentioned Danielle and they all seemed to accept Ellen freely, although a couple of people gave her curious looks. Eventually, Ellen relaxed and smiled up at Reed.

"That wasn't so bad, was it?" he asked, his voice tender.

"Not at all."

"Would you like something to drink?"

"Please."

"Wine okay?"

"Of course."

"I'll be right back."

Ellen watched Reed cross the room toward the bar. She was absurdly proud of him and made no attempt to disguise her feelings when he returned to her, carrying two glasses of white wine.

"You shouldn't look at me like that," he murmured, handing her a glass.

"Why?" she teased, her eyes sparkling. "Does it embarrass you?"

"No. It makes me wish I could ignore everyone in this room and kiss you right this minute." A slow, almost boyish grin spread across his features.

"That would certainly cause quite a commotion."

"But not half the commotion it would cause if they knew what else I was thinking."

"Oh?" She hid a smile by taking another sip of wine.

"Are we back to that word again?"

"Just what do you have in mind?"

He dipped his head so that he appeared to be whispering something in her ear, although actually his lips brushed her face. "I'll show you later."

"I'll be waiting."

They stood together, listening to the music and the laughter. Ellen found it curious that he'd introduced her to so few people and then only to those who'd approached him. But she dismissed her qualms as petty and, worse, paranoid. After all, she told herself, she was here to be with Reed, not to make small talk with his friends.

He finished his drink and suggested another. While he returned to the bar for refills, Ellen wandered through the crowd, walking over to the windows for a glimpse of the magnificent view. But as she moved, she kept her gaze trained on Reed.

A group of men stopped him before he could reach the bar. His head was inclined toward them, and he seemed to be giving them his rapt attention. Yet periodically his eyes would flicker through the crowd, searching for her. When he located her by the huge floor-to-ceiling windows, he smiled as though he felt relieved. With an abruptness that bordered on rudeness, he excused himself from the group and strolled in her direction.

"I didn't see where you'd gone."

"I wasn't about to leave you," she told him. Turning, she faced the window, watching the lights of the ferry boats gliding across the dark green waters of Puget Sound.

His hands rested on her shoulders and Ellen leaned back against him, warmed by his nearness. "It's lovely from up here."

"Exquisite," he agreed, his mouth close to her ear. "But I'm not talking about the view." His hands slid lazily down her arms. "Dance with me," he said, taking her hand and leading her to the dance floor.

Ellen walked obediently into his arms, loving the feel of being close to Reed. She pressed her cheek against the smooth fabric of his jacket as they swayed gently to the slow, dreamy music.

"I don't normally do a lot of dancing," he whispered.

Ellen wouldn't have guessed that. He moved with confident grace, and she assumed he'd escorted Danielle around a dance floor more than once. At the thought of the other woman, Ellen grew uneasy, but she forced her tense body to relax. Reed had chosen to bring *her,* and not Danielle, to this party. That had to mean something—something exciting.

"Dancing was just an excuse to hold you."

"You don't need an excuse," she whispered.

"In a room full of people, I do."

"Shall we wish them away?" She closed her eyes, savoring the feel of his hard, lithe body against her own.

He maneuvered them into the darkest corner of the dance floor and immediately claimed her mouth in a kiss that sent her world spinning into orbit.

Mindless of where they were, Ellen arched upward, Reed responded by sliding his hands down her back, down to her hips, drawing her even closer.

He dragged his mouth across her cheek. "I'm sorry we came."

"Why?"

"I don't want to waste time with all these people around. We're hardly ever alone. I want you, Ellen."

His honest, straightforward statement sent the fire roaring through her veins. "I know. I want you, too." Her voice was unsteady. "But it's a good thing we aren't alone very often." At the rate things were progressing between them, Ellen felt relieved that the boys were at the house. Otherwise—

"Hey, Reed." A friendly voice boomed out a few feet away. "Aren't you going to introduce me to your friend?"

Reed stiffened and for a moment Ellen wondered if he was going to pretend he hadn't heard. He looked at her through half-closed eyes, and she grinned up at him, mutely telling him she didn't mind. Their private world couldn't last forever. She knew that. They were at a party, an office party, and Reed was expected to mingle with his colleagues.

"Hello, Ralph." Reed's arm slid around Ellen's waist, keeping her close.

"Hello there." But Ralph wasn't watching Reed. "Well, aren't you going to introduce me?"

"Ellen Cunningham, Ralph Forester."

Ralph extended his hand and held Ellen's in both of his for a long moment. His eyes were frankly admiring.

"I don't suppose you'd let me steal this beauty away for a dance, would you?" Although the question was directed at Reed, Ralph didn't take his eyes from Ellen. "Leave it to you to be with the most beautiful woman here," the other man teased. "You sure do attract them."

Reed's hand tightened around Ellen. "Ellen?" He left the choice to her.

"I don't mind." She glanced at Reed and noted that his expression was carefully blank. But she knew him too well to be fooled. She could see that his jaw was rigid with tension and that his eyes showed annoyance at the other man's intrusion. Gradually he lowered his arm, releasing her.

Ralph stepped forward and claimed Ellen's hand, leading her onto the dance floor.

She swallowed as she placed her left hand on his shoulder and her right hand in his. Wordlessly they moved to the soft music. But when Ralph tried to bring her closer, Ellen resisted.

"Have you known Reed long?" Ralph asked, his hand trailing sensuously up and down her back.

She tensed. "Several months now." Despite her efforts to keep her voice even and controlled, she sounded slightly breathless.

"How'd you meet?"

"Through his brother." The less said about their living arrangements, the better. Ellen could just guess what Ralph would say if he knew they were living in the same house. "Do you two work together?"

"For the last six years."

They whirled around, and Ellen caught a glimpse of Reed standing against the opposite wall, studying them like a hawk zeroing in on its prey. Ralph apparently noticed him, as well.

"I don't think Reed was all that anxious to have you dance with me."

Ellen merely shrugged.

Ralph chortled gleefully, obviously enjoying Reed's reaction. "Not if the looks he's giving me are any indication. I can't believe it. Reed Morgan is jealous," he said with another chuckle, leading her out of Reed's sight and into the dimly lit center of the floor.

"I'm sure you're mistaken."

"Well, look at him."

All Ellen could see was Reed peering suspiciously at them across the crowded dance floor.

"This is too good to be true," Ralph murmured.

"What do you mean?"

"There isn't a woman in our department who wouldn't give her eyeteeth to go out with Reed."

Ellen was shocked, yet somehow unsurprised. "Oh?"

"Half the women are in love with him and he ignores them. He's friendly, don't get me wrong. But it's all business. Every time a single woman gets transferred into our area it takes her a week, maybe two, to fall for Reed. The rest of us guys just stand back and shake our heads. But with Reed otherwise occupied, we might have a chance."

"He *is* wonderful," Ellen admitted, managing to keep a courteous smile on her face. What Ralph was describing sounded so much like her own feelings that she couldn't doubt the truth of what he said.

Ralph arched his brows and studied her. "You too?"

"I'm afraid so."

"What's this guy got?" He sighed expressively, shaking his head. "Can we bottle it?"

"Unfortunately, I don't think so," Ellen responded lightly, liking Ralph more. His approach might have been a bit overpowering at first, but he was honest and compelling in his own right. "I don't imagine you have much trouble attracting women."

"As long as I don't bring them around Reed, I'm fine." A smile swept his face. "The best thing that could happen would be if he got married. I don't suppose that's in the offing between you two?"

He was so blithely serious that Ellen laughed. "Sorry."

"You're sure?"

Ralph was probably thinking of some rumor he'd heard about Danielle. "There's another woman he's seeing. They've known each other for a long time and apparently, they're quite serious," she explained, keeping her voice calmly detached.

"I don't believe it," Ralph countered, frowning. "Reed wouldn't be tossing daggers at my back if he was involved with someone else. One thing I suspect about this guy, he's a one-woman man."

Ellen closed her eyes, trying to shut out the pain. She didn't know what to believe about Reed anymore. All she could do was hold on to the moment. Wasn't that what she'd told him earlier—that they'd have to take things day by day? She was the one who hadn't wanted to talk about Danielle. In any case, she didn't want to read too much into his actions. She couldn't. She was on the brink of falling in love with him…if she hadn't already. To allow herself to think he might feel the same way was asking for trouble. For heartbreak.

The music ended and Ralph gently let her go. "I'd better return you to Reed or he's likely to come after me."

"Thank you for…everything."

"You're welcome, Ellen." With one hand at her waist, he steered her toward Reed.

They were within a few feet of him when Danielle suddenly appeared. She seemed to have come out of nowhere. "Reed!" She was laughing delightedly, flinging herself into his arms and kissing him intimately. "Oh, darling, you're so right. Being together is more important than any ski trip. I'm so sorry. Will you forgive me?"

CHAPTER EIGHT

"ELLEN," RALPH ASKED. "Are you all right?"

"I'm fine," she lied.

"Sure you are," he mocked, sliding his arm around her waist and guiding her back to the dance floor. "I take it the blonde is Woman Number One?"

"You got it." The anger was beginning to build inside her. "Beautiful, too, you'll notice."

"Well, you aren't exactly chopped liver."

She gave a small, mirthless laugh. "Nice of you to say so, but by comparison, I come in a poor second."

"I wouldn't say that."

"Then why can't you take your eyes off Danielle?"

"Danielle. Hmm." He looked away from the other woman and stared blankly into Ellen's face. "Sorry." For her part, Ellen instinctively turned her back on Reed, unable to bear the sight of him holding and kissing another woman.

"Someone must have got their wires crossed."

"Like me," Ellen muttered. She'd been an idiot to assume that Reed had meant anything by his invitation. He'd just needed someone to take to this party, and his first choice hadn't been available. She was a substitute, and a second-rate one at that.

"What do you want to do?"

Ellen frowned, her thoughts fragmented. "I don't know yet. Give me a minute to think."

"You two could always fight for him."

"The stronger woman takes the spoils? No, thanks." Despite herself she laughed. It certainly would've created a diversion at this formal, rather staid party.

Craning his neck, Ralph peered over at the other couple. "Reed doesn't seem too pleased to see her."

"I can imagine. The situation's put him in a bit of a bind."

"I admit it's unpleasant for you, but, otherwise, I'm enjoying this immensely."

Who wouldn't? The scene was just short of comical. "I thought you said Reed was a one-woman man."

"I guess I stand corrected."

Ellen was making a few corrections herself, revising some cherished ideas about Reed Morgan.

"I don't suppose you'd consider staying with me for the rest of the evening?" Ralph suggested hopefully.

"Consider it? I'd say it's the best offer I've had in weeks." She might feel like a fool, but she didn't plan to hang around looking like one.

Ralph nudged her and bent his head to whisper in her ear. "Reed's staring at us. And like I said, he doesn't seem pleased."

With a determination born of anger and pride, she forced a smile to her lips and gazed adoringly up at Ralph. "How am I doing?" she asked, batting her lashes at him.

"Wonderful, wonderful." He swung her energetically around to the beat of the music. "Uh-oh, here he comes."

Reed weaved his way through the dancing couples and tapped Ralph on the shoulder. "I'm cutting in."

Ellen tightened her grip on Reed's colleague, silently pleading with him to stay. "Sorry, buddy, but Ellen's with me now that your lady friend has arrived."

"Ellen?" Reed's eyes narrowed as he stared at her intently. The other couples were dancing around them and curiously watching the party of three that had formed in the center of the room.

She couldn't remember ever seeing anyone look more furious than Reed did at this moment. "Maybe I'd better leave," she said in a low, faltering voice.

"I'll take you home," Ralph offered, dropping his hand to her waist.

"You came with me. You'll leave with me." Reed grasped her hand, pulling her toward him.

"Obviously you were making provisions," Ellen said, "on the off-chance Danielle showed up. How else did she get in here?"

"How am I supposed to know? She probably told the manager she was with me."

"And apparently she is," Ellen hissed.

"Maybe Reed and I should wrestle to decide the winner," Ralph suggested, glancing at Ellen and sharing a comical grin.

"Maybe."

Obviously, Reed saw no humor in the situation. Anger darkened his handsome face, and a muscle twitched in his jaw as the tight rein on his patience slipped.

Ralph withdrew his hand. "Go ahead and dance. It's obvious you two have a lot to talk about."

Reed took Ellen in his arms. "I suppose you're furious," he muttered.

"Have I got anything to be angry about?" she asked calmly. Now that the initial shock had worn off, she felt somewhat distanced from the whole predicament.

"Of course you do. But I want a chance to explain."

"Don't bother. I've got the picture."

"I'm sure you don't."

Ellen stubbornly refused to look up at him, resisting for as long as she could, but eventually she gave in. "It doesn't matter. Ralph said he'd take me home and—"

"I've already made my feelings on that subject quite clear."

"Listen, Reed. Your Porsche seats two. Is Danielle supposed to sit on my lap?"

"She came uninvited. Let her find her own way home."

"You don't mean that."

"I certainly do."

"You can't humiliate Danielle like that." Ellen didn't mention how *she* felt. What was the point? "Don't—"

"She deserves it," he broke in.

"Reed, no." Her hold on his forearm tightened. "This is unpleasant enough for all of us. Don't compound it."

The song ended and the music faded from the room. Reed fastened his hand on Ellen's elbow, guiding her across the floor to where Danielle was standing with Ralph. The two of them were sipping champagne.

"Hello again," Ellen began amicably, doing her utmost to appear friendly, trying to smooth over an already awkward situation.

"Hello." Danielle stared at Ellen curiously, apparently not recognizing her.

"You remember Ellen Cunningham, don't you?" Reed said.

"Not that college girl your brother's renting a room to—" Danielle stopped abruptly, shock etched on her perfect features. "*You're* Ellen Cunningham?"

"In the flesh." Still trying to keep things light, she cocked her head toward Ralph and spoke stagily out of the side of her mouth, turning the remark into a farcical aside. "I wasn't at my best when we met the first time."

"You were fiddling around with that electrical outlet and Reed was horrified," Danielle inserted, her voice completely humorless, her eyes narrowed assessingly. "You didn't even look like a girl."

"She does now." Ralph beamed her a brilliant smile.

"Yes." Danielle swallowed, her face puckered with concern. "She looks very...nice."

"Thank you." Ellen bowed her head.

"I've made a terrible mess of things," Danielle continued, casually handing her half-empty glass to a passing waiter. "Reed mentioned the party weeks ago, and Mom and I had this ski party planned. I told him I couldn't attend and then I felt guilty because Reed's been so sweet, escorting me to all the charity balls."

Ellen didn't hear a word of explanation beyond the fact that Reed had originally asked Danielle to the party. The other woman had just confirmed Ellen's suspicions, and the hurt went through her like a thousand needles. He'd invited her only because Danielle couldn't attend.

"There's no problem," Ellen said in a bland voice. "I understand how these things happen. He asked you first, so you stay and I'll leave."

"I couldn't do that," Danielle murmured.

Reed's eyes were saying the same thing. Ellen ignored him, and she ignored Danielle. Slipping her hand around Ralph's arm, she looked up at him and smiled, silently thanking him for being her friend. "As I said, it's not a problem. Ralph's already offered to take me home."

Reed's expression was impassive, almost aloof, as she turned toward him. "I'm sure you won't mind."

"How understanding of you," Danielle simpered, locking her arm around Reed's.

"It's better than hand-to-hand combat. I don't really care for fighting."

Danielle looked puzzled, while Ralph choked on a swallow of his drink, his face turning several shades of red as he struggled to hide his amusement. The only one who revealed no sense of humor was Reed, whose face grew more and more shadowed.

The band struck up a lively song and the dance floor quickly filled. "Come on, Reed," Danielle said, her blue eyes eager. "Let's dance." She tugged at Reed's hand and gave a little wriggle of her hips. "You know how much I love to dance."

So Reed *had* done his share of dancing with Danielle—probably at all those charity balls she'd mentioned. Ellen had guessed as much and yet he'd tried to give her the impression that he rarely danced.

But noticing the stiff way Reed held himself now, Ellen could almost believe him.

Ralph placed a gentle hand on her shoulder. "I don't know about you, but I'm ready to get out of here."

Watching Reed with Danielle in his arms was absurdly painful; her throat muscles constricted in an effort to hold back tears and she simply nodded.

"Since we'll be skipping the banquet, shall we go have dinner somewhere?"

Ellen blinked. Dinner. "I'm not really hungry," she said.

"Sure you're hungry," Ralph insisted. "We'll stop at a nice restaurant before I drive you home. I know where Reed's place is, so I know where you live. Don't look so shocked. I figured it out from what you and Danielle were saying. But don't worry, I understand—impoverished students sharing a house and all that. So, what do you say? We'll have a leisurely dinner and get home two hours after Reed. That should set him thinking."

Ellen didn't feel in any mood to play games at Reed's expense. "I'd rather not."

Ralph's jovial expression sobered. "You've got it bad."

"I'll be fine."

He smiled. "I know you will. Come on, let's go."

The night that had begun with such promise had evaporated so quickly, leaving a residue of uncertainty and suspicion. As they neared the house, her composure gradually crumbled until she was nervously twisting the delicate strap of her evening bag over and over between her fingers. To his credit, Ralph attempted to carry the conversation, but her responses became less and less animated. She just wanted to get home and bury her head in her pillow.

By the time Ralph pulled up in front of the Capitol Hill house, they were both silent.

"Would you like to come in for coffee?" she asked. The illusion she'd created earlier of flippant humor was gone now. She hurt, and every time she blinked, a picture of Danielle dancing with Reed came to mind. How easy it was to visualize the other woman's arms around his neck, her voluptuous body pressed against his. The image tormented Ellen with every breath she took.

"No, I think I'll make it an early night."

"Thank you," she said affectionately. "I couldn't have handled this without you."

"I was happy to help. And, Ellen, if you want a shoulder to cry on, I'm available."

She dropped her gaze to the tightly coiled strap of her bag. "I'm fine. Really."

He patted her hand. "Somehow I don't quite believe that." Opening the car door, he came around to her side and handed her out.

On the top step of the porch, Ellen kissed his cheek. "Thanks again."

"Good night, Ellen."

"Night." She took out her keys and unlocked the front door. Pushing it open, she discovered that the house was oddly dark and oddly deserted. It was still relatively early and she would've expected the boys to be around. But not having to make excuses to them was a blessing she wasn't about to question.

As she removed her coat and headed for the stairs, she noticed the shadows bouncing around the darkened living room. She walked over to investigate and, two steps into the room, heard soft violin music.

Ellen stood there paralyzed, taking in the romantic scene before her. A bottle of wine and two glasses were set out on the coffee table. A fire blazed in the brick fireplace. And the music seemed to assault her from all sides.

"Derek," she called out.

Silence.

"All right, Pat and Monte. I know you're here somewhere."

Silence.

"I'd suggest the three of you get rid of this…stuff before Reed comes home. He's with Danielle." With that,
she marched up the stairs, uncaring if they heard her.

"With Danielle?" she heard a male voice shout after
her.

"What happened?"

Ellen pretended not to hear.

THE MORNING SUN sneaked into her window, splashing
the pillow where Ellen lay awake staring sightlessly
at the ceiling. Sooner or later she'd have to get out of
bed, but she couldn't see any reason to rush the process. Besides, the longer she stayed up here, the greater
her chances of missing Reed. The unpleasantness of
facing him wasn't going to vanish, but she might be
able to postpone it for a morning. Although she had
to wonder whether Reed was any more keen on seeing her than she was on seeing him. She could always
kill time by dragging out her algebra books and studying for the exam—but that was almost as distasteful
as facing Reed.

No, she decided suddenly, she'd stay in her room
until she was weak with hunger. Checking her wristwatch, she figured that would be about another five
minutes.

Someone knocked on her bedroom door. Sitting up,
Ellen pulled the sheet to her neck. "Who is it?" she
shouted, not particularly eager to talk to anyone.

Reed threw open the door and stalked inside. He
stood in the middle of the room with his hands on his

hips. "Are you planning to stay up here for the rest of your life?"

"The idea has distinct possibilities." She glared back at him, her eyes flashing with outrage and ill humor. "By the way, you'll note that I asked who was at the door. I didn't say, 'come in.'" Her voice rose to a mockingly high pitch. "You might have walked in on me when I was dressing."

A smile crossed his mouth. "Is that an invitation?"

"Absolutely not." She rose to a kneeling position, taking the sheets and blankets with her, and pointed a finger in the direction of the door. "Would you kindly leave? I'd like to get dressed."

"Don't let me stop you."

"Reed, please," she said irritably. "I'm not in any mood to talk to you."

"I'm not leaving until we do."

"Unfair. I haven't had my cup of tea and my mouth feels like the bottom of Puget Sound."

"All right," he agreed reluctantly. "I'll give you ten minutes."

"How generous of you."

"Considering my frame of mind since you walked out on me last night, I consider it pretty generous."

"Walked out on you!" She flew off the bed. "That's a bit much!"

"Ten minutes," he repeated, his voice low.

The whole time Ellen was dressing, she fumed. Reed had some nerve accusing her of walking out on him. He obviously didn't have any idea what it had cost her to leave him at that party with Danielle. He was thinking only of his own feelings, showing no regard for hers. He hadn't even acknowledged that she'd swallowed her pride to save them all from an extremely embarrassing situation.

Four male faces met hers when she appeared in the kitchen. "Good morning," she said with false enthusiasm.

The three boys looked sheepishly away. "Morning," they droned. Each found something at the table to occupy his hands. Pat, who was holding his basketball, carefully examined its grooves. Monte read the back of the cereal box and Derek folded the front page of the paper, pretending to read it.

"Ellen and I would like a few minutes of privacy," Reed announced, frowning at the three boys.

Derek, Monte and Pat stood up simultaneously.

"I don't think there's anything we have to say that the boys can't hear," she said.

The three boys reclaimed their chairs, looking with interest first at Reed and then at Ellen.

Reed's scowl deepened. "Can't you see that Ellen and I need to talk?"

"There's nothing to discuss," Ellen insisted, pouring boiling water into her mug and dipping a tea bag in the water.

"Yes, there is," Reed countered.

"Maybe it would be best if we did leave," Derek hedged, noticeably uneasy with his brother's anger and Ellen's feigned composure.

"You walk out of this room and there will be no packed lunches next week," Ellen said, leaning against the counter. She threw out the bag and began sipping her tea.

"I'm staying." Monte crossed his arms over his chest as though preparing for a long standoff.

Ellen knew she could count on Monte; his stomach would always take precedence. Childishly, she flashed Reed a saucy grin. He wasn't going to bulldoze her into any confrontation.

"Either you're out of here *now*, or you won't have a place to *live* next week," Reed flared back. At Derek's smug expression, Reed added, "And that includes you, little brother."

The boys exchanged shocked glances. "Sorry, Ellen," Derek mumbled on his way out of the kitchen. "I told Michelle I'd be over in a few minutes anyway." Without another moment's hesitation, Reed's brother was out the door.

"Well?" Reed stared at Monte and Pat.

"Yeah, well… I guess I should probably…" Pat looked to Ellen for guidance, his resolve wavering.

"Go ahead." She dismissed them both with a wave of her hand.

"Are you sure you want us to go?" Monte asked anxiously.

Ellen smiled her appreciation at this small display of mettle. "Thanks, but I'll be okay."

The sound of the door swinging back and forth echoed through the kitchen. Ellen drew a deep, calming breath and turned to Reed, who didn't look all that pleased to have her alone, although he'd gone to some lengths to arrange it. His face was pinched, and fine lines fanned out from his eyes and mouth. Either he'd had a late night or he hadn't slept at all. Ellen decided it must have been the former.

"Well, I'm here within ten minutes, just as you decreed. If you've got something to say, then say it."

"Don't rush me," he snapped.

Ellen released an exaggerated sigh. "First you want to talk to me—and then you're not sure. This sounds like someone who asked me to a party once. First he wanted me with him—and then he didn't."

"I wanted you there last night."

"Oh, was I talking about you?" she asked in fake innocence.

"You're not making this easy." He ploughed his fingers through his hair, the abrupt movement at odds with the self-control he usually exhibited.

"Listen," she breathed, casting her eyes down. "You don't need to explain anything. I have a fairly accurate picture of what happened."

"I doubt that." But he didn't elaborate.

"I can understand why you'd prefer Danielle's company."

"I didn't. That had to be one of the most awkward moments of my life. I wanted you—not Danielle."

Sure, she mused sarcastically. That was why he'd introduced her to so few people. She'd had plenty of time in the past twelve hours to think. If she hadn't been so blinded by the stars in her eyes, she would have figured it out sooner. Reed had taken her to his company party and kept her shielded from the other guests; he hadn't wanted her talking to his friends and colleagues. At the time, she'd assumed he wanted her all to himself. Now she understood the reason. The others knew he'd invited Danielle; they knew that Danielle usually accompanied him to these functions. The other woman had an official status in Reed's life. Ellen didn't.

"It wasn't your fault," she told him. "Unfortunately, under the circumstances, this was unavoidable."

"I'd rather Danielle had left instead of you." He

walked to her side, deliberately taking the mug of tea from her hand and setting it on the counter. Slowly his arms came around her.

Ellen lacked the will to resist. She closed her eyes as her arms reached around him, almost of their own accord. He felt so warm and vital.

"I want us to spend the day together."

Her earlier intention of studying for her algebra exam went out the window. Despite all her hesitations, all her doubts and fears, she couldn't refuse this chance to be with him. Alone, the two of them. "All right," she answered softly.

"Ellen." His breath stirred her hair. "There's something you should know."

"Hmm?"

"I'm flying out tomorrow morning for two days."

Her eyes flew open. "How long?"

"Two days, but after that, I won't be leaving again until the Christmas holidays are over."

She nodded. Traveling was part of his job, and any woman in his life would have to accept that. She was touched that he felt so concerned for her. "That's fine," she whispered. "I understand."

Ellen couldn't fault Reed's behavior for the remainder of the weekend. Saturday afternoon, they went Christmas shopping at the Tacoma Mall. His choice of shopping area surprised her, since there were several in the immediate area, much closer than Tacoma, which was a forty-five-minute drive away. But they had a good time, wandering from store to store. Before she knew it, Christmas would be upon them and this was the first opportunity she'd had to do any real shopping. With Reed's help, she picked out gifts for the boys and her brother.

"You'll like Bud," she told him, licking a chocolate ice-cream cone. They found a place to sit, with their packages gathered around them, and took a fifteen-minute break.

"I imagine I will." A flash of amusement lit his eyes, then he abruptly looked away.

Ellen lowered her ice-cream cone. "What's so funny? Have I got chocolate on my nose?"

"No."

"What, then?"

"You must have forgiven me for what happened at the party."

"What do you mean?"

"The way you looked into the future and said I'd like your brother, as though you and I are going to have a long relationship."

The ice cream suddenly became very important and Ellen licked away at it with an all-consuming energy. "I told you before that I feel things have to be one day at a time with us. There are too many variables in our... relationship." She waved the ice cream in his direction. "And I use that term loosely."

"There *is* a future for us."

"You seem sure of yourself."

"I'm more sure of you." He said it so smoothly that Ellen wondered if she heard him right. She would have challenged his arrogant assumption, but just then, he glanced at his wristwatch and suggested a movie.

By the time they returned to the house it was close to midnight. He kissed her with a tenderness that somehow reminded her of an early-summer dawn, but his touch was as potent as a sultry August afternoon.

"Ellen?" he murmured into her hair.

"Hmm?"

"I think you'd better go upstairs now."

The warmth of his touch had melted away the last traces of icy reserve. She didn't want to leave him. "Why?"

His hands gripped her shoulders, pushing her away from him, putting an arm's length between them. "Because if you don't leave now, I may climb those stairs with you."

At his straightforward, honest statement, Ellen swallowed hard. "I enjoyed today. Thank you, Reed." He dropped his arms and she placed a trembling hand on the railing. "Have a safe trip."

"I will." He took a step toward her. "I wish I didn't have to go." His hand cupped her chin and he drew her face toward his, kissing her with a hunger that shook Ellen to the core. She needed all her strength not to throw her arms around him again.

MONDAY AFTERNOON, WHEN Ellen walked into the house after her classes, the three boys were waiting for her. They looked up at her with peculiar expressions on their faces, as though they'd never seen her before and they couldn't understand how she'd wandered into their kitchen.

"All right, what's up?"

"Up?" Derek asked.

"You've got that guilty look."

"*We're* not the guilty party," Pat said.

She sighed. "You'd better let me know what's going on so I can deal with it before Reed gets back."

Monte swung open the kitchen door so that the dining-room table came into view. In the center of the table stood the largest bouquet of red roses Ellen had ever seen.

A shocked gasp slid from the back of her throat. "Who...who sent those?"

"We thought you'd ask so we took the liberty of reading the card."

Their prying barely registered in her numbed brain as she walked slowly into the room and removed the small card pinned to the bright red ribbon. It could have been Bud—but he didn't have the kind of money to buy roses. And if he did, Ellen suspected he wouldn't get them for his sister.

"Reed did it," Pat inserted eagerly.

"Reed?"

"We were as surprised as you."

Her gaze fell to the tiny envelope. She removed the card, biting her lip when she read the message. *I miss you. Reed.*

"He said he misses you," Derek added.

"I see that."

"Good grief, he'll be back tomorrow. How can he possibly miss you in such a short time?"

"I don't know." Her finger lovingly caressed the petals of a dewy rosebud. They were so beautiful, but their message was even more so.

"I'll bet this is his way of telling you he's sorry about the party," Derek murmured.

"Not that any of us actually knows what happened. We'd like to, but it'd be considered bad manners to ask," Pat explained. "That is, unless you'd like to tell us why he'd take you to the party and then come back alone."

"He didn't get in until three that morning," Monte said accusingly. "You aren't going to let him off so easy are you, Ellen?"

Bowing her head to smell the sweet fragrance, she closed her eyes. "Roses cover a multitude of sins."

"Reed's feeling guilty, I think," Derek said with authority. "But he cares, or else he wouldn't have gone to this much trouble."

"Maybe he just wants to keep the peace," Monte suggested. "My dad bought my mom flowers once for no reason."

"We all live together. Reed's probably figured out that he had to do something if he wanted to maintain the status quo."

"Right," Ellen agreed tartly, scooping up the flowers to take to her room. Maybe it was selfish to deprive the boys of their beauty, but she didn't care. They'd been meant for her, as a private message from Reed, and she wanted them close.

THE FOLLOWING DAY, Ellen cut her last morning class, knowing that Reed's flight was getting in around noon. She could ill afford to skip algebra, but it wouldn't have done her any good to stay. She would've spent the entire time thinking about Reed—so it made more sense to hurry home.

She stepped off the bus a block from the house and even from that distance she could see his truck parked in the driveway. It was the first—and only—thing she noticed. She sprinted toward the house and dashed up the front steps.

Flinging open the door, she called breathlessly, "Anyone here?"

Both Reed and Derek came out of the kitchen.

Her eyes met Reed's from across the room. "Hi," she said in a low, husky voice. "Welcome home."

He advanced toward her, his gaze holding hers.

Neither spoke as Ellen threw her bag of books on the sofa and moved just as quickly toward him.

He caught her around the waist as though he'd been away for months instead of days, hugging her fiercely.

Ellen savored the warmth of his embrace, closing her eyes to the overwhelming emotion she suddenly felt. Reed was becoming far too important in her life. But she no longer had the power to resist him. If she ever had…

"His plane was right on time," Derek was saying. "And the airport was hardly busy. And—"

Irritably, Reed tossed a look over his shoulder. "Little brother, get lost."

CHAPTER NINE

"I'VE GOT A game today," Pat said, his fork cutting into the syrup-laden pancakes. "Can you come?"

Ellen's eyes met Reed's in mute communication. No longer did they bother to hide their attraction to each other from the boys. They couldn't. "What time?"

"Six."

"I can be there."

"What about you, Reed?"

Reed wiped the corners of his mouth with the paper napkin. "Sorry, I've got a meeting. But I should be home in time for the victory celebration."

Ellen thrilled at the way the boys automatically linked her name and Reed's. It had been like that from the time he'd returned from his most recent trip. But then, they'd given the boys plenty of reason to think of her and Reed as a couple. He and Ellen were with each other every free moment; the time they spent together was exclusively theirs. And Ellen loved it. She loved Reed, she loved being with him...and she loved every single thing about him. Almost. His reticence on the subject of Danielle had her a little worried, but she pushed it to the back of her mind. She couldn't bring herself to question him, especially after her own insistence that they not discuss Danielle. She no longer felt that way—she wanted reassurance—but she'd decided she'd just assume that the relationship was over. As far as she knew, Reed hadn't spoken to Danielle since the night of the Christmas party. Even stronger evidence was the fact that he drove his truck every day. The Porsche sat in the garage, gathering dust.

Reed stood up and delivered his breakfast plate to the sink. "Ellen, walk me to the door?"

"Sure."

"For Pete's sake, the door's only two feet away," Derek scoffed. "You travel all over the world and all of a sudden you need someone to show you where the back door is?"

Ellen didn't see the look the two brothers exchanged, but Derek's mouth curved upward in a knowing grin. "Oh, I get it. Hey, guys, they want to be alone."

"Just a minute." Monte wolfed down the last of his breakfast, still chewing as he carried his plate to the counter.

Ellen was mildly surprised that Reed didn't comment on Derek's needling, but she supposed they were both accustomed to it.

One by one, the boys left the kitchen. Silently, Reed stood by the back door, waiting. When the last one had departed, he slipped his arms around Ellen.

"You're getting mighty brave," she whispered, smiling into his intense green eyes. Lately, Reed almost seemed to invite the boys' comments. And when they responded, the teasing rolled off his back like rain off a well-waxed car.

"It's torture being around you every day and not touching you," he said just before his mouth descended on hers in an excruciatingly slow kiss that seemed to melt Ellen's very bones.

Reality seemed light-years away as she clung to him, and she struggled to recover her equilibrium. "Reed," she whispered, "you have to get to work."

"Right." But he didn't stop kissing her.

"And I've got classes." If he didn't end this soon, they'd both reach the point of no return. Each time he held and kissed her, it became more difficult to break away.

"I know. I know." His voice echoed through the fog that held her captive. "Now isn't the time or place."

Her arms tightened around his middle as she burrowed her face into his chest. One second, she was telling Reed they had to stop and in the next, she refused to let him go.

"I'll be late tonight," he murmured into her hair.

She remembered that he'd told Pat something about a meeting. "Me, too," she said. "I'm going to the basketball game."

"Right. Want to go out to dinner afterward?" His breath fanned her temple. "Just the two of us. I love being alone with you."

Ellen wanted to cry with frustration. "I can't. I promised the boys dinner. Plus exams start next week and I've got to study."

"Need any help?"

"Only with one subject." She looked up at him and sadly shook her head. "I don't suppose you can guess which one."

"Aren't you glad you've got me?"

"Eternally grateful." Ellen would never have believed that algebra could be both her downfall and her greatest ally. If it weren't for that one subject, she wouldn't have had the excuse to sit down with Reed every night to work through her assignments. But then, she didn't really need an excuse anymore....

"We'll see how grateful you are when grades come out."

"I hate to disappoint you, but it's going to take a lot more than your excellent tutoring to rescue me from my fate this time." The exam was crucial. If she didn't do well, she'd probably end up repeating the class. The thought filled her with dread. It would be a waste of her time and, even worse, a waste of precious funds.

Reed kissed her lightly before releasing her. "Have a good day."

"You, too." She stood at the door until he'd climbed inside the pickup and waved when he backed out of the driveway.

Ellen loaded the dirty dishes into the dishwasher and cleaned off the counter, humming a Christmas carol as she worked.

One of the boys knocked on the door. "Is it safe to come in yet?"

"Sure. Come on in."

All three innocently strolled into the kitchen. "You and Reed are getting kind of friendly, aren't you?"

Running hot tap water into the sink, Ellen nodded. "I suppose."

"Reed hasn't seen Danielle in a while."

Ellen didn't comment, but she did feel encouraged that Derek's conclusion was the same as hers.

"You know what I think?" he asked, hopping onto the counter so she was forced to look at him.

"I can only guess."

"I think Reed's getting serious about you."

"That's nice."

"*Nice*—is that all you can say?" He gave her a look of disgust. "That's my brother you're talking about. He could have any woman he wanted."

"I know." She poured soap into the dishwasher, then closed the door and turned the dial. The sound of rushing water drowned out Derek's next comment.

"Sorry, I have to get to class. I'll talk to you later." She sauntered past Pat and Monte, offering them a cheerful smile.

"She's got it bad," Ellen heard Monte comment. That was the same thing Ralph had said the night of the party. "She hardly even bakes anymore. Remember how she used to make cookies every week?"

"I didn't know love did that to a person," Pat grumbled.

"I'm not sure I like Ellen in love," Monte flung after her as she stepped out the door.

"I just hope she doesn't get hurt."

The boy's remarks echoed in her mind as the day wore on. Ellen didn't need to hear their doubts; she had more than enough of her own. Qualms assailed her when she least expected it—like during the morning's algebra class, or during the long afternoon that followed.

But one look at Reed that evening and all her anxieties evaporated. As soon as she entered the house, she walked straight into the living room, hoping to find him there, and she did.

He put some papers back in a file when she walked in. "How was the game?"

"Pat scored seventeen points and is a hero. Unfortunately, the Huskies lost." Sometimes, that was just the way life went—winning small victories yet losing the war.

She hurried into the kitchen to begin dinner preparations.

"Something smells good." Monte bounded in half an hour later, sniffing appreciatively.

"There's a roast in the oven and an apple pie on the counter," she answered him. She'd bought the pie in hopes of celebrating the Huskies' victory. Now it would soothe their loss. "I imagine everyone's starved."

"I am," Monte announced.

"That goes without saying," Reed called from the living room.

Gradually, the other boys trailed in, and it was time to eat.

AFTER DINNER, THE evening was spent at the kitchen table, poring over her textbooks. Reed came in twice to make her a fresh cup of tea. Standing behind her chair, he glanced over her shoulder at the psychology book.

"Do you want me to get you anything?" she asked. She was studying in the kitchen, rather than in her room, just to be close to Reed. Admittedly, her room offered more seclusion, but she preferred being around people—one person, actually.

"I don't need a thing." He kissed the top of her head. "And if I did, I'd get it myself. You study."

"Thanks."

"When's the first exam?"

"Monday."

He nodded. "You'll do fine."

"I don't want fine," she countered nervously. "I want fantastic."

"Then you'll do fantastic."

"Where are the boys?" The house was uncommonly silent for a weekday evening.

"Studying. I'm pleased to see they're taking exams as seriously as you are."

"We have to," she mumbled, her gaze dropping to her notebook.

"All right. I get the message. I'll quit pestering you."

"You're not pestering me."

"Right." He bent to kiss the side of her neck as his fingers stroked her arms.

Shivers raced down her spine and Ellen closed her eyes, unconsciously swaying toward him. "Now...now you're pestering me."

He chuckled, leaving her alone at the kitchen table when she would much rather have had him with her every minute of every day.

THE NEXT MORNING, Ellen stood by the door, watching Reed pull out of the driveway.

"Why do you do that?" Pat asked, giving her a glance that said she looked foolish standing there.

"Do what?" She decided the best reaction was to pretend she didn't have any idea what he was talking about.

"Watch Reed leave every morning. He's not likely to have an accident pulling out of the driveway."

Ellen didn't have the courage to confess that she watched so she could see whether Reed drove the pickup or the Porsche. It would sound ridiculous to admit that she gauged their relationship by which vehicle he chose to drive that day.

"She watches because she can't bear to see him go,"

Derek answered when she didn't. "From what I hear, Michelle does the same thing. What can I say? The woman's crazy about me."

"Oh, yeah?" Monte snickered. "And that's the reason she was with Rick Bloomfield the other day?"

"She was?" Derek sounded completely shocked. "There's an explanation for that. Michelle and I have an understanding."

"Sure you do," Monte teased. "She can date whoever she wants and you can date whoever you want. Some *understanding*."

To prove to the boys that she wasn't as infatuated as they assumed—and maybe to prove the same thing to herself—Ellen didn't watch Reed leave for work the next two mornings. It was pointless, anyway. So what if he drove his Porsche? He had the car, and she could see no reason for him to not drive it. Except for her unspoken insecurities. And there seemed to be plenty of those. As Derek had said earlier in the week, Reed could have any woman he wanted.

She was the first one home that afternoon. Derek was probably sorting things out with Michelle, Pat had basketball practice and no doubt Monte was in someone's kitchen.

Gathering the ingredients for spaghetti sauce, she arranged them neatly on the counter. She was busy reading over her recipe when the phone rang.

"Hello," she said absently.

"This is Capitol Hill Cleaners. Mr. Morgan's evening suit is ready."

"Pardon?" Reed hadn't told her he was having anything cleaned. Ellen usually picked up his dry cleaning because it was no inconvenience to stop there on her way home from school. And she hadn't minded at all. As silly as it seemed, she'd felt very wifely doing that for him.

"Is it for Reed or Derek?" It was just like Derek to forget something like that.

"The slip says it's for Mr. Reed Morgan."

"Oh?"

"Is there a problem with picking it up? He brought it in yesterday and told us he had to have it this evening."

This evening? Reed was going out tonight?

"From what he said, this is for some special event."

Well, he wouldn't wear a suit to a barbecue. "I'll let him know."

"Thank you. Oh, and be sure to mention that we close at six tonight."

"Yes, I will."

A strange numbness overpowered Ellen as she hung up. Something was wrong. Something was very, very wrong. Without even realizing it, she moved rapidly through the kitchen and then outside.

Reed had often told her the importance of reading a problem in algebra. Read it carefully, he always said, and don't make any quick assumptions. It seemed crazy to remember that now. But he was right. She couldn't jump to conclusions just because he was going out for the evening. He had every right to do so. She was suddenly furious with herself. All those times he'd offered information about Danielle and she'd refused to listen, trying to play it so cool, trying to appear so unconcerned when on the inside she was dying to know.

By the time she reached the garage she was trembling, but it wasn't from the cold December air. She knew without looking that Reed had driven his sports car to work. The door creaked as she pushed it open to discover the pickup, sitting there in all its glory.

"Okay, he drove his Porsche. That doesn't have to mean anything. He isn't necessarily seeing Danielle. There's a logical explanation for this." Even if he *was* seeing Danielle, she had no right to say anything. They'd made no promises to each other.

Rubbing the chill from her arms, Ellen returned to the house. But the kitchen's warmth did little to chase away the bitter cold that cut her to the heart. Ellen moved numbly toward the phone and ran her finger down the long list of numbers that hung on the wall beside it. When she located the one for Reed's office, she punched out the seven numbers, then waited, her mind in turmoil.

"Mr. Morgan's office," came the efficient voice.

"Hello…this is Ellen Cunningham. I live, that is, I'm a friend of Mr. Morgan's."

"Yes, I remember seeing you the night of the Christmas party," the voice responded warmly. "We didn't have a chance to meet. Would you like me to put you through to Mr. Morgan?"

"No," she said hastily. "Could you give him a message?" Not waiting for a reply, she continued, "Tell him his suit is ready at the cleaners for that…party tonight."

"Oh, good, he wanted me to call. Thanks for saving me the trouble. Was there anything else?"

Tears welled in Ellen's eyes. "No, that's it."

Being reminded by Reed's assistant that they hadn't met the night of the Christmas party forcefully brought to Ellen's attention how few of his friends she did know. None, really. He'd gone out of his way *not* to introduce her to people.

"Just a minute," Ellen cried, her hand clenching the receiver. "There *is* something else you can tell Mr. Morgan. Tell him goodbye." With that, she severed the connection.

A tear rolled down her cheek, searing a path as it made its way to her chin. She'd been a fool not to have seen the situation more clearly. Reed had a good thing going, with her living at the house. She was close to falling in love with him. In fact, she was already there and anyone looking at her could tell. It certainly wasn't any secret from the boys. She cooked his meals, ran his errands, vacuumed his rugs. How convenient she'd become. How useful she'd been to the smooth running of his household.

But Reed had never said a word about his feelings. Sure, they'd gone out, but always to places where no one was likely to recognize him. And the one time Reed did see someone he knew, he'd pretended he wasn't with her. When he *had* included her in a social event, he'd only introduced her to a handful of people, as though…as though he didn't really want others to know her. As it turned out, that evening had been a disaster, and this time he'd apparently decided to take Danielle. The other woman was far more familiar with the social graces.

Fine. She'd let Reed escort Danielle tonight. But she was going to quit making life so pleasant for him. How appropriate that she now used the old servants' quarters, she thought bitterly. Because that was all she was to him—a servant. Well, no more. She would never be content to live a backstairs life. If Reed didn't want to be seen with her, or include her in his life, that was his decision. But she couldn't...she *wouldn't* continue to live this way.

Without analyzing her actions, Ellen punched out a second set of numbers.

"Charlie, it's Ellen," she said quickly, trying to swallow back tears.

"Ellen? It doesn't sound like you."

"I know." The tightness in her chest extended all the way to her throat, choking off her breath until it escaped in a sob.

"Ellen, are you all right?"

"Yes...no." The fact that she'd called Charlie was a sign of her desperation. He was so sweet and she didn't want to do anything to hurt him. "Charlie, I hate to ask, but I need a friend."

"I'm here."

He said it without the least hesitation, and his unquestioning loyalty made her weep all the louder. "Oh, Charlie, I've got to find a new place to live and I need to do it today."

"My sister's got a friend looking for a roommate. Do you want me to call her?"

"Please." Straightening, she wiped the tears from her face. Charlie might have had his faults, but he'd recognized the panic in her voice and immediately assumed control. Just now, that was what she needed—a friend to temporarily take charge of things. "How soon can you talk to her?"

"Now. I'll call her and get right back to you. On second thought, I'll come directly to your place. If you can't move in with Patty's friend, my parents will put you up."

"Oh, Charlie, how can I ever thank you?"

The sound of his chuckle was like a clean, fresh breeze. "I'll come up with a way later." His voice softened. "You know how I feel about you, Ellen. If you only want me for a friend, I understand. But I'm determined to be a good friend."

The back door closed with a bang. "Anyone home?"

Guiltily, Ellen turned around, coming face to face with Monte. She replaced the receiver, took a deep breath and squared her shoulders. She'd hoped to get away without having to talk to anyone.

"Ellen?" Concern clouded his face. "What's wrong? You look like you've been crying." He narrowed his eyes. "You *have* been crying. What happened?"

"Nothing." She took a minute to wipe her eyes with a tissue. "Listen, I'll be up in my room, but I'd appreciate some time alone, so don't get me unless it's important."

"Sure. Anything you say. Are you sick? Should I call Reed?"

"No!" she almost shouted at him, then instantly regretted reacting so harshly. "Please don't contact him…. He's busy tonight anyway." She rubbed a hand over her face. "And listen, about dinner—"

"Hey, don't worry. I can cook."

"You?" This wasn't the time to get into an argument. How messy he made the kitchen was no longer her problem. "There's a recipe on the counter if you want to tackle spaghetti sauce."

"Sure. I can do that. How long am I supposed to boil the noodles?"

One of her lesser concerns at the moment was boiling noodles. "Just read the back of the package."

Already he was rolling up his sleeves. "I'll take care of everything. You go lie down and do whatever women do when they're crying and pretending they're not."

"Thanks," she returned evenly. "I'll do that." Only in this case, she wasn't going to lie on her bed, hiding her face in her pillow. She was going to pack up everything she owned and cart it away before Reed even had a hint that she was leaving.

Sniffling as she worked, Ellen dumped the contents of her drawers into open suitcases. A couple of times she stopped to blow her nose. She detested tears. At the age of fifteen, she'd broken her leg and gritted her teeth against the agony. But she hadn't shed a tear. Now she wept as though it were the end of the world. Why, oh why, did her emotions have to be so unpredictable?

Carrying her suitcases down the first flight of stairs, she paused on the boys' floor to shift the weight. Because she was concentrating on her task and not watching where she was going, she walked headlong into Derek. "Sorry," she muttered.

"Ellen." He glanced at her suitcases and said her name as though he'd unexpectedly stumbled into the Queen of Sheba. "What…what are you doing?"

"Moving."

"Moving? But…why?"

"It's a long story."

"You're crying." He sounded even more shocked by her tears than by the fact that she was moving out of the house.

"It's Reed, isn't it? What did he do?"

"He didn't do a thing. Stay out of it, Derek. I mean that."

He looked stunned. "Sure." He stepped aside and stuck his hand in his pocket. "Anything you say."

She made a second trip downstairs, this time bringing a couple of tote bags and the clothes from her closet, which she draped over the top of the two suitcases. There wasn't room in her luggage for everything. She realized she'd have to put the rest of her belongings in boxes.

Assuming she'd find a few empty boxes in the garage, she stormed through the kitchen and out the back door. Muttering between themselves, Monte and Derek followed her. Soon her movements resembled a small parade.

"Will you two stop it," she shouted, whirling around and confronting them. The tears had dried now and her face burned with the heat of anger and regret.

"We just want to know what happened," Monte interjected.

"Or is this going to be another one of your 'stay tuned' responses?" Derek asked.

"I'm moving out. I don't think I can make it any plainer than that."

"Why?"

"That's none of your business." She left them standing with mouths open as she trooped up the back stairs to her rooms.

Heedlessly she tossed her things into the two boxes, more intent on escaping than on taking care to ensure that nothing was broken. When she got to the vase that had held the roses Reed had sent her, Ellen picked it up and hugged it. She managed to forestall further tears by taking deep breaths and blinking rapidly. Setting the vase down, she decided not to bring it with her. As much as possible, she wanted to leave Reed in this house and not carry the memories of him around with her like a constant, throbbing ache. That would be hard enough without taking the vase along as a constant reminder of what she'd once felt.

The scene that met her at the foot of the stairs made her stop in her tracks. The three boys were involved in a shouting match, each blaming the others for Ellen's unexpected decision to move out.

"It's your fault," Derek accused Monte. "If you weren't so concerned about your stomach, she'd stay."

"My stomach? *You're* the one who's always asking her for favors. Like babysitting and cooking for you and your girlfriend and—"

"If you want my opinion…" Pat began.

"We don't," Monte and Derek shouted.

"Stop it! All of you," Ellen cried. "Now, if you're the least bit interested in helping me, you can take my things outside. Charlie will be here anytime."

"Charlie?" the three echoed in shock.

"Are you moving in with him?"

She didn't bother to respond. Once the suitcases, the bags, two boxes and her clothes had been lugged onto the porch, Ellen sat on the top step and waited.

She could hear the boys pacing back and forth behind her, still bickering quietly. When the black sports car squealed around the corner, Ellen covered her face with both hands and groaned. The last person she wanted to see now was Reed. Her throat was already swollen with the effort of not giving way to tears.

He parked in front of the house and threw open the car door.

She straightened, determined to appear cool and calm.

Seconds later, Reed stood on the bottom step. "What's going on here?"

"Hello, Reed," she said with a breathlessness she couldn't control. "How was your day?"

He jerked his fingers through his hair as he stared back at her in utter confusion. "How am I supposed to know? I get a frantic phone call from Derek telling me to come home right away. As I'm running out the door, my assistant hands me a message. Some absurd thing about you saying goodbye. What is going on? I thought you'd hurt yourself!"

"Sorry to disappoint you."

"Ellen, I don't know what's happening in that over-worked mind of yours, but I want some answers and I want them now."

"I'm leaving." Her hands were clenched so tight that her fingers ached.

"I'm not blind," he shouted, quickly losing control of his obviously limited patience. "I can see that. I'm asking you *why.*"

Pride demanded that she raise her chin and meet his probing gaze. "I've decided I'm an unstable person," she told him, her voice low and quavering. "I broke my leg once and didn't shed a tear, but when I learn that you're going to a party tonight, I start to cry."

"Ellen." He said her name gently, then shook his

head as if clearing his thoughts. "You're not making any sense."

"I know. That's the worst part."

"In the simplest terms possible, tell me why you're leaving."

"I'm trying to." Furious with herself, she wiped a tear from her cheek. How could she explain it to him when everything was still so muddled in her own mind? "I'm leaving because you're driving the Porsche."

"What!" he exploded.

"You tell me," she burst out. "Why did you drive the Porsche today?"

"Would you believe that my truck was low on fuel?"

"I may be confused," she said, "but I'm not stupid. You're going out with Danielle. Not that I care."

"I can tell." His mocking gaze lingered on her suitcases. "I hate to disillusion you, but Danielle won't be with me."

She didn't know whether to believe him or not. "It doesn't matter."

"None of this is making sense."

"I don't imagine it would. I apologize for acting so unreasonable, but that's exactly how I feel. So, I'm getting out of here with my pride intact."

"Is your pride worth so much?"

"It's the only thing I have left," she said. She'd already given him her heart.

"She's moving in with Charlie," Derek said in a worried voice. "You aren't going to let her, are you, Reed?"

"You can't," Monte added.

"He won't," Pat stated confidently.

For a moment, the three of them stared intently at Reed. Ellen noticed the way his green eyes hardened. "Yes, I can," he said at last. "If this is what you want, then so be it. Goodbye, Ellen." With that, he marched into the house.

CHAPTER TEN

"I'M SWEARING OFF men for good," Ellen vowed, taking another long swallow of wine.

"Me, too," Darlene, her new roommate, echoed. To toast the promise, Darlene bent forward to touch the rim of her wineglass against Ellen's and missed. A shocked moment passed before they broke into hysterical laughter.

"Here." Ellen replenished their half-full glasses as tears of mirth rolled down her face. The world seemed to spin off its axis for a moment as she straightened. "You know what? I think we're drunk."

"Maybe you are," Darlene declared, slurring her words, "but not me. I can hold my wine as well as any man."

"I thought we weren't going to talk about men anymore."

"Right, I forgot."

"Do you think they're talking about us?" Ellen asked, putting a hand to her head in an effort to keep the walls from going around and around.

"Nah, we're just a fading memory."

"Right." Ellen pointed her index finger toward the ceiling in emphatic agreement.

The doorbell chimed and both women stared accusingly at the door. "If it's a man, don't answer it," Darlene said.

"Right again." Ellen staggered across the beige carpet. The floor seemed to pitch under her feet and she placed a hand on the back of the sofa to steady herself. Facing the door, she turned around. "How do I know if it's a man or not?"

The doorbell sounded again.

Darlene motioned languidly with her hand to show that she no longer cared who was at the door. "Just open it."

Holding the knob in a death grip, Ellen pulled open the door and found herself glaring at solid male chest. "It's a man," she announced to Darlene.

"Who?"

Squinting, Ellen studied the blurred male figure until she recognized Monte. "Monte," she cried, instantly sobering. "What are you doing here?"

"I... I was in the neighborhood and thought I'd stop by and see how you're doing."

"Come in." She stepped aside to let him enter. "What brings you to this neck of the woods?" She hiccuped despite her frenzied effort to look and act sober. "It's a school night. You shouldn't be out this late."

"It's only ten-thirty. You've been drinking."

"Me?" She slammed her hand against her chest. "Have we been drinking, Darlene?"

Her roommate grabbed the wine bottle—their second—from the table and hid it behind her back. "Not us."

Monte cast them a look of disbelief. "How'd your exams go?" he asked Ellen politely.

"Fine," she answered and hiccuped again. Embarrassed, she covered her mouth with her hand. "I think."

"What about algebra?"

"I'm making it by the skin of my nose."

"Teeth," both Darlene and Monte corrected.

"Right."

Looking uncomfortable, Monte said, "Maybe I should come back another time."

"Okay." Ellen wasn't about to argue. If she was going to run into her former housemates, she'd prefer to do it when she looked and felt her best. Definitely not when she was feeling…tipsy and the walls kept spinning. But on second thought, she couldn't resist asking about the others. "How's…everyone?"

"Fine." But he lowered his gaze to the carpet. "Not really, if you want the truth."

A shaft of fear went through her, tempering the effects of several glasses of wine. "It's not Reed, is it? Is he ill?"

"No, Reed's fine. I guess. He hasn't been around much lately."

No doubt he was spending a lot of his time at parties and social events with Danielle. Or with any number of other women, all of them far more sophisticated than Ellen.

"Things haven't been the same since you left," Monte added sheepishly.

"Who's doing the cooking?"

He shrugged his shoulders. "We've been taking turns."

"That sounds fair." She hoped that in the months she'd lived with them the three boys had at least learned their way around the kitchen.

"Derek started a fire yesterday."

Ellen couldn't conceal her dismay. "Was there any damage?" As much as she tried to persuade herself that she didn't need to feel guilty over leaving the boys, this news was her undoing. "Was anyone hurt?" she gasped out.

"Not really, and Reed said the insurance would take care of everything."

"What happened?" Ellen was almost afraid to ask.

"Nothing much. Derek forgot to turn off the burner and the fat caught fire. Then he tried to beat it out with a dish towel, but that burst into flames, too. The real mistake was throwing the burning towel into the sink because when he did, it set the curtains on fire."

"Oh, good grief." Ellen dropped her head into her hands.

"It's not too bad, though. Reed said he wanted new kitchen walls, anyway."

"The walls too?"

"Well, the curtains started burning the wallpaper."

Ellen wished she hadn't asked. "Was anyone hurt?"

Monte moved a bandaged hand from behind his back. "Just me, but only a little."

"Oh, Monte," she cried, fighting back her guilt. "What did you do—try and pound out the fire with your fist?" Leave it to Monte. He'd probably tried to rescue whatever it was Derek had been cooking.

"No, I grabbed a hot biscuit from the oven and blistered one finger."

"Then why did you wrap up your whole hand?" From the size of the bandage, it looked as though he'd been lucky not to lose his arm.

"I thought you might feel sorry for me and come back."

"Oh, Monte." She reached up to brush the hair from his temple.

"I didn't realize what a good cook you were until you left. I kept thinking maybe it was something I'd done that caused you to leave."

"Of course not."

"Then you'll come back and make dinners again?"

Good ol' Monte never forgot about his stomach. "The four of you will do fine without me."

"You mean you won't come back?"

"I can't." She felt like crying, but she struggled to hold back the tears stinging her eyes. "I'm really sorry, but I can't."

Hanging his head, Monte nodded. "Well, have a merry Christmas anyway."

"Right. You, too."

"Bye, Ellen." He turned back to the door, his large hand gripping the knob. "You know about Pat making varsity, don't you?"

She'd read it in the *Daily*. "I'm really proud of him. You tell him for me. Okay?"

"Sure."

She closed the door after him and leaned against it while the regrets washed over her like a torrent of rain. Holding back her tears was difficult, but somehow she managed. She'd shed enough tears. It was time to put her grief behind her and to start facing life again.

"I take it Monte is one of the guys," Darlene remarked. She set the wine back on the table, but neither seemed interested in another glass.

Ellen nodded. "The one with the stomach."

"He's so skinny!"

"I know. There's no justice in this world." But she wasn't talking about Monte's appetite in relation to his weight. She was talking about Reed. If she'd had any hope that he really did care for her, that had vanished in the past week. He hadn't even tried to get in touch with her. She knew he wouldn't have had any problem locating her. The obvious conclusion was that he didn't *want* to see her. At first she thought he might have believed the boys' ridiculous claim that she was moving in with Charlie. But if he'd loved her half as much as she loved him, even that shouldn't have stopped him from coming after her.

Apparently, presuming that Reed cared for her was a mistake on her part. She hadn't heard a word from him all week. Exam week, at that. Well, fine. She'd wipe him out of her memory—just as effectively as she'd forgotten every algebraic formula she'd ever learned. A giggle escaped and Darlene sent her a curious look. Ellen carried their wineglasses to the sink, ignoring her new roommate, as she considered her dilemma. The trouble was, she wanted to remember the algebra, which seemed to slip out of her mind as soon as it entered, and she wanted to forget Reed, who never left her thoughts for an instant.

"I think I'll go to bed," Darlene said, holding her hand to her stomach. "I'm not feeling so great."

"Me neither." But Ellen's churning stomach had little to do with the wine. "Night."

"See you in the morning."

Ellen nodded. She was fortunate to have found Darlene. The other woman, who had recently broken up with her fiancé after a two-year engagement, understood how Ellen felt. It seemed natural to drown their sorrows together. But…she missed the boys and— Reed.

One thing she'd learned from this experience was that men and school didn't mix. Darlene might not have been serious about swearing off men, but Ellen was. She was through with them for good—or at least until she obtained her degree. For now, she was determined to bury herself in her books, get her teaching credentials and then become the best first-grade teacher around.

Only she couldn't close her eyes without remembering Reed's touch or how he'd slip up behind her and hold her in his arms. Something as simple as a passing glance from him had been enough to thrill her. Well, that relationship was over. And just in the nick of time. She could have been hurt. Really hurt. She could be feeling terrible. Really terrible.

Just like she did right now.

SIGNS OF CHRISTMAS were everywhere. Huge decorations adorned the streetlights down University Way. Store windows displayed a variety of Christmas themes, and the streets were jammed with holiday traffic. Ellen tried to absorb some of the good cheer that surrounded her, with little success.

She'd gone to the university library to return some books and was headed back to Darlene's place. Her place, too, even though it didn't feel that way.

She planned to leave for Yakima the next morning. But instead of feeling the pull toward home and family, Ellen's thoughts drifted to Reed and the boys. They'd been her surrogate family since September and she couldn't erase them from her mind as easily as she'd hoped.

As she walked across campus, sharp gusts of wind tousled her hair. Her face felt numb with cold. All day she'd been debating what to do with the Christmas gifts she'd bought for the boys. Her first inclination had been to bring them over herself—when Reed wasn't home, of course. But just the idea of returning to the lovely old house had proved so painful that Ellen abandoned it. Instead, Darlene had promised to deliver them the next day, after Ellen had left for Yakima.

Hugging her purse, Ellen trudged toward the bus stop. According to her watch, she had about ten minutes to wait. Now her feet felt as numb as her face. She frowned at her pumps, cursing the decrees of fashion and her insane willingness to wear elegant shoes at this time of year. It wasn't as though a handsome prince was likely to come galloping by only to be overwhelmed by her attractive shoes. Even if one did swoop Ellen and her frozen toes onto his silver steed, she'd be highly suspicious of his character.

Smiling, she took a shortcut across the lawn in the Quad.

"Is something funny?"

A pair of men's leather loafers had joined her fashionable gray pumps, matching her stride. Stunned, Ellen glanced up. Reed.

"Well?" he asked again in an achingly gentle voice. "Something seems to amuse you."

"My...shoes. I was thinking about attracting a prince...a man." Oh heavens, why had she said that? "I mean," she mumbled on, trying to cover her embarrassment, "my feet are numb."

"You need to get out of the cold." His hands were thrust into his pockets and he was so compellingly handsome that Ellen forced her eyes away. She was afraid that if she stared at him long enough, she'd give him whatever he asked. She remembered the way his face had looked the last time she'd seen him, how cold and steely his eyes had been the day she'd announced she was moving out. One word from him and she would've stayed. But the "might-have-beens" didn't matter anymore. He hadn't asked her to stay, so she'd gone. Pure and simple. Or so it had seemed at the time.

Determination strengthened her trembling voice as she finally spoke. "The bus will be at the corner in seven minutes."

Her statement was met with silence. Together they reached the pavement and strolled toward the sheltered bus area.

Much as she wished to appear cool and composed, Ellen's gaze was riveted on the man at her side. She noticed how straight and dark Reed's brows were and how his chin jutted out with stubborn pride. Every line of his beloved face emanated strength and unflinching resolve.

Abruptly, she looked away. Pride was no stranger to her, either. Her methods might have been wrong, she told herself, but she'd been right to let Reed know he'd hurt her. She wasn't willing to be a victim of her love for him.

"Ellen," he said softly, "I was hoping we could talk."

She made a show of glancing at her watch. "Go ahead. You've got six and a half minutes."

"Here?"

"As you so recently said, I need to get out of the cold."

"I'll take you to lunch."

"I'm not hungry." To further her embarrassment, her stomach growled and she pressed a firm hand over it, commanding it to be quiet.

"When was the last time you ate a decent meal?"

"Yesterday. No," she corrected, "today."

"Come on, we're getting out of here."

"No way."

"I'm not arguing with you, Ellen. I've given you a week to come to your senses. I still haven't figured out what went wrong. And I'm not waiting any longer for the answers. Got that?"

She ignored him, looking instead in the direction of the traffic. She could see the bus approaching, though it was still several blocks away. "I believe everything that needed to be said—" she motioned dramatically with her hand "—was already said."

"And what's this I hear about you succumbing to the demon rum?"

"I was only a little drunk," she spat out, furious at Monte's loose tongue. "Darlene and I were celebrating. We've sworn off men for life." Or at least until Reed freely admitted he loved her and needed her. At the moment that didn't appear likely.

"I see." His eyes seemed to be looking all the way into her soul. "If that's how you want it, fine. Just answer a couple of questions and I'll leave you alone. Agreed?"

"All right."

"First, what were you talking about when you flew off the handle about me driving the Porsche?"

"Oh, that." Now it just seemed silly.

"Yes, that."

"Well, you only drove the Porsche when you were seeing Danielle."

"But I wasn't! It's been completely over between us since the night of the Christmas party."

"It has?" The words came out in a squeak.

Reed dragged his fingers through his hair. "I haven't seen Danielle in weeks."

Ellen stared at the sidewalk. "But the cleaners phoned about your suit. You were attending some fancy party."

"So? I wasn't taking another woman."

"It doesn't matter," she insisted. "You weren't taking me, either."

"Of course not!" he shouted, his raised voice attracting the attention of several passersby. "You were studying for your exams. I couldn't very well ask you to attend an extremely boring business dinner with me. Not when you were spending every available minute hitting the books." He lowered his voice to a calm, even pitch.

The least he could do was be more unreasonable, Ellen thought irritably. She simply wasn't in the mood for logic.

"Did you hear what I said?"

She nodded.

"There is only one woman in my life. You. To be honest, Ellen, I can't understand any of this. You may be many things, but I know you're not the jealous type. I wanted to talk about Danielle with you. Any other woman would've loved hearing all the details. But not you." His voice was slightly raised. "Then you make these ridiculous accusations about the truck and the Porsche, and I'm at a loss to understand."

Now she felt even more foolish. "Then why were you driving the Porsche?" Her arms tightened around her purse. "Forget I asked that."

"You really have a thing for that sports car, don't you?"

"It's not the car."

"I'm glad to hear that."

Squaring her shoulders, Ellen decided it was time to be forthright, time to face things squarely rather than skirt around them. "My feelings are that you would rather not be seen with me," she said bluntly.

"What?" he exploded.

"You kept taking me to these out-of-the-way restaurants."

"I did it for privacy."

"You didn't want to be seen with me," she countered.

"I can't believe this." He took three steps away from her, then turned around sharply.

"Don't you think the Des Moines Marina is a bit far to go for a meal?"

"I was afraid we'd run into one of the boys."

More logic, and she was in no mood for it. "You didn't introduce me to your friend the night we went to that French film."

His eyes narrowed. "You can bet I wasn't going to introduce you to Tom Dailey. He's a lecher. I was protecting you."

"What about the night of the Christmas party? You only introduced me to a handful of people."

"Of course. Every man in the place was looking for

an excuse to take you away from me. If you'd wanted to flirt with them, you should've said something."

"I only wanted to be with you."

"Then why bring up that evening now?"

"I was offended."

"I apologize," he shouted.

"Fine. But I didn't even meet your assistant...."

"You left so fast, I didn't exactly have a chance to introduce you, did I?"

He was being logical again, and she couldn't really argue.

The bus arrived then, its doors parting with a swish. But Ellen didn't move. Reed's gaze commanded her to stay with him, and she was torn. Her strongest impulse, though, was not to board the bus. It didn't matter that she was cold and the wind was cutting through her thin coat or that she could barely feel her toes. Her heart was telling her one thing and her head another.

"You coming or not?" the driver called out to her.

"She won't be taking the bus," Reed answered, slipping his hand under her elbow. "She's coming with me."

"Whatever." The doors swished shut and the bus roared away, leaving a trail of black diesel smoke in its wake.

"You *are* coming with me, aren't you?" he coaxed.

"I suppose."

His hand was at the small of her back, directing her across the busy street to a coffee shop, festooned with tinsel and tired-looking decorations. "I wasn't kidding about lunch."

"When was the last time *you* had a decent meal?" she couldn't resist asking.

"About a week ago," he grumbled. "Derek's cooking is a poor substitute for real food."

They found a table at the back of the café. The waitress handed them each a menu and filled their water glasses.

"I heard about the fire."

Reed groaned. "That was a comedy of errors."

"Is there much damage?"

"Enough." The look he gave her was mildly accusing.

The guilt returned. Trying to disguise it, Ellen made a show of glancing through the menu. The last thing on her mind at the moment was food. When the waitress returned, Ellen ordered the daily special without knowing what it was. The day was destined to be full of surprises.

"Ellen," Reed began, then cleared his throat. "Come back."

Her heart melted at the hint of anguish in his low voice. Her gaze was magnetically drawn to his. She wanted to tell him how much she longed to be…home. She wanted to say that the house on Capitol Hill was the only real home she had now, that she longed to walk through its front door again. With him.

"Nothing's been the same since you left."

The knot in her stomach pushed its way up to her throat, choking her.

"The boys are miserable."

Resolutely she shook her head. If she went back, it had to be for Reed.

"Why not?"

Tears blurred her vision. "Because."

"That makes about as much sense as you being angry because I drove the Porsche."

Taking several deep, measured breaths, Ellen said, "If all you need is a cook, I can suggest several who—"

"I couldn't care less about the cooking."

The café went silent as every head turned curiously in their direction. "I wasn't talking about the cooking *here*," Reed explained to the roomful of shocked faces.

The normal noise of the café resumed.

"Good grief, Ellen, you've got me so tied up in knots I'm about to get kicked out of here."

"Me, tie *you* in knots?" She was astonished that Reed felt she had so much power over him.

"If you won't come back for the boys, will you consider doing it for me?" The intense green eyes demanded a response.

"I want to know why you want me back. So I can cook your meals and—"

"I told you I don't care about that. I don't care if you never do another thing around the house. I want you there because I love you, damn it."

Her eyes widened. "You love me, damn it?"

"You're not making this any easier." He ripped the napkin from around the silverware and slammed it down on his lap. "You must have known. I didn't bother keeping it secret."

"You didn't bother keeping it secret…from anyone but me," she repeated hotly.

"Come on. Don't tell me you didn't know."

"I didn't know."

"Well, you do now," he yelled back.

The waitress cautiously approached their table, standing back until Reed glanced in her direction.

Hurriedly the girl set their plates in front of them and promptly moved away.

"You frightened her," Ellen accused him.

"I'm the one in a panic here. Do you or do you not love me?"

Again, it seemed as though every customer there had fallen silent, awaiting her reply.

"You'd better answer him, miss," the elderly gentleman sitting at the table next to theirs suggested. "Fact is, we're all curious."

"Yes, I love him."

Reed cast her a look of utter disbelief. "You'll tell a stranger but not me?"

"I love you, Reed Morgan. There, are you happy?"

"Overjoyed."

"I can tell." Ellen had thought that when she admitted her feelings, Reed would jump up from the table and throw his arms around her. Instead, he looked as angry as she'd ever seen him.

"I think you'd better ask her to marry you while she's in a friendly mood," the older man suggested next.

"Well?" Reed looked at her. "What do you think?"

"You want to get married?"

"It's the time of year to be generous," the waitress said shyly. "He's handsome enough."

"He is, isn't he?" Ellen agreed, her sense of humor restored by this unexpected turn of events. "But he can be a little hard to understand."

"All men are, believe me," a woman across the room shouted. "But he looks like a decent guy. Go ahead and give him another chance."

The anger washed from Reed's dark eyes as he

reached for Ellen's hand. "I love you. I want to marry you. Won't you put me out of my misery?"

Tears dampened her eyes as she nodded wildly.

"Let's go home." Standing, Reed took out his wallet and threw a couple of twenties on the table.

Ellen quickly buttoned her jacket and picked up her purse. "Goodbye, everyone," she called with a cheerful wave. "Thank you—and Merry Christmas!"

The amused customers broke into a round of applause as Reed took Ellen's hand and pulled her outside.

She was no sooner out the door when Reed hauled her into his arms. "Oh, Ellen, I've missed you."

Reveling in the warmth of his arms, she nuzzled closer. "I've missed you, too. I've even missed the boys."

"As far as I'm concerned, they're on their own. I want you back for myself. That house was full of people, yet it's never felt so empty." Suddenly he looked around, as though he'd only now realized that their private moment was taking place in the middle of a busy street. "Let's get out of here." He slipped an arm about her waist, steering her toward the campus car park. "But I think I'd better tell you something important."

"What?"

"I didn't bring the truck."

"Oh?" She swallowed her disappointment. She could try, but she doubted she'd ever be the Porsche type.

"I traded in the truck last week."

"For what?"

"Maybe it was presumptuous of me, but I was hoping you'd accept my marriage proposal."

"What's the truck got to do with whether I marry you or not?"

"*You're* asking me that? The woman who left me—"

"All right, all right, I get the picture."

"Okay, I don't have the truck *or* the Porsche. I gave it to Derek."

"I'm sure he's thrilled."

"He is. And…"

"And?"

"I traded the truck for an SUV. More of a family-friendly vehicle, wouldn't you say?"

"Oh, Reed." With a small cry of joy, she flung her arms around this man she knew she'd love for a lifetime. No matter what kind of car he drove.

* * * * *

THE RAIN SPARROW

Linda Goodnight

In memory of Travis Goodnight and with gratitude for the time we had. Though your life was far too short, you made a difference in so many others, especially in those of your family. We miss your larger-than-life personality, your brilliance and wisdom, your giant laugh and your bigger heart.

Love you forever and always.

CHAPTER ONE

*I'm tired, boss...tired of bein' on the road, lonely
as a sparrow in the rain.*

—The Green Mile

Present Day, Honey Ridge, Tennessee

BRODY HATED FRIDAYS.

He knew what would happen if he went home. So
he didn't. He hung out at the library until it closed, and
then, wishing he had money for a hamburger, he wandered down to his spot on Magnolia Creek. It was a
pretty good hike, a couple of miles out of town past the
Griffin sisters' peach orchard and through a hundred
yards of tangled weeds, but at eleven, he was up for it.
He could have run that far and not been out of breath.

When the night surrounded him and clouds gathered in the inky sky, he once more contemplated going
home. He was hungry, but food wasn't always worth
the trouble. He wasn't afraid of the dark or of being
alone deep in the country. Home was a whole lot scar-
ier.

Stretched out on the cool earth with his hands
stacked behind his head, he listened to the peaceful night sounds, the sawing rhythm of katydids that
sometimes grew so loud he felt as if they were in-

side him, and the splash of bullfrogs diving from the nearby bank.

A rumble of thunder sounded in the distance. It was probably somewhere far off, clean over in the mountains. He wouldn't worry about that. He didn't mind a little rain. If he had to, he could hightail it past the inn to the abandoned gristmill, even though the place was kind of spooky.

The mill was probably haunted. That's what his buddy Spence said. The last time they'd gone there to explore, Spence had heard something and freaked out, so Brody would rather not go to the mill unless he had to.

Would the old man be passed out by now? Or would he be waiting with clenched fist and a hankering to take out his hatred of life on the good-for-nothing son of the good-for-less woman who'd left them both so long ago the boy had forgotten her? Mostly. Somehow it was Brody's fault that his mother had left, and the old man never let him forget it, though he never gave a reason. Brody was pretty much clueless about his absentee mother. His angry father he understood, but thoughts of his mother left him lonely and nursing guilt he didn't understand. He must have done something really bad to make her up and leave that way.

A mosquito buzzed somewhere in the humid darkness. He listened close while the pest came in for a landing, waited until the sound stopped and then he swatted. A few bug bites was better than the alternative.

He didn't like killing anything, even bugs, but as the old man would say, "It's a dog-eat-dog world. Eat the dog before he eats you."

Something about that didn't sound right to Brody, but what did he know? That's what the old man always said. A punk kid like Brody didn't know nothing.

He sighed at the moon and closed his eyes.

Better catch some z's and wait awhile longer. The old man was a bull, and once enraged, he had blood in his eyes. Clint Thomson was seldom anything but enraged on payday, especially when it came to his good-for-nothing son.

CHAPTER TWO

IT WAS A dark and stormy night, a cliché Hayden Winters dearly loved. These broody, moody nights of lightning and thunder and violent wind fueled his imagination like no other. A man intent on committing murder...

The storm had moved in around midnight, interrupting his original plans to sleep. He could never sleep on a night like this. Didn't want to, especially here in a house filled with memories and secrets.

Everyone, he believed, had a secret, and the South was filled with them. That's why he'd come.

Hayden had a secret, too, a psychological cankerworm. One that was eating a raw, black hole in his soul. Not that he'd ever let anyone see inside to know that much about him. To the world, Hayden Winters was a winner, a success, a man who brushed problems away with a charming smile. He was a man invited to the best parties he seldom attended and who gave rare but coveted interviews. A man with a charmed life.

But on these dark, moody, broody nights the demons danced around the edges of his fertile mind. He wondered at his sanity, and he knew it was only by a merciful God that he was strong of constitution and could keep the demons in their rightful place. Most of the time.

So he killed people. Dozens of them. Books littered with bodies fed some perverse need in the populace and kept his bank account fat and happy.

In the elegant rented bedroom—the Mulberry Room—lit only by the glow of his laptop, Hayden rose, went to the windows to watch and listen as rain lashed the sides of Peach Orchard Inn with its silver-on-black fingers clawing to get in.

The view outside was far different from what it had been upon his arrival earlier today. An Australian shepherd, graying around the edges, had drowsed on the long and glorious antebellum veranda. Hayden had immediately envisioned himself on the wicker furniture, feet up on the railing with a glass of Julia Presley's almost-famous peach tea and his imagination in flight.

The two-story columned mansion had shone in the sun, glowing in its whiteness with dark-trimmed shutters, flowers spilling everywhere and thick vines twining like great green arms around the oak trees. He'd driven down the winding lane of massive magnolias right into an antebellum past, far from the distractions and manic pace of the modern world.

Peach Orchard Inn, a simple name for a magnificent house, restored, he would bet, to better than its former glory. His assistant, who knew him better than most, though not well, had discovered the inn while on vacation and suggested he write the next bestseller here. Exhausted by the city bustle and another romance gone sour, he'd jumped at the idea. His ex should have taken him at his word. He'd told her from the beginning that he was neither husband nor father material. The reasons for this aversion he'd kept to himself, more for her protection than his. She didn't know that, though, and had been hurt.

He hated hurting people. Other than in his books. And the latest episode had driven him deeper into himself. A man like him ought not to need other people.

He could work here, rest here, research small-town secrets for the next thriller. There were plenty of interesting places to commit murder.

Across the road, a single light glowed like a beacon in the storm. The source was the abandoned, dilapidated gristmill that had once been part of this farm. He knew this because he was ferociously curious and knowing was his business. Abandoned buildings provided perfect places to get away with murder. He'd be suitably inspired here among the hills and hollows of southern Tennessee.

A blue-fire javelin of lightning, fierce as a bolt straight from the hand of Zeus, slit the night like a fiery blade. Gorgeous stuff.

Hayden stretched, rolled his neck, considered a walk in the violence.

He'd be up most of the night during a wild thunderstorm of this magnitude. He could feel the yet-unformed story brewing in his blood, a bubbling cauldron of energy and creativity.

Coffee, and plenty of it, was a must. He wasn't a Red Bull kind of guy. Something about it seemed addictive to him, and if there was anything he feared greater than losing his only useful resource—his fertile mind—it was addiction. Addictions came, he knew, in many forms.

Leaving the laptop curser to blink a blind eye, he let himself out of the luxurious Mulberry Room and made his way down shadowy stairs carpeted in bloodred, his hand on the smooth wooden banister, taking care on the creaky third step he'd noticed earlier. No self-respecting author of murder and mayhem missed a creaky step.

Lightning illuminated the curved staircase, and thunder rumbled like a thousand kettle drums. The house stood steady, quiet even, as if it had weathered too much to be bothered by a thunderstorm. There were stories here. He could feel them.

Hayden's Scots-Irish blood heard the dance of his ancestors in the thunder, saw wave-tossed fishing vessels on storm-gray seas and imagined a woman standing on the shore, hand to her forehead, watching while in the misty shadows lurked the equally watchful predator, biding his time.

Hayden tucked away the image for future reference. The new book was to explore the dark undercurrents hidden behind the welcoming smiles and sweet tea of a small town in the rural South, not the storm-tossed coasts of Ireland.

At the base of the stairs, he crossed the foyer through to an area the proprietress had termed the front parlor, a room of times past with a marble fireplace enclosure and Victorian decor, and into the much more modern kitchen. He fumbled for a light switch, mildly concerned about waking the sister-owners who resided somewhere on the first floor, but dismissed the concern in favor of coffee.

A quick survey of the brown granite countertops revealed no coffeemaker. He cursed himself for not remembering to ask about essential coffee equipment in his rented room, of which there was none. Here, in the large copper-and-cream kitchen, the coffee machine could be anywhere. He had no luck locating it but found a tea bag caddie, a discovery that made him snarl.

While he pondered the usefulness of lemon zinger tea, his cell phone buzzed against his hip. He winced at the sudden racket, though if the thunder didn't wake the house, a ringtone shouldn't. Still, out of consideration and being the new guest in the place, he slapped the phone silent. He'd intended to dump the device in the bottom of his suitcase and forget it for a few days, but out of habit, he'd stuck the phone in his back pocket.

"A pity," he grumbled. "And stupid."

He knew who the caller was. The only person who ever called him in the dead of night. She'd been the one who taught him never to sleep too soundly.

"Hello, Dora Lee."

He heard her quivery intake of breath and braced himself for the histrionics or cursing. One or the other was inevitable.

When she didn't respond, a tingle of worry forced a regrettable question. "Are you all right?"

"No, I'm not all right, though a lot you care. I'm sick. You know I'm sick, and you don't help me. How am I supposed to get my medicine?"

Hayden closed his eyes and leaned against the hard counter edge. He could imagine her there in the cluttered trailer among unwashed dishes and fast-food containers filled with dry, half-eaten meals, hair wild and eyes wilder, hands shaking in desperation. "What did you do with the last money?"

"You think that's enough? You think I can pay rent and buy food and keep the lights on with that?"

His sigh was heavy. "Is the electricity off again?"

"Been off. I had to have my medicine. What good is lights if a body hurts too bad to open her eyes."

"Dora Lee, I won't send money for any more pills." God knew, he'd contributed to her addiction too long already with the ever-raw hope that she'd change, a hope that even now burned with a flickering flame. "You're killing yourself. I'll come to Kentucky, get you into a clinic—"

The scream in his ear was louder than the thunder. "Shut up! Shut up—you hear me? You ungrateful scum. I should have drowned you when I had the chance, for all the good you've done me. Keep your filthy money."

The line went dead in his ear.

Weariness of the past few months pressed in. His stir of creative energy seeped out like lifeblood on the kitchen tile.

He should never have given her his cell phone number, but the desperate little boy inside him still yearned to make things better with his embittered, addicted nightmare of a mother. Even when he was small, before the dark and deadly underbelly of a coal mine had killed his gentle father, Dora Lee had popped illegally gotten pills for imaginary headaches and hated her only child. And he didn't know why.

His mother had no idea the same hated son was now Hayden Winters, successful novelist. It was a secret he would never share with her. Could never share. The ramifications were too deep and disturbing to consider.

Long ago, he'd changed his name and re-created his past in an effort to become something besides the dirtiest little boy in the worst part of Appalachia. Suave, confident Hayden Winters was as fictitious as the novels he wrote. Dora Lee wouldn't have cared anyway. All she cared about was that he sent money.

For her unconcerned ignorance, Hayden would ever be grateful to the God who'd rescued him from the mines and Dora Lee Briggs. If the press got hold of his mother, Hayden could kiss his tightly controlled privacy goodbye.

He was glad she couldn't read, though as a needy boy, hoping to please his mother, he'd offered to teach her. For his offer, she'd battered him with the book until the binding loosened and the pages ripped, raging that she wasn't as stupid as he thought.

At least a couple of times a year, he made the trek to see her, again out of some psychological wound that needed to be fed. Each time, he'd leave behind another piece of himself along with a parting gift that she would trade, in addition to her monthly draw, for Oxycontin or whatever pills she could get that would take her away from reality for a while.

Dora Lee Briggs was his ugly secret. One of them.

With the wound in his soul open and throbbing, Hayden stuck a cup of water in the microwave. Lemon zinger would have to do.

CARRIE RILEY TIPTOED down the stairs, shivering in her bare feet and lightweight pajamas. Storms made her nervous. *Really* nervous. She couldn't sleep. Couldn't begin to sleep with all that fierce wind whipping the trees and thunder making her jump out of her skin. How anyone else could sleep boggled her well-ordered mind.

She didn't know where she was going, considering the late hour, but since the family parlor housed the inn's only downstairs television to check the weather, she'd head there. What if a tornado was coming? Didn't anyone in this house think about that?

Carrie hated storms. Absolutely hated them. Even in infancy, according to her mother, Carrie had screamed like a banshee, inconsolable, at the first thunderclap. She didn't scream anymore, but she did quake and shake and long for someone to hold her.

Penlight aimed at the floor, she gripped the banister and made her way down. The third step squeaked. She stopped, winced and then went on. She was such a wimp. Such a mouse.

A sleepover was a silly thing for grown women to do, but yesterday in the light of day, before the storm, time spent with sisters and friends had sounded like the perfect respite. She and her two sisters, lifelong friends of the inn's sister-owners, Valery Griffin and Julia Presley, had decided on a weekend retreat to reconnect and have some fun. Julia was making a fresh effort to reclaim old friends and move forward after the terrible abduction of her son six years ago, and Carrie was pleased to be part of her friend's healing.

They'd had a great time, exchanging stories and giggling over a bit too much Moscato as they painted toenails and discussed Julia's engagement to Eli Donovan of *the* Knoxville Donovans and urged her to have a big, fancy wedding right here at Peach Orchard Inn.

Now the others were snoozing like fossil rocks while she trembled in fear over the storm and nursed the teeniest headache. Wine had a tendency to do that to plain old Carrie of the boring life who rarely drank anything stronger than a single-shot espresso. She couldn't even tolerate a double. *Wimp.*

At the bottom of the steps, she noticed a light in the kitchen. Curious and eager for human companionship, Carrie hurried on shaky knees across the cool wood floors, but skittered to a stop in the arched doorway when she spotted him. For the person in the kitchen was definitely a him. A lean, rangy, masculine him.

He obviously had not yet been to bed. Still in casually expensive jeans she recognized only by the label on the back pocket, holding a cell phone and a long-sleeved navy pullover with the sleeves pushed back, he was turned away from her, lifting a tea bag in and out of a China cup. His wide shoulders, like his forearms, were muscled, his hands long and strong-looking as if he worked outside for a living. But not in those jeans. Or with that haircut.

He wore a rich man's haircut. She knew this because her sister Nikki was the most fashion-conscious woman in Honey Ridge. Boutique owner Nikki knew fashion, knew haircuts, knew high-end anything, unlike Carrie, who couldn't tell Gucci from a gunnysack and basically didn't care. The man's straight brown hair was casually shoved off his forehead in a loose, sexy muss that probably cost a bazillion dollars to maintain.

Carrie couldn't decide whether to speak or wait until he noticed her. In her case, that might be another fifty years. Men did not notice Carrie Riley. Not unless they wanted to check out a book.

The loudest clap of thunder ever heard, at least to Carrie, rocked the countryside. The house trembled. More lightning followed on its tail, a blinding explosion of light and sound that crackled the air.

Carrie jumped, fists raised, and squeaked.

The spoon clattered against the counter. The man

stilled and then slowly turned his head. He was good-looking, darn it. Romantic-looking, like one of the poets she read incessantly with a deep longing for *that* kind of love to find its way to her house. Now she'd be a bumbling, stuttering mess for more reasons that the storm.

"Sorry. I didn't mean to startle you." She crossed her arms tightly over her chest.

A very nice, full-lipped mouth curved. Eyes the color of fog and smoke and mystery watched her. "You squeaked."

Like a mouse. Stupid. Stupid.

"Storms scare me. I thought I'd better check the weather."

"It's raining."

Carrie rolled her eyes, almost smiled, though she was still too shivery. "What if there's a tornado?"

He shook his head. "Not going to happen."

Something about the easy way he rejected the idea of a tornado soothed her. Maybe he was a meteorologist.

Carrie took a few steps into the kitchen. She didn't know this man, but she could always scream if he tried something, though not a soul in this house would hear her over the storm.

Comforting thought.

"Want some—" he saluted her with one of Julia's delicate white cups and a wry arch of eyebrow, sipped and made a face "—lemon zinger tea?"

At times like this she wished she was as outgoing as Nikki or gorgeous like Bailey or even a little wild and easy with men like Valery. But she was none of those things. She was plain Carrie, the librarian, wishing she could say something snappy and clever.

"If you don't like lemon zinger, pick a different kind." *Very snappy and clever.* No wonder she was past thirty and still single.

"I wanted caffeine," he said with a shrug.

"You won't get it from lemon zinger. Make coffee."

"I would if I knew where the machine was."

She lifted a finger. "*That* I can help you with."

He dropped his head back. "Praise the saints and Maxwell House."

Bare feet soundless on the cool tile flooring, Carrie moved to a pantry and removed one of Julia's sterling silver French press urns. "We'll have to grind the beans. Julia's a bit of a coffee snob."

"Won't the noise disturb the others?"

Thunder rattled the house. Carrie tilted her head toward the dark, rain-drenched window. "Will it matter?"

"Point taken. You're a lifesaver. What's your name?"

"Carrie Riley." She kept her hands busy and her eyes on the work. The fact that she was ever so slightly aware of the stranger with the poet's face in a womanly kind of way gave her a funny tingle. She seldom tingled, and she didn't flirt. She was no good at that kind of thing. Just ask her sisters. "Yours?"

"Hayden Winters."

"Nice to meet you, Hayden." She held up a canister of coffee beans. "Bold?"

"I can be."

She laughed, shocked to think this handsome man might actually be flirting a little. Even if she wasn't. "Bold it is."

As she'd predicted, the storm noise covered the

grinding sound and in fewer than ten minutes, the silver pot's lever was pressed and the coffee was poured. The dark, bold aroma filled the kitchen, a pleasing warmth against the rain-induced chill.

Hayden Winters offered her the first cup, a courteous gesture that made her like him, and then sipped his. "You know your way around a bold roast."

"Former Starbucks barista who loves coffee."

"A kindred spirit. I live on the stuff, especially when I'm working, which I should be doing."

She didn't want him to leave. Not because he was hot—which he was—but because she didn't want to be alone in the storm, and no one else was up. "You work at night?"

"Stormy nights are my favorite."

Which, in her book, meant he was a little off center. "What do you do?"

He studied her for a moment and, with his expression a peculiar mix of amusement and malevolence, said quietly, matter-of-factly, "I kill people."

CHAPTER THREE

HAYDEN DIDN'T KNOW what possessed him to say such a thing when this pleasant woman was already a nervous wreck and had saved his night with a terrific cup of coffee, but he'd given his standard glib answer when asked about his line of work. The press seemed to love it. Carrie, not so much.

She squeaked again. Cute. Mouse-like. Her eyes widened to two huge, espresso-colored circles. He had the random thought that those soft eyes could melt concrete.

Hayden set the cup aside and took a step toward her. "Metaphorically speaking."

She took a step back, arms tight over her chest. "Excuse me?"

"I'm a writer. Thrillers."

"Oh." The big doe eyes blinked. "You're a writer. You don't kill people *literally*."

"Only in the pages of my books."

She put a hand to her heart and blew out a breath. "Thank goodness. I thought for a minute…stormy night, thunder, lightning, murder." She arched her back in a body shrug.

"Bad habit of mine."

"Murdering people?"

"That, too." He smiled. She was pretty cute.

"Wait a minute." She held up a finger. "What did you say your name was again?"

"Hayden Winters."

"Well, do I ever feel stupid." Fists on hips, she shook her head in self-disgust. "Hayden Winters. The novelist. We have all your books in the library—very popular, too, I might add—but apparently my brain did not register an actual bestselling author here in Honey Ridge."

He braced for it, fully expecting her to fawn over him and make all kinds of gushy noises before an onslaught of tedious questions about the easy way to get published and why he'd chosen to write thrillers. He hadn't. They'd chosen him.

Why couldn't he have a conversation with a woman without things getting awkward?

"Now that I know you're not going to kill me," she went on, "I'll share a secret with you. I know where Julia keeps the cookies." She clinked her cup on the countertop, stood on tiptoe and opened an overhead cupboard. "Oreos or pecan sandies?"

The back side of her intrigued him, threw him off. Everything about her threw him off. She wasn't impressed by Hayden Winters, and he didn't know if that bothered or pleased him.

He let his eyes roam, taking her in, a writer's habit of observing nuances, gestures. And yet something essentially male stirred, just a bit, as he watched Carrie Riley stretch up high for the cookies. He should have offered to reach them, but he'd rather watch her.

She wasn't tall—average height, maybe, with ample curves, maybe a little extra in the hips that he found... comforting. Her hair was the color of roasted pecans, short and shoved behind her ears and messy on top. Side bangs fell across her forehead. She looked good sleep-mussed, her classic pajamas in an almost see-through shade of pink cupcakes.

And her feet were pretty.

He must be asleep and dreaming because he didn't have a foot fetish. Never noticed women's feet unless they were in shoes sky-high and strappy at the end of very long legs. But Carrie's bare feet were perfectly shaped, feminine and smooth, and her toes polished a shiny pearl. Around her left ankle was a delicate silver chain he found particularly intriguing.

She turned her head and looked over one shoulder at him. "Which kind?"

He snapped his eyes to hers. "You choose."

She handed down the sandies and then reached back for the Oreos, grinning. "Who says we can't have both?"

Plastic crinkled as she ripped open the packages and offered him first dibs. He took his mind off the interesting little ankle bracelet to help himself to an Oreo.

"Julia prefers to bake from scratch. This is her emergency stash."

"Is this an emergency?"

"In a storm of this proportion? You bet it is." She crunched down on a sugary sandie, scattering crumbs.

He saluted her with the Oreo and thought how pleasant and comfortable this unexpected late-night encounter had become. She had no idea she'd saved him from a bout of melancholy after the conversation with his mother.

He was about to pry into her life, a natural result

of his writer's curiosity, when a sound from outside caught his ear.

He tilted his head. "Did you hear something?"

Carrie's espresso eyes got bigger. "No. Did you?"

"A clatter. On the porch. As if a chair fell over."

Thunder rolled, and rain gushed against the house as loud as Niagara Falls. "How can you hear anything over the storm?"

He shrugged. "Probably nothing."

"It's your murderous writer's brain."

She wasn't wrong about that, but he walked to the window anyway and peered out.

"Black as the heart of a coal mine." He started to turn back to his bold coffee and chocolate cookie when a shadowy bulk caught his eye.

"What is—?" He tensed, leaned in, squinted. "Turn the light off."

"What? What do you see?"

"Turn the light off so I can be certain."

"You're making me nervous."

"It's probably some poor animal trying to get out of the storm."

"A mountain lion. Or a bear."

He smirked at her. "You have a vivid imagination."

"From the mouth of Hayden Winters." She clicked off the light. "Don't do something juvenile and try to startle me. I'll scream and wake the whole house."

But Hayden's attention was focused on the dark lump against the wall of the porch. "There's someone on the veranda."

"No way." She flipped the light back on. "No one would be out in this."

"No one should be." He strode to the entry leading

out onto the veranda, flipped on the porch light and jerked the door open.

Rain and wind battered the flowers along the railing and sprayed mist against the entry. Hayden felt Carrie's warmth close behind him, felt her shiver.

Her sharp intake of breath matched his.

"Oh, my gravy," she whispered.

Storm or no storm, Hayden strode outside. A wind gust sprayed him with fat drops of rain, and cold prickled the skin on his arms.

A boy, drenched to the bone and shivering, huddled against the wall, a soggy bundle of plastered hair and pale skin.

"What are you doing out here?" Hayden demanded.

The kid's teeth chattered. "I—I got lost."

"On a night like this?"

Miserably, the boy nodded but glanced away, either lying or too chilled to hold eye contact. No kid would be out alone in a storm without good reason.

Hayden grabbed him by the arm and said, "Come inside."

The boy came willingly, eagerly, and stood in the entry dripping water everywhere. He shivered like a wet Chihuahua.

Hayden pulled the door closed and blocked out the chilly wet air.

"We'll need towels." Carrie rushed away.

While she was gone, Hayden quietly assessed the young boy. He was slender built, close to skinny, with a heart-shaped face kissed by a sprinkle of brownish freckles. A Huckleberry Finn kind of kid who was trying to look anywhere except in Hayden's eyes. There was something frighteningly familiar about the kid, so much so that Hayden softened.

In a patient voice, he said, "I'm Hayden. Who are you?"

"Brody." He rubbed a soggy hand across his wet eyes. His rain-darkened eyelashes stuck straight out above cheeks pale as sand.

"So you got lost?"

The boy stared down at the ever-widening puddle on the floor. "Um...yeah."

Lost didn't feel right to Hayden. He was reasonably sure the boy was hiding something. The question was, why?

"What were you doing out in this kind of weather?" A beeping sound came from the kitchen. Hayden kept his focus on the child.

"Camping out." Brody's voice was soft and uncertain. "I wasn't expecting the storm."

Camping out. Okay, that made sense. Country boys did that kind of thing. He'd done it plenty of times.

"By yourself?"

"Yeah."

Carrie appeared with two snow-white towels and draped one around the boy's shoulders. "I warmed them for you in the microwave."

That explained the beep.

"Smart." Hayden glanced at her in appreciation.

"Thank you." Brody shivered and huddled beneath the fluffy towel while Carrie patted at his face and soggy hair with the other. Kind. Tender. Her actions stirred something in Hayden's chest. He couldn't remember anyone ever drying him off.

"What's your phone number, Brody? I'll give your folks a call."

"Uh, they're, uh—" The boy fidgeted. "They're not home."

"No?" Suspicion, like a hairy spider, crawled over Hayden's scalp.

Brody flashed pale blue eyes at Hayden before letting them slide away. But in that instant, Hayden saw the truth. The kid didn't want to go home. He preferred a stormy, cold, wet night alone.

An icy feeling of déjà vu lodged in Hayden's chest.

He'd camped out in the woods dozens of times to avoid going home.

Carrie disappeared again to make noises in the kitchen. Lightning flickered against the windows, less intense than earlier.

"You camp by yourself often?"

"I like the woods." Brody's quiet words were almost imperceptible.

If the kid knew the woods well enough to camp, he likely had not been lost at all.

"How old are you, Brody?"

"Eleven."

"You live close by?" The lopsided conversation felt more like an interrogation, which Hayden supposed it was.

"In town."

Hayden had stopped in the picturesque town of Honey Ridge, a couple of miles down the road, when he'd come through on his way to the inn. "Pretty long walk."

"I don't mind it." A glint of humor showed in the

blue eyes Brody flashed his way. "Except when it storms."

"Can't say I don't feel the same."

Carrie returned, carrying a steaming white cup and the bag of Oreos. "Here you go, Brody. A mug of hot cocoa should warm you up."

Shaky hands took the offered treats. "Thanks."

The kid gobbled a cookie in two bites. *Hungry*, Hayden thought, when he dispatched a second one every bit as quickly. Pondering, Hayden munched on his Oreo while the boy ate and drank.

"You're welcome to all the cookies you want." Carrie urged the package toward Brody.

"I should…go." But he made no move to shed the now-damp towels or move toward the door.

Carrie put another cookie in his hand. "Drink your cocoa, and we'll figure something out."

The kid had nowhere to go. Hayden had already figured that out even if Carrie hadn't. A thought danced through his head, and he latched on.

"I have a perfectly good room upstairs that I won't be using tonight," Hayden offered. "Why don't you bunk there until morning?"

Brody shook his head. "I couldn't do that."

"Why not? I paid for the bed, but I won't be in it. Someone might as well sleep there."

"But—"

"He works at night, Brody." Carrie flashed Hayden a look of gratitude. "It'll be okay. Julia won't mind."

Hayden didn't know if the innkeeper would mind or not, and he didn't much care. The kid was cold, hungry and too exhausted to be any trouble. He was staying. If Julia wanted to charge extra on Hayden's tab, fine.

"I'll take my laptop into the front parlor close to the coffeemaker. The bed's all yours."

The boy looked relieved, hopeful. "You sure? I wouldn't bother nothing."

"Drink up, and let's get you upstairs."

Brody took a long swig and drained the cup, handed it off to Carrie. "Thank you. You make delicious cocoa."

Carrie touched his wet hair. She was, Hayden noticed, a toucher. "You're welcome."

"Ready?"

The boy nodded, and Hayden led the way up the stairs, whispering, "Watch the third step. It creaks."

With a solemn nod, Brody imitated Hayden's path and nothing squeaked.

Inside the bright and pretty Mulberry Room, Brody stood awkward and silent while Hayden dug out a pair of drawstring sweats and a T-shirt. The air was thick and humid from the damp night and a wet boy who smelled of river and woods.

"They'll be too big, but they're dry." He motioned toward the bathroom. "In there. You can grab a hot shower if you want to."

"I'm pretty tired."

"I bet you are. Change, then, while I gather my work gear."

Hayden needed less than a minute to organize his laptop, charger and notebook. For good measure, he added the extra blanket from the closet and pocketed his wallet. Sometimes a kid did things out of desperation.

Brody reappeared, a waif in oversize clothes, the gray sweats rolled up at the ankle and the shirt hang-

ing below his hips. He'd scrubbed at his hair with a
towel and it stuck out like porcupine quills. He held the
wet clothes in his hands. "Where should I put these?"

"I'll take them. They'll have a dryer." Carrie would
know, and he hoped she hadn't gone to bed. She was
apparently a friend of the innkeeper and knew her way
around the inn.

Hayden added the jeans and shirt to the items he'd
take downstairs, then flipped back the mulberry-print
comforter and gestured. The boy climbed in, his cold
feet brushing Hayden's hand. Tucking in a kid brought
an odd sensation, and he had a sudden gray-edged
memory of his father, the scent and soot of the mines
imprinted in his pores, snugging a blanket beneath
Hayden's chin.

Brody's pale fingers gripped the edge of the cover.
His eyes drooped and he sighed, a pitiful sound of relief and exhaustion.

Hayden stepped back to leave.

"Mister?"

"Yes?"

"Thanks." Brody's lips barely moved as his eyelids
fluttered shut.

Full of a pity he didn't want to feel, Hayden waited
less than a minute before the skinny chest rose and fell
in rhythmic sleep. Softly he murmured, "Good night,
Brody." What was left of it.

He clicked the switch and sent the room into darkness lit only by the flicker of leftover lightning. So
much for writing during the storm. The best part was
nearly gone.

Skirting the third step, he made his way back to the

kitchen, where Carrie cleaned up the evidence of the night's activities.

When he entered the room, she paused, closed Oreo package in hand, to nod at Brody's wet garments. "Let me have those."

Hayden handed over the soggy clothes and followed Carrie down a short hall behind the kitchen to a laundry room.

"That was nice of you," she said.

"What else was I going to do? Toss the kid back out in the storm?"

"I could have woke up Julia and gotten the key to a vacant room."

He shrugged. "No need. I'm up anyway."

"Right." She tossed the clothes into the dryer, added a softener sheet, clicked the door shut and hit a button that set the tumbler into humming motion and the warm humid smell of peaches swirling about the space. "So you can kill people."

"Uh-huh." *Starting with the parents of a certain half-drowned boy*, he thought with grim satisfaction.

Carrie headed back to the kitchen to finish the cleanup. A neat freak with the neurotic need to be cleaner than his boyhood, Hayden joined in.

"I know that boy," Carrie said as she sponged down the countertop. "He comes in the library nearly every day after school for our tutoring program."

"Why didn't you say something?"

She shrugged. "He probably doesn't know who I am. Kids don't notice librarians."

He did. "What do you know about him?"

"He hangs out and plays on the computers, reads some but rarely checks out a book. He likes mysteries and adventure." She flashed the charming dimple. "Librarians always notice reading preference. He doesn't say much or bother anyone, but he generally stays awhile, as if he has no place else to be. We get our share of those at the library."

"Do you know his parents?"

"He lives with his father. No mother in the picture. Brody's one of the street kids around Honey Ridge. I don't believe for one minute that he was lost."

Hayden filled a coffee carafe and started another pot. "That was my take, as well. His father isn't out of town, either."

"Why would he lie about a thing like that? If his dad is at home, why didn't he let us call him?"

There were plenty of reasons, and Hayden, unfortunately, knew too many of them.

LONG AFTER CARRIE trudged up the stairs in hopes of a few hours' sleep, Hayden contemplated the night's events and stared at a blank word processor. Fueled by the cookies and strong coffee, his mind whirled, though not in the direction he'd hoped. Carrie, Brody and Dora Lee wouldn't leave him alone.

He stretched, rolled his neck and roamed the parlor.

Finally, frustrated by the lack of progress, he grabbed the blanket and a throw pillow and flopped down on a curved, skinny Victorian sofa clearly not intended for napping. Especially by a man with long legs.

After fifteen minutes of misery, he rolled off onto the area rug, taking the pillow and cover with him. *Much better.*

The pillow smelled of peaches and the floor of wood polish, though a dark stain spread from the rug to the fireplace. The wood was old, likely original to the house, but he wondered why this section hadn't been replaced.

He sifted through the memories of the day, tossed out the conversation with his mother, which was guaranteed to keep him awake and suffering from dyspepsia, and focused on the fascinating old house.

His fingers grazed the stain, interestingly cool to the touch. With a weary sigh, he closed his eyes and let himself feel the memories clinging to the fireplace and the floor, searching for that one kernel of story that would become a novel. His last conscious thought was the low vibrating rumble of a distant train.

CHAPTER FOUR

It is said that some lives are linked across time, connected by an ancient calling that echoes through the ages.

—Prince of Persia

1867

HEAT SEARED HIS lungs and scorched his skin. Flames leaped and clawed. His shirt melted against his back. He coughed, once, twice, as hot tears rolled down his face.

Amelia! Grace! Where are you? Their names stuck in his throat, burned shut by the hungry flames.

"Sir! Wake up. You's havin' a bad dream."

Thaddeus Eriksson opened his eyes with a start. A broad black face, as dark and shiny as a coat button and most certainly not his wife or daughter, stared down at him. Thad sat up straighter, reorienting to the inside of the Tennessee passenger train. The metallic click of the tracks rumbled below him. Smoke puffed past the windows. He was on a train bound for southern Tennessee, not in the burning house in Ohio.

He dragged a shaky hand down his face. "I was dreaming."

He'd not had the dream in weeks. The engine smoke must have set him off.

"Yes, sir. You sure was. You all right now?"

Thaddeus saw kindness in the obsidian eyes of Abram, an ex-slave, fit and strong like a field-worker, not old but old enough to be on his own on a south-bound train, though from the haughty glances and grumbles, there were plenty on board who disapproved of his presence. The slaves were all free now that the war had ended and a bumpy kind of peace had descended on the country. Still, a black man alone on a train was taking a risk.

From the moment Abram had boarded the train, Thaddeus had kept a watchful eye until fatigue and the train's rhythm had lulled him to sleep. He hadn't intended to doze. A former Union soldier and a freed slave on a Southern train weren't especially welcome, and he knew better than to let down his guard. He tried to keep his voice low to hide the Ohio accent, but Abram couldn't hide who he was.

Surrender may have come, but the nation was far from being united.

Even now, a rotund man with a cigar squinted at them in hostile speculation.

The scarlet padded seat gave as Thaddeus twisted toward the friendly freedman. Abram sat behind him, but they'd exchanged a cordial conversation on the long ride. No one else seemed inclined to pass the time.

"I'm obliged you woke me."

He'd slept for five nights on a series of conveyances on his way from Ohio to Honey Ridge, Tennessee. The train cars were noisy, dirty, and the interruptions unpredictable but the ride was still a luxury considering the miles he'd marched and places he'd slept during the war.

Like most of the South, railroad service had yet to fully recover, and the flood of Northern profiteers into the South had raised the hackles of former Confederates.

"Bad dreams can be an omen. That's what my mama always said." Abram's rough, weathered hands gripped the seat back as he leaned forward, speaking low. "You were hollering out to somebody named Amelia."

Sometimes bad dreams were reality. The hard knot of pain tightened in Thad's gut. "My wife. She died."

Even after a year, the words shocked him.

"Now that right there is a pure shame, Mr. Thaddeus. I sho is sorry for yo' loss. Do you have any chilren?"

"Grace. She died, too." He was the only survivor of the fire that had taken his home and family, and Thaddeus knew he should be thankful to the Almighty for sparing him. But after a year alone, a year of strangling grief and regret, he often wished he'd died with them. "What about you, Abram? You got a wife and children?"

"No, sir. I had me a sweetheart once, but the masta' sold her off somewhere when the war started. My mama and brothers, too. Pappy, he died in the fightin'."

Abram's words were a useful reminder that others had lost as much or more in the long, painful War Between the States, a struggle he still believed was righteous.

"That's a shame."

"Yes, sir. I'm gonna find them, though."

"Is that where you're headed now?"

"Uh-huh. Chattanooga. Miz Malden, she couldn't pay us no more after Mr. Malden passed. The war done took everything." He laughed softly. "Even us workers, thank the Lawd. But she looked in Mr. Malden's book, and told every one of us where our families was sold off to."

"Kind of her." Thad's heart had returned to a steady rhythm as the dream faded. He was grateful for Abram's distracting conversation. "You think your family is still there?"

"Yes, sir. Hoping so. My mama and my brother, Jesse."

Since emancipation former slaves were scattered, searching for one another and for a new start to a way of life few of them understood. There was no telling where Abram's family was now. But Thaddeus didn't have the heart to steal the man's hope.

"Chattanooga sounds like the place to start."

"Won't be long now."

Thad removed his pocket watch, a timepiece he'd carried since before the war. A long-ago Christmas gift from Amelia, it was his most treasured possession. Even as the polished silver glinted in the sunlight, he recalled her smile, her joy at presenting him with such a fine watch. The memory both hurt and comforted.

"Ought to be coming up on my stop soon and then Chattanooga not long after."

He'd no more than spoken than the train began to slow and the brakes squealed. A shrill whistle nearly split his eardrums.

"This yo' stop right here?"

"This is it." A water stop for the train, and a place for passengers to disembark or board that wasn't much more than a handful of clapboard buildings. "I hope you find your family, Abram. If you ever get up around Honey Ridge, stop in and say hello."

Thaddeus hoisted his satchel and rose, turning to offer a hand to Abram. The ex-slave seemed momentarily taken aback before he clasped Thad's hand with a grin. "Good luck to you, Mr. Thaddeus."

Steam smoke swirled around Thad's face as he disembarked, and the strong odor made him anxious. He knew the scent came from the train and yet the memory of the fire that had stolen too much haunted him more than the years of unrelenting battle.

He glanced around at the tiny town, then toward the rising blue haze that would be the Smokies to the east and the rolling countryside that spread in every direction in undulant shades of green. The landscape across Tennessee was beautiful, even though too many burned farms and ravaged villages littered the countryside like the dead Confederacy.

Weary but hopeful, Thad aimed toward a sign proclaiming General Store in search of information. If he was fortunate, someone would share an easy route to Honey Ridge. If he was very lucky, he might even find a wagon headed in that direction.

His boots echoed in the hot afternoon as he stepped through the doorway into the tiny store. The inside was dim and smelled of coffee and leather and hog grease. Shelves stuffed tight with an array of goods lined the walls of the narrow room, a promising sign. Three men stood talking around a spittoon, while a white-haired merchant wrapped a length of brightly printed calico in brown paper.

Thaddeus approached the merchant. "I'm headed

for Honey Ridge. Might you direct me toward the best route?"

Nimble fingers paused in tying the package. "I might."

Thaddeus waited, but the merchant didn't say more.

One of the tobacco chewers, a short, squat man with a big nose, approached. "Where you from, boy?"

It wasn't the first time he'd answered that question, though not everyone across the South had been unkind to a former Yankee soldier. There were sympathizers in Tennessee, including the rosy-cheeked woman who'd sold him a loaf of bread and thrown in some dried apples for good measure. Thaddeus had a feeling this man wasn't one of those.

He sighed. "Ohio."

The man spat a long stream of tobacco, narrowly missing Thad's boots. Thad followed the insult with his eyes.

"Yankee." The man bit off the word as if it left a nasty taste. He looked to his friends, both of whom stared at Thad with more than a little animosity. The one in red suspenders tilted back to stare and Thad saw what he'd missed. One of the men was missing a leg. A soldier, no doubt. A Rebel. Probably all three of them had been.

"I'm not looking for trouble," Thaddeus said. "Just directions."

"You won't find them here." The man ran his hands under his suspenders. "You best head on back to where you come from."

The tiny hope that he might purchase some food or even share a ride on a farmer's wagon dissipated in the dark confines of the general store.

The merchant kept his attention on the parcel now neatly wrapped and tied with string.

Thaddeus gave a head bob and walked outside. A hundred yards down the track, the train chugged onward toward Chattanooga, its smoke a gray feather tickling the blue sky.

The air was sticky and thick. Nights would be cooler, though every bit as humid. Will had sent him a map, drawn by his own hand. A former army captain who'd campaigned all over Tennessee, William Gadsden would be accurate. The trip to Peach Orchard Farm was a long one, especially without food, but nothing to a man who had marched with a hungry infantry for three years.

He shouldered his satchel and started walking.

"You can't. I won't have it."

Josie Portland tossed down her napkin to glare at Will Gadsden across a long oak table that had fed four generations of Portlands. Portlands, not Gadsdens. The former Union captain had married her late brother's widow, and now the uppity Yankee thought he owned Peach Orchard Farm and Mill.

"Josie, please," Charlotte said mildly. "Don't fuss."

"Fuss? You expect me to sit back and let more and more of the enemy invade my home? Haven't we lost enough?"

Will's jaw tightened. "The war is over, Josie. We are not enemies."

"Tell that to Tom!" The chair scraped against a floor where dozens of wounded had once sprawled in bloody misery. Josie bolted upright. Heat swamped her, burning her cheeks. She fought hot tears, ever present at the mention of Tom.

Four pairs of eyes watched her. Her sister, Patience, as sweet and holy as Mother Mary herself, looked baffled as she usually did by any kind of disturbance, while her nephew, Benjamin, clearly sided with Captain Will. He always did. Admittedly, Will had been good to the eleven-year-old after the tragic death of Ben's father.

Lizzy's dark face appeared at the kitchen door, eyes wide. Charlotte's former maid was one of the few slaves who'd stayed behind to work for provisions and little else. They were all like slaves now, doing what they could to survive.

"Josie, sit down please and let's speak of this sensibly." Charlotte folded her hands together on the edge of the table as calm as bath water. Ever serene, the British vicar's daughter was too pious for Josie's liking. Never a bad word, never a complaint, no matter how awful things had been since the war. At times, she didn't know how Charlotte had kept the farm and the mill going, though her sister-in-law gave credit to God and the handful of crippled Yankees and former slaves who'd stayed to help.

Certainly, Josie comprehended all that her brother's widow had done. She wasn't a fool. If not for Charlotte's stiff resolve and clever wrangling, they would have lost the farm and mill to Yankee carpetbaggers. Nevertheless, Josie wanted her life back the way it was before the hated war, before Father and her brother, Edgar, had died.

"Why couldn't you hire someone from Honey Ridge?" Her chest heaved beneath the hatefully dull brown dress. She was so angry her face must be as red as her hair. "Why do you have to hire a Yankee?"

"Because no one here has Thad's skills. He's from a family of millers. He is a millwright as well as a miller, which means he can repair the machinery and make improvements. He can teach us what we need to know to make the operation smoother and more profitable." Will lifted the letter he'd received earlier that day. The hateful letter he'd read to them over a supper of dumplings and stewed fruit. "We are fortunate he's agreed to come."

"You've been doing fine by yourself," she spat, though the compliment cost her. Will was a decent man for a Yankee, but he was still a Yankee. Men like him were the reason her Tom had never come home from the bloody, horrible war. They were the reason so many women like her cried for sweethearts still missing or buried in some remote place without so much as a name marker. They were the reason she would never wear Mother's wedding gown.

"I've barely kept things going, Josie. The mill needs repairs that I can't do, and even if I could, I haven't any more hours in the day. I need Thad, and he is already on his way. He's a fine man who's had his share of loss, and I expect you to treat him with respect."

Helpless fury shook her. Let Thaddeus Eriksson come if he must, but Josie would do her best to make his visit short and miserable.

She would choke before she'd show respect to another bloody Yankee.

CHAPTER FIVE

You must stay drunk on writing so reality cannot destroy you.

—Ray Bradbury

Present

HAYDEN AWOKE WITH a jerk, disoriented as he stared into a nineteenth-century fireplace. Where was he?

He sat up, heart chugging with the hard rhythm of a train. Except for the blue glow from his laptop, asleep but powered on, heavy darkness shrouded the room.

The dream had been so real. Even now when he was awake, Thaddeus's sorrow lay heavily in his chest, as real as if *he* had suffered the loss of a wife and child. He'd smelled the smoke, looked into the eyes of the ex-slave and sat at the dinner table with the Portland family.

"Weird," he muttered. He'd dreamed scenes from his work before but never anything like this. These characters were realistically familiar, as if he knew them. As if he *was* them.

Blowing out a shaky breath, Hayden tapped the keyboard to shed more light on his surroundings. The tiny digital clock in one corner said he'd slept a few hours. Dawn would break soon.

His senses slowly returned as he recognized the antebellum inn and recalled why he was in the parlor instead of in the cushy bed upstairs in the Mulberry Room. Still, the dream lingered and the strong emotions persisted.

In his imagination, the computer clock morphed into a silver pocket watch, glinting in the Tennessee sun.

He scrubbed his face with both hands, uncomfortably aware that the dream man, Thaddeus, had done the same.

Thaddeus, Abram, Josie. Three fascinating characters who had nothing to do with the kind of book he was contracted to write.

Yet the rich images prodded at his imagination, stirring the creative hunger.

Before the gauzy cobweb dream was cleaned away by the hand of wakefulness, Hayden grabbed his computer and began to write.

By the time he purged his memory, morning had broken through the drapes in September's pure yellow-white streaks, and delicious scents wafted from the kitchen, waking his senses and his taste buds. If Julia had found his presence in the parlor odd when she'd come through at dawn, she'd said nothing. A short time later, she'd placed a fresh cup of coffee next to him. He'd called her a goddess.

The classy blonde innkeeper had simply smiled and padded quietly away, a courtesy he appreciated. He didn't like interruptions when he worked. In fact, he didn't like people when he worked. He supposed his assistant had relayed that persnickety piece of information when she'd booked the room for an indefinite period of time for enough money to get him anything

he wanted. Today he would express his desire for a coffeemaker. Or he'd go into town and buy one. He wasn't
a purist. Any old cup of java worked, though he appreciated Julia's freshly ground beans.

He sipped the rich, bold grind, a reminder of Carrie,
the squeaky cute librarian, his fellow storm watcher
from last night. He wondered if her jittery nerves had
finally settled enough to sleep.

When he heard a man's voice in the kitchen, his curiosity got the better of him. Ready for a refill, he hit
Save and closed the laptop. Forget the dream. He didn't
write historical novels.

Right now he needed coffee.

Upon reaching the kitchen door, he stopped,
amused. Innkeeper Julia and a dark-haired man were
locked in a passionate kiss. If Hayden were polite, he'd
do the well-bred thing and slip out again. But he was
a writer and therefore fascinated by the innate bonds
that attract male and female, sometimes to their joy
and every bit as often to their detriment.

As the pair broke apart, rather reluctantly if he was
any judge, the man noticed him and said, "Caught
again."

Julia made a soft noise, flushing slightly, as she
turned and offered a sheepish but glowing smile.

"Hayden Winters, this is my fiancé, Eli Donovan,
who apparently returned to the carriage house late last
night without warning me." Her June-blue eyes flashed
adoration at her fiancé. "Eli, Hayden is a newly arrived guest."

Eli extended a hand, though he seemed to regret releasing his hold on Julia. Who could blame him? Love
was a beautiful thing. For other people.

"A pleasure, Hayden. I read your books."

"Thank you. I apologize for interrupting." Not that he meant it. "Mind if I snitch another cup of coffee?"

"She makes the best." Eli took Hayden's cup and refilled it. "How was your room?"

"I'm not sure."

Julia, who now peered into the oven, looked up with a frown. "Was something wrong?"

"Not at all." He told her about Brody but skipped the dream.

"For heaven's sake." She gazed up at the ceiling as if she could see the boy wrapped in sleep and the plush bedding of the Mulberry Room. "That poor child."

"I hope you don't mind." Being a good guest often reaped benefits. "You can charge me extra if you'd like."

"For what? Being nice enough to rescue a little boy from the storm? For giving up your own night's rest?"

"I slept a little," he said, and the dream pushed in. He pushed back.

"Speaking of kids," Eli said to Julia. "How's my son?"

"Good as gold and sweet as pie. He missed his daddy, though."

"I'll run up and see if he's awake." Eli grabbed her for another kiss that left him grinning and her flustered. "Save me some bacon."

Hayden took his coffee out on the long wraparound veranda, propped up his feet and watched morning slide across the emerald-green magnolias. The large shady yard was littered with leaves dispatched by last night's wind, the grass glistened, still wet, and the flowers along the porch front drooped, too battered by the storm to lift their colorful heads. But the rain-washed air smelled glorious-fresh and moist and clean like the Appalachian woods in spring.

He found it interesting, if a bit pathetic, that even after all the years away, after all the fabrications, the success and money, he missed the green hills and deep, secret hollows, the crystal creeks and thick woods of Appalachia. Coming to Tennessee reminded him starkly of the home from which he'd escaped at sixteen. He could almost smell the Smoky Mountains to the east, like his Kentucky Mountains, a part of the long Appalachian chain that had once split east from west. With a kind of nauseating nostalgia, he'd driven the rental car around the curves of roads populated only by horse pastures or thick woods and shadowy secret trails the country boy still hiding in him longed to explore.

At his back, an old-fashioned wooden door opened and the blue Australian shepherd he'd seen yesterday trotted out for his morning business, black nose to the sparkling wet grass. Carrie appeared, carrying her own cup of coffee. Hayden whiffed the spike of vanilla flavoring she'd added, along with Carrie's own scent, fresh and clean with a spicy edge of mystery.

"Good morning." Her voice was throaty, a rough morning sound that sent his mind spinning down inappropriate avenues, to tumbled beds and warm, sleep-drenched interludes.

His head lolled in her direction. Her short hair was slicked back in a headband, her pale skin scrubbed pink and void of makeup. Over a blue print dress, she'd tossed a jean jacket against the morning chill. Simple and charming.

"You didn't sleep long," he said, not minding that she'd interrupted his solitude.

"When the sun rises, so do I. It's a nasty habit left over from college when I'd get up early to cram before class."

He arched an eyebrow. "Late nights?"

"Uh-huh. Slinging macchiatos."

"Ah, yes, the wild midnight barista," he said with a slight smile.

With an answering curve of bowed lips, she leaned against the veranda railing and sipped at her coffee. "Get any writing done?"

The dream rushed in, the people, the train, the watch, disturbing in a way that carried undercurrents he hadn't quite put his finger on. The dream itself had not been terrible, not like the killers who stalked the edges of his thoughts and littered the pages of his books. Those didn't disturb him at all.

"Some."

"Did you kill anyone? Metaphorically speaking."

"Will you be disappointed if I say neither metaphorically nor literally?"

She laughed, and a single dimple flashed at the corner of her mouth. She had a sweet face, made even more innocent by her round puppy-dog eyes and fresh-scrubbed style. She was doubtless younger than him by several years and a lifetime of experiences he wouldn't wish on anyone. A small-town woman protected by and comfortable in the bosom of familiarity.

"Have you checked on Brody yet?" she asked.

"Later. He needs the sleep."

"That's what I thought, too."

"Great minds." He stretched his legs out on the porch, propped his crossed ankles on the railing.

"When he wakes up, I'll drive him home."

"Nice of you," he said, though he would have made the same offer. He was curious about Brody's home life, curious to know why the kid had lied and didn't want to go home. He was also gritty-eyed from lack of sleep and wouldn't mind a few hours' sack time on the pillow top upstairs.

"I'm going that way. Might as well give him a ride." She sipped again, dainty and ladylike, fingers on the handle and the opposite hand beneath the cup. "Thank you for keeping me company last night."

"Storms really scare you that much?" He wanted to probe deep, his usual response to anyone's fears because, quite frankly, he could use the information in a book. Psychology, even one's own, provided powerful motivation.

"The fear is silly, I know, but they do. Always have. I owe you one."

"Count us even." He toasted her. "You knew where to find the coffee and cookies."

He thought of her pretty pink toes and hid his grin with the coffee mug. The lack of sleep and the bizarre dream were giving him weird thoughts.

THE KID DIDN'T want to go home.

Hayden figured that out about two minutes after stepping into the Mulberry Room with Brody's dry clothes.

Still in the baggy sweats, the Huck Finn look-alike stood in front of the bathroom mirror. He'd wet his sandy-colored hair and was doing his best to slick down a frontal cowlick with both hands.

Hayden tossed him a comb. It would wash.

"When you get dressed, come down to the dining room. Julia has breakfast ready." Hayden hung the dried clothes over the towel bar. "After breakfast, Miss Carrie will drive you home."

The kid tensed, the comb flush against his wet hair. He kept his focus on the mirror, but Hayden could see the wheels turning. The kid's body language spoke volumes.

"I'm okay. She doesn't need to do that. I can walk."

"A ride's no problem. She lives in town and is going that way. See you downstairs."

Hayden left before Brody could argue or come up with an excuse, though he didn't know why it mattered. He was here to write a book, not get tangled up with some wayward kid.

The chatter of too many voices met him at the bottom of the crimson-carpeted stairs. He'd expected other guests, but when he walked into the red-walled dining room, one china-laden table was flooded with animated, laughing, gesturing women. Carrie was one of them.

The only males in the room, Eli Donovan and a small black-haired boy who could only be his much-missed son, sat next to a double window overlooking a backyard garden. Their plates were loaded with French toast, fruit and bacon, and the smell was enough to make Hayden's mouth water.

"You're surrounded," Eli said wryly with a tilt of his head toward the female contingency. "Might as well enjoy it." He pushed at an empty chair. "You're welcome to join us."

Hayden did, though he overheard the women's chatter, gleaned bits of gossip, catalogued names. Julia slipped away from the others to bring his breakfast and more coffee.

When Brody appeared in the arched doorway, Hayden almost laughed. The kid looked shell-shocked, either by the abundance of estrogen or the opulence of the breakfast room.

Carrie saw the boy, too, and sent a smile in his direction. "Good morning, Brody. You look better."

Brody offered a shy grin and made his way, silent as a memory, to what Hayden thought of as the guys' table.

"They don't bite," he promised.

With a flourish, Valery placed a glass of orange juice in front of the boy. "In fact, girls can be kind of handy. Do you like bacon?"

"Yes, ma'am."

"French toast?"

This time the boy floundered. He stared at his juice.

"Ever had French toast, Brody?" Hayden asked gently.

The boy shook his head.

"Might as well try it," Valery said. "Julia makes the best."

"It's sort of like pancakes, only better," Hayden said.

This brought Brody's head up. "I love pancakes."

"There you go, then. French toast with plenty of powdered sugar and syrup coming right up." Valery flounced out of the room like a flamenco dancer. The innkeeper was flashy, a head turner, with dark hair curling around her shoulders and bright red lipstick.

Food was served, and Brody ate like a starved pup, speaking only once to say, his mouth stuffed with French toast, "This is good."

The exceptional meal made Hayden sleepy and lethargic. If he ate like this every day for the next few months, he would have to do some serious walking or find a gym.

During the meal, he made polite conversation with Eli and listened to sweet exchanges between the father and son that stirred thoughts of his own father. Donald Briggs had been his light in a dark childhood and when that light went out, Hayden had been lost. If not for an English teacher who had seen his talent, he'd still be lost, likely in the same drug-dulled world that had sucked Dora Lee under.

Eli's son, Alex, finished his meal, hopped down from his chair and hugged his father. "I missed you, Daddy."

Hayden experienced a pinch beneath his breastbone. He missed his daddy, too.

Hayden tossed his napkin on the table. He must need sleep worse than he'd thought.

BRODY WAS STUFFED. He couldn't remember when he'd tasted anything as good Miss Julia's French toast.

With both hands on his full belly, he leaned back in the seat of Carrie Riley's Volkswagen Bug. The inside smelled good, like something strawberry coming from a little tree dangling from the rearview mirror. Miss Riley smelled good, too. He always noticed that about her when she helped him with something at the library. She smelled like cinnamon, he thought. Or maybe gingerbread. The smell was nice, like her. She was always nice to him, and sometimes he imagined his mother had been like her or like Mrs. Timmons, the art teacher, who told him he had talent.

He liked drawing animals, especially wildlife like Max, but the Sweat twins let him draw their parrot, too. Mrs. Timmons said Binky was his best work, and she'd entered the picture in the county art show.

"What grade are you in this year, Brody?" Miss Carrie asked as they pulled out of the driveway onto the pavement leading into Honey Ridge.

"Fifth."

"Who's your teacher?"

"Mrs. Krouper."

"You like her?"

He hiked one shoulder. "She's okay."

"I've heard she's pretty strict."

"Yeah. She sent me to detention for a whole week." He didn't know why he'd told her that. Maybe because his belly was full and he'd slept in that soft bed last night, where he'd dreamed of riding a horse. He'd always wanted to ride a horse.

Miss Riley grinned at him. "Uh-oh. What did you do?"

"Nothing."

When she hiked an eyebrow, he felt compelled to explain. He didn't know why. He just did.

"There's this boy. He's a bully, but no one does anything about it. He was picking on this little kid named Jacob, so I told him to stop and he kicked me. We kind of got in a fight." He hated fighting, but when Jacob cried and looked all helpless, he had to do something.

Like the time he'd found a cat with its head stuck in a soup can.

"Did you tell your dad? Maybe he could have talked to the teacher?"

"He wouldn't." Why'd she have to bring up his dad? Now he was thinking about him again. Would the old man be sober yet? Or would he still be drunk enough to be mad that Brody had been out all night?

Miss Riley cut him a curious look, so he hurriedly said, "My dad works a lot. He's real busy."

"Where does your dad work?"

"Big Wave, on the second shift. I don't know what he does."

"Something to do with boats, I'm sure." And she laughed. She had a pretty laugh with a little hiccup on the end that made his chest tickle.

"Which way?" She pulled the VW Bug to a stop at the red light in the center of Honey Ridge.

"My house is not far. I can walk from here." Brody reached for the door handle.

"Brody," she said gently. "Which way?"

She was so nice, he didn't want to hurt her feelings or look like some kind of ungrateful kid without a lick of manners, so he guided her down the side streets, across the railroad track.

His heart beat hard enough to hurt in his belly. If he was lucky, the old man would still be asleep. He wasn't lucky very often.

"Right there." He pointed. "Where the white car is."

"Looks like your dad is home now."

"Yeah."

Brody hoped Max was okay, still safely tucked in a shoe box under the bed. He should have brought him camping like usual, but the old man had already been drunk when school let out, and he'd been afraid to chance a return to the house.

"Was he really gone somewhere last night, Brody?"

She was hard to lie to. "He might have been."

"I see."

He sure hoped not. He tugged at the door handle and stepped out. No sign of his father. "Thank you, Miss Riley."

"See you at the library."

He slammed the door and hustled across the mowed grass, tension in his neck slowly easing. The old man was probably still sleeping it off. His relief was short-lived when Clint Thomson appeared in the doorway without his shirt, his black eyebrows pulled low in a frown of displeasure at the sight of his son. No big surprise there.

"Where you been?"

Brody heard Miss Riley's car backing out of the driveway and hoped she'd leave quickly.

He searched for a lie that would appease his father but finding none, told the truth. "I went camping."

"Why is someone driving you home?" His dad listed to one side, wobbly. He slapped the door to catch himself, and Brody jumped. "You're not supposed to ride with strangers."

"That's Miss Carrie from the library." Knowing a glance could be mistaken for defiance, he kept his eyes trained on the porch. "She's not a stranger."

His dad cuffed the back of his head. "Don't get smart with me."

Brody snuck a fast glance at the street and saw the blue Volkswagen turn the corner. Relieved, he ducked inside the house before his father could really get going.

CHAPTER SIX

If truth is beauty, how come no one has their hair done in the library?

—Lily Tomlin

THE LIBRARY WAS always busy after the weekend.

The small one-story building in the middle of Honey Ridge was Carrie's domain, her vocation and avocation. She loved the tidy rows, loved reading and sharing books and loved that the library sponsored adult literacy classes. In fact, she loved everything about the library, including her sometimes troublesome patrons.

Herman Peabody, bless his heart, couldn't hear a freight train if it ran over his foot, but he forgot his hearing aids as often as he remembered them. Whenever that happened, his voice never dropped below bullhorn level.

Patrons of the library looked at him with either annoyance or resignation.

Wearing a jaunty tam angled on his semi-bald head and in blue overalls that could use a good scrub, Herman Peabody was one of the afternoon regulars.

"Am I talking too loud again?" he asked.

She leaned close, refusing to insult him by wrinkling her nose at his less-than-pleasant scent. "Did you forget your hearing aids?"

He slapped at his ears. A twinkly smile wrinkled an already-wrinkled cheek. "I guess I did."

Carrie aimed an eye at his overalls. "Maybe in your pocket?"

He squinted and leaned closer. "What?"

She pointed. "Your pocket."

Recognition dawned, and he patted the overall bib, coming up with a small pair of flesh-colored hearing aids. He popped them in, winced, made an adjustment and then said, "All better?"

Carrie smiled. Most people didn't bother to know Mr. Peabody had been a Nashville studio musician back in the day when self-trained artists played by ear and before time took away his ability to do exactly that. Now he had nothing to fall back on and barely eked by on a meager Social Security check. She knew this because she volunteered at Interfaith Partnership, a social charity that collected and distributed food and clothing to the needy.

After Mr. Peabody settled onto one of the couches with a sigh and a groan, grabbing at his left knee, she handed him the Honey Ridge Register. "Do you need some aspirin for that knee?"

"Nah. Just an old man's stiff joints. I must have sat too long with the good ol' boys down at the café."

The café was the coffee klatch of retired men who gathered at the Miniature Golf Café every morning without fail to shoot the breeze and resolve the political and social ills of the universe.

"Did you fellas come up with a solution to world peace?"

"Just about." He nodded, chuckling. "Just about.

Mr. B. says we'll never get out of this world alive, so what difference does it make?"

Carrie laughed. Mr. B., short for Bastarache, a name few of them could pronounce, was the town undertaker. His fatalistic views were legendary.

"Well, that's Mr. B. for you," she said. "You tell me if you need some aspirin for that knee, okay? I have a bottle in my purse."

He patted her hand. "You're a good girl, Miss Carrie. Your mama raised you right."

Carrie's chest squeezed in affectionate sympathy for the man as she returned to the front desk.

"Why doesn't he loiter somewhere else?" Tawny Brown, the other media specialist, ran the scanner gun across the bar code on the back of *The Cat in the Hat*. The computer beeped, and she crammed the book onto a roller cart for reshelving.

Carrie offered a sympathetic glance but said nothing. Tawny got all stirred up about the computer hogs and the regulars who hung out for lack of anything better to do. In Carrie's opinion, everyone needed time in the safe haven of a library.

The thought of a safe haven brought Brody Thomson to mind, which brought Hayden Winters to mind, as well. The boy concerned her, but she didn't know what to do about it. The man—well, he *was* a famous writer and she was a book person.

Beyond his incredible gift of words and the stormy night encounter at Peach Orchard Inn she didn't know anything about him. He was an enigma even to book lovers.

Out of curiosity, she'd read his website bio, which was primarily about his novels and devoid of personal information. Because of his profession and hers, she also followed him, along with other popular authors, on Facebook and Twitter. Again, no personal information on Hayden Winters. Only book talk. A writer of his stature probably had an assistant handling social media anyway.

She'd had coffee, in her pajamas no less, with Hayden Winters.

Laughing at herself a little, she focused on work. The man had probably put her out of his mind the moment she'd driven away.

At noon, her sister Nikki came flying in, a swirl of energy and beauty. All the Riley siblings had dark hair, but Nikki took hers to a whole other dimension. Sleek as a mink and layer-cut in the latest style, Nikki's hair gleamed. Today, the fashionista sister wore eggplant heels as high as the biography stacks. Carrie's back hurt to look at them. No matter how hard she'd tried in high school, she'd never been able to pull off the beauty-queen look.

"What are you doing?" she asked. "Taking me out to lunch or jumping off into the deep to actually read something besides *Fashion and Fad* magazine?"

Nikki ignored the jab.

"Wasn't this weekend at Peach Orchard Inn fun?" Her sister leaned an elbow on the circulation desk.

"Except for the tornado."

Nikki rolled luminous brown eyes. "Don't be a ninny. I slept right through it."

"Two glasses of wine will do that to you."

"Three, but who's counting."

"The hammer in my head was counting." Carrie thanked a patron who dropped a couple of books on the desk and left. "One reason I seldom drink anything stronger than espresso."

Hayden Winters flashed through her head again. Bold. He liked his coffee bold.

Nikki was nodding, her face repentant. "I don't think Julia was particularly pleased that I'd brought wine in the first place. After we poured Valery into her bed, I understood why."

"She did get a little crazy."

"A little? Carrie, she was smashed. Having a glass of wine is one thing, but Valery didn't seem to have a cutoff point."

Carrie bit down on her bottom lip. "You sound as if you think she has a drinking problem."

Nikki's shoulders arched. "I've heard rumors, but you know how people like to talk in Honey Ridge."

Yes, Carrie knew. She'd been the object of those rumors at one time, and the experience had made her cautious. The memory pressed in and caused an ache beneath her rib cage.

"If Valery has a problem, gossip won't help. Nor will friends who come bearing wine. So, to be on the safe side, no more vino at our get-togethers."

"Which means we have to have more."

"Wine or get-togethers?" She beeped the wand across a bar code.

"Get-togethers, silly. Pedicures, weird hairdos and that hilarious Reese Witherspoon movie. Did I ever tell you about the time I saw her in Knoxville? We were in the same boutique, and she bought the exact scarf I had my eye on?"

"About a million times," Carrie said, glad they'd moved away from the rumor mill topic.

She didn't want Nikki rehashing *the incident*, which always brought on a painful slew of sympathetic hugs and the false assurance that nobody remembered anymore. *She* remembered.

"Some things are worth repeating." Her sister hitched a purse Carrie recognized as a Coach only because it said so right on the front. "So are you in for some more fun?"

Carrie's hand stilled on the two books she was now checking in. "Shoot! I let Maggie get out without paying her fine again."

"Are you listening to me?"

"What? Oh, sure. Reese Witherspoon."

Nikki exhaled in a long, beleaguered sigh. "Fun, Carrie. You know, something besides this musty library."

Insulted, Carrie drew back. "My library is *not* musty."

But that was the way things went with her sisters. Carrie's choice in clothes, occupation and lifestyle was stodgy and musty. Theirs was perfection.

Most of the time she even agreed with them but not when they criticized her library.

"Bailey and I think we need a break, all three of us," Nikki was saying. "Chad's on board and Ricky doesn't count."

Ricky was her longtime on-again, off-again boyfriend who pretty much let her do anything she wanted and was always waiting when she returned. That she took advantage of the easygoing man never crossed Nikki's mind.

Carrie beeped a book and added a worn copy of

Laura Ingalls Wilder to the cart. "What are you talking about?"

"Let's plan a winter getaway to somewhere warm and wet. A Christmas gift to ourselves. What do you think of Hawaii?"

"Christmas is still months from now." She beeped another book.

"Plans, darling. Plans." Which in Nikki's world meant planning her wardrobe.

"Hawaii sounds beautiful," Carrie said hesitantly. "But it's a long way from here with water in between."

"That's the whole point. Water, beaches, shirtless men, getting a tan in the dead of winter." Nikki circled a finger in the air. "Water's not a problem. You can swim."

"Not hundreds of miles across the ocean."

"Don't start with that. Flying is safer than riding in a car."

"Crashing isn't."

"We won't crash. I promise. So what do you say?"

"You know how I hate flying." Carrie's pulse got all rickety at the mere mention of stepping on a plane. She'd flown once. *Once.* And thrown up twice, an experience she never wanted to repeat. "Besides, I don't think I can take the time off."

Nikki snorted so loudly, Carrie had to shush her.

"You probably have a hundred years of vacation time coming."

Tawny whisked past, pausing long enough to say, "Go, Carrie. I'll cover."

"Eavesdropper," Carrie groused.

Tawny tilted a shoulder and grinned.

Nikki's lips curved in triumph. "There you go. No

excuses. The three of us will have such fun. You might even meet a hunky Hawaiian who'll teach you to surf."

"Sharks eat people who surf."

Nikki pursed her lips and got serious. "What's the deal, Carrie? You don't want to hang out with your big sisters for a week of fun in the sun?"

Carrie dropped her head back.

"I love the idea of the three of us doing more things together." She touched her sister's hand. "Really, Nik. I just…" Hated the idea of hanging over an ocean for hours in a plane held up only by invisible air. Hated the unknown and unexpected, where men lied and people assumed things that weren't true and left you with a hole in your heart.

She preferred her predictable world of Dewey decimals and alphabetical order.

"I'm saving for a house. A trip to Hawaii is not in my budget."

"Oh." Nikki looked deflated. For once, the whirlwind sister had no argument. "I didn't know you were planning to buy a house."

That's because she'd only this moment decided to start saving. Maybe it *was* time to move forward and stop looking back and dreaming of something that was never going to happen. She was a career woman now. She had a stable, steady income. She certainly wasn't going anywhere else. Not even Hawaii.

To ease the disappointment on her sister's face, she said gently, "You and Bailey go. I'll help Chad with their kids while you're gone."

Nikki pouted pink lips. "The whole sister bond thing. Come on, Carrie. Nearly four years have passed since—"

Carrie pointed a finger, expression stern. "Do not go there, Nikki."

"Then get over it. No one even remembers anymore."

"You do."

Nikki huffed. "I wouldn't if you'd move on and get a life."

"I *am* over it. I have moved on. That's why I'm saving for a house."

Hers wasn't Nikki's or Bailey's idea of a life, but Carrie had learned to be content. She'd accepted the fact, thanks in large part to "the incident," that she was as ordinary and uninteresting as a slice of plain white bread. And she was okay with that. Most of the time.

"Go to Hawaii," she said. "Get a great tan, see a real volcano and a rain forest." All the reasons Carrie would love to visit Hawaii. "You can Skype me from Waikiki Beach with a hunky Hawaiian on your arm and say, 'I told you so.'"

Nikki's eyes squinted in suspicion. "You're a coward, Carrie Leanne. You're scared to death to get out of this town and do something. You're terrified of making the same mistake—"

Carrie quickly interrupted. "Remember when we went to Graceland? That was fun."

"Out of Tennessee, Carrie." Nikki rolled her well-mascaraed eyes. "You're going to spend the rest of your life stuck in this library if you don't branch out a little. Really, Carrie, don't you want to meet people?"

"I meet people every day."

"I meant people as in the single male variety, not the shut-ins and bookworms and computer geeks you meet through the library."

"Hey!"

"Sorry. But did you see those shoes Maggie had on?"

"No, I didn't. And you shouldn't be so shallow as to judge a woman by her shoes." Carrie fought the urge to glance at her own discount store flats. "Don't you have a boutique to run?"

Nikki flipped a nonchalant hand. "Bailey's in the shop today. She can handle the customers."

Carrie's two older sisters co-owned the Sassy Sisters Boutique. Nikki coordinated the fashion end while Bailey managed the business details and kept spendthrift Nikki firmly in check. Theirs was the perfect partnership and one they'd tried to interest Carrie in, another case of the oddball sister who couldn't quite fit.

The week had barely begun and already she'd had too many reminders of how drab and pathetic she was. Like a sharp knife in the throat, she'd never forget the moment she'd accepted the truth. No one needed to remind her ever again.

Yet she knew they would.

"Then you'll excuse me," Carrie said. "I have work, even if you don't."

"You're overwhelmed with customers." Nikki's index finger bobbed up and down as she counted. "Seven."

Though she loved them, her sisters had the power to drain her.

"Patrons. And computer three needs to move on so the next patron can take over." Happy for an excuse to escape, Carrie went to the computer section and quietly reminded the bearded man that his time was up.

He scowled, thick eyebrows coming together. "I'm not done."

"You're playing a game, sir." *"Zombie Zap," for pity's sake.* "Other patrons are waiting for the computer. So please, log out."

With a growl, the man logged out, shoved back his chair and stalked out of the library. If he'd been a real zombie, she'd be toast right now.

Carrie tooled through the library, shelving a book here and there, stopping to point out the biography section to a woman in shorts and flip-flops before returning to the front.

She was sliding a weathered copy of *Wuthering Heights* into its exact spot—823.8—when her sister rounded the end of the stack.

"I thought you left," Carrie said.

"Isn't it cool having a famous novelist staying in Honey Ridge? At Julia's inn, no less."

A little jitter danced in Carrie's stomach. "He's researching a book."

"Really? Then I guess that explains why he just walked in the door."

"Here? In the library?" From her spot behind several rows of books she couldn't see the front, but she craned her head in that direction anyway.

"He's not a rock star, Carrie. I didn't even recognize him."

He was a star in the literary world, though Nikki wouldn't know that.

"Most people wouldn't recognize John Grisham or Nicholas Sparks if they met them on the street, either. Authors' names and books, yes, but their faces? Not so much."

"I guess that's true."

"Have you ever read one of his novels?"

Nikki looked shocked at the very idea. "All that violence? Not on your life. Valery had to tell me who he was. She thinks he's hot."

"Valery thinks anyone with testosterone is hot." So what if Carrie had thought the same thing the other night in Julia's kitchen. She had an excuse. The storm had rattled her nerves and he'd been kind, not only to her but to Brody. He'd given up his bed and his rest for the pitiful little boy. In Carrie's book, a man who showed kindness was hot with a capital *H*.

Nikki, still standing at the end of the stack, gaped toward the entrance. "Oh, my goodness."

"What?"

"Ferragamo!"

"Who?"

Nikki tossed her head and made a disgusted noise. "I swear, sometimes I wonder if we share any DNA at all. The man is wearing Ferragamo loafers."

"What man?"

"Hayden Winters! The man we're discussing." Nikki let out a long sigh. "Ferragamo. Such fabulous taste. His hotness rating has officially sailed off the meter."

"He's more than a pair of shoes, Nikki. He's a nice, ordinary guy who likes strong coffee and Oreo cookies and isn't afraid of storms."

Nikki eyed her sister with speculation. A perfectly groomed pair of black eyebrows rose in a higher arch.

Carrie could never get her eyebrows to look that good.

"I thought you were busy rescuing the drenched boy."

"Before that. The storm scared me. Don't roll your eyes. I can't help it. I came downstairs to watch the weather on TV."

"And your hottie writer pal was already there?"

"He was trying to find the coffeepot. I showed him. We made coffee."

"You must have nearly fainted when you learned who he is. I mean, you being a bookworm and all. Valery's right. He's not hard to look at, even if he's older by a few years."

Late thirties. Maybe even forty. When a guy looked that good, age didn't matter.

"It was *storming*, Nikki," Carrie said in exasperation. "You know how I feel about storms. I would have hung out with anyone wearing skin. I didn't care if the guy was a writer or a skid-row bum."

She might be stretching the truth a little, but she *had* been deeply relieved at finding a living, breathing, unterrified human in the kitchen. The fact that he was Hayden Winters was icing on the cake.

"Are you ever going to stop being a ninny about a little thunder and lightning?"

"One can only hope." But how could she, when she lived with memories of that one particular stormy day, of the helpless dread and shattering humiliation that came with every thunderclap? All her life, she'd known something terrible would eventually happen during a storm. She'd been right.

Her sister glanced at her cell phone. "Aren't you going up there? See what he wants?"

"Tawny's got the front desk. She can assist him."

Nikki made a hissing noise and shook her head in

dismay. "You are the most hopeless female in Honey Ridge."

Carrie laughed. "Bye, Nikki. See you."

Her sister rolled her eyes for the tenth time, tossed her sleek hair and departed, eggplant stilettos tip-tapping on the indoor-outdoor carpet.

As Nikki disappeared from sight, Tawny whipped around the end of the stacks. "Someone wants to see you at the desk."

Carrie suffered a little swell of energy, quickly tamped down.

He might be Hayden Winters, the most celebrated name in killer thrillers, but to Carrie, he was the guy who liked bold coffee and books and kept the tornadoes away. A pleasant and passing acquaintance.

Keep telling yourself that, and maybe you'll believe it.

"Be right there."

CHAPTER SEVEN

Libraries raised me.

—Ray Bradbury

HAYDEN SCANNED THE LIBRARY, taking in the small computer bay, the cozy sections of brown vinyl couches and chairs, the study tables, and the rows and rows of books tidily divided into sections. Along the east wall, a rack of current magazines overlooked round tables littered with various newspapers.

With each breath, he drew in the redemptive smell of books. Places like this had saved his life.

At the circulation desk Hayden asked for Carrie. A tiny blonde librarian, after giving him a puzzled stare as if she couldn't quite place him but knew she should, took off toward the rows of books. Apparently, Carrie hadn't mentioned his presence at Peach Orchard Inn, and he couldn't decide if he was grateful or wounded.

He liked his midnight barista. Had been intrigued by her. Had found an excuse to see her again.

While he waited, Hayden perused the new releases shelf, flipping through Mary Higgins Clark's latest as he kept half an eye out for Carrie.

When she came into view, a quick kick deep in his gut caught him off guard. His glance drifted to her ankle, noting the bracelet she'd worn a few nights ago was there again above simple black flats. Even in his sleeplessness, he hadn't imagined Carrie Riley's fresh appeal. Dressed in black skinny slacks and a white button-down, she'd tucked her short dark hair behind pearl-studded ears.

She was like the library, neat and orderly.

"You looking for a cup of coffee?" Her mouth curved.

"Might be. You have a few minutes?"

"Not for coffee. Sorry."

So was he.

"Another time, then." He slid a hand into the pocket of his chinos. "I wondered about Brody. Did you get him home all right?"

A crease appeared between Carrie's eyes. She motioned toward a round table nearby, and they sat down across from each other.

Hayden had an uncomfortable feeling about the kid, and he was seldom wrong in his character analyses. Whether fictional or real, he discerned people. Right now, he discerned trouble for Brody Thomson and concern in Carrie Riley.

Posture erect, the tidy librarian clasped her hands together on top of the table. Her fingernails were unpolished, unlike the pearl-pink toes from Friday night. She wore no jewelry on her slim fingers, either. Another point of interest he filed away.

"Brody acted very uncomfortable about me driving him home," she said in her soft-as-rainwater voice. "He wanted me to drop him off in town. He said he'd rather walk."

"You let him?"

"No. I insisted on driving him all the way to his

house." She shrugged, dark eyes widening. "I had a funny feeling."

"As did I. Any sign of his father?"

"He came to the door. Brody was anxious for me to leave."

An oily feeling curled in his belly. "That doesn't sound good."

"This may seem silly—" she glanced up at him and then back down, absently picking at the curled corner of the *Knoxville News Sentinel* "—but as I drove away, I tried to keep watch in my mirrors without being too obvious."

"Not silly at all. See anything?"

"When I turned the corner, I thought I saw his father slap the side of his head." She exhaled a little breath of frustration. "I'm not sure, though, and it might have been a friendly thing like dads do sometimes."

"You mean like a welcome home, a love pat?"

"Exactly. My dad used to put my brother, Trey, in a headlock and they'd wrestle around. Guy stuff. That's probably what I saw." She nibbled her bottom lip.

"But you don't think so?"

"Something's not right, or Brody would have let us call his father that night. His dad was not out of town."

"The kid lied." He wasn't surprised. No drowned rat of a boy refused to go home to dry clothes and a warm bed without good reason.

"I think so. I asked him directly and he sidestepped the question with a vague reply that was all but an admission."

Hayden inhaled deeply and sat back in the chair.

Home was hell for some kids. A few were lucky enough to escape. He'd lied about a lot of things, too, usually to his mother but often to others. Lies he passed off as excuses. His mama was out of town. She was sick. He'd forgotten to ask her.

He swallowed back the intruding thoughts. They were discussing Brody, not him.

"I talked to Trey," Carrie said. "He couldn't recall any problems from that address, not since he's been on the force."

"Did he know anything about the kid's father?"

"Basically common knowledge stuff and what Brody told me. Clint Thomson is employed at the Big Wave boat factory. He hangs out at Brannon's bar on Second Street. No record of arrest except for a DUI a few years ago."

"An alcoholic?"

"Or maybe a man who has a few beers after work and got caught once."

"What about Brody's mother?"

"She left before Trey came back to Honey Ridge, but I asked my mother. Brody's mom, Penny, was the quiet type who didn't socialize much. She didn't even attend church, which is a social no-no in Honey Ridge. Mama didn't recall anything about their divorce."

"No close friends or job or anything?"

"I didn't ask, but apparently not, because Mama, who basically knows everyone and his dog in Honey Ridge, was barely acquainted. Apparently, the breakup was one of those private things that happen. She was unhappy in her marriage and left."

"But she left her son, too."

"Sad, isn't it? Maybe she thought Brody, being a boy, would be better off with his father. I've known couples who did that. Mama took custody of the girl. Daddy took the boy."

"But wouldn't she care if the old man is knocking him around? I wonder if he hears from her. If she knows things are rocky?"

"I think your writer's brain is kicking into gear."

"Meaning?"

"We don't know if Brody is being mistreated, Hayden. Maybe he and his dad had a disagreement that night. Maybe he got in trouble at school and didn't want to face the music at home. Kids do that."

Hayden rubbed the back of his neck. "I guess that's possible."

His fertile mind *did* overreact at times and suspect trouble where none existed. That was how he got his story ideas. Experience had taught him that beneath every smile was a heartache. Behind every cloud was a tornado. Not that he'd mention a tornado to Carrie.

"When Trey was about that age, he got in trouble with Dad for something. I don't remember what he'd done, but he ran away and hid in Grandpa's barn all day." She spread her hands. "And I can promise you, the Riley kids were not abused."

All of what she said was true, but Hayden's instincts, honed for survival, rarely let him down. "If he doesn't complain and no one sees anything illegal going on, his dad could get away with hurting him."

"He goes to school. His teachers would notice."

Hayden didn't smirk. He didn't even react. Once in a great while a teacher noticed, but mostly not. Hayden knew better than anyone. Teachers were only human, and if a kid kept his mouth shut and wasn't a class disturbance, no one noticed; no one asked the uncomfortable questions.

That was the problem with home situations. A stranger, even an interested one, couldn't see what was happening behind closed doors. "Perhaps you're right and it's nothing serious."

For all her reasoning to the contrary, the small frown between Carrie's eyebrows said she still worried.

"Does he come into the library much?"

"Almost every day after school."

Hayden glanced at his watch. "Which can't be too long from now."

"What if he does? How is that helpful?"

A muscle jerked below his eye. He reached up and rubbed as if he had an itch. A tic. A twitch. A mental hiccup in a man with crazy in his genetic code. "If something is happening to him at home, he's safe here."

Knowing the kid had a refuge, even for little while, brought Hayden a measure of peace.

"Tawny and I set up a cookie tray in the foyer for after school." Carrie gestured toward the front of the library. "I think that may be his dinner."

"Another reason to be concerned."

"Maybe. But maybe I'm wrong. All of the kids, especially the older boys, gobble the cookies like hungry wolves."

"Gut feelings count." Especially his gut. She wouldn't understand, and he certainly couldn't explain.

"I care about kids, Hayden. If his home situation is bad—" she bowed her shoulders "—well, I want to be alert to any signs. He's a nice little boy. Puts the books and magazines neatly back where they belong or brings them to the reshelf cart. Doesn't turn down the page corners."

"Librarians get testy about those page corners." His lips quivered.

She arched an eyebrow at him. "Defacing a perfectly wonderful book is a serious thing, especially when we have bookmarks at the desk. Free!"

Letting the grin slip through, he lifted both hands from the tabletop. "Won't get an argument from me."

Mr. Franks had taught him that people who respect themselves respect public property, too. This was after Hayden had carved his name on a bathroom stall. He'd never forgotten that lesson or how the event had begun the change that saved his life.

Carrie silently slid her chair back from the table and started to stand.

"If you need any help with your research, let me know."

"Can you point me to archives of the town's history?"

"Sure, but you can learn more, especially the colorful, gossipy stuff, from the good ol' boys down at the Miniature Golf Café. You are guaranteed to get an earful any day of the week."

"Would you be willing to come along and introduce me? I'll buy your breakfast."

Carrie tucked an invisible strand of hair behind her ear. "The good ol' boys have no trouble talking, but I understand what you're saying. Someone to break the ice, so to speak."

"Exactly. Tomorrow morning at eight?"

"I can't tomorrow. We have an early staff meeting."

"You pick the day."

"I don't work until ten on Thursdays."

"Thursday it is. I'll swing by and pick you up at eight."

"I can meet you at the cafe."

"You're safe with me." He grinned. "I only kill people in my books."

She tilted her head, mouth pursed, amused. "You think I'm afraid to be alone with a man who devises ways to commit murder?"

"Are you?"

"You saved me from the tornado. That's nearing hero status in my book."

He laughed, flirting, enjoying her. "I'll need your address."

"I'll write it down before you leave. Anything else I can help you with?"

Reluctant to lose her company, though not needing anything in particular, Hayden said the first thing that popped into his head.

"Tell me about the dark side of Honey Ridge. Every place has dirty little secrets. Unexplained deaths. Suicide pacts. Murders."

"In my library?" She drew up straight, pretending insult though her brown eyes sparkled with humor.

"Perfect place to find an unsuspecting victim," he said. "Her attention is riveted on a book. The villain sneaks up behind her and—" In pure melodrama, he slid a finger across his throat. *"Murder in the Stacks."*

She grimaced. "How about *Death by Dewey Decimal*?"

"Hey, that's not bad." His mind started racing with the possibilities. "A serial killer. I'm good at those."

"Don't you dare! There are plenty of places in

Honey Ridge to commit homicide." She gave an overly dramatic shudder. "Please no murder in my library."

A passing patron shot a strange glance in their direction. Carrie backpedaled. "Don't worry, Mrs. Mayes. We're talking about books."

Mrs. Mayes waved both hands. "No need to explain. Nothing like a good suspense."

Carrie shot a wry glance at Hayden. "We have the latest Hayden Winters novel, *The Last Blackbird*, two stacks over."

"Oh, I haven't read that one yet. Thank you, Carrie."

The woman disappeared behind a wall of books, and Carrie followed her with her gaze.

"He's here," she said quietly.

Hayden swiveled his body in that direction. The Huck Finn look-alike stood in the entry, wolfing down cookies, a camo backpack over his shoulders.

Brody had lost the battle with the cowlick. The sprout of hair waved like a blond feather.

Hayden watched the boy with his usual curiosity, memorizing the little details. After a few cookies, four of which went into his backpack, Brody came into the library and looked around. When his gaze met Hayden's, his expression flickered.

Hayden lifted a hand and motioned at him. To Carrie, he said, "A conversation won't hurt anything. Maybe I can learn something to allay our concerns."

"Sounds good. Want me to go or stay?"

"Suit yourself."

"I'll check the desk and be back in a few minutes." With her easy, quiet manner, she strode toward Brody. As she passed, she smoothed his hair, said something to him and pointed toward Hayden.

Brody blinked a couple of times and glanced behind him before hitching the backpack higher and approaching Hayden's table.

"Miss Carrie said you wanted to talk to me?"

"I'm Hayden. Remember from the other night?"

"Sure." Pale, cautious eyes questioned why Hayden wanted to speak to him. "At Peach Orchard Inn."

"That's right. During the big storm."

"Yeah. It was a good one."

A kindred spirit, perhaps, in more ways than one? "You like thunderstorms?"

Brody hiked a shoulder. The dirty camo backpack rustled against a faded black Honey Ridge Raptors T-shirt. "They're okay. Do you?"

"Love them. They're wildly exciting."

"Especially when you're asleep in the woods." A tiny smile crooked the corners of Brody's mouth, drawing attention to his cleft chin. Pale eyes twinkled above a splatter of tan freckles. "Camping, I mean."

"I've done that a few times, but I don't think I've ever been caught in a storm that powerful. Did you get home okay?"

Brody's chipper countenance changed. His gaze dropped to the table. "Fine. Miss Carrie dropped me off. Thanks for letting me stay in your room." He glanced up again. "Did you write your book?"

"Not yet." The strangely realistic dream pressed in, messing with his head. "I'm still thinking about it. Want to sit down?"

"I gotta do my homework." Brody made a face. "English is hard."

"I feel your pain." Hayden kicked the chair back. "Go ahead. Sit. I might know a thing or two."

Brody slouched out of his backpack and took the offered chair. "Did you hate English?"

Loved it, which infuriated his mother. He, she claimed, was sneering at her with his fancy vocabulary and fat books. All he'd wanted to do was learn… and to escape. Books offered both.

"Math," he said.

"Math is not so bad. It's just numbers."

"Do you like to read?"

"Reading's okay, I guess. Not the stuff they want us to read in school, but Miss Carrie helps me find cool books." He reached into his backpack and dragged out an English literature text. A golden cheetah sleeked across the cover with verbs falling from his tongue.

Hayden placed a hand on top of the book. "Could we talk a minute before we start on homework?"

Uncertainty flitted across Brody's face. He fidgeted. "What about?"

I want to know if your old man is knocking you around. I want to know if your mother calls or visits.

Instead, Hayden kept the conversation neutral. "You know your way around Honey Ridge pretty well—don't you?"

"Lived here all my life." Brody sounded as if he was ancient instead of eleven.

"I'm new to Honey Ridge, so maybe you could tell me about your town."

Brody looked bewildered. "Like what?"

Hayden had the fleeting notion that he was about to jump off into uncharted territory. He didn't get involved, certainly not with kids that reminded him too much of himself. He donated to causes, to literacy, to poverty programs, but he never got involved. Not personally and never more than necessary. He observed, he pried into other people's business to get what he needed for his books and felt no guilt for refusing to allow them to pry in return. Then he quietly disappeared to write his stories.

Involvement was temporary and surface only. Involvement danced too close to the fire of revelation.

He studied the boy and had a painful flashback of being ten years old and feeling completely alone in the world.

Dora Lee had gone somewhere with her latest boyfriend, which was always a relief to Hayden. Boyfriends tended to dislike Dora Lee's bookish brat.

The trailer had no heat, no food, and he'd slept huddled inside a sour-smelling quilt between the mattress and box springs for warmth. His gnawing belly kept him awake.

He'd never told a living soul of those cold, hungry days alone. It had been Christmas.

He suppressed the urge to ask the hard questions, knowing Brody would lie the same as Hayden would have. Protect the guilty because they were all you had.

One person, one calm oasis in a world of chaos, could change everything.

Brody needed an oasis.

But Hayden was no one's savior. He didn't have the hero gene. His time in Honey Ridge was limited. Brody's situation, if there was one, was like a knife pressed too close to the bone.

Do the right thing, Hayden.

What if Mr. Franks had been a coward? Where would Hayden be today?

With an inward sigh and confident he'd live to regret the decision, he said, "I have a proposition for you."

"What's a proposition?"

"A deal. I need a guide to show me around town sometimes. Got any ideas for me?" Not that he actually needed a guide any more than he needed to get involved with a boy from a troubled home. *Potentially* troubled, as Carrie had reminded him.

Hayden felt compelled to find out one way or the other. He didn't need a shrink to know the reasons.

The boy tilted his head and squinched his face. Nose freckles consolidated into a patch of tan across his cheekbones. "The Sweat twins know everything, but they're really old. They might not have the energy."

Carrie reappeared. She didn't say a word, but Hayden felt the quiet freshness of her presence. Brody looked up. "Hi, Miss Carrie."

She smoothed a hand down the back of the boy's head. Hayden felt her touch all the way to his toes. Pathetic that he should still long for what he'd never had. He, a man with everything he'd ever wanted. Except that.

Steeling himself against the bizarre thoughts, he turned his attention back to the boy. "I was thinking about you."

There. He'd done it. Jumped into the deep, aware that he was projecting his own sorry past and angry parent onto Brody.

Being wrong was acceptable. Being right and doing nothing wasn't.

Brody lit up. Sitting up straighter, he tapped a hand against his chest, expression equal parts incredulous and excited. "Me?"

"Why not? You can do the job, can't you?"

"Sure. I guess. I'm not doing anything anyway. And I know everybody in town. Mostly."

"Great. We have a deal, then. After school on the days you're not too busy with homework and while your dad is working, I'll pick you up at your place and you can show me around."

Brody's mood darkened. "My dad might not like it."

"I'll talk to him first and explain that you'd be doing me a favor and getting paid at the same time. How about that?"

Brody shook his head. "I come to the library every day after school anyway. We can meet up here. My dad won't have to know."

That worked for Hayden. Sometimes keeping your mouth shut was the safest way.

Carrie's soft voice intruded. "Not a good idea, Brody. Your dad would worry if he doesn't know what you're doing or who you're with."

"Nah, he don't care about that. He just gets mad if I bother him about stupid stuff that don't matter to him." Then, as if he'd said too much, Brody slunk down in his chair and went silent, arms crossed tightly over the raptor logo.

Hayden huffed a frustrated breath. This was between him and Brody. Carrie should stay out of it.

He shot her a warning look and then said to Brody, "Is your dad working tonight?"

"Yeah."

"What are you doing for dinner?"

"I don't know." The words were mumbled.

"Can you recommend a good burger place?"

Brody's head came up. "Plenty of them around here."

"I'm starved. Let's grab a burger and talk this over. We'll figure out something."

The boy looked to Carrie. Her lips had thinned as if she was annoyed with Hayden for pushing. But pushing was how he'd gotten to where he was. No risk, no reward.

Soften a kid up with food and they'd tell you things. He knew about that, too.

"I guess I can do my homework later." Brody jammed the English book back into the bag.

"You should do your homework first, Brody." Carrie glared at Hayden with those soft eyes now glittering with annoyance.

Hayden held up both hands in surrender. "I guess you're stuck, Brody. We don't want to make Miss Carrie mad. I don't know about you, but I'm going to need this library over the next couple of months."

"Yeah. Me, too. Miss Carrie's usually real nice."

Teeth bared, Carrie flared her fingers like claws. "They don't call me the dragon lady for nothing."

Hayden offered his most charming smile, wanting back on her good side. "The dragon lady wins. Homework first, Brody, my man. We'll hang around until closing time and feed Miss Carrie a burger, too. Maybe some ice cream. Sweeten her up."

"The library doesn't close until five," she said.

"Which gives my pal and me time to wrestle out the English assignment. Then we can drive around Honey Ridge, and you can show me the sights."

Carrie shook her head. The light caught the pearly luminescence of her earrings. "We already have breakfast on Thursday."

"You only eat once a week?"

She huffed, amused. "I have books to drop off after closing. Shut-ins that live up on the ridge."

"Mind if I tag along?"

She blinked, puzzled. "Why would you want to?"

Because you intrigue me. All buttoned up, neat and tidy, and fresh as a flower. When his curiosity was roused, he never backed off until it was satisfied.

If he was truthful, he felt a connection with Carrie, whether because of Brody or their obvious shared love of books or something else. He wanted to know her better.

"Research," he lied, smooth as warm butter. "I need to get the lay of the countryside anyway."

"Oh, right." Her eyes twinkled. "A place to commit murder."

His smile was intentionally diabolical. "Exactly."

"In that case, you're staying across the road from the creepiest place in Honey Ridge. You should check that out first."

"Yeah," Brody piped up. "The old gristmill. People say it's haunted."

"Haunted, is it?"

The South was full of supposedly haunted places. Hayden had never given the stories credence. But then the dream flashed in his head, the dream about a Yankee miller and the Portland Grist Mill.

CHAPTER EIGHT

Victory is an illusion of philosophers and fools.
> —William Faulkner

1867

IF THE WATCH was an omen, Thaddeus faced a dismal future.

Late in the evening on the first hot, sticky day of walking, he'd reached inside his vest to check the time only to come away empty. A search of his carpetbag proved every bit as futile. His silver pocket watch was gone.

Distraught to lose this final link to Amelia and the past he never wanted to leave behind, Thad considered turning back to retrace his journey.

Sweat trickled between his shoulder blades as he contemplated a long, hungry walk that would likely turn up nothing. He didn't even know where to look. The last he'd seen the timepiece was on the train before disembarking. A train bound for Chattanooga and beyond.

For an hour, he sat under an oak by the side of the dusty trail, head in his hands, and mourned. More than the loss of his timepiece, Thad mourned what the watch represented. Amelia. Their love. Their life together.

Gone. Everything that mattered gone.

He'd given up the familiar and his future in Ohio to come to this hostile state. Losing the pocket watch felt as if he was giving up the last vestige of who he'd been, of who he was. It felt like letting go of Amelia and Grace all over again.

He considered making camp for the night, but night was still hours away, so he finally roused himself and, weary now in a way he hadn't been, trudged onward.

Without the watch, he kept time by the morning and evening of each day as God had done in Genesis, though he quaked to compare himself to the God who gave and took away.

Each night he lay his head beneath the oaks and willows, listened to their whispers, thankful he traveled in summer, though mosquitoes and chiggers feasted on his flesh until he had no place left that wasn't covered in itchy bumps. Last night, he'd stolen an ear of corn from a farm and gnawed the raw kernels after river fishing proved unsuccessful. He'd found blackberries growing along the river's edge, but too many berries pained a man and he'd learned to be careful.

At the third daybreak, after a night on ground soppy with southern dew, he ate a handful of those same berries, then dipped in the river, the cold water soothing his insulted, itchy skin. Then he hiked up and over a long, wooded ridge, confident that a township wasn't far away. Yesterday, the number of farms had increased, and he'd stopped to ask directions. The cautious-eyed occupants had mercifully obliged, though not one single Southern soul had offered the Northern wayfarer a meal or shelter.

Now with the sun blistering his neck and his belly

snarling around the berries, he entered the edge of a town that according to William's map must be Honey Ridge, Tennessee.

Outside a tidy cottage a pair of chickens pecked. Thaddeus fought the urge to wring a neck in the name of survival as he had done during the war even though *thou shalt not steal* was as ingrained in him as his belief that all men were created equal. The cottage owner, no doubt, needed the birds every bit as much, and they were not his to take. Not since the war ended. He and the Union might be the victors, but the vanquished foes would soon be his neighbors and his employers. He'd best not steal their chickens.

As he hurried on, a young widow, evidenced by her black-dyed dress and veil, tossed a dishpan of water out her front door, barely missing him. She looked up and smiled an apology, her face tired already this morning. He touched the brim of his hat, aching a little as he suspected she was a war widow and wondering if he or Will or someone he knew had taken the life of her man.

A wagon rumbled past, drawn by a single mule. Horses were in short supply, seized by the armies and never replaced. Like towns and cities everywhere across the war-torn regions, Honey Ridge had seen better days. Only a handful of businesses had survived the lean times, others were boarded up, and the charred remains of a large building scarred the town square.

A melancholy hung over the South as thick and oppressive as humidity.

Beneath the shady porch of the mercantile, an aproned man swept the boardwalk. Hoisting his bag, Thaddeus approached.

"Good morning, sir."

The merchant stopped sweeping to stare at him, his squinted gaze taking in Thad's unshaven face, rumpled clothes and carpetbag.

"Morning."

"Is this Honey Ridge?"

"What's left of her." The man, eyes cautious beneath a wrinkled brow, his brown beard salted with gray, leaned his broom against the wall. "Looks like you've been traveling."

"Yes, sir." Thad rested a boot on the edge of the boardwalk. "Name's Thaddeus Eriksson. I've come to work at the Portland Grist Mill."

"Jess Merriman. This is my store." He jerked a thumb toward the dark entryway behind him. "Gadsden mentioned a cousin millwright."

"That would be me."

"From up North?"

Thad tensed. "Yes, sir. Ohio."

"Well, son, you're either brave or a fool. The war's not over to some, but you'll find welcome at my store. The wife has kin in Pennsylvania."

Tension seeped out. Thad's shoulders relaxed. "I'm obliged."

On the opposite side of the road, a woman exited a milliner's shop, a basket in hand, and started across in a jaunty, purposeful stride, her head held high, hair as bright as a copper penny gleaming in the sunlight.

He watched her, mesmerized by her energy and hair. She was color to the town's tired drab, a slender redbird on a bland canvas of dust and unpainted buildings. Even the dull gray of her dress couldn't hide her vibrancy. Her skin was pale peaches and cream, and her bright hair, though tucked up on the sides, sprang loose in headstrong ringlets along her cheeks and neck.

She was, in short, a stunning beauty.

At that moment, a wagon, going much too rapidly, sped down the dirt thoroughfare. The woman, halfway across, looked up in alarm, too late to get out of the way.

The mules kicked up a dust devil, and the woman cried out. The wagon barreled on past, the driver yelling at the out-of-control mules. Thad dropped his carpetbag and rushed to the woman's side. She was on the ground, struggling to sit upright.

Thaddeus went to his knees beside her. "Ma'am, are you injured?"

Her chest rose and fell in breathy gasps. Her peach cheeks had turned as red as summer roses. She shook her head. Her bonnet was askew, her ribbons untied.

"I don't think so. I am, however," she said with a jut of her chin, "quite furious."

A smile tugged at Thad's lips. There was fire beneath that red hair.

"Allow me to assist you." Without waiting for her reply, he slid both hands around a very narrow waist and easily lifted her to her feet.

She landed with her hands gripping both his arms to steady herself, and he couldn't help noticing how utterly feminine and fragile she seemed to his superior height. Closer now, her beauty struck him like a blow. He'd not noticed a woman other than Amelia since he was eighteen. Noticing this one disturbed him. He loosened his hold and stepped back. Her hands still rested on his arms, too close, close enough that her rose scent tickled his nose and sent a hot spiral of memory through his body.

"Thank you, sir," she said, in a drawl as thick and sweet as honey. "You are too kind."

"Glad to be of service. Looks like the wagon had a runaway."

"Sterling Bridges couldn't drive a wagon if his life depended on it, and the silly man doesn't have the decency of a field rat. He should be flogged. But you, sir, are clearly a gentleman." She pouted prettily, and Thad had the uncomfortable feeling that she was flirting.

"Your bonnet," he said, with a pointed glance. The garment skewed toward her left ear, dislodging handfuls of copper hair. Thad battled an overwhelming and altogether undesirable urge to smooth the mesmerizing curls.

To his relief, she released her hold on his arms to straighten her bonnet.

"Oh, dear," she murmured as she bent to dust her skirt. "Would you look at that?"

The basket she had carried now lay crumpled in the dirt, at least a half-dozen eggs broken and seeping yellow.

"A shame," he said, though he was tempted to scoop up the raw yolks, dirt and all, and gulp them down. "Let's see if we can salvage any."

They crouched together and gingerly picked through the sticky mess. Thad removed his handkerchief. "Use this to wipe off the unbroken ones."

"Oh, I couldn't." But she did, and another smile tugged at his mouth.

When at last they'd salvaged thirteen eggs, she said,

"You've saved my morning, sir, and I don't even know your name."

"Thaddeus Eriksson, ma'am." He handed her the damaged basket. "Just arrived in town. I've come to work with my cousin Will at the Portland Grist Mill. Perhaps you could direct me there."

Her hand flew to her lips. She shrank back. "No!"

Puzzled at her violent reaction, he offered his best smile. "Yes, ma'am. My apologies for the way I must look. I'm a mite rusty around the edges from the long trip but eager to see my cousin again and be of service."

As if the air had suddenly taken on a nasty smell, she tossed her nose up high. Thad resisted the urge to sniff his armpits.

"No one around here needs your services, Mr. Eriksson. Go back to Ohio." Giving an insulted toss of her head, she stalked to a wagon parked in front of the milliner.

Thad stood in the middle of the main street with his mouth open and a furrowed brow. Had he mentioned Ohio to her? Had William changed his mind? Was Thad's skill no longer needed at the mill? Who *was* she?

When the fiery woman slapped the reins and drove away, wagon rumbling like a distant storm, Thad heard laughter. Turning toward the sound, he saw the apron-clad merchant leaning on his broom, his salt-and-pepper mustache curled above a wide grin.

"Ran into a wildcat, didn't you, son?"

Embarrassed, Thad dusted his cap against his britches. "What did I do?"

"'Sakes, man, you ought to know by now. It's not

what you did. It's who you are. Nothing that woman hates more than a Yankee."

Thad stifled a sigh. "Who is she?"

"That furious little firebrand is Miss Josephine Portland."

"Portland?" Realization dawned and dread seeped into his tired, hungry body.

"Yes, sir." Merriman chuckled again and pointed in the direction of the now distant wagon. "If you're looking for the Portland Mill, just follow her trail of dust."

CHAPTER NINE

THE PORTLAND MILL operation was a handsome endeavor. Nestled in a thick green wood with vines growing up the sides of the white-mortared red brick and with the sound of clean creek water bubbling over the wheel, the mill stirred a passion in Thaddeus that nearly erased the hostile meeting with one Miss Josephine Portland.

The woman engendered any number of feelings in him, most of which he didn't know what to do with. Amusement, annoyance and, though it made him feel disloyal, attraction.

Seeing her again at the farmhouse could prove... interesting. But for now, his focus was his cousin and the gristmill.

With Will grinning at his side and his belly filled with cold corn bread, he roamed through the mill works, pausing to smooth his hands over the fifteen-hundred-pound runner stone, immobile now as the wheel waited for his expertise.

"Who's been running this place?" He turned to the second cousin on his father's side who'd brought him here.

William Gadsden was a fine specimen of man. At two years Thad's senior, he maintained his regal military bearing and air of command. Lean and dark-haired with a wisdom born of sorrows, Will was a man to trust and respect, and the fact that they'd once climbed trees together and prowled on bare feet through Grandfather's marble factory making a nuisance of themselves made him a man to like.

"Charlotte before I came. Now mostly myself."

Thad heard the tenderness and admiration in William's voice. "Charlotte? A woman ran the mill?"

"Wait till you meet her, Thad. She's the strength that kept the farm and gristmill going when others would have faltered. She's beautiful and kind and—"

Thad clapped him on the shoulder. "And you are a happy husband."

"In a way I thought impossible during the campaign years and even for a time thereafter. Though God spared my life from the twin hells of combat and Confederate prison, Charlotte gave me a reason to live again."

Forever and always, I will love you.

Thad turned away, pretending to study the pulley system used to move the grain to the upper floor. The iron needed oiling, parts needed cleaning, repair and replacing. There was much to do here. But it was not the mill that occupied Thad's mind. Though he rejoiced in Will's good fortune, he selfishly despaired in his lack thereof. What plan did the Almighty have for one such as him?

As if he knew he'd touched a tender spot, Will said, "I am truly grateful that you've come, cousin. The burden you carry does not go unnoticed."

"As I am truly happy for you and Charlotte. You seem to have found your anchor."

"I have."

He, on the other hand, flailed in the winds of happenstance like a feather on a stormy sea. His foundation had been yanked from beneath him, and he had no solid rock on which to stand. He, like his cousin before him, sought a reason to live again.

"I never would have picked you for a farmer and a mill operator," he said.

"That, my friend, is where you come in. The farm thrives. On the other hand, the mill limps along like a hobbled mule. I'm convinced we can do better with the right man at the wheel."

"The family thought you'd return to the marble factory. Grandfather's business would have been yours."

A soft smile lit Will's face. "Love is stronger than commerce."

"Stronger than the anger and resentment a Northerner encounters here in the broken South?"

His cousin cocked his head and squinted. "Your journey was not a pleasant one, I take."

"Nor my arrival. I met one of the Portland women in Honey Ridge this morning."

Will's eyebrows rose. "Did you now? Who would that be?"

"A beautiful redhead named Josephine." He unwittingly recalled her rose scent, the fire in her eyes and the heat in her touch that had made him feel alive again, if only for those few seconds.

With a strange expression, part amusement and the other parts dismay and pity, William carefully asked, "How did that go?"

Thad smirked in self-derision. "Not too well. She wasn't happy to make my handsome acquaintance, if you can imagine."

"Josie bears strong opinions about most things… and people."

"So I hear." He relayed the manner of their meeting, ending with Josie's abrupt departure and his walk to the mill in her cloud of dust.

William chuckled but quickly pinched his lip twixt finger and thumb and sobered. "Forgive me. I, more than anyone, understand the icy fire of Josie Portland."

"She's beautiful."

"No man with eyes can deny that, but beauty is deceptive. Josie has a heart, but it is buried deep beneath her resentment and anger."

"Perhaps she needs to come down off her high horse."

Will frowned slightly, studying him. "Tread lightly, cousin. You're a Union man." Then he smiled. "Josephine Portland would happily slit your throat."

Thad realized then that he'd been teetering on the edge, wondering if he should turn around and go back to Ohio, where, at least, he was not the enemy. But the aptly spoken jest, instead of deterring him, was exactly the impetus he needed to stay, if only to prove himself worthy of the challenge.

With a resurrected twig of his former self, Thad experienced the stirring of purpose along with the gossamer thread of something else, something long buried beneath a pile of ashes.

"Yes." His lips curved. "I do believe she would."

JOSIE KNELT ON the pine floor of the sewing room, scissors in hand as she salvaged worn shirts and discarded dresses collected from neighbors and friends, saving the buttons and cutting the still-serviceable pieces of fabric into precise squares for a new quilt top.

She chafed at this morning's wasted trip to Honey Ridge, squarely placing the blame on *him*, the odious Yankee. She'd gone to trade eggs for a bolt of red yard goods to use as quilt binding. Since the surrender, the whole world seemed drab and dark, but color brought cheer and liveliness to the women's faces. Yesterday, Sarah O'Clary had absolutely beamed at the blue bordered shawl made by Josie's hand. The poor woman had worn nothing but black long after the period of mourning had passed simply because she had nothing else. Not even a ribbon.

In her fury at meeting *him*, Josie had not only wasted a trip to town; she'd endured a needless frown of disapproval from Charlotte. Young maiden ladies did not travel unaccompanied into town. A suitable escort was essential, especially since Tennessee was now riddled with an influx of scalawags and strangers and all sorts of unsavory characters. An unmarried woman's virtuous reputation was to be protected at all costs.

Little did her sister-in-law understand that such conventions were long dead, had died with the Confederacy, and Josie refused to be afraid anymore.

Fear had gained her nothing. Indeed, her greatest fear had come to pass.

Tom and dozens of other vital Honey Ridge men— boys she'd danced with and a few she'd kissed beneath the stars—had marched grim faced to a war from which they did not return. She bore the burden of Tom's loss as much as the Yankees bore the responsibility. No Yankee would ever make her afraid again.

"You're starting another quilt?" Patience gathered her skirt and settled beside her. "Have you the time?"

Josie paused to look at her sister, her chest squeezing with love and tenderness. She'd always thought of Patience as the other part of her soul. The good part. If she was a muddy, raging river, Patience was a pure, clear stream.

Though a woman grown, Patience had never quite left behind her childlike sweetness. Add the wide, guileless blue eyes and baby-fine corn-silk hair, and Patience was a misplaced angel who only saw the good in everyone. She was every bit as pious as Charlotte, though far less irritatingly so.

Josie added a green square to her tidy stack and ignored Patience's concern about time. Work was never ending without the slaves anyway. "This is to be a gift for Margaret."

"Tom's mother?"

"She sent every quilt and scrap of extra clothing she owned to Tom during the war, always worried her son was cold or in need. Did you know she covered herself with an old horse blanket, having told not a soul of her deprivation on Tom's behalf?"

"Mrs. Foster is a dear lady. Let me help." Patience took up a faded shirt with ripped elbows.

"I thought Charlotte assigned you to the peach orchard." Josie had trouble keeping the snarl out of her voice.

After Edgar's death and even now, after Charlotte had wed the Yankee captain, the woman organized the household and farm chores like an army general. Everyone had duties that kept them slaving from dawn to dusk. Thankfully, Josie sewed better than either Patience or Charlotte did and spent many hours in that pursuit, though she did her part in the fields and mill whenever necessary.

Everyone did. They had no choice. Thanks to the hateful, thieving Yankees.

Patience began to snip the buttons. "Peaches are picked, Josie. Can't you smell the jam?"

She sniffed the air and caught the scent, though she'd missed the sweet, sticky smell in her fury at *him*. Lizzy and Charlotte would be in the kitchen, and if she was fair, she'd admit that no one worked harder than Charlotte Portland Gadsden. The fact that circumstances forced such labor was the thing that kept Josie at a rolling boil much of the time.

If not for the hideous war and the greedy Northerners who were bent on destroying her Southern lifestyle, she and Patience could focus on parties and beaus and pretty clothes.

Now the Yankee interlopers bought up farms and businesses for a few dollars, grabbing what didn't belong to them, showing their true colors, so that gentle Southern women were reduced to hoeing corn and wearing rags.

Let them brag of emancipation and equality. She knew the truth hiding in their black hearts. The North had always been jealous of the South.

They were here, stealing, taking over. Like Will and his cousin.

"I met the Yankee in town this morning," she said, and her harsh tone brought Patience's worried eyes to hers.

"What Yankee?"

"The captain's cousin." She never called William

Gadsden by his given name. To do so might indicate she liked the man, and she refused to give him that honor. He was, by all rights, a usurper.

"The miller? Mr. Eriksson?"

"That's him. Ugly as a mud puppy."

Patience's eyes widened more. "He's green?"

A giggle burst forth at her sister's gentle wit.

"Green, slimy and crawls on his belly. Like all Yankees."

"I daresay he's handsome like Will."

"You think the captain is handsome?"

"Don't you?"

"Don't be silly." She did, however, think the new millwright might be handsome beneath his traveler's untidiness. For those few minutes when she'd deemed him a savior, she'd almost found him attractive. Indeed, her pulse had fluttered at the sheer strength of the tall, muscular man and at the way he'd easily lifted her off the ground with warm concern in his voice and light blue eyes. Why, she absolutely shuddered to remember.

All along he was another Yankee scalawag come to take what her family had worked to build since the Revolution. They were like rats, these Unionists, nibbling away at the South.

"I don't wish to speak of him or *to* him ever again."

"He's going to be living here, Josie. You can't be rude to a guest."

"Can't I? Were the Yankees not rude when they invaded our home and stole our food and everything we couldn't hide?"

Let Reverend Watley preach of loving the enemy and praying for those who despitefully used her. Josie would never dishonor Tom's memory with Union sympathies, and she could not believe a just God expected her to.

Patience sighed and reached for a tattered pale green skirt. "Look, Josie, a color that's lovely with your hair."

Josie gave her sister a soft smile. "I know what you're doing, Miss Patience, but I will not be kind." She put her scissors aside. "Let me see the cloth. I do so love green."

She held the silken fabric below her chin, admiring the softness and color. Inwardly, she debated. So many woman and children of her acquaintance did without adequate clothing. Did she have a right to be selfish with goods donated through the church? "I could make a lovely blouse for someone. Perhaps the reverend's daughter."

"The color makes your eyes as green as leaves. Keep it, Josie, as payment for all the many dresses and shawls and quilts you've made for others."

"I don't know if I should."

"But you want to."

"Of course I do." She laughed, closing her eyes in jest as she rubbed the silky fabric along her cheek. "I look positively fetching in green!"

Footfalls and the rustle of movement jerked her eyes open. Standing in the doorway were the captain and *him*, Thaddeus Eriksson.

She dropped the green silk onto her lap, good humor as gone as her happy childhood.

"Josie. Patience," Will said, stepping closer. "This is Thaddeus Eriksson, my cousin, who's come to take charge of the mill."

"Miss Patience, a pleasure, I'm sure." The insufferable Yankee bowed slightly as if he were a gentleman.

Josie rolled her eyes toward heaven.

She would not rise. She would not be polite or welcoming, for he was *not* welcome. Not at all.

"Miss Josie. We meet again." Amusement danced in eyes the color of a summer sky.

A most undesirable shiver ran through Josie and infuriated her further.

She tossed her head and sniffed. "Unfortunately." Her nose tilted ever higher. "I hoped you'd get lost en route. Or be eaten by a tiger."

Patience sucked in a gasp, sweet eyes as round as cornflowers. "Josie!"

Instead of seeming insulted, Thaddeus laughed. "Should I be afraid of tigers in Tennessee? Or only of the tigress?"

Josie's chest tickled with the need to laugh. Insufferable, amusing, handsome, dastardly Yankee. He could laugh all he wanted, but neither his laughter nor hers would change who he was.

CHAPTER TEN

A cat is more intelligent than people believe, and can be taught any crime.

—Mark Twain

Present

CARRIE EASED HER foot off the gas pedal, aware that she was driving too fast around curves and over hills and up the mountain leading to the ridge for which Honey Ridge was named.

Flashes of green flickered in her peripheral vision as she zipped past lush, verdant meadows bracketed by thick, dark woods and bisected by lazy creeks shining in the September sun.

Hayden, the enigma, sat in the pushed-back passenger seat, his long legs stretched out as far as possible in the VW Bug.

She was still surprised that he'd wanted to ride along. He didn't know her, and other than his brilliance with words, she didn't know him.

Except she liked him and they shared a mutual concern for Brody. And she'd agreed to breakfast Thursday morning.

Hayden seemed so...normal. Not like a rich and famous person with an elitist attitude.

Nevertheless, those Ferragamo loafers Nikki had pointed out and the fancy watch glinting from his left wrist were dead giveaways that he was a successful man who lived in the stratosphere, not down here on planet small town with mere mortals such as the town librarian.

He was far from the average Joe.

What bothered her most about him wasn't his penchant for death, nor was it his fault. It was the tingly sensation on her arms and neck whenever those smoke-colored eyes locked on hers.

She knew the danger of those tingly sensations. If she ever married, and the jury was still out on that unlikely event, she wasn't looking for tingles. Never again. She wanted a friend, a man who could discuss books and work beside her in charities and hold her through the storms of life, both figuratively and literally.

A man of Hayden's status would never look twice at a plain Jane librarian who barely knew Ferragamo from Freddy Krueger. To Hayden she was a resource, a living Google search. Carrie got that. She had no illusions about herself.

Yet, here she was, driving along these narrow, hilly roads with Hayden Winters wedged into the seat of her Beetle. If she felt a little thrill of pride at being with one of the country's favorite authors, she was, after all, a book person and a public librarian.

A confused librarian with tingly arms.

Following a brief drive through Honey Ridge and a meal of burgers, tots and ice-cream sundaes, they'd driven Brody to his empty house. He had to get home, he'd said, to feed Max, his pet lizard. Following this statement, he and Hayden had launched into a lengthy discussion about the care and feeding of the five-lined skink.

The fact that Mr. Thomson was at work eased any immediate concern she had about the boy. If he was being mistreated, and she still wasn't convinced on that front, Brody was safe with his father gone. An awful thought, come to think of it, that a child was better off alone than with a parent.

She glanced toward Hayden. "I hope we're wrong about Mr. Thomson."

He shifted as much as possible in the cramped seat to look at her. "We're not."

There he went again. Laying those smoky eyes on her.

He sounded so sure, the way he had the night of the storm.

"Oh, Hayden." She bit her lip and frowned his way.

Hayden's lips tightened; his nostrils slightly flared. "He said his dad doesn't cook and isn't home much. Where does the kid get his meals?"

"School?"

"He gets lunch. And if he's lucky breakfast."

"Surely there's food in the house." She glanced at him, heart bleak. "Sandwich makings. Frozen pizza. PB and J."

"Are you confident of that?"

Frustrated, she said, "No," and vowed to find out. "His dad works. He can afford groceries."

"Admit it, Carrie. We both suspect something's wrong in that house. Brody sends out signals."

"All I'm saying is that we shouldn't rush to judgment. I wouldn't be happy if someone assumed terrible things about me that weren't true." In fact, she'd hated it.

Clint Thomson might be a hard man, even neglectful, but that didn't necessarily make him an abuser.

"Look, I don't want to get involved, either, but the kid came to us." His jaw was tight and maybe a little angry. "Hard to turn your back."

"There's no law against befriending him," she offered, conciliatory against his vehemence, a vehemence she found curious. Why would Hayden Winters, here for peace and quiet to write a novel, push so hard on the subject of a boy he didn't even know?

At the signal light's clicking, Carrie turned down a dirt road, narrowed by the lush vegetation tumbling out of the woods.

"The cat lady lives here."

He looked at her with interest. "An eccentric old woman with a million cats and not much else?"

She brought the car to a halt in front of a row of native rocks placed neatly around the perimeter of the small house as if someone had intended to build a wall and had run out of steam. Knowing the cat lady, that was likely the case.

"Not old but certainly eccentric. Coy Than Travers. Originally from Cambodia but married an American. Turns out his Cambodian business trips netted him more than a wife. He died a few years ago in a bad drug deal."

"Did she know he was trafficking?"

"Hard to tell. The police don't think so. Her English isn't great, so she doesn't communicate with too many people."

"Why would a librarian be delivering books to someone who can't read English?"

"I special-order for her in Cambodian. She'd like to improve her English, but since she never leaves the property..."

A puzzled frown knit his brow. "Why not?"

"Anxiety."

"Understandable after what happened to her husband, especially with her limited English."

"She says she can't breathe in town and feels like she's having a heart attack."

"That sounds like agoraphobia."

Carrie flashed a grin. "When I said that word to my sister, she shuddered and said she hated spiders, too."

Hayden's lips curved. "I take it your sister's not a word person like us?"

Like us. The inclusion felt intimate.

"Please don't think Nikki's dumb. She spotted your Ferragamo shoes right away, and she can identify the year and designer of every Oscar gown since 1980."

His steady gaze was both unsettling and reassuring. "No judgment from me. Your family's close?"

"Very." She put the car in Park and cut the motor. "What about you? Any brothers and sisters?"

"Only child," he said lightly.

"Being an only must be great, not that I'd trade the Riley brood for anything."

His eyes glazed and went empty. He turned his attention toward the little blue cottage, pointing. "Your cat lady. Should I stay in the car?"

"Probably the best idea. She's a bit skittish, and she totes a shotgun."

"Fascinating."

"Lots of women around here own guns, especially those who live alone."

"Do you?" His mouth twitched. "And should I be afraid?"

In her best Terminator voice, Carrie teased, "Very afraid."

Hayden laughed, and the frost in his expression melted.

She reached for the bundle of books on the backseat. The movement brought her in close proximity to the man filling up her passenger seat. Her shoulder brushed his.

"Let me get them." His voice came from very close to her ear. "I want to see how good my Cambodian is."

A pesky tingle skittered over her skin. Her pulse kicked up a notch. "You read Khmer?"

The words came out breathy and soft.

"Not a word."

Amusement filtered like sunlight past the attraction.

"Silly. You can't even move in this car. I'll get the books."

She pushed open the door, but before she could pop the seat he grabbed the stack and handed it across the console.

"Here you go." His eyes held hers. The air hummed, and the space in the tiny car shrank until she could hear him breathe. A spell. He cast a spell.

"Next time." He sounded far more normal than she felt. "I'd like to meet her if she doesn't mind."

Their hands brushed, and the subtle scent of expensive cologne swirled around in her senses.

Next time. He planned to make more trips up the mountain with her?

She snatched the stack and headed toward the small cropped-haired woman waiting tense as a fiddle string on the porch.

Hayden Winters was a dangerous man. Dangerous not because of the dark and murderous imagination that made him famous, but because of the light he cast on her loneliness and the foolish infatuation that sprang up like dandelion weeds in her tidy inner garden.

CHAPTER ELEVEN

What does not kill you will likely try again.
                    —Mr. B., undertaker

HAYDEN WANDERED ALONG the creek bank bisecting the quiet woods that stretched behind Peach Orchard Inn. This morning his head was full of too many things.

He'd dreamed again about Peach Orchard Farm and the old mill across the road. Except the mill hadn't been old in his dreams. It had thrived, the big wheels grinding under the hand of Thaddeus Eriksson, a Yankee in a land of Confederates, a misfit. It was the only comparison between himself and Thaddeus he could find.

This morning the memory was as thick as fog and about as easy to hold on to. Yet the scene lingered in the back of his brain and gave him an uneasy feeling he didn't understand.

He wanted to blame the haunting dreams on the late-night helping of Mississippi Mud Brownies Julia had placed in the parlor for guests. Wanted to but couldn't. A man didn't dream about the same people and place more than once without believing his subconscious was trying to tell him something.

What, he didn't know.

Against his hip, his cell phone vibrated, but he didn't answer or even check caller ID. Earlier he'd spoken to his agent and emailed with his assistant and editor. That was enough business contact for one day. His few friends knew he'd disappeared to write as always and respected his privacy.

He'd been called enigmatic, quiet or reserved. None of those were true. He was cautious.

Brody was cautious, too.

The boy haunted him every bit as much as the bizarre dreams and sent his mind down dark alleys he'd prefer to avoid.

He'd attempted to start the new book last night, but Brody kept intruding. Brody and Carrie and a pair of fictional dream people. Everything in him wanted to write the nineteenth-century story, but the talk with his agent reminded him again of his obligations. Readers expected and paid for certain things in a Hayden Winters novel. Changing horses in the middle of the stream could derail his lucrative career.

The idea of losing everything he'd worked for frightened him more than a serial killer with a penchant for torture. Those he understood. Their twisted psychology kept him writing, kept him digging deeper to know more about how their minds worked.

He understood broken minds.

After several false starts at the computer that included a bomb squad renegade and a psychotic zookeeper, he'd come away uninspired, leaving his psychologically wounded hero to work out his frustration with a second helping of brownies.

Bad decision.

His editor expected something on his desk soon.

And he had nothing other than a fragmented story outside his moneymaking genre.

He rolled his shoulders to stretch tight muscles and crouched on the creek bank. His clean-shaven face stared back, mirrored in the clear water. An honest face full of lies.

What would the people of Honey Ridge say if they knew?

He felt a connection here. With the town, the house, the people. Especially the people.

He blamed Carrie Riley, the squeaky librarian with the big brown eyes and the pretty feet. He'd enjoyed their trek up on Honey Ridge, liked being with her.

He didn't form attachments, not normally, but he was feeling far from normal since his arrival.

At the bottom of the shallow creek bed, pale, ghostly minnows darted in bunches above the brown rocks.

Had Brody camped here that stormy Friday night? Had he stared into the mirrored pool and watched the minnows?

Hayden blew out a frustrated breath. He wanted to ignore the warning signs and focus on work. Carrie, whom he considered his ally in the quest to know more about Brody, vacillated between assurances that nothing was amiss and fear that it very much was.

Carrie. Warmth edged into his somber mood.

The curvy, hilly trip up on the ridge had proved interesting in a number of ways, especially getting to know Carrie. She was more than a cute librarian who jumped at her own shadow and squeaked at the sound of thunder. She was a caring person who worried about kids and special-ordered books for an agoraphobic cat lady whose husband died smuggling drugs into the United States.

Drugs. Death. Crime. And an intriguing dose of

agoraphobia. If the cat lady didn't get his imagination flowing, nothing would.

Mulling as he was inclined to do when ideas brewed like dark coffee in his veins, Hayden walked away from the stream and pressed deeper into the shadowy woods. Maybe something more would develop here among the dying leaves and deadly silence.

Deadly Silence, a good title, already taken. Too bad.

The idea of a mute victim rattled around in his head. Silent. Alone. Unable to cry out.

Or squeak.

Carrie again.

How was he to create scenes of depraved evil when her fresh, warm smile and big doe eyes kept crowding in?

Down an incline his loafers slipped, reminding him to wear hiking boots the next time he ventured away from the house. Tennessee landscape, like Kentucky, could be rugged, and he hadn't hiked the woods and mountains in a very long time.

A love-hate relationship.

The leaves showed signs of changing—a few here and there had yellowed—foreshadowing deep fall when the woods would break out in sunset colors as surely as the warbler serenading his solitary walk broke out in song.

He examined the ground, covered in leaves and twigs and the occasional bit of paper, a shiny gum wrapper, an aluminum can. He wasn't sure what he looked for, but sometimes the strangest or simplest thing triggered a twist or a plot point that poured out of him onto the page.

A squirrel scolded from a sugar maple, and next to

it a persimmon tree hung heavy with green fruit. The seeds, he'd learned, were roasted, ground and used as a coffee substitute during the Civil War. He'd never tried the coffee, but he'd eaten his fill of persimmons, some orange and sweet, while others puckered his mouth and made his belly hurt.

Hunger pushed the bounds of good taste and common sense.

He thought again of Brody. The boy appeared as healthy and clean as any fifth grader, especially one who liked the outdoors. Yet Hayden wondered who fed him, what he ate besides cookies at the library.

Hayden dodged a tree limb, shoving the branch to one side as he passed. A silvery-white spiderweb bright as a snowflake stretched above his head. A moth had met his doom there.

He thought of the web he'd spun around himself and wondered if someday he'd be caught like the moth with no hope of escape.

Up ahead in the thick underbrush Hayden spotted a rudimentary shelter of some kind, definitely created by human hands. An A-frame made entirely of broken limbs and wilting pine boughs, it was fairly well designed, using the trunk of a huge oak as an anchor. The shelter was not tall enough to stand up in, so Hayden crouched low to peer inside. The interior was dark, lighted only by sun rays slanting through the roof. It smelled of pine and wet earth but of warmth, too.

"What have we here?" he murmured softly.

When his eyes adjusted to the dimness, Hayden saw an empty butter bowl, a cardboard box and what appeared to be a lidless tackle box next to a neatly folded piece of blue plastic tarp.

His chest clutched like a clenched fist around his windpipe.

The sense of tumbling backward through time made him dizzy.

He put one hand on the damp ground to keep from falling sideways.

A scratching sound caught his attention and brought him back from the brink. Something rummaged for crumbs inside a deep cardboard box. Curiosity won out, and Hayden ducked inside the enclosure, hunched over like Quasimodo.

Nestled in a leafy bed, a young cottontail looked up at him with button eyes and quivering nose. A crude bandage, some sort of white cloth, was wrapped around a back leg. Blood had seeped through, leaving a brown spot on the outside. Someone had tended the injured rabbit, adding a plastic lid of water and a handful of gnawed carrots.

Someone like Brody Thomson.

CHAPTER TWELVE

If you don't believe in the resurrection of the dead, be here at closing time.

— Lynn, café owner

THE MORNING SMELLS of bacon and coffee permeated the interior of the Miniature Golf Café and stirred Carrie's stomach to life.

She and Hayden were early, but the good ol' boys had already gathered, and Hayden seemed to be soaking up the small-town atmosphere like a fresh biscuit in hot gravy.

Hayden, with his smooth charm and easy smile, had fielded a few questions about writing and then sidestepped anything personal with a finesse that Carrie wouldn't have noticed if she hadn't been listening intently to get a hint about his life beyond his career. In five minutes' time, he'd had the good ol' boys running off at the mouth while he sat back and listened.

Carrie sipped at her cream-laden coffee while Poker Ringwald regaled Hayden and anyone else who'd listen with a tale from Honey Ridge's storied past. This one about the Frederick brothers, who'd squared off in an epic fight at town center over a prize watermelon. One of the pair had ended up pumping three bullets not into his brother, but into the melon.

"To this day, those fellas live in this town with ad-joining farms and never speak to each other."

"Human nature is a funny thing," said Sugar Bo Jackson, a former pugilist with the flat nose and cauliflower ear to prove it.

Sugar Bo sat across from Poker, shoveling pancakes into a Latino face that had probably been handsome before opponents had battered it flat. Now he suffered seizures and could neither box nor work a regular job, but he did odd jobs all over Honey Ridge. Occasionally, Carrie hired him to set up tables and chairs for events at the library.

Poker and his wife, magenta-haired Lynn, owned and operated the Miniature Golf Café. If truth was told, Lynn operated while Poker shuffled a deck of cards, played solitaire and kept the customers coming back for friendly conversation.

Poker *flrrred* his cards against the table and tapped the ends. One, two, three times. In the chair next to him was Judge Rutherford Black, who'd sat on the bench at the county seat for years until his retirement. Now he sported a beard and played President Lincoln for the occasional history lesson at Honey Ridge school. His wife was suitably eccentric as Mary Todd Lincoln.

The keepers of the past, as she'd described them to Hayden on the way over, gathered every day at the retro café with its green vinyl booths and checkerboard floors. They told stories, rehashed history and politics, drank Lynn's coffee by the vat and held sway in the small café forgotten by time but not by Honey Ridge.

"You all ready to order, Carrie, honey?"

Lynn had left behind two plastic menus, although Carrie wondered why she bothered. Today's offerings were written in black marker on a whiteboard that hung over the register beneath the thought for the day: *If at first you don't succeed, don't go skydiving.*

"The smell of bacon is torturing me. I'd better have some."

Lynn scribbled on her pad. "With biscuits and gravy?"

"You know me too well." To Hayden, she said, "Anything you order is good."

"Bacon and eggs over easy."

"Biscuits and gravy?" Lynn asked without looking up.

"Grits, too." Hayden handed her the menu with his charmer's smile, the one that made Carrie's stomach jitter. "Might as well go straight for the arteries."

Lynn laughed, scribbled and hustled away.

With a smile, Carrie said, "You can't get food like this in New York City."

"I'm not sure if that's bad or good."

She chuckled softly. "Both, I imagine. A steady Southern diet is tasty but hard on the waistline."

"You don't seem to have a problem with that." His smoky gaze held hers for two beats and caused the jittery thing to happen again.

The compliment flustered her. Her cheeks heated, and her pulse kicked up. She didn't like it, didn't want to feel anything remotely resembling attraction.

Yet she did.

Carrie dragged her eyes away from his and pretended interest in the café.

The door opened, a bell jingled and a man who resembled a depressed version of Morgan Freeman slumped inside.

"Our pessimistic funeral director, Mr. B.," she whispered.

"If you think about it, optimism in an undertaker might be off-putting."

"I guess that's true. Not many of us are optimistic about being in a coffin. Well, except you maybe."

"Only for a character in my books."

"Preferably a villain."

"Or not," he said with an ornery twinkle.

"Mr. B., who you got down to the funeral home?" Lynn held the coffeepot in midair. A pencil stuck out of stiffly sprayed hair. "I saw the hearse creep past the nursing home last night."

"Shelton Vandyke. A stroke, poor soul, took him to the other side." The undertaker took the final seat at Poker's table and looked respectfully solemn. In a dramatic orator's voice, he intoned, "Life is short and full of sorrows."

"Short?" Poker *flrrred* his deck of cards against the tabletop. "Wasn't Shelton in his nineties?"

"Yes, he was. Yes, he was." Mr. B.'s body rocked with the melancholy affirmation. "But a vapor, we are, Poker. Here today and gone tomorrow. No one gets out alive."

"Well, God rest his soul." Lynn topped off Carrie's coffee without asking and leaned in with a mischievous grin. "The crooked old skinflint."

Poker shuffled the cards again and straightened the edges. *Thwack, thwack,* against the vinyl tablecloth. "Now, darlin', don't speak ill of the dead."

Lynn didn't pay the mild rebuke a bit of mind. "Old Vandyke's so crooked Mr. B. will probably have to screw him in the ground."

Carrie, ready for anything, laughed, but Hayden nearly spit out his coffee. Lynn barked her rowdy guffaw and whacked him once on the back before moving on.

Sugar Bo pushed a wad of napkins across the space between their tables, his teeth bright white in a dark face.

"You gotta be prepared around here," Sugar Bo said. "No telling what somebody might say."

"That's why he's here, Sugar Bo. So don't hold back." As if holding back was in their blood.

"That a fact? You gonna put us in a book, Mr. Winters?"

Carrie answered for him. "Probably not. He murders people. You don't want to get killed off—do you?"

"Just like in a good TV show," Lynn said. "You get to liking the hero and next thing you know, he's dead and gone."

"Life is but a vapor," intoned Mr. B.

Fighting a giggle, Carrie sat back in her chair and watched Hayden take it all in, satisfied he was getting exactly what he'd come for and fully aware she was getting way more than she bargained for.

HAYDEN CHEWED A bite of crispy bacon and listened to the conversation swirling around the small space. They were an entertaining group; Carrie was right about that. But the man who'd been introduced as Judge Rutherford Black fascinated him. Beneath a dark beard, the Abe Lincoln look-alike bore faint scars up the sides of his neck.

There was a story there.

Hayden experienced a sudden flash of Thaddeus,

the man in his dreams. The miller had been burned in a house fire in a frantic attempt to rescue his wife and daughter.

The bell over the door jingled again, and six heads plus Lynn's big hair swiveled in that direction. Two ladies bustled inside, dressed in identical shirtwaist dresses sprigged with lilacs, a black purse dangling from each left elbow. Probably in their eighties, the spry pair sported painted-on eyebrows and rolled hair in an impossible shade of daffodil yellow. They were as wrinkled as a pair of shar-peis, and their eyes snapped with wit and energy.

"Good morning, ladies," Lynn called. "Come on in. I'll rustle up some tea."

"The Sweat twins," Carrie told him quietly. "Miss Vida Jean and Miss Willa Dean, though only a few can tell the difference. Anything you want to know about Honey Ridge, ask the twins. They'll know or make it up."

Introductions were made, and the elderly twins turned fascinated eyes on him. "Hayden Winters, the novelist."

"Yes, ma'am." Though he doubted these white-gloved, proper Southern ladies read his genre.

"Vida Jean loved the way you stuffed that barber in a freight mailer and had him shipped to his ex-wife."

"They were both such bullies." Vida Jean nodded. "Served them right. Delicious, the way you dispatched them. Purely delicious, I tell you. Didn't I say that, sister?"

"Delicious. Yes, you did."

Hayden's chest tickled with amusement. A writer never knew where he'd meet a fan.

Sugar Bo and Abe Lincoln aka Judge Black pushed out of their chairs. "You ladies take our seats. We can sit over by the window."

"Not necessary, gentlemen, though we thank you kindly. We can procure an extra." Willa Dean—or was it Vida Jean?—looked over one shoulder. "Poker, get your lazy carcass up and find Willa Dean a chair."

Hayden studied the speaker—obviously Vida Jean—trying to tell the pair apart. Even in identical twins, something would be different.

Poker nearly turned the table over in his eagerness to obey. "Yes, ma'am."

"The twins were schoolteachers for many years," Carrie told him as he watched with interest. "I think they taught every person in here."

"Ah. That explains the sudden rush to obedience."

"They were disciplinarians, let me tell you, though always with a spoonful of sugar."

"They taught you, too?"

"Miss Willa Dean for art. Music with Miss Vida Jean."

"What instrument?"

"Piccolo. I marched in the band, but she never awarded me first chair."

"Vicious old lady."

"Shh." Carrie suppressed a giggle and cut her eyes toward the scooting chairs. "They're lovely, really. The matriarchs of Honey Ridge society."

Though Carrie was not his intended focus this morning, Hayden's gaze drifted to her often. He'd rather look at her than listen in on the good ol' boys, as interesting as they were.

She was smart and witty and unassumingly pretty.

Maybe that was why she interested him. No pretense. No airs. No effort to impress. Carrie was who she was.

Unlike him.

He sipped his coffee, swallowed hard and forced his attention back to the newcomers. Fine arts teachers, cultured ladies, eccentrics.

"Now. Mr. Winters." Vida Jean folded her gloved hands on the tabletop. "As women with Tennessee roots as far back as the American Revolution, we officially welcome you to Honey Ridge. This is terribly exciting for us."

Willa Dean nodded, folding her hands in exactly the same pose as her sister. "We're huge fans."

"Huge," Vida Jean agreed.

"Hayden's here to research and write his next novel," Carrie told them.

Vida Jean turned owl eyes on the novelist. "Really? Oh, my gracious. How thrilling."

Willa Dean pressed both hands to her heart. "Our uncle Claremont was a writer, you know."

"Yes, he was. A wonderful writer for the Tennessean back in the fifties. We have storytelling in our blood."

"Yes, we do, and we would dearly love to help with your research. We know a story or two."

The old ladies exchanged glances. Then, as if some invisible agreement passed between them, one of them—Willa Dean, he thought—said, "Since you're staying at the Peach Orchard Inn, you probably know about the kidnapped boy, Mikey."

The other twin's lips thinned as she pressed them together. "Julia's little boy, though he'd be a teenager now. Bless his precious heart. He's been gone a long time."

"Yes, ma'am," Hayden said. "Carrie told me. A tragedy."

"I do hope you won't write about that, Mr. Winters. Julia can't bear it."

Both ladies leaned forward, peering at him intently, willing him with their schoolteacher stare to do the right thing.

He wrote thrillers, murder and gore. No mother wanted to think of her child in those terms, though kidnapping was a common topic in his genre. Julia Presley was convinced Mikey was still alive and would eventually find his way home. Hayden suspected she was wrong, but who was he to dash her hope?

The new proposal would not be a child abduction story.

"No," he said simply.

Usually anything was game, but Hayden drew the line when he was living under the woman's roof. Julia wanted her privacy respected. He got that.

"What about all those nasty drug dealings up in the hills?" one of them asked. Vida Jean, he thought. "Somebody gets killed every few years."

Nothing he didn't already know from scanning the newspaper files. Drug deals were old news unless they came with a twist. Was it possible that the cat lady ran a Cambodian connection and agoraphobia was a cover for a drug ring?

Inwardly he groaned. He was stretching, straining for something, anything that would stir the muse. The only muse that stirred these days was 150 years old.

Maybe he'd chosen the wrong place. Maybe he should forget the small-town South and head to the ocean, away from the antebellum influences.

While his mind wandered, the Sweat twins chattered about the history of Honey Ridge, the scourge of illegal drugs and the time some preacher died of unnatural causes. When Hayden tuned back in, the ladies were off on another rabbit trail.

"Porter Walenta was an itinerant peddler in the thirties. Vacuum cleaners, wasn't it, sister?"

"Vacuum cleaners. And pots and pans." The other twin leaned in and whispered, though every ear in the place was close enough to hear. "He was a philanderer. Cheated on his wife all over the county and beyond."

"He'd knock on a door, smile that toothy snake oil salesman grin and get himself invited in. Next thing you know, that woman had the cleanest rugs around and the messiest sheets."

"Willa Dean! I declare." Vida Jean looked suitably scandalized.

"Well, that's what Virginia Washington told me." Cheeks blushing crimson, Willa Dean warmed to her topic. "One day a farmer came in from the fields unexpectedly—his mule harness broke—and beat old Porter with a buggy whip. Messed up his handsome face and various other parts real good."

The room erupted with laughter. Hayden exchanged amused glances with Carrie, whose cheeks were also rosy.

Vida Jean fanned her face with the plastic menu. "Lord have mercy, sister. You ought not to tell that story in mixed company."

"Oh, don't be prudish."

Vida Jean sat up primly, lips pursed, unhappy with her sister's admonishment as much as the indiscreet story.

Lynn sailed in to save the moment with a flowered teapot and two cups. "Here you go, ladies. Earl Grey."

Around the small café, the locals resumed talking among themselves.

Itinerant salesman. Drug dealers. Nothing to jiggle the muse. Hayden struggled with the misery of pushing at his brain and coming away empty. He needed to relax, focus elsewhere and let his subconscious work on the next book. Stress and deadlines were creativity killers.

Hayden sipped his coffee and listened to the chatter around him.

Carrie ate with proper manners, left hand in her lap and back straight. It was ingrained, he could see, a natural habit she didn't even notice but one he'd had to practice over and over again.

Carrie. He let his thoughts settle on her for a while. So pretty and fresh when she'd bounced out of her small house that morning and crossed the lawn to his rental car. She wore a skirt, one of the swirly kind that made him watch her walk.

"Lynn, dear," one of the twins said, "do you have wilting veggies we can carry home?"

Lynn jabbed the ever-present pencil into the top of her hair. "For the Thomson boy?"

Hayden shot a surprised glance at Carrie, who widened her eyes and shrugged.

"For his critters," the twin said. "He's got a new one."

Hayden's shoulders relaxed as he considered the hideout he'd found in the woods. They weren't asking for wilted veggies to feed the boy. They were asking for the rabbit.

"I'll have a look-see and box up what I have."

"So kind," Vida Jean said. "If you have any leftover cinnamon rolls, I wouldn't mind one for Binky. You know how he loves them."

"Binky?" Hayden mouthed to Carrie.

"Their parrot."

"Ah." Somehow it didn't surprise him at all that the old ladies owned a parrot.

When Lynn moved off toward the kitchen, he said to the twin he'd marked as Vida Jean by the tiny mole next to her nose, "Do you ladies know Brody Thomson well?"

Vida Jean removed the tea bag from her cup and gingerly placed it in her saucer. "Why, yes, we do. He's a dear little boy."

"He visits our Binky sometimes and even runs errands for us. Such a tender heart. Always rescuing some creature."

"Though we despair at that father of his."

"Awful man."

Hayden's fork paused in midbite. "In what way?"

Willa Dean stiffly replied, "We are not given to gossip, Mr. Winters. It is a sin."

"A pure sin," her sister concurred.

"However." Willa Dean smacked her lips. "Fact is not gossip. And it is a known fact that Clinton Thomson is given to strong spirits."

"On a regular basis." Vida Jean huffed with indignation.

"Does he treat Brody well?"

"Can't say I've heard anything to the contrary, but he treated his wife poorly."

Willa Dean nodded emphatically. "Very poorly."

Hayden tensed. "What happened?"

Willa Dean's impossible eyebrows shot into her hairline. "Most people think she left him."

Vida Jean's head bobbed. "But sister and I have given the situation a great deal of thought, and we are convinced she did not."

"No?"

"No." Willa Dean paused for effect, making eye contact with each listener. "She was murdered."

CHAPTER THIRTEEN

"MISS VIDA JEAN, what are you talking about?" Poker turned his chair around and dragged it to Hayden's table. "Don't pay her no mind, Hayden. She watches too much TV."

A mortified Willa Dean pressed a hand to her heart. "You hush, Poker Ringwald. Remember that time you swore up and down we were senile when we claimed Billy Roy Peterson broke into the golf course and played a round every single night? Isn't that right, sister?"

"Right as rain. He said we were senile. Shame on you, Poker."

"Then one night Officer Riley caught Billy Roy dead to rights with a golf club in one hand and one of Lynn's cinnamon rolls in the other."

Sugar Bo laughed. "Is that true, Poker?"

Poker scratched behind his ear. "I guess it is."

"No guessing to it." Vida Jean was clearly incensed. "So you listen to us, Mr. Winters. We know a thing or two about that Clinton Thomson."

"And we think he murdered her."

Hadn't he wondered the same thing? "Why would you think that?"

"Woman's intuition. We never liked that man. Did we, Vida Jean?"

"No, we didn't. Poor Penny. She kept to herself most of the time, but we'd see her now and then. Always so shy. Nervous as a long-tailed kitty at a rocking chair convention. We'd wonder why she didn't leave him."

"Maybe she did."

"She did," Lynn said emphatically as she warmed up Hayden's coffee. "The poor thing went home to Mama and never looked back." To Hayden, she said, "The ladies get carried away."

"Most people didn't even notice she was gone." Poker dealt a card, turned it over and groaned.

"Her leaving was their business." The judge hoisted his coffee cup toward Lynn, indicating a need for a refill. "In my years on the bench, I saw plenty of divorces, but folks don't have to get divorced to be apart. Troubled marriages break up, people move away and that's that. The woman left him, and it wasn't anyone's business. People have a right to privacy."

"In this town?" Shocked, Willa Dean sat up as prim and straight as a tea rose. "I think he murdered her and buried her in the backyard like in that Lifetime movie. What was the name of it, Vida Jean?"

"I don't remember, but a backyard burial is too obvious. Like a key under the welcome mat. Anyone knows where to look." Vida Jean frowned and shook her head. "We've had this discussion before. He took her somewhere back in the woods. Remember that episode of *Hawaii Five-0*?"

"Oh, now, Miss Vida Jean, cut that out. Movies and TV ain't real life. Penny Thomson finally wised up and left her sorry husband. End of subject." Poker shuffled his deck again, this time with a toothpick in the corner of his mouth. "Everybody knows that."

Hayden observed the ping-pong conversation with interest.

"We say he killed her, and it's a pure shame the police didn't do a thing about it."

"Nothing to investigate, ladies," the judge said. "No evidence. No complaints. No case."

"That's because he was clever."

"Y'all are not being very nice here." Lynn's hair quivered in magenta indignation as she slid a cinnamon roll in front of Mr. B. "Clint Thomson has lived in this town as long as I have, and other than getting three sheets to the wind like plenty of others, he's never caused any trouble. No disrespect, ladies, but you got no business spreading tales about him."

"Well." Both twins pursed their lips in identical expressions of insult. One of them pushed her teacup aside. The other opened the clasp on her purse and whipped out the exact change, laid it on the table, and, with quiet dignity, the pair walked out.

Chatter followed their departure, but Hayden turned his attention to Carrie. "What do you think?"

"The twins are dear ladies, but Lynn's right. They can get carried away."

"You don't buy their accusation?"

"Not at all. Things like that don't happen in Honey Ridge. Someone would notice."

Hayden bit down on a buttery biscuit, wondering.

Even if there wasn't a grain of truth in the twins' suspicions, they'd gotten the wheels turning in his head.

One way or the other, he was keeping an eye on Brody…and on his father.

CHAPTER FOURTEEN

*Take the proverb to thy soul! Take and clasp it
fast: "The mill cannot grind with the water that
has passed."*

—Sarah Doudney

1867

A WEEK WENT by and Thaddeus spent such long hours
at the gristmill he had little time for brooding about his
cold Tennessee welcome or the Ohio home he dearly
missed. A home that was no longer there.

He was grateful for the distraction William's new
family provided. Each day at noon Will ordered the
work stopped, and they hiked across the fields to the
farmhouse for dinner, leaving Oscar, the hired man,
to serve any customers.

Thaddeus understood William's need to rush home
to the big house. His cousin was in love, and if he'd
learned anything, it was that life was fragile and people were to be cherished. Will had found happiness
again. Thad was determined to be glad for his cousin
and his gentle bride with the iron spine. Charlotte had
made him welcome and had given him his own space
near the other former soldiers who'd stayed behind to
work the farm.

Each night, when darkness made work impossible even in lamplight, he joined the family's table, where he seemed to find ways to annoy the red-haired Josie whether he intended to or not. Most times he intended to.

Will teased that enough sparks flew between Josie and Thad to light a campfire, and Thad found himself looking forward to the match of wits. The fiery redhead would rather see him drawn and quartered, and when she said as much one evening in the parlor while Patience soothed them with Chopin and lamplight created a relaxing glow, he'd laughed. Her furious fire and sharp tongue amused him for some reason. At his laughter, Josie looked up from her needlework, caught his eye, and he was certain he saw a sparkle, a twinkle of humor as her cheeks grew pink and her mouth twitched.

With all the problems at the mill, sparring with Miss Josie had become the pinnacle of his very long days. He was, he mused, in a sorry state.

Josephine Portland was a vain woman, as he'd discovered the first day when he'd come into the parlor to find her gushing over her own beauty and bragging about how wonderful she looked in green. That he agreed with her assessment had no bearing on his opinion of her vanity. She spent hours sewing pretty things for herself and fawning over bits of ribbons and lace.

Men must surely dance at the end of her lead. But not him. His heart was taken, and he was wise to the false charms of a woman like Josie, amusing as she was.

On this particular noon when the sun blazed hotter than a blacksmith's forge, Thaddeus wiped sweat from his brow and considered sending his hired man across the fields with word that he would not be at the dinner table. This morning William had remained at the farm to repair a barn door broken by the wind, a forceful storm that ushered in this cursed humidity.

After spending the better part of the morning grinding corn, a gear had broken. Add this to a host of other repairs and the steady flow of business and he fought against discouragement. He hadn't expected the mill to need this much attention.

"Oscar!" he called to the hired man as he threaded his way past the grinding stones and bins and up the stairs to the loft.

A cat meowed and trotted up the wooden steps beside him. When he paused on the landing, she rubbed against his pants leg, and he bent to scratch her ears.

"She and her kittens are doing the job." Oscar nodded toward the gray tabby. "I saw her trot off toward the woods with a mouse a while ago."

Keeping the rodent population at bay was essential to a mill's operation, and cats were the solution. Every grain mill had at least one.

"Giving her the bowl of cream didn't slow her down. Did it?" Thad asked.

Oscar protested the waste of food on a cat when she could get her meals by doing her job. Oscar protested a lot of Thad's ideas, come to think of it. The man had worked for Edgar Portland and thought he knew more than anyone about the mill's workings. He knew the community and Thad tried to appreciate that, but the man rubbed against the grain.

Big and brawny with a full head of black hair, Oscar Pitts was around forty years old, but his strength had not diminished with the passage of time. Though a married man, he had a leering eye toward women who came to the mill. Thad was troubled because the Portland women frequently joined the workforce when the need arose. He'd seen the way Oscar studied them, and though he had kept the observation to himself, he put a watch on the hired man.

"Old lady Beacon's meal and grits is sacked and ready." Arms bulging, Oscar easily lifted and poured a full sack of corn into the hopper. Powdery dust flew up to stick on sweaty skin, and the smell of ground meal was thick in their nostrils. "You needin' me for something else, boss man?"

"I wasn't planning to grind any more today, Oscar," he said, eyeing the filled hopper. "Got a broke gear."

"Want me to scoop the grain back out?"

Thad contemplated the full bin, a temptation to mice and vermin. "Leave Tabby up here as guard. Maybe I can get this gear repaired at the blacksmith shop in town—"

Before he could finish the thought, a voice called from down below. "Hello. Anybody here?"

Oscar cocked his head and groused. "Sign clearly says we ain't taking any more grain this week."

Thad's nostrils flared in irritation. Not everyone could read. "Haul Mrs. Beacon's sacks over to her farm, and I'll see what our visitor wants."

"I ain't no delivery boy."

"She's an old woman, Oscar, a widow. A man's Christian duty is to take care of widows and orphans."

Oscar huffed. "Then send me over to Elizabeth Cower's farm. I'd be mighty pleased to take care of *that* particular widow and add a star in my heavenly crown at the same time." A sly grin slid up his cheeks. "Yes, sir. I believe the Lord is calling me to Miz Cower's place."

Thad frowned. The young, pretty Mrs. Cower had been left with three children and not much else. She didn't need Oscar's wandering eye to point in her direction. "Deliver to Mrs. Beacon, Oscar, and leave the other women alone."

The burly man spun on his boot heel and tromped down the stairs, showing his displeasure in every heavy step.

The tall double doors that made up the entrance of the mill stood open to let in the breeze blowing over the falls, a relief from the heat. There in the dust-mote sunlight stood a very black man.

He stepped forward, peering upward. "Mr. Thaddeus? Is that you, sir?"

"Abram?" Thad's displeasure dissipated. He hurried down the remaining steps. "I didn't expect to see you again."

"No, sir, I 'spect not."

"Did you find your family in Chattanooga?"

The young man's face saddened. "No, sir. They'd moved on after the emancipation."

"I'm sorry to hear that. What brings you to Honey Ridge?"

"You do, Mr. Thad. I remembered what you told me about the mill and how you'd be working here. Sure is glad to find you." He stood with faded black hat in hand, shiny with sweat. "I knowed this here watch was important to you after what you told me about your woman."

Abram reached into his pocket and extracted a

pocket watch. Thad gazed, stunned, at the silver time-piece. It was his, all right. He'd recognize Amelia's gift anywhere. "Where did you find this?"

Footsteps on the stairs turned their attention to a smirking Oscar. "He probably stole it."

"No, sir." Abram's expression darkened. His eyes flickered to Oscar, then to Thad and to the ground.

Irritation rose on the back of Thad's neck. He shot Oscar a sharp look.

"I believe you, Abram. Why else would you come all this way to return it?"

Oscar harrumphed and pushed around the freed-man, whispering something crude as he jostled the ex-slave's arm and stomped out into the sunlight.

Thad glared at the departing man. Some days were better than others with Oscar Pitts, but today he'd been on a tear since his arrival at dawn.

Abram kept his eyes downcast, his shoulders slumped in subservience. The notion that he expected to be ill-treated cramped in Thad's gut worse than a gallon of wild berries.

"You must have dropped your timepiece when you was getting off the train, Mr. Thad, sir. I didn't see it 'til the train started up again and it was too late to holler at you."

Thad took the beloved watch into hands dusty white with meal flour. He turned it over to read the inscrip-tion on back, and his heart turned over with it. Sweet words. Loving words. He ran his rough fingertips over the fine engraving.

Forever and always, I will love you.

"I thought I'd lost her again," he murmured softly, throat thick with emotion.

Except for the trickle and rush of water over the falls, the mill was silent, resting up for farmers who would come later in the day to pick up or drop off their corn for processing.

Thad's heart beat against his chest, a reminder that he lived on, the only legacy of a good woman and a beautiful child. He was as adrift as Abram, but at least he had the mill and honest work.

"Did you walk all the way from Chattanooga?"

Abram lifted his head with a slight, wry smile. "Yes, sir."

A silent understanding passed between them. Of course he had.

"Then you're weary. Hungry, too. I was about to go to the farm for dinner. Can you walk another half mile?"

Abram glanced down at his dusty, worn boots. "Yes, sir. Thank you, Mr. Thad. I'm obliged."

No, Thad thought. *He* was obliged. Regardless of the problems at the mill, the troublesome hired man or the animosity from Josie, having the watch returned was a balm to a sore soul. He owed Abram.

JOSIE GLANCED IN the cheval mirror in the corner of her bedroom and then out the window to the long lane of magnolias planted years ago for her great-grandmother Hattie Portland, a Georgia native who was also responsible for the peach orchard. Both, she was said to claim, reminded her of home.

After living off the peaches and peas for most of a year until new crops could be produced and livestock recovered and fattened, Josie appreciated her ancestor's efforts more than before the war.

From the fields to the right of the lane, she saw Thaddeus and another man walking toward the house. A charge, like soft lightning that jumped from cloud to cloud, flickered through her. Not that she found the man attractive—that would be disloyal to Tom—but Thaddeus was a change in her dull routine. He annoyed her no end. That was a fact. Annoyed her enough that she spent long moments at her sewing table pondering ways to upset his applecart. Vexing each other was the game they played, this Yankee and her, and though she despised a Yankee, Josie had always loved games.

From her sewing basket, she extracted a length of bonny blue ribbon. Eventually, the ribbon would adorn a shawl for Henrietta Baskin, but today Josie threaded it into her hair and went downstairs to help get supper on the table.

Lizzy was there, bossing everyone around, and Josie took her orders in stride. The uppity maid, now a free woman, had always been a favorite of Charlotte's and these days she ran the household and took her pay in room, board and a share of the farm profits. Charlotte also paid two Yankee leftovers, as Josie called them, as well as Hob, an arthritic old man who wasn't good for much other than tending the chickens and fishing with Benjamin. Everyone loved old Hob. Even her.

"Where's Charlotte?" she asked, noting the missing sister-in-law.

Patience slid a pan of corn bread out of the oven. The smell of catfish, fresh from the river and crispy fried with cornmeal, saturated the kitchen. "She and Ben went to the cemetery. Will went to call them for dinner."

"Oh." Charlotte paid regular respects to her late hus-

band and their lost babies, as well as the handful of
Yankee soldiers who'd died in this house. Josie shivered at the memories. So much grief and blood. Even
now, blood stained the parlor floor and the smell lingered and clung, especially in summer when the air
was thick and hot. She hoped the freed slaves appreciated all who'd died on their behalf.

Plates clattered. Silverware, saved from the Yankees
by Lizzy and Hob, who had buried it beneath the slave
cabins, gleamed from a fresh polish.

Will, Charlotte and Benjamin came inside. Eleven-
year-old Ben was quiet as always after visiting his father's grave. In pity and affection, Josie touched his
pale cowlick as she passed by carrying the plate of
catfish. A bag of marbles given to him by the captain
hung from her nephew's waist. The boy was rarely
without them, though he was without the best friend
with whom he'd played the game. Tandy was gone,
sold. One of many sins on Josie's account.

So many regrets. So many sins laid to her charge.
She'd likely never get to heaven. But if Yankees strolled
the streets of gold, perhaps she didn't want to go anyway. Not that she would express those thoughts to
Charlotte or Patience, both of whom feared the wrath
of God. Josie feared nothing. Not one single thing.
Never again.

From the parlor, the *thump-tap* of Logan's walking
sticks announced that the other men had come inside
the house. Yankees, every one of them. Legless Logan
and blind Johnny, a pitiful pair, remained at Peach Orchard Farm and showed absolutely no intent of ever
leaving. The other wounded soldier, Brinks, had healed
and returned to the North after Will's arrival.

That she might respect Captain Gadsden's ex-soldiers who'd stayed to help the women of Peach Orchard Farm in their time of need allowed her to remain civil. She would not, however, betray her beloved Tom or his Confederacy by liking any of them. They were a boil on the back of the South, an ever-present reminder of the ultimate price too many had paid.

As the table was laid and diners tromped in, hair slicked and wet and faces shiny damp from the well, Thaddeus and another man entered. The room fell silent as all eyes stared. The dark stranger dropped his head as if trying to disappear. Thad clapped him on the back, treating him as an equal, which she grudgingly supposed he was in a twisted sort of way. She had yet to fully understand the new rules of emancipation.

"I'd like you to meet Abram," Thaddeus said. "We met on the train where I lost my pocket watch. He found it and walked all the way from Chattanooga to return it to me."

Will, from his place at the head of the table, stood. "We're obliged to you, Abram."

"He's had a long trip and is hungry and tired. I invited him to supper."

Josie stared, aghast.

Charlotte's hands rested at her waist, her usually serene face disturbed. Even she saw the predicament. Surely even barbaric Northerners did not sit at the table with their servants?

Lizzy placed a plate of sliced corn bread on the table. She flashed obsidian eyes at the discomfited stranger. "Abram will be wanting to wash up and rest a spell, I suspect. I'll show him to the kitchen."

An inaudible sigh worked its way around the dining room. Abram nodded, hat in hand, and followed Lizzy.

Chairs scraping, the family settled in to eat. Josie peeked at Thaddeus while Will said grace. Yankees had strange ways.

When the prayer ended, Josie took a slice of golden corn bread and reached for the butter.

"Could I see your pocket watch, Mr. Thad?" Ben's eager face proved irresistible.

Thad pulled the timepiece from his pocket and passed it across the table to the boy, who studied the silver case with curiosity. "There's writing on the back."

"The watch was a gift," Thad said. "I am fortunate to have it returned."

"A pocket watch is valuable," Charlotte said in her soft, reasonable voice. "Abram could have sold it and saved himself the walk."

Thad nodded. "And had money in his pocket."

"An honest man is hard to find." Will forked a crispy catfish fillet and passed the dish to his cousin.

William nodded and reached for the butter. "We're agreeable. There's plenty to do, if he's inclined to work."

"I figure he is. He's searching for his family, but a man's got to rest and eat."

"It's settled, then. You'll speak to him?"

"I will."

Josie stared at her plate, her appetite diminished and replaced by remorse.

Abram searched for his family, separated by the bonds of slavery. Lincoln could declare the slaves free, but who would put their families back together? Was Lizzy searching for her son even as Abram searched for his family? Would Tandy try to find his way home again? Would the child know how?

And if he never returned, would she ever stop feeling guilty?

CHAPTER FIFTEEN

All that we see or seem is but a dream within a dream.

—Edgar Allan Poe

Present

SATURDAY MORNING, CARRIE finished her work at Interfaith Partnership and loaded two boxes of kid-friendly nonperishables in the small trunk of her car, stopping at Kroger for milk, eggs and bread before heading to Brody's house.

Her sister Bailey, who also volunteered at the charity, had offered to ride along, but this was something Carrie wanted to do on her own. She was a little nervous, but a meeting with Clint Thomson was in order, if nothing else to introduce herself and allay the worries about Brody's environment.

After the Sweat twins' bizarre conversation at the café, her curiosity and her concern were elevated to red alert.

Hayden had taken the twins seriously, gnawing over the conversation like a dog with a new bone.

Bones. Burial in the backyard. Such things were too grizzly for a librarian.

Yet there was a child to consider.

Mr. Thomson's car, an older-model white sedan, was parked in the driveway, so she marched up to the door and knocked with one hand while juggling a box in the other.

Though she avoided looking toward the backyard, a shiver tingled her spine.

The Sweats and their wild imaginations.

Inside the house, the television blared.

She knocked again, and the door opened. Scowling out at her was a shirtless Clint Thomson, his torso pale white and hairy.

Carrie was careful to keep her focus on his face. "Mr. Thomson, I'm Carrie Riley. I work at the library."

Did you bury your wife in the backyard?

His squint raked up and down her. He leaned a bare arm on the doorjamb. "I know who you are."

Well, that was certainly friendly. She swallowed, hiked her chin. She might be a mouse, but this was broad daylight in Honey Ridge.

"Brody comes to the library often."

The man's expression darkened. "He's not bothering you, is he? If that boy makes a nuisance of himself, I'll tear his hide up."

"No, sir. Not at all. Brody's a nice boy, and I'm happy to have him at the library anytime. In fact, I have a nephew his age and wondered if Brody might come over sometime and play."

The idea had appeared out of thin air, but her family had a cookout planned for Dad's upcoming birthday, so why not?

Clint Thomson's scowl deepened. "You sure he's not a pest? He can be a sneaky little troublemaker if you don't watch him. I never know what he's up to next."

The snide reference from the child's own father sent anger shooting up Carrie's backbone. She bit down on her back teeth to remain civil.

"I assure you—that is not the case. We'd be delighted to have his company."

The man scratched at the side of his head. "I guess that would be okay, then. He don't hang around here much anyway."

Was it any wonder?

"Excellent." This was going better than she'd expected. Breathing a sigh of relief, she held out the box of food. "I also volunteer at Interfaith Partnership and thought you and Brody might find a use for these items."

He took the box and glanced inside. His body stiffened.

"Charity?" He looked up at her, his color going dark red. "You think I'm some kind of charity case?"

"No, sir, not at all. I only wanted to help—"

"That stupid boy say something to you? Did he say I don't feed him? 'Cause that's a lie!" A vein popped out on his forehead. He spun his head toward the interior of the house. "Brody! Get out here right now!"

Brody's white face appeared behind his father. His pale blue eyes stared at Carrie in fear and dismay, but he said not a word.

Carrie reached for the man's arm. "Mr. Thomson, please. This was my idea. Brody didn't say anything. He had nothing to do with this."

Thomson turned back toward her, bulging eyes taking in her fingers on his skin. "No? You sure about that?"

"Yes, sir. Absolutely, and if I have offended you,

I apologize." Oh, what had she done? Her heart stuttered wildly.

He shook her off. "I don't need some highbrow librarian looking down on me and my kid. I take care of my own."

"Completely understood. No one is making judgments, Mr. Thomson." But she had. So had Hayden. "I wanted to be friendly in case—"

He shoved the box toward her. "Take your charity to someone else."

"But, sir, I—"

He slammed the door in her face.

WITH A CREEPING sense of déjà vu, Hayden stared at the shadow box of keepsakes hanging above a mahogany credenza in the foyer of Peach Orchard Inn. All the items, according to the caption, had been found during the refurbishing of the antebellum inn and dated back before 1900.

A silver spoon. A faded leather-bound journal next to a book of sheet music. Buttons and coins and a brooch with a missing jewel. A medicine bottle with stopper intact. But it was the pocket watch that gave Hayden pause, that stirred the hair on the back of his neck and that seemed eerily familiar.

He squinted to read the inscription, a fine, flowing script engraved on aged silver.

Bingo, the blue merle shepherd, wandered in, sniffed Hayden's shoes and collapsed with a sigh on the heart pine flooring. Hayden bent down to scratch the patient ears.

He'd had a dog once long ago, a slick black stray

that had followed him everywhere and loved him un-
conditionally. He'd stolen to feed that dog.

Hayden rubbed a weary hand over his face. Dora
Lee had called again last night. The voice mail still
lingered on his phone, unanswered, haunting him, a
reminder that he was a liar and a fraud and a worthless excuse for a son.

He normally didn't think about those things, about
the past he'd left behind or the life he'd fabricated. He
blamed the inn and the crazy dreams, the stubborn
book proposal and the surrounding woods and creeks
and mountains that reminded him too much of home.

Perhaps he'd made a mistake in coming to rural
Tennessee to write. He'd been off balance since the
night he'd arrived.

The very truth of his existence required he remain
aloof from places and people, but this place and these
people wouldn't let him. It scared him. Though he'd
learned to sustain fear like an old friend, this fear was
different. Honey Ridge was different. It both soothed
and unsettled.

"Intriguing, isn't it?" a cultured voice asked.

He straightened to find Julia at the base of the staircase. The blonde innkeeper looked cool and refined
even with a load of towels in her arms.

"Very. To think these items survived more than a
hundred and fifty years." He pointed. "The watch in-
terests me most. I can't quite make out the engraving."

She came up beside him to look in at the memora-
bilia of former residents' lives. Peaches, the prevailing
scent of the inn, clung to her.

"The inscription says, 'Forever and always, I will
love you.' Incredibly romantic, I think."

A chill ran through him, as if a ghost had trailed icy fingers up his spine. Last night's dream flickered behind his eyes.

He swallowed, stunned. "Thaddeus."

Julia cocked her head. "I'm sorry?"

Hayden shook away the cobwebs of the dream. He didn't want her to think he was crazy, though he was beginning to wonder if his greatest fear had begun its insidious work, if his mother's genes had finally come to life and even now ate away at the only thing of value he possessed. "Who owned it? Do you know?"

She shook her head. "Eli found the watch, along with some of the buttons and coins, buried in the backyard when he was excavating for Michael's garden. An antique appraiser confirmed it dates back to the 1800s. Perhaps one of the early owners of Peach Orchard Farm lost it there."

"Who were they?" With dread as strong as the need to know, he waited, suspecting before she spoke that he would not like her answer.

"The original owners were the Portland family. We've found letters and artifacts from Edgar and his wife, Charlotte, and his sisters, Josie and Patience, along with others. Every time we renovate something, we find more."

The hairs stood on the back of Hayden's neck. Familiar names, but all of them were figments of his imagination. They were dream people.

Yet, according to Julia, they weren't.

He cleared a throat gone powder dry. "Interesting."

The telephone jangled, and Julia hurried to answer, leaving him reeling from the news that his dream people were real. And if they were, this watch could very well have belonged to Thaddeus Eriksson.

But how would a novelist from the mountains of Kentucky know any of that?

He was pondering the bizarre turn of events when a knock sounded behind him. He turned to see Carrie through the front glass and suffered an overwhelming desire to tell her about the crazy dreams.

Carrie stepped inside, a frown between her eyebrows. He must have looked as shell-shocked as he felt because she said, "Are you all right?"

Hayden couldn't tell her. She'd think he was losing his grip on reality. And he feared she might be right.

He forced a smile. "Perfect. And yourself?"

Her face was glum. "Not so perfect."

In dark jeans and a fitted yellow shirt, she looked as beautiful as a daffodil in spring.

"What's wrong?"

"Brody."

He let the dreams go for now. The present was more pressing. He could go crazy later.

"Did something happen?"

"I think I messed up." She blinked at him, all big brown eyes and worry lines.

He touched her arm. A light touch that only meant empathy, but it shimmied up his sleeve and into his chest, easing him somehow. "Come in and tell me what happened before you chew your bottom lip off."

"Oh!" Her hand went to her mouth. Then she laughed a little and lightened his mood. The problem couldn't be too severe if she could laugh. The kid was okay. He had to be.

"Want some coffee?" he asked. "I'm a pretty fair

barista, and I happen to be friendly with a former professional."

"I'd rather have some of Julia's peach tea if she's made any."

Julia stuck her head into the parlor, her gaze bouncing from Hayden to Carrie. "I thought that was your blue Bug out there. Are you looking for me or Valery?"

Carrie shook her head and pointed. "Hayden."

Julia's warm hostess smile radiated at both of them. "He told me you'd been introducing him around. Well, help yourself in the kitchen. Fresh tea in the pitcher, and you know where the coffee carafes are." She started to leave and then popped back in. "Oh, I was going to call you later. What are you doing tomorrow after church?"

"The usual." Carrie made a cute face as if Julia knew exactly what she meant.

"Good. I talked to your sisters. All of us are getting together tomorrow afternoon to pick out flowers and colors and such for the wedding."

Carrie's face lit up. "You've set a date?"

"December 14."

Carrie ticked the months off her fingers. "Julia, that's less than three months!"

The innkeeper didn't seem the least rushed. "We're not getting too elaborate. Already booked the venue." She looked lovingly around the inn. "Since I own the perfect place for a wedding, that part was easy. So, we have plenty of time for decorations, cake and all the rest."

"I'm really happy for you, Julia. Eli's a great guy."

"Isn't he? You'll be here, then? To help make plans?"

"Nikki and Bailey are the mavens of fancy events,

flowers and fluff, but I'll do whatever you want. Happy to take part."

"Tomorrow at one." With a jaunty wave, Julia disappeared again.

Once they were alone, Hayden pointed toward the parlor. "Sit. I'll get the drinks."

"Let me help. We can talk as we work." A tiny smile pierced the worry lines around her mouth. "Just like at Starbucks."

While he primed the coffeemaker, she relayed the visit to Brody's house.

"I realize now that going there with boxed groceries was a mistake. I insulted the man, and I'm afraid I made things worse for Brody." Taking a glass from the cabinet, she turned to lean on the counter. "His little face was as white as new paper."

"Do you think Thomson will hurt him?" Hayden's whole body tensed. He wanted to drive into Honey Ridge now and squeeze the truth out of Clint Thomson.

"I don't know. I did my best to convince him that the boxes of food were my idea alone and that Brody hadn't told me anything."

A knot formed in Hayden's belly. He put the lid on the French press and set the timer before taking his own spot against the opposite counter to face her.

"Brody's talked to me a little."

Her eyes grew wider. "What did he say?"

Hayden held up a hand. "First, let me be clear about what he *didn't* say. In fact, he was guarded and careful not to say his father hits him, but he admitted Thomson gets mad and yells a lot. According to Brody, he says mean things, especially when he's drunk."

"How did you get him to tell you that?"

"I'm a nosy writer. I pry." And he knew which buttons to push, when to push and when to back off. He knew the way of kids with secrets. "He was showing me around Second Street, and we passed the bar." He glowered at the coffeemaker, hurrying it up while remembering the hurt on Brody's face. "Thomson gets drunk every Friday night and stays that way pretty much all weekend."

Carrie's face was stricken. "Oh, Hayden. The night he was on Julia's porch during the thunderstorm was a Friday."

He was tempted to touch her again, to reassure her, though he had no reassurances to offer.

"Whether Brody is being hit or not, and even if the refrigerator is full, his home life isn't a good place."

"Being drunk in your own house isn't a crime."

It was in his book. Especially when a child was involved. A man with serious mother issues understood the damage emotional and psychological abuse could do. Any kind of abuse. He'd studied it. He'd lived it. He didn't go swimming because of it.

"He agreed to let Brody spend time with you, and he's already coming and going as he pleases," he said. "You've given Brody a way out of the house safely."

"You're still thinking about what the twins said."

"Can't get it off my mind. No matter if it's writer's curiosity, I'm poking around. Thomson's a creep even if didn't kill his wife."

"He didn't seem to care at all where Brody goes as long as he isn't a bother." Her shoulders slumped. "I feel like such a failure."

"You were trying to do a good thing, and you *did* receive permission for us to hang out with him. That's a big score." The timer dinged. Hayden pressed the plunger and poured himself a steaming cup, the smell alone worth the time and effort.

Carrie exhaled a long sigh. "I'm glad I drove out to talk to you."

"Even if I think murderous thoughts?"

She rolled her eyes. "You're not so bad. You listen *and* you make a good cup of coffee."

He toasted her with the bold brew. "Glad to be of service."

In truth, he was glad she was here. She kept him from thinking too much about the watch and the man who had worn it. Carrie was a ray of sun in his darkness.

He frowned, troubled by the random, needy thought. He'd worked hard to never need anyone again.

Suddenly, the coffee tasted bitter on his tongue.

What was happening to him? What was this place doing to him?

"I'm going to invite him to a family gathering," Carrie said, interrupting his troubled thoughts. "We're having a cookout for Dad's birthday. An afternoon of food, family and fun, Honey Ridge style, that I think will be good for Brody." She dropped her gaze to the condensation gathered on her glass. "Would you like to come? We'd love to have you there, and I'm sure Brody would be more comfortable. Plus, you might pry some more background on Penny Thomson from my brother."

A zing of anticipation shot through him. He studied it, worried over it before closing the sweet emotion carefully behind the door of caution.

A desire to spend time with an interesting woman

was normally not an issue, but Carrie Riley came from a close-knit family in a small town. She was a sweetness-and-light kind of girl who deserved more than a writer of darkness could offer. He'd go, but he'd have to be careful.

BRODY'S HANDS TREMBLED as he opened the shoe box, lifted Max out and held the little lizard against his cheek.

For once Max was calm as Brody stroked a finger down his slick, lined back.

"It's okay, Max," he whispered. "It's okay."

He hoped he wasn't lying.

The old man had been really mad when Miss Carrie stopped by with the box of food. Why had she done that?

As still as possible, he listened hard for any sound that indicated his father had returned. He'd stormed out not long after letting Brody know exactly how unhappy he was with the nosy librarian.

No stupid whelp of a dog in heat was going to shame Clint Thomson. That was what the old man had said. He worked like a horse to make a good living and if that wasn't enough for Brody, he could hit the road like his mother had.

Brody sniffed, long and shaky. Someday he would. He'd pack Max and his clothes and hit the road. He'd find his mama. And she'd kiss him and smooth his hair and tell him how smart he was. She'd never, ever cuss him and call him ugly names.

The old man had laughed, that mean laugh that smelled like whiskey and made Brody's stomach sick. He'd reminded Brody for about the millionth time that his own mama hadn't wanted him, that she'd preferred the company of other men.

He hated when the old man talked like that because he had no defense and yet he wanted to defend his mother.

His eyes stung as he eased Max onto the floor, letting him race around the room in the fits and starts that usually made Brody smile. The mean words cut him and played over and over inside his head.

He rubbed his forearm across his face, still shaking.

The old man probably wouldn't be back until late. He'd have peace and quiet now. Maybe Brody wouldn't sleep in the hideout again tonight. The bunny was mending. He'd be fine until tomorrow.

He thought of Miss Carrie and how nice she'd been to worry about him. Hayden, too. He wished they'd been his parents, though he didn't think they were girlfriend and boyfriend or anything as mushy as that. They were friends, and the old man had said he didn't care if Brody hung out with them as long as he didn't go whining and begging. Well, that's not exactly what he'd said. He'd said he didn't care what Brody did as long he didn't drag the Thomson name through the mud the way his mama had.

When his father got like that, Brody always wanted to ask about her. Where had she gone? Why had she left? Why didn't she call or write or come for a visit?

But he didn't. Some things were too scary to know.

CHAPTER SIXTEEN

SUNDAY AFTERNOON, THE family parlor of Peach Orchard Inn was an explosion of sample books, fabrics and female chatter. Julia's mother, Connie Griffin, fluttered around with a wedding veil in each hand while Julia and Bailey had their heads together over a bridal book Nikki had brought from the boutique. Valery had disappeared to somewhere a long time ago with the promise to "be right back."

After two hours of lists, menus, colors and flowers, Carrie needed a break, too. She slipped out of the room and, smiling a little because no one would even notice she was gone, headed for the kitchen.

She'd be more use with a tea tray and cookies in hand than being asked if a lace veil was preferable to a garland. She had an opinion, but really, wasn't Julia's the only one that mattered?

Eli, she noticed, had made himself scarce by taking Alex to play in the city park with Bailey's sons.

There were four other guests at Peach Orchard Inn this weekend besides Hayden, but they were all out and about enjoying the fading days of summer.

Carrie wound through the guest parlor toward the kitchen, but movement caught her eye in the small library Julia used as an office.

"Valery?" She stepped in as Julia's sister lowered a

bottle of whiskey from her lips. Not a glass. The whole bottle. A fifth.

Valery turned defiant eyes in her direction. She held out the bottle. "Want to join me?"

Carrie shook her head. "I wondered where you went."

"Yeah, well, now you know." Val's laugh seemed brittle. "All that sweet and gooey wedding stuff is enough to drive anyone to drink."

Carrie was no expert, but from the glassy look in Val's eyes, she suspected she'd been in here with Jack Daniel's the whole time.

"I know what you mean."

"Join me, then. We'll celebrate the upcoming nuptials and the joy of remaining miserably single in this one-horse town."

Carrie shook her head. "I don't do so well with the hard stuff."

Valery's expression hardened. "Oh, don't be a Goody Two-shoes."

When Carrie shook her head again, Valery's nostrils flared. "I swear your sister is right. You're as much fun as dental floss."

Carrie blinked; her mouth dropped open at the uncharacteristically rude remark. Her sister had said that about her?

The hurt must have showed, because Valery's posture changed. She set the bottle on Julia's tidy desk, shoulders slumped and said, "Oh, honey, I'm sorry. I'm stupid sometimes." Her words slurred. "Stupid and worthless."

"Don't say that."

"Why not? It's what you're thinking. It's what everyone thinks about that *youngest* Griffin sister." She shoved her long dark hair out of her face. Her eyes welled with tears, and her beautiful mouth quivered. "Isn't that what they say? Valery is the trashy, worthless Griffin girl."

Carrie was out of her element. There was clearly more going on here than she understood. Valery was drunker than she'd been the night of the storm, and she'd been maudlin and crying then.

"Valery," she said, touching her friend's arm. "What's going on? Are you okay? Is there a problem I can help you with?"

Valery jerked back and slashed her hands across her tear-streaked cheeks. "The only problem I have is people sticking their noses in my business. Why couldn't you stay in the parlor where you belong? Why'd you have to come in here poking around? Your mama taught you better."

"Our mamas taught us a lot of good things, Valery," she said softly. "I want to help."

"I don't need your help, Carrie." Valery gave a bitter laugh. "Trust me—I get enough crap from Julia."

This conversation was not going to get better, not as long as Valery was intoxicated.

"I'll go, then, and leave you alone." She turned as if to leave.

Valery's voice stopped her, turned her around. "Don't turn up your prissy nose at me, Carrie Riley. You're no better than I am. You're…" She sniffed, her face the picture of dejection, her red mouth pulled down. "We used to be friends." And then pitifully, "Didn't we used to be friends?"

Carrie twisted her hands together, afraid of saying

the wrong thing. "We still are, Val, and that's why I'm worried."

Valery reached for the whiskey bottle, took another long drink, shuddered and pressed a hand to her lips. "Nothing to worry 'bout. I'm celebrating. Can't a girl celebrate a happy occasion?"

Getting drunk by herself on a Sunday afternoon while her sister was in the other room choosing between poinsettias and roses seemed more self-destructive than celebratory. "You don't seem very happy."

Valery's snort was harsh. "What's not to be happy about? I live in my sister's house. Oh, sure, I own a third, but trust me, this is Julia's inn. *I* work for *her*. She's marrying a terrific man. A rich man, if you didn't know. Julia has it all, and I don't have a frigging thing."

A look of horror crossed Valery's face. She slapped a hand to her mouth. "What's wrong with me?" She lurched toward Carrie, face white. "I am such a loser. Please, please, don't repeat that. It's the booze talking. I only meant to have one drink. One drink to settle my nerves."

Was Valery an alcoholic? Her beautiful, vivacious, talented friend who could snap her fingers and have any guy she wanted?

While she grappled to say something worthwhile, Valery rambled on.

"I love my sister. She's been through hell, and now she's finally happy again with a really sweet guy." The troubled brunette gripped Carrie's arm. "Don't breathe a word of this to anybody. I won't ruin this for her. Promise me."

Carrie knew the rule of families like theirs, especially families in Honey Ridge. They took care of their own dirty laundry, hid their problems under the bed or locked them away in closets and pretended the bad things didn't happen. Julia knew Valery sometimes drank too much. Apparently, more often than anyone else realized, but family issues were no one else's business. Not Carrie's. Not anyone's.

Pity welling, she said the only thing she could. "I won't say anything."

Valery began to cry and turned her back. Carrie touched her shaking shoulder in comfort, but her friend shook her off. "Go away, Carrie. Just go."

With a lump in her chest, Carrie left the library and refreshments forgotten, went outside. She needed air. She needed to think.

She and Valery had hung out in high school before Val discovered boys and left Carrie with her books. They'd been friends. Still were, but time and different styles had put a gulf between them. A far greater gulf than she'd realized until today.

Yesterday's fiasco with Mr. Thomson should have taught her to keep her nose to herself.

But she cared.

That was the problem with being Carrie Riley. She cared, but when faced with trouble, she got all shaky and ran away. Her sisters would never have walked out. They would have known what to do.

But she was Carrie, the sister who was as exciting as dental floss.

Mulling, worried, she walked out through the kitchen. The peach orchard spread in the distance, dormant now until spring, when the pink blossoms filled the air with scent and beauty.

At the back of the house was Michael's garden, a

memorial of sorts to Julia's abducted son created by Eli Donovan in a labor of love that told the whole town he'd fallen for the innkeeper.

Theirs was a bittersweet story of grief and healing.

But what had happened to Valery? How had she come to this?

The bitterness had shocked Carrie more than the drinking. The Griffin girls had always seemed so together.

Worried, pensive, she found a quiet place on the grass where she could see the comforting hills rising around Honey Ridge, kicked off her shoes and sat down.

When had life become so complicated?

HAYDEN SHUT THE LAPTOP, frustrated at the snail's pace of this new project. He'd dumped an entire chapter and started fresh again.

Killing people for a living was murder in more ways than one.

He'd holed up in his guest room after a buffet lunch at Miss Milly's Café with Brody. Chicken and dumplings with all the fixings.

The boy had ambled along the road, hands deep in his pockets, a shoe box under one arm, looking as if he carried the weight of the world when Hayden drove past. He'd stopped, pushed open the door and said, "Get in."

Brody hadn't questioned the command. He'd been going fishing he claimed, but he'd had no fishing gear. Showing Hayden his lizard, he'd grown animated. Hayden had asked him about the hideout, and they'd talked of the rabbit and wounded creatures and night noises.

The boy's affection and care for animals reminded Hayden painfully of the stray black dog.

The mulberry walls of the B and B pressed in. He'd been planning to explore the old gristmill across the road as much to assure himself that it was not the mill in his dreams as to generate a book idea.

This was as good a time as any.

He jogged down the stairs, hopping over the bloodred squeaker.

Maybe he'd kill somebody on that step. Someone like Clint Thomson.

The thought of Penny Thomson flashed through his head. Where was the woman? Dead? Hiding?

The young couple staying in the Blueberry Room passed him on the stairs.

"I picked up a copy of your new book," the man said. "Would you sign it for me?"

"Be happy to."

The woman beamed. "We'll bring it down to breakfast in the morning."

They moved on up the stairs, heads together, murmuring to each other, and Hayden suffered a pang of loneliness, of being one in a world of couples and family. His thoughts drifted to Carrie. She was here somewhere at the inn, holed up with the other women in a wedding frenzy.

He veered into the long hallway that bisected the house, intending to go out the front way until he spotted her in the backyard.

She sat on the lawn in the afternoon shade, a vision of quiet and peace, with her knees pulled to her chest, blue floral dress demurely tugged to her ankles. She'd kicked off a pair of tan flats to dig her toes into the lush green grass. The slender ankle bracelet glinted in the sunlight.

She was a picture, a scene for a movie or a book. But not the kind he wrote.

He stepped out onto the veranda, its timeworn planks painted the blue of yesteryear, and crossed the expanse of green between himself and the woman who captured his interest. A sugar maple with a trunk the girth of an elephant dappled the ground in shades of gold and shadow.

When he drew close, Carrie looked up.

He went to his haunches beside her.

"I thought you were plotting a wedding with the other women."

"Plotting." She turned her head toward him and smiled. A pearl earring winked at him. "Is that how you view marriage? As a plot?"

The topic made him melancholy, pinched a spot in the center of his chest, but he put on a good front by teasing, "Weddings are the ultimate diabolical plot. The poor groom is trussed up in a monkey suit on display for all the world to learn that he can't dance. Then he stutters over the vows and forgets the bride's name, forever damned."

Instead of the expected laugh, she gazed at him mildly, curiously, with that half smile lingering around her softly bowed mouth. "Why aren't you married, Hayden?"

The question didn't bother him. He'd been asked before. "Never wanted to be."

She picked at a piece of grass. "That diabolical plot thing?"

"Exactly." He folded his body and sat down beside her, ankles crossed, knees up to match hers. He brushed her arm as he plucked a piece of bluestem; the grass reminded him poignantly of Kentucky. "So why aren't you in there with them?"

She hesitated, picking at the grass. Something troubled her. He felt her worry as sure as he felt a pleasant hum of attraction.

"I'm not good at that sort of thing, and after a while…" She lifted a shoulder, the strap of her sundress pressing into creamy white skin that looked as soft as down.

"You needed some fresh air."

She nodded, and again he got the feeling that she was worried. "Weddings can be diabolical for a woman like me, too."

But that wasn't the only thing bothering her. He was intuitive enough to read conflict in her brown eyes.

"Why aren't *you* married?" he asked, really wanting to know.

"Same reason as you, I suppose." She shook her head. "No. That's not true. I wanted to get married, to have a terrific husband to keep the storms away and send me gardenias on my birthday." The single dimple returned, poking fun at her ambition, and he found it endearing.

"Why didn't you?"

"It just never happened. The right guy never came along."

"No one special?"

"No."

"I don't believe you."

She turned her face toward him, the slope of cheekbone elegant and appealing. He resisted the urge to trace the shape with his finger.

"Why not?"

"If you're fishing for a compliment, you have it."

"I wasn't." But she looked pleased, softened by his words.

She was a uniquely beautiful woman. Didn't she know that?

He tickled her arm with the grass. "Tell me."

"No." She gave a light laugh as if she couldn't believe he was serious.

"Did he break your heart?"

"I'm not sure."

"Mysterious." He tickled her again. "Should I ask one of your sisters? Or the good old boys?"

"Don't you dare. I've already lived down enough rumors without starting them up again."

He grew serious. She'd been hurt, and the truth of that hurt him, too. "He *did* break your heart."

For a moment, her brown eyes clouded and her throat worked. She glanced away and back again but didn't quite meet his gaze.

Rumors, she'd said, an indicator of something colossal.

She shrugged off the heartache, but the action didn't convince him. "It's no big deal. A college guy I was dating. My sister came to visit. He took one look at Nikki, and I was out like yesterday's newspaper."

Nothing colossal in that. His sharp second sense didn't believe this was *the* event that had broken her heart and made her skittish. "What a jerk."

"Not really. My sisters, I'm sure you've noticed, are irresistible. The man didn't stand a chance."

"You're *not* yesterday's newspaper." Hayden brushed a knuckle over her arm.

"And you're a nice man, Hayden Winters." She pointed a finger. "A man who had better swear never to use that pathetic tale in a book."

"I promise."

She rose up on her knees and thrust out a crooked finger. "Pinkie swear."

He crooked his much larger pinkie and hooked it with her smaller one. "Pinkie swear. I will never use that in a book. At least not with your name."

"Hayden!" She laughed and whacked his arm. "A pinkie swear is serious business. God will get you if you break a pinkie swear. And I will hunt you down and do something…terrible. Something…"

He rubbed his arm, pretending pain while he grinned at her. "Diabolical?"

"Yes!" She whacked at him again for good measure, and this time he caught her hand and held on. He liked his barefoot librarian and contemplated the next couple of months with her. And he *would* have her company, though her comments about marriage lodged uncomfortably beneath his breastbone.

Carrie was the marrying kind.

The guy who'd broken her heart was a fool. There was more, a lot more than a college boy who'd dropped her for her sister. He recognized avoidance when he saw it because he did it himself all too often.

"You want to tell me what's really bothering you?" he asked gently. "About the man who caused the rumors."

Her mouth opened in a mini-gasp of surprise. "No."

He gently prodded her foot with the tip of his shoe. "More than a pinkie swear, Carrie. I'm sorry for whatever happened. You're a kind and beautiful woman. Any man that didn't see that didn't deserve you."

She looked at him for a long, considering moment and must have read the genuine empathy and caring in his eyes.

"There *was* someone. I thought we'd get married and have a wonderful life together. But he turned out to be…different than I believed."

And he'd damaged her confidence, left her believing she was not as special in her own right as her sisters.

"Want to talk about it?"

She looked out at the barren peach orchard and sighed. "No."

"Is that why you're sitting out here by yourself? Memories? Wishing it was you and the brainless idiot planning a wedding?"

Her lips curved. "No."

"But you're out here alone and maybe a tad depressed for some reason."

He waited her out, curiosity too strong for him to play the Southern gentleman, a role he embraced when the need suited, though he'd never actually be one. Breeding, as they said, prevailed.

"I have a friend who is in trouble," she said finally, softly. "At least I think she is, and I don't know how to help her."

"Anything I can do?"

"I don't know how you could. She's a friend, Hayden. We've been friends since we were kids."

"Valery or Julia?" When she blinked at him, he

shrugged. "You're here with the two of them. Easy analysis that it's one or the other."

"I promised not to tell."

"You didn't. I guessed. And if my radar is correct, Julia is a happy woman. Valery isn't."

She dropped her hands from her knees and shifted toward him. "We used to be close. We had sleepovers, hung out and even took dance together."

"I can see Valery as a dancer. The way she moves is…musical."

Carrie nodded her agreement. "In high school, she was so good people assumed she'd end up on Broadway or in Vegas. She was on the dance team, danced in local theater and some plays in Knoxville and Chattanooga. Her parents even sent her to New York for a year of dance school."

"What happened?"

"I don't know. Our lives went different directions. I went to college and lost touch for a while."

"And met the brainless idiot."

She smiled. "Valery…changed."

"She didn't continue her dance?"

"I heard once that she might open her own studio here in Honey Ridge, but she never did. Today I realized she's really hurting about something. Not that she'd tell me."

"Any guesses?"

"None. But she drinks too much."

"I've noticed." When she looked up, brown eyes swimming with sadness, he tilted his head. "Especially late in the evenings after the guests settle."

"Every guest except you."

"I keep strange hours. Noticing things makes me a better writer."

"I wish there was something I could do for her."

He had little sympathy for the innkeeper. Addictions infuriated him. All she had to do was put down the booze, but, like Dora Lee, she chose herself over others. The ultimate selfishness.

"Her family knows. The only thing you can do is continue to be her friend."

Exactly as he continued being Dora Lee's son, no matter how badly he wanted to forget her. Dad would have expected him to watch over his mother.

"You're right. I know. It's just—" She lifted a hand to her forehead. "Don't tell anyone we talked about this. Please."

Having her confidence made him feel close to her. "You have more than a pinkie promise on that."

She glanced up, serious. "You're a good listener."

He didn't tell her that listening was a skill he'd honed intentionally. When he listened, he wasn't talking and in danger of revealing too much.

"Come on." He leaped to his feet and tugged her up. "Walk with me."

Using him for balance, she slipped into her flats. "I should let them know."

"Text them."

"My cell's in the house with my purse."

"Will they send out the hounds?"

"I doubt they'll even miss me."

"Don't worry, then. We won't go far. I want to explore that abandoned mill across the road."

"Are you scared to go in alone?" she teased. "The mill *is* kind of spooky."

"Something like that." He tugged her along, across the front lawn past the orchard and down the long road flanked by whispering trees that leaned close to listen and gossip.

The hum of late summer sounded around them. An orange-and-black butterfly—a swallowtail, he thought—dipped and danced as if leading the way across the main road and down a trail nearly obliterated by overgrown bushes and kudzu vines.

"What's that?" He pointed to a shaft of red berries growing along the trail.

"Jack-in-the-pulpit. The berries are poisonous."

"To humans?"

She rolled her eyes. "Yes, Mr. Murder and Mayhem, but I don't know how potent. When I was a kid, Daddy took us on nature hikes and pointed out the poisonous berries so we didn't eat them and get sick."

"Good dad."

"The best."

"What's he do?"

"Electrician. He rewired the inn when Julia and Valery first bought it." A soft breeze fluttered a wispy lock of hair around her cheek. "What about your dad? You never say much about family."

The question caught him off guard. It shouldn't have. He was normally more careful than to travel down conversational roads that lead to killer dead ends. Carrie's natural manner made talking too easy. He'd have to tread more carefully with her.

"He died when I was small."

Sympathetic eyes met his. "I'm so sorry. That must have been awful for you."

He shrugged, but his chest burned. His father's

death had opened up an ugly Pandora's box from which he'd almost not escaped. *Awful* didn't begin to describe losing his daddy.

Before she could dig deeper and ask more questions he didn't want to answer, he looked toward the west, across the road toward the abandoned gristmill. "Do you know who owns the mill?"

"It used to be part of Peach Orchard Farm but not anymore. The place has been abandoned as long as I can remember. I don't know if it belongs to anyone." Her face wrinkled up. "But I guess someone has to hold the title. Long-lost heirs maybe?"

Though sadly neglected, the abandoned mill had charm. Surrounded by lush overgrown plants, the wood and natural rock structure perched on the edge of a creek with a clear, rocky bottom and a small frothy waterfall. The property intrigued him, especially given the dreams he'd been having.

"Then they won't mind if we explore?"

"This place gets explored all the time. Kids trying to scare each other, hikers, picnickers, ghost hunters."

"Ghost hunters? Hmm."

She gave a tiny squeak. "Don't try to scare me in there."

"Would I do that?" he asked with such studied innocence that Carrie bumped his shoulder with hers.

"Proceed with caution," she said.

In a dangerous tone, he warned, "And a machete."

"Hayden!" She shrank back, and he laughed, pleased to see her teasing again.

The dilapidated building was gray with age. Grass grew into the cracks left by missing boards. The waterwheel stood silent and still, the sluice box filled with leaves, dirt and broken limbs. The heavy wooden doors leading into the main section of the three-story structure hung on one hinge, unlocked.

Carrie shuddered as they stepped inside the dim confines of the once-productive mill. "I understand where the ghost stories get started."

"See what I mean about the machete?" he asked and laughed again when she made a mean face at him. "Watch your step here."

He assisted her over a gap in the floor.

"Sure you want to explore this place?" Cautiously, she gazed around. "The whole structure looks pretty shaky. Not to mention creepy."

He gave his best evil eyebrow pump. "Absolutely."

Old equipment he couldn't identify lay about, rusted and broken. A series of interesting cupboards rose through the ceiling into the upper floor, and the remnants of the horizontal grinding wheel, a giant of a thing on a raised dais, took up one end of the room. Much of the interior had been stripped over the years, and only a few damaged remnants of the past remained. A small room, probably once an office, opened to the left, rickety stairs to the right and, directly in front of them, a dirt-coated window looked out at the creek.

An eerie sensation crept over Hayden, slow and spidery and suggestive. He imagined Abram trotting down those steps and Thaddeus standing in the door of the little office, meal flour coating his white apron and dark hair.

Was this the gristmill he'd dreamed about? Had seeing the mill from afar somehow stirred his imagination and sent his subconscious into overdrive?

He'd feel saner if that was the case.

But Thaddeus had been a real person, not a figment of a writer's dreams. And how could Hayden possibly know about a man who'd lived nearly 150 years ago?

"I wonder what's through that door," Carrie said.

Hayden barely glanced before answering. "The loading dock and storehouse."

She looked at him quizzically. "You sound so positive. Have you been here before?"

Blood pounded in his temples. "Only a guess."

But he knew. Exactly as he knew how bolting machines had once stretched in long canvas conveyers across one end of the upstairs.

No, that was crazy thinking. Crazy.

He sucked in a troubled breath of musty air, trembling inside. *Crazy* was the scariest word he knew.

What was happening to his mind?

CHAPTER SEVENTEEN

Here lies an honest miller and that is Strange.
                    —Epitaph in Essex churchyard

1867

JOSIE HATED TO SWEAT, but running the corn sheller at the mill was far cooler than working in the field, and those had been her choices that morning.

She jabbed another ear of Bernard Stinson's corn into the sheller and cranked. Her dress was covered in specks of yellow, and her lips and throat were parched from the dust. She looked a mess, no doubt, and if Thaddeus said one word, she'd chuck a corncob at him.

He was running the grinding wheels, his nose to the grindstone as he carefully monitored the process to be certain the grain was properly ground without burning. The rumble and whir of the stones ceased, and Josie glanced down the long length of the building to where Thad bent over the enormous bedstone.

Oscar and Abram were somewhere upstairs. Occasionally she heard the thump and drag of something heavy, probably sacks of meal or corn or chicken feed. She wouldn't be surprised if Oscar was ogling her backside through the cracks in the floorboards, but if she caught him, she'd poke his eye out with a dry corncob.

In the days since his arrival, Abram had established himself as a quiet, steady laborer both on the farm and with Thaddeus at the mill. As a former blacksmith apprentice, he and Thad repaired pulleys and cogs and kept the machinery running. The pair had even lifted the stones for dressing—an onerous, dangerous task.

She hoped the man would stay. He made the load lighter for the rest of them. But so many of the former slaves preferred to ramble, seeking greener pastures.

She cranked the sheller, heard the corn hit the wooden bin, but her attention remained on Thaddeus. Strong shoulder muscles bulged as he made adjustments to the grindstone and ran his fingers through the fine cornmeal in the trough.

"Mercy, I'm hot." Josie dropped the crank handle and went to the water bucket. After a long drink, she filled the dipper and carried it to Thad.

"You look thirsty."

He grinned, his face moist with sweat and pale with meal as he swigged deeply from the dipper. "Be careful, Miss Josie. Drinking from the same dipper as a Yankee might poison you."

"I drank first," she said. "Perhaps I'll poison you."

His grin widened, a devilish glint in his eyes. "You're looking pretty today."

She curtsied. Corn tumbled from the folds of her skirt. She looked hideous and knew it. *The scoundrel.* "You, sir, are a barbarian with no manners."

He laughed. She wanted to do the same but was too stubborn to let him know how stimulating she found their conversations. Instead, she took the dipper and flounced back to the sheller.

JOSIE PORTLAND SURPRISED HIM. He'd thought her vain as well as deeply hostile toward his kind and just about anyone else who was different.

Yet she was here again today shelling corn for the grinder. Will teased that she trekked across the fields only to torment and admire the millwright, a jest that made Thad feel both uncomfortable and pleased. The days seemed shorter when Josie was in the building.

His own thoughts troubled him. Was he being disloyal to Amelia to be in constant thought about another woman? Especially one that claimed to despise the very air he breathed.

Yet she didn't despise him. He'd daresay she liked him.

Thoughtful, he went out to the waterwheel to adjust the sluice gate. Did he want her to like him?

Abram joined him. Thad tensed. Abram was not a complainer, but his dark, nervous eyes and solemn frown indicated that something was wrong. Thad prayed the man was not about to leave Honey Ridge. Though the thought was selfish, given Abram's desire to find his family, Thad trusted and needed the hardworking freedman.

"Mr. Thad, sir. I got something I need to tell you."

Thad ran his arms through the flow of water, relishing the cool against his hot flesh. "You're not leaving us, are you, Abram?"

"No, sir. Not yet. Not unless you say so." He shifted on his worn boots and glanced toward the adjacent building. "Something's fretting me fierce. I got to tell you. Don't want to cause no trouble, though."

Relieved that Abram wasn't leaving, Thad turned to face him. Water dripped from his scarred arms. "Say it."

Again Abram glanced toward the doorway. Then, his voice low and covered by the splash and rumble of the waterwheel, he said, "Mr. Oscar, he don't measure the meal right. He got him a sack he fills for hisself and hides back. He tells the customers that's all the meal their corn made, but that ain't right. I measured Miz Cower's myself. Two hundred thirty pounds. He done gave her two hundred. Miz Cower, she got little chilren to feed and no man."

Thaddeus frowned, recalling Oscar's interest in the widow. "Was the two hundred before or after the miller's toll?"

"After, sir. I measured the mill's share like you showed me and sacked it for sale. Miz Cower shoulda got all two thirty."

"Maybe the man made a mistake."

"Yes, sir. Sure could have. Folks make mistakes." Abram rubbed thick fingers over his chin. "Mr. Oscar, he sure makes a lot of them."

Thad frowned, considering the implications. "You've seen him do this before?"

"Most every time when you or Mr. Will or the customer ain't watching."

Dread settled into the pit of Thad's stomach. The last thing he needed was trouble. Already many of the local farmers looked askance at a Union man running what most considered their gristmill. He'd known

Oscar had an eye for the ladies, but he hadn't expected him to be a thief.

"You did the right thing by bringing this to me, Abram. Don't say anything to Oscar. I'll keep a watch."

"Yes, sir." Abram started to turn and the paused. "Sir?"

"What is it?"

"Miss Lizzy, she come over yesterday for some grits." He glanced out at the tumbling falls as if searching for the right words amid the foaming waters. "He said some things to her."

The hackles stood up on Thad's neck. "What did he say?"

"Things a man ought not to say to a good woman like Miss Lizzy. First off, I thought maybe she liked him, too. They was standing real close, so I didn't hear all the words, but I heard her tell him to leave her be. He laughed and made a grab for her. Jerked her up kind of close. She gave him a push and then she hurried off real fast like as if he scared her." Abram's mouth worked, and when he spoke again his voice was deathly quiet. "I ain't never hit a white man—"

Fear shot through Thad. He put a hand to Abram's powerful upper arm. "Don't start now. They'd hang you. I'll take care of this. You have my word."

Abram held his gaze for several seconds as if determining his credibility. Then he nodded and headed back inside.

Thad stood at the waterwheel pondering. The clackety rumbling rhythm melded with the splash and roar of the falls. His insides churned, too, as he considered the best course of action. A hornets' nest of trouble had just burst open, and he was the man in charge.

He made his way back inside to the grindstones and settled in to finish his job. If what Abram said was true, he'd find out soon enough.

OPPORTUNITY KNOCKED THE next day when a farmer, his wife and four sons arrived to collect their ground corn. Thad pretended to be busy and sent Abram out to shut the sluice gate. He wanted the ex-slave as far away from suspicion as possible. Josie was bagging corncobs to take home to the hogs when Oscar strutted out to meet the farmer.

Thad quietly made his way up the stairs to the loft and stood inside the opened doorway out of sight. Voices drifted upward. He listened to the cordial exchanges and watched Oscar tote the white cotton sacks to the wagon. Seeing or hearing nothing out of the ordinary, Thad was about to turn away when the farmer's voice rose in protest.

Thad stepped into the opening and gazed down. Baker stood on the loading porch, while the woman and children waited in the wagon. Mrs. Baker appeared mildly concerned, and the children watched in open curiosity as Baker and the hired man talked.

"Look here, Baker." Oscar shoved a paper at the farmer. "Says right here how much your corn weighed. Take out the miller's share and this is what's left."

"Don't look right to me, Pitts." Baker lifted his hat and scratched behind his ear. "But I never was too good at figures. If you say that's all, I reckon I calculated wrong."

Oscar clapped him on the back. "We been doing business for years, Baker. Would Portland Mill cheat a good customer like you?"

"No, no, I reckon not."

Would Portland Mill cheat a good customer? That was the question Thad needed to answer.

He bounded down the stairs, past a startled Josie, who watched him nearly stumble over Tabby in his haste. He heard her giggle behind him but was in no mood to tease. If Oscar truly was shortchanging this customer, his cheating stopped now.

"Is there a problem with the order, Mr. Baker?" he asked as he stepped out onto the loading dock.

Baker glanced from Thad to Oscar and back again. "Well—"

Oscar gave Thad a cocky smirk. "Everything is fine, boss man. Go on back to your grindstones. Mr. Baker is all fixed up and ready to leave."

"Is that right?" Thad remained outwardly calm, casual but determined. If Pitts had nothing to hide, he shouldn't mind the interruption. "Mind if I have a look at your sale bill, Mr. Baker?"

"'Preciate it, Mr. Eriksson." Baker handed over the sales slip.

Oscar's confidence faltered. "Now, see here—"

Thad tuned him out as he studied over the figures. He'd measured the incoming grain himself and measured it again after grinding. At the figures before him, his heart dropped into his belly. He didn't need the conflict, but hardworking farmers trying to recover from years of war deserved fair treatment.

"I think Mr. Baker's short a sack, Oscar. Go ahead and get that for him."

Oscar shook his head, face darkening, feet planted firmly on the weathered boards. "He's not short."

"Everybody makes mistakes now and then." Thad

kept his voice cordial and controlled, though his insides tumbled like the waterwheel. "We wouldn't want good customers to leave with bad feelings. A sack of meal won't break us. Get it."

"But—"

He aimed a sharp, steady stare at the hired man. "*Now*, Pitts."

Jaw tight and face mottled, Pitts did as he was told while Thad carried on an easy conversation with the farmer about crops and weather and anything else he could think of. Let the man believe this was truly a onetime error. He didn't want word to circulate that Portland Grist Mill overcharged customers.

Seething and silent, Oscar returned and dumped the extra bag into the farmer's wagon, then stood back, meaty fists on his hips.

With a genial nod, Thad thanked the customer and waited until the loaded wagon was out of earshot before he turned on his hired hand.

"You intentionally held back, didn't you?"

"*Ppff.* I don't know what you're talking about."

Thad stared him down. Only thing he despised worse than a thief was a liar. "The truth, Pitts."

Oscar shrugged carelessly. "So what if I did? It's part of doing business. A miller takes a share."

"You're not the miller."

His eyes narrowed. "I've been here a lot longer than you, Eriksson. I got a right to that grain. Customers don't miss a little here and there, but the extra makes a big difference to me."

"How long have you been stealing from our customers?"

"Taking a share ain't stealing." The square jaw tightened. "It's part of doing business. Most folks don't even notice."

"Baker noticed."

"Old Baker's a skinflint. Probably counts the corn kernels."

Thad's blood hummed like a beehive, ready to burst loose in a hot swarm. He opened and closed his fists, drawing in a deep breath of composure. His mind had been made up long before he'd come down the stairs. He'd never liked Pitts, didn't like the way he ogled women or his insubordinate attitude, but he'd had no reason to fire him. Now he did.

"You're not needed here anymore, Pitts. Take your thieving ways and go home. Don't come back."

"You're firing me?" Oscar's eyes bugged, incredulous. "Over a handful of cornmeal?"

"A handful?"

The man broadened his stance, spreading his feet like an eager pugilist. His fists tightened at his side. "You can't run this mill without me."

Thaddeus braced himself. He didn't want to fight, but he wouldn't back down. "We'll manage."

"We? Gadsden ain't never here anymore." His beady eyes flickered toward the open doorway. Abram stood in the shadows. "You don't mean the likes of *him*."

"He's a free man and an *honest* one who's not afraid to earn his pay."

Oscar's voice rose. "You ain't hiring him over me."

"I will if he'll accept the job." The answer surprised him. He hadn't given a thought to who would take Oscar's position, but now that Abram came to mind, he warmed to the idea.

Fury reddened Oscar's face. "Gadsden will have

something to say about this. He's the boss of this out-fit. Not you."

"Then go on over and talk to him. Remember to tell him about the grain you stole from elderly neighbors, widows and friends. I'll be right behind you."

Pitts's mouth worked. Hatred shot out of his glare as potent as cannon fire.

"You'll pay for this, Eriksson." He hawked and spat, then wiped his hand across his lips. "You'll be sorry you ever messed with Oscar Pitts."

LONG AFTER PITTS stomped off down the road, dusk gathered along the banks of the creek and hovered like a thin gray curtain over the fields. Josie finished the last of the corn and, shoulders aching, went out to the creek to wash away the meal dust. Thaddeus was al-ready there, doing the same.

"You're going to get yourself killed." She'd over-heard the confrontation.

Water dripping from his face and hair, he whirled at her voice. "What?"

"Firing Oscar."

"He stole from Mr. Baker and no telling how many others."

"I know, but that won't keep you alive when word gets out that a Yankee fired a local, especially if you were serious about putting Abram in his place." She shuddered to think what stories Oscar would spread in Honey Ridge.

"Would *you* object to Abram working here? As a gainful employee in Pitts's position?"

Josie understood his meaning. Did she mind if the mill paid good money to a former slave when there were plenty of white men in Honey Ridge who could use the work? Folks wouldn't like it. "No. I wouldn't object. Abram's a hard worker."

In fact, she admired Thad's stand. Not that she'd tell him as much. She worried, too.

"Where is Abram anyway?" She looked back toward the darkened building and the bolted doors. "Already gone to the house?"

"Mmm-hmm." Thad ran his fingers through his hair. He had nice hair, sandy brown and tipped in sun gold. "I think maybe he's sweet on Lizzy."

"On our Lizzy?" She widened her eyes. "Well, I declare."

"He said something about helping her repair a table leg, but I think she's the reason he's not moved on in search of his family."

"Did he say anything to you? About being sweet on her, I mean."

"No, but he wasn't happy that Oscar had…upset her."

"Oscar?" Josie blinked, suddenly chilled. "What did he do?"

Thad told her about the incident.

"I've never liked that man. He—" Her cheeks heated. Should she be telling him this?

"What?" Thad's blue eyes flamed. "Has he bothered you? Touched you?"

"No, no, not like that, but he…stares and stands too close." The heat under her collar nearly roasted her. "He makes me uncomfortable, and I do not like to be alone with him."

"You won't have to be. We've seen the last of Oscar Pitts."

Josie hoped he was right. Oscar was not the kind of man to take insult lightly. And Thad had insulted him deeply.

She stuck her arms down into the cool creek and closed her eyes. "Oh, that feels wonderful. I am near to baking."

Sleeves rolled back, Thad did the same, splashing water onto his face and neck. She slid a glance toward him and her breath froze. Long, puckered scars ran from the backs of his hands up to his elbows.

"Thaddeus," she whispered and, before propriety stopped her, reached to touch the scars.

He jerked away and gripped his sleeve in an effort to cover the damaged skin. Josie put a hand on his, stopping him.

"What happened?" Her heart beat a strange, thick rhythm in her chest.

Thad glanced down at his arms, face grim. "A fire." *Burns. But from what?* "The war?"

He shook his head and swallowed, his throat working. "No."

Seeing his discomfort, a polite, well-bred woman like Charlotte or Patience would have let the topic end.

"How, Thaddeus? Tell me." She held his blue eyes with her green ones and saw the hurt and horror that lingered there.

He pushed down his sleeves and sighed as though he knew she was not the kind of woman to take silence for an answer. "A house fire."

"Yours?"

"Yes." His face worked and he rubbed a hand over his eyes.

"Something terrible happened, didn't it? Someone else was involved."

"My wife and daughter." He turned his back. A turtle slid into the creek.

She knew the rest before he told her. No man could look so utterly lost without having suffered beyond endurance.

"I couldn't save them." The words came out flat and emotionless as if he'd grieved so long and hard, he could not bear to go there again.

She moved in front of him, tender inside in a way that wasn't comfortable for Josie. She didn't like to feel tenderness. Tender blooms got crushed.

"You tried, Thad. You did everything you could." She knew that about him. As with the unpleasant situation concerning Oscar, Thad was not the kind of man who stepped away from the hard things.

He made a harsh sound. "They died, Josie. Trying didn't matter."

She had no words of consolation, so she took his arm, first one and then the other, and rolled up his sleeves again until the scars stretched between them. She wanted to skim her fingertips over the puckered evidence of his devotion, but her bravery in shunning propriety only went so far. Touching his skin would mean feeling something she couldn't allow.

"When Will said you'd been through a lot, I didn't understand…"

Guilt gripped Josie as if her aversion to anyone from the Northern states had caused his heartbreak. She'd been adamant about him not coming to Honey Ridge, about making him miserable enough to leave. Now that she knew him and knew of his losses, she felt so very, very small.

Tenderness, that unwanted emotion, crept ever upward, winding, vining, threatening to choke her.

"I asked Will to say nothing," he murmured.

Of course. Pride. Say nothing. Soldier on. Carry the loss and grief, but weep in great gulping gasps into sleep's pillow.

"Oh, Thaddeus, I am deeply sorry."

She could feel his eyes on her and couldn't bear to look up. His physical wounds were only a fraction of the internal ones. She knew. Yes, she knew.

"I don't want your pity, Josie."

Shivery, aching, she tugged his sleeves back into place and wished she'd never seen the horrifying scars.

Pity was not the emotion swirling in Josie's chest.

CHAPTER EIGHTEEN

I cannot fix on the hour, or the spot, or the look, or the words, which laid the foundation... I was in the middle before I knew that I had begun.
—Jane Austen, *Pride and Prejudice*

Present

"HAYDEN?"

Someone called his name and he tried to focus.

"Earth to Hayden."

Hayden blocked the imagines flashing like an old sixteen-millimeter movie in his head. Carrie's puzzled face came into focus.

He blinked, rubbed at the pain pulsing in his temple. Something bizarre was happening to him, but he wasn't ready to accept insanity.

It was only a dream. A dream that became strikingly true the second he'd stepped inside the two-hundred-year-old mill.

He'd dreamed portions of his books before.

But not like this.

"Sorry," he said through lips gone dry as cornmeal. "My mind wandered."

Carrie tweaked an eyebrow. "Plotting something devious?"

If she only knew.

"This is a great place for it." Hands on his hips, he gazed around, pretending interest but really needing time to regain his composure. This uncanny familiarity had him shaken. "Want to check out what's behind that door?"

"We have a book in the library with a story called *The Lady or the Tiger*." She splayed her fingers on either side of her face in a pretend scream. "Opening a mystery door always reminds me of that book."

"The original choose-your-own-ending story." He remembered the tale of terrible decision and was grateful for the distraction. "A princess falls for an unworthy hero, and her father sends him into the arena to decide his fate. Behind one door is a tiger. Behind the other is a woman the king has chosen for him to marry but *not* the usually indulged princess. Either way, the princess loses her lover. So, does she choose, out of love, to let her lover marry another? Or does she, out of jealousy and loss, send him to his death by opening the tiger's door?"

"Which do you think happened?"

Hayden shrugged. "He's at the mercy of a disappointed woman. He gets eaten."

"No way! The princess truly loves him. She'll let him go to another rather than hurt him."

Hayden scoffed. "I write thrillers, not romance. Death makes more sense and is undeniably more certain."

"Cynic." She put one hand on the closed door and looked over her shoulder at him, eyebrow lifted. "Tiger or lady? Will I be eaten?"

Testing the boards as he moved behind her, he said, "Be careful."

She paused and in a spooky voice asked, "Because of the weak floors or the doom that awaits me behind that door?"

He smirked. "Your imagination is as active as mine." *Almost.*

"I love books, too. Just because I don't write them doesn't mean I have no imagination."

She pushed on the handle. As the tall door swung open, Hayden let out a loud growl and goosed her.

Her scream ripped the silence. She whirled on him, eyes wide and face pale. "Hayden Winters! I swear—"

He couldn't hold back his laughter. "Sorry. I couldn't resist. I haven't done that since I was a kid."

"You will pay for this, buster. I mean it." She shook a small fist at him, but she was laughing, too.

Pleasure bloomed. "You really are a scaredy-cat."

"Card carrying." She put a hand to her chest. "My heart is jumping out."

Her chest heaved, and her breath came in short bursts. He had the overpowering desire to hold her and let her know he'd never really allow anything to hurt her.

This day was getting weirder by the minute.

His mind veered off track, off the mill, off the crazy dreams and onto her, his jumpy librarian with the big brown eyes.

"I wouldn't let the tiger get you," he murmured, aware that his voice had lowered and his pulse had picked up.

Her eyes flickered as if she, too, felt the mood

change. He could see her sudden awareness, the caution, the uncertainty.

She licked her lips. "You wouldn't?"

"You're safe with me." His throat felt full and hoarse, as if his heart was pushing up inside it. The symptom was unfamiliar, and he logged the feeling somewhere in the back of his brain. Fodder for a novel.

Carrie was not his type. She was too sweet. Too nice. Too good. And he was losing his grip.

Her lips, which looked as lush and enticing as any he'd ever seen, curved. "Defender against tigers and thunderstorms?"

His hands felt too big for his body, and he was suddenly a gangly adolescent, uncertain of what to say to a pretty girl.

Hayden Winters was rarely unsure with women, not out of arrogance but out of knowing exactly what they wanted from him and he from them.

But he didn't know what he wanted from Carrie. Or if he did know, he dared not go there. Not in a million years.

If he let this moment drag out, he might do something foolish, like kiss her and start an affair right here and now. *Foolish. Selfish.* He didn't know if Carrie was the affair kind, but one thing he did know. He did not want to hurt Carrie Riley.

And he was an expert at hurting people.

He cleared his throat, tamped down the mad rush of hormones and dragged his focus toward the now-opened room. "The coast is clear. Look out for the dust bunnies."

His voice still sounded weird. He cleared his throat

again, swallowing down the unwanted and unexpected desire coursing through him.

Relationships were sticky. He was here to plot and write a book.

If she felt the throb between them, she ignored it, a good reason for him to do the same.

She stepped inside the long divided space with doors at each end, and Hayden followed.

His heart still behaved weirdly.

"Don't scare me again," Carrie was saying, her finger pointed at his face. "There's a window over there I can push you out of."

"I'm beginning to wonder which of us plots thrillers," he said.

She smirked and turned her attention to the room. "Someone else has been in here recently."

"Good observation." He stuck his hands in his pockets. "No spiderwebs."

"The junk has all been moved to one side."

"Homeless?" A place like this would be well visited in the inner city or even deep in the poverty-stricken hollers of eastern Kentucky. Any shelter was better than none.

"I don't know. Most likely kids camping out."

The remark put him in mind of Brody. Had the kid been heading here the night of the storm?

Their shoes tapped on the hollow flooring. Dust motes rode in through the windows on shafts of sunlight. He went to the window, filthy with time and age, to gaze out at the peaceful creek. From the corner of one eye, he spotted the edge of the waterwheel.

"I wonder if a person were pushed from this window, if he would fall onto the wheel, onto the rocks or elsewhere."

"We could do an experiment."

He arched an eyebrow. "Are you volunteering to let me push you?"

She laughed, eyes flashing. "Toss something out the window besides me."

He displayed his empty hands. "Got nothing else."

"Let's look in the other rooms. Maybe we'll find something." She shoved open the door to the left, stepped inside and disappeared.

"CARRIE!"

Hayden thrust himself toward the dark yawning doorway, heart in his throat.

She was there, on what was left of the collapsing floor, hands pressed against the broken boards as she tried to extract one foot and leg from a splintered hole.

"I'm okay," she said, voice shaky. "The floor gave way."

Without stopping to think of the danger of more collapse, he slid his hands beneath her arms and gently pulled.

"Easy now. Easy. Are you hurt?" He scooped her into his arms and carried her back into the bigger room and found that he was trembling, too.

"I don't think so. A scrape maybe."

Carefully, he settled them both on the floor, holding her, loath to let go. His chest thundered still.

"If the floor had given completely, you would have fallen through to the basement." A full fifteen feet. He sickened to think of the damage a fall like could do, given the amount of junk and debris lying around. "You could have been injured, Carrie. Seriously injured."

"Calamity Carrie." She tried for a tremulous smile, self-deprecating as always. "I didn't think before I leapt."

"Could have been either of us." In fact, he'd rather the accident had happened to him. "I shouldn't have let you go in there."

"You aren't my boss, Mr. Winters," she said softly, though her tone was sweet.

He only allowed people to get hurt in his books. She mattered.

Needing to regain his breath and calm his heart rate, he wrapped his arms around her and leaned his chin on top of her head.

She fit nicely against his shoulder. He cradled her there, comforted by her closeness.

"I scared you." Her hand rubbed the small of his back in comforting circles.

Emotions stirred, powerful and disturbing. He longed for her comfort like a child longed for his mother's love.

"Yes. And I don't scare easily." He pondered that, realized that Carrie got to him in ways he wasn't used to. He felt this need to protect, all the while drawing comfort from her. *Irony. Oxymoron.* He could use that in a book. "Any place hurting? Any broken bones?"

"My leg burns a little. Probably only a scrape."

"Let me see." Reluctantly, he released her from his embrace. Holding Carrie was…nice. The editor in his head said the description wasn't strong enough, but he was afraid to say more than nice.

With endearing modesty Hayden found sexy, she

slowly tugged her skirt up to knee level, giving him full few of a shapely ankle and calf. He tried to stay detached, realizing he'd never have been a good doctor. Female skin was too intriguing.

"Right there." She pointed to the side of her shinbone. A long, red, raw abrasion streaked four inches or more up her leg. "I'm okay, though, Hayden. Really. Stop fretting."

"Looks like a broken board got you, but I don't see any splinters left behind." He carefully, purposely, tugged her skirt down to her feet, but let his fingers linger on her smooth curvy ankle. "You've lost your bracelet."

"Oh." She leaned forward, bumping the top of her head with his. "Darn."

He looked up from her smooth, curvy ankle, lamenting the broken ankle bracelet as much for him as for her. Her eyes met his, and a shiver of need moved through him.

Carrie was a dangerous woman. She made him wish for things he'd long ago put on a shelf.

"Was the bracelet special?"

"Only to me. Don't worry about it."

"I liked it."

"You did?"

He touched her cheek, which proved every bit as soft and smooth as her ankle.

"I noticed it the first night we met," he said softly, reminiscing about the moment he'd laid eyes on her and the tingly sensation she and her pajamas and her ankle bracelet had aroused. "Unintentionally sexy. The most appealing kind."

Beneath his fingertips, her skin warmed in a blush.

She tipped her head to one side so that he cupped her face.

Again Hayden considered kissing her, taking this interest to the next level, but when he looked into enormous brown eyes so full of warmth toward a man she couldn't begin to understand, a man he could never let her know, he retreated to his carefully erected lie, the facade that was Hayden Winters.

He dropped his hand and backed away from her tempting personal space. "I'll see if I can find it."

"Don't you dare go back in there. The floor is too unstable."

Hayden was already up and heading that way. The distance was what he needed to clear his head, though he held out little hope. His head had been anything but clear since coming to Honey Ridge, Tennessee.

CHAPTER NINETEEN

We are all ready to be savage in some cause. The difference between a good man and a bad one is the choice of the cause.

—William James

1867

FOR MANY DAYS after what Thad came to think of as the incident at the creek, Josie was different. She no longer seethed with anger, but she didn't sparkle, either. Thad had come to like when Josie got all stirred up and sparkled.

She'd stopped coming to the mill, too.

He shouldn't have let her see the scars. Tired, and mulling the confrontation with Oscar Pitts, he'd been distracted.

Will and Charlotte had stood firmly behind his decision to fire the cheating mill worker. He was thankful for that, but he worried about repercussions. The Yankee miller had yet to find acceptance in Honey Ridge, and this would only deepen the rift.

So far, business continued as usual. Farmers had little choice if they wanted their meal ground. If customers weren't particularly friendly, they never had been. At church on the Sabbath, he'd received some sly glances and snide comments and figured word had circulated. Hopefully, he'd seen the last of Oscar Pitts and the rest would blow over in time.

As Thursday wound down, sweat seeped from his pores like water from a spring, and even the breeze off the waterwheel didn't provide relief from the heat generated by the spinning stones and the constant, cloying fog of meal dust. Abram worked the bolting cloths upstairs, sifting the cornmeal from the grits with Tabby and the kittens alert for mice.

They would require more hands when the heavy harvest began later in the fall, though Will assured him the family was up to the task. They'd been doing it for years. Thad thought of Josie at the sheller with yellow corn bits stuck in her bright red hair.

He wished he'd not frightened her away with his grief and damaged flesh.

He took out his pocket watch and rubbed his fingers over the inscription. Forever and always had ended too soon. Even now, he struggled to remember the faces of his family. Their voices had long since disappeared from memory, no matter how he strained to hear them. How deeply he longed to hear Grace's childish giggle and Amelia's sweet melody as she hummed in the kitchen.

Starting over in a new place had provided distance, but no number of miles erased the dark emptiness inside his chest.

He realized then that Josie, as well as hard labor at the mill, had proved a distraction from his heartache. Now, as he held Amelia's gift, he felt vaguely sinful as if enjoying another woman's company was disloyal to Amelia. His wife was worth grieving over, worth clinging to, worth loving forever and always as they'd promised.

With a sigh, he replaced the watch, grateful again to the man who had walked across less-than-friendly territory to return it. A man he'd come to consider a friend.

He strode to the water bucket and drank deeply and then went into the office to go over Logan's figures for the day. Logan was a fine bookkeeper, but the incident with Oscar had taught Thad to keep an eye on everything.

So engrossed was he in the ledgers that he only vaguely heard footsteps tap against the hardwood. Accounting the sounds to Abram, he continued his perusal of the names and amounts until a voice said, "I thought you should know."

Josie stood in the doorway, her cheeks rosy and green eyes glistening beneath a plain straw hat tied with emerald-green ribbons.

A bolt of energy shot through his weary body. He pushed back from the desk and stood. "Well, look what the wind blew in."

She made a derisive noise and fanned a hand in front of her face. "In case you haven't noticed, there's hardly a breath of air stirring."

A grin tickled his chest. She was here…and in a prickly mood.

He came around the mercifully silent potbellied stove to where the redhead gripped the doorjamb of the tiny office and stood close enough to see the rise and fall of her buttoned bodice.

"Got a bee in your bonnet?"

She sniffed. "I have no idea what you mean."

"Haven't seen you around here in a while."

"I've been busy. Hannah Ogden had twins and not a stitch to put on them." Which clearly made her furious. She tossed her head, eyes flashing lightning. "Federals stole everything they had."

Ah, the hated Federals. Again. "Never figured you for a midwife."

"Don't be foolish. I wouldn't know how to deliver so much as a kitten. But I know how to sew."

Realization turned over in his chest. "You sewed for her babies?"

"Gowns and flannels. Patience knits the booties and caps." A tenderness he'd not noticed before softened her sharp edges. "The darlings looked precious, and poor Hannah cried. I don't know why she did such a thing." She waved a dismissing hand. "Over a few leftover scraps of cloth."

Thad stood dumbstruck. He'd thought she sewed only for her own vanity. The truth caught on the jagged edges of his mind, and he left it hanging. Something to ponder later, this new layer of Miss Josie Portland.

"So what brings you to the mill? Miss my company?"

Green eyes rolled upward. "Don't flatter yourself. I relish the fragrance of enterprise."

At that, he laughed, and she joined him.

Abram tromped down the steps covered in fine white powder, a black ghost. "Mr. Swartz is here for his order."

"Jim Swartz?" Josie swiveled in the direction of the mill road.

"Yes, ma'am."

"Go ahead and load his wagon, Abram," Thad said. "I'll write out his bill."

Abram headed around the staircase toward the side of the mill where processed grain was stamped and stored until retrieved by its owner or sold to paying customers. From there, a double door led out to the loading porch.

"Jim Swartz," Josie said softly as she stared with interest toward the dock. "Why, I haven't seen him in a month of Sundays."

A former beau, perhaps?

Suddenly disgruntled, Thad hitched his chin. "Then, by all means, you must pay your respects to the man. I'll be there in a minute."

After she left, he realized she'd never told him why she'd come.

With a shrug, he figured up Jim Swartz's account, all the while wondering at Josie's connection with the man, and then wondering why he was wondering.

Shaking his head, he tossed the stub of pencil on the desk and started toward the loading dock.

As he stepped out into the sunshine, tension simmered in the air thicker than lima bean soup.

Thad slowed his steps, taking in the situation as he gazed from the two farmers to Abram. He recognized the short, stocky man with the slick mustache as Jim Swartz from the day he'd brought in his corn. The other, tall and lanky with pocked scars, was a stranger. Both glared at Abram.

"Everything all right out here, gentlemen?"

"No, sir." Swartz propped a boot on the sack at Abram's feet. "It's not."

"What seems to be the problem?"

"Him." Chest thrust out, Swartz poked a stubby finger toward Abram. "Must not have been Oscar Pitts doing the cheating around here. This here—" he curled his lips as if something stank "—*gentleman* stole from me. Or tried to. George saw him do it, saw him hide this bag of cornmeal when he thought we wasn't paying attention."

Thad drew in a weary breath. As much as he trusted Abram, a man never knew for sure. "That true, George?"

George's face was red as fresh beets. He flicked a nervous glance toward Abram. "Yep."

"Abram, did you short this man?"

Abram's arms hung limply at his sides, shoulders stooped. A black man arguing with a white one could get him beaten or worse.

"The truth, Abram."

In a whisper, eyes on the ground, the freedman said, "No, sir."

Thad let out a slow, thoughtful breath. He was caught between a rock and a hard place. Trouble was bad for the mill, and taking sides with a black man over a white was nothing but trouble. Yet he couldn't shake the feeling that Abram was telling the truth. Something about the two men didn't ring true.

"Abram's been an honest employee, Mr. Swartz. Perhaps a mistake was made. These things happen from time to time, and as we want to keep our customers happy, how about we deduct the price of grinding this bag from your account and call it square?"

"It weren't no mistake, Eriksson. He stole from me sure as I'm standing here, and I want him fired. Horse-whipped, too." He stabbed the air again, face mottled.

"I found my sack, marked with my name, right over there behind that barrel where he hid it."

"Because you put it there, Jim."

All heads swiveled toward Josie. In the commotion, he'd barely noticed her below the dock near the millpond.

She came up the steps toward the gathered men, green eyes troubled, her skirts swishing softly in the sudden silence that followed her declaration.

"What are you talking about, Josie? You standing up for the likes of them?" Swartz seemed incredulous. "Over Tom's best friend?"

Something painful flashed across Josie's face, and Thad watched her struggle, but she stood her ground.

Chin tilted up, she said, "This is my family's mill. If Abram had stolen from us, I would fire him myself. You know I would, but he didn't. I saw what happened." Some of her composure slipped. "Please, don't do this, Jim."

When her lip trembled, Thad figured he'd heard enough. "Mr. Swartz, I don't want any trouble."

"Should have thought of that when you fired Pitts." Expression venomous, Jim glared at Abram. "He told us how you accused him when he hadn't done anything wrong so you could hire...*him*."

Thad held up a hand. He could argue all day, but neither this man nor any other friend of Oscar Pitts would hear the truth.

"You have your order. Take what's yours and go. The next time you need a miller's services, take your business elsewhere."

Swartz pulled back as if struck. "Nearest mill is fifty miles!"

Thad crossed his arms. "You should have considered that before bringing false witness against an innocent man."

Hate-filled eyes first raked over Abram and then Thaddeus. "You're getting in over your head around here, Union boy. Better watch out."

The other farmer, who had looked nothing but miserable throughout the confrontation, jerked a hand toward the loaded wagon. "Come on, Jim—it's getting late."

"Yeah, and the air around here stinks." Jim pointed a finger at Josie. "I wonder what Tom would think about you right now, girl."

Josie sucked in a gasp, her hands going to her midsection as if the man had punched her.

Thad clenched his fists. From the corner of his eye, he saw Abram tense.

He stepped forward, but the two farmers had done their damage and stomped down the steps to the waiting wagon. Jim shot one last simmering glare toward Abram, then slapped the reins and drove away.

CHAPTER TWENTY

*It has been said, "time heals all wounds." I do
not agree. The wounds remain. In time, the mind,
protecting its sanity, covers them with scar tissue and the pain lessens. But it is never gone.*
                                        —Rose Kennedy

Present

BRODY DRAGGED HIS backpack across the front porch,
reluctant to go inside the house, but the old man had
told him to come straight home from school.

He hoped he wasn't in trouble again. Maybe the old
man had heard about the lunch he'd had with Hayden.
Maybe he was mad about that, thinking Brody had
shamed him again by letting the rich writer pay for his
meal. That's what the old man said, his face twisted and
red. He'd called Hayden a bad word and said Hayden
was a rich man looking down on a bunch of hillbillies.

A terrible thought made his knees quake. Had the
old man found out about the things Brody told Hayden?

But how could he have? Hayden promised not to
tell a soul.

Unless Hayden lied.

Belly heavy as a lead pipe, he pushed silently
through the door and tiptoed toward his room.

"Brody! That you, boy?"

Brody froze in midstep. He swallowed. "Yes, sir."

"Get in here."

He left the backpack where it fell and, head down, trudged toward the kitchen, where his dad sat at the table. He didn't know why the old man was off work today, and he didn't dare ask.

What his father did was no business of a stupid, useless kid.

From the doorway, he murmured, "Yes, sir?"

"Come over here. I got something for you." His father didn't sound drunk. He sounded...pleased.

Brody's head popped up.

He didn't look drunk, either. He wasn't swaying or glassy-eyed. He had a box in front of him on the table.

Brody eased closer. "What's that?"

"Go on. Open it." The old man pushed the box toward him, his eyes gleaming with a strange light. A good kind of light that Brody only saw when his father had sobered up after being drunk and crazy and breaking stuff. Like this past weekend. "Go on now."

The excitement of a rare gift was too much for Brody. He tore into the box and when he saw the Nintendo 3DS, a small gaming system, his heart leaped.

"Dad," he breathed, looking into his father's face.

"You like it?"

"Yeah. I mean, yes, sir." He held the little plastic box reverently. Several boys at school had them, but he'd barely dreamed of owning one. "Today's not my birthday."

His father hooked an elbow around his neck and squeezed, but for once the squeeze was light and didn't hurt. His dad wasn't mad at him.

"Can't a man buy his kid something if he wants to?"

"I guess so." But Brody wondered. Would the old man throw the gift in his face later or break it on a drunken tear?

Clint scrubbed his knuckles across the top of Brody's head with enough pressure to let him know he meant business. "So what do you say?"

"Thank you, sir. I love it." The pleasure felt hollow and insecure, like an empty stomach.

"Comes with a few games, too." Clint scratched himself. "I was thinking. That library woman, Carrie Riley."

Brody tensed but didn't say a word.

"She invited you to a cookout with her nephew. You know him?"

"Yes, sir. Landon. He's in sixth."

"He a troublemaker?"

"Landon's pretty nice. He lets fifth graders play soccer on his team at recess." Landon was Mr. Popular. All the girls liked him, and he wore cool clothes and shoes, but he didn't act snotty about it like some boys did.

"Well, you go to that cookout, then. Being around class won't hurt you none."

"Thanks, Dad." He was afraid to show too much enthusiasm. If he really wanted to do something, his dad would change his mind.

"All right, then." Clint ran a hand through greasy hair. "We're okay? Everything's square?"

He understood his father's meaning. Not that he'd ever tell anyone else but Hayden that his father screamed and cussed and broke stuff when he got drunk. That he scared Brody so much he didn't sleep all night.

Hayden had promised not to tell, and he believed him. He didn't know why but the rich man from New York seemed to understand. Probably because he was a writer and writers knew stuff.

Brody had known a kid once who went to foster care and never came back. He didn't want to go there. That was what he'd told Hayden. He could always hide in the woods now that he had his own place. Or maybe go visit Hayden at the inn. Hayden liked him.

"Yes, sir. All square."

"You hungry, boy?"

"Yes, sir."

"Come on, then—let's go out and celebrate. Me and you, father and son."

Brody didn't know what they were celebrating, but a cautious hope sprouted in his chest. A Nintendo *and* supper? Maybe his dad didn't hate him as much as he thought...

CHAPTER TWENTY-ONE

*The man who can keep a secret may be wise,
but he is not half as wise as the man with no secrets to keep.*

—E. W. Howe

CARRIE EASED A glance at the man seated behind the
steering wheel of a huge gray Chrysler. His long legs
stretched out, hands relaxed on the wheel, confident
and easy in his own skin.

Hayden turned his head toward her and smiled.

Something in her chest turned over.

Since the afternoon at the mill, her head buzzed
with thoughts of Hayden Winters. Impossible thoughts.
Ridiculous thoughts.

He'd almost kissed her, but then he'd backed away.
Since then he'd been very careful to keep a friendly
distance.

Friendly. But guy friendly. The kind of friendly that
opened doors and rested his hand at the small of her
back. The kind of friendly that looked at her too long
and had her pulse clattering and her brain winging off
into fantasyland.

He was here to write a book, not have a fling with
the local librarian.

Because of Brody's and Hayden's keen use of her library, she saw him nearly every day.

Some days he researched through books or pecked away at his laptop. Notes and photos, quotes and reference links. Several times she'd noticed articles on agoraphobia.

He'd ask her a question, and she'd settle into a chair across from him to answer, though rarely did they talk about anything remotely related to a killer thriller. He asked about the town, the quirky good ol' boys, Brody and the Riley family. He told of her his apartment in New York, which sounded so glamorous, though the idea of living with strangers mere inches away through a wall gave her hives. He told of escaping to Central Park for quiet moments amid nature. He asked about her family, and she talked until she was sure he must be bored, but he wasn't. He seemed to lap up the funny memories, the holidays, pressing for more.

His curiosity, as he liked to say, was insatiable.

Very little of this seemed to have a thing to do with writing a novel.

Today they were on their way to pick up Brody for Dad's birthday cookout. Hayden wanted to meet Clint Thomson.

Carrie didn't look forward to another unpleasant encounter with the man. Call her wimpy, but having Hayden along for backup felt…safe.

He'd listened so patiently while she worried about Valery, a confidence she hadn't expected to share with anyone. But she'd felt such relief in the telling.

Then at the mill when she'd fallen. *Oh, my.* Those moments cradled in his arms had set her head spinning in crazy circles.

When they'd headed back to the inn, Hayden had treated her like a fragile bird with a broken wing, even offering to carry her. Though her leg smarted and she'd laughed at him, the offer seemed incredibly romantic and protective. A man caring for his woman.

For that quivering, glimmering moment, she'd wanted him to kiss her. Had wished they were more than friends. If she wasn't such a ninny, she would have thrown caution to the wind and done the kissing.

But what if he didn't want that? What if he rebuffed her? What if he mocked her in public and ruined her reputation?

The timid sparrow retreated to her safe nest of friendship.

She studied Hayden's strong, manly profile as he drove through town, two fingers lifting from the steering wheel as they passed the Golf Café and two of the good ol' boys, Poker and Mr. B., standing outside in the sunshine.

Hayden Winters was a mystery. But she knew enough about who he was, just as she knew who *she* wasn't. She knew what falling for the wrong man could do. She would never be delusional again. Handsome, successful men didn't fall for small-town women who were as ordinary as a Savannah sparrow.

But looking and enjoying didn't cost a penny.

Outside the Thomson house, they parked and walked to the porch with Hayden a protective strength at her side. Before they could knock, Brody bolted out the door.

"I'm ready." The boy had shined up, and the cute cowlick was slicked down with water, his freckles scrubbed pink.

"I'll let your dad know we're leaving." Hayden strode to the door and knocked. "Will you introduce me, Carrie?"

Brody shifted from one foot to the other, eyes darting around, making no contact with the adults. Carrie's chest squeezed. The child was a nervous wreck.

Clint Thomson came to the door, clear-eyed and tidy, wearing a T-shirt and jeans. Carrie made the introduction, and the two men exchanged head nods. She could tell Hayden was making an assessment of the other man. That inquisitive brain of his missed very little.

"Brody's excited about this cookout," Thomson said, his gaze landing on Carrie. "I appreciate you taking him, Miss Riley."

"My pleasure. Thanks for letting him go."

"Well, now, that's all right. Kid don't have much else to do around here with only his old man for company, if you know what I mean."

She had no idea.

"We'll bring him back when the cookout is over, but it may be close to bedtime. When my family starts playing games, we can go on half the night."

Thomson scratched at his ear. "He can walk. His legs ain't broke."

Hayden's jaw twitched. "We'll drop him off after the cookout. No problem."

"Nice of you." He pointed a finger at Brody. "You be good, boy. You hear?"

"Yes, sir." Brody scuffed the porch with his tennis shoe. "I will."

The trio turned and headed across the small patchy lawn to the Chrysler. Brody quickly slid inside and slammed the door as if he was afraid his father would change his mind.

When they arrived at the Riley home, Brody spotted her nephew Landon and hopped out of the car. Carrie started to follow suit, but Hayden put a hand on her arm.

"Hold on a minute, okay?"

The yard was already filled with cars and pickup trucks. Everyone was there.

"Are you nervous about meeting my crazy family?" she asked, though she couldn't imagine him being uncomfortable anywhere.

"Should I be?"

She made a face. "Look out for my sisters. They think you're hot."

His eyes sparkled. "Yeah?"

"And given the fact that you have a Y chromosome, they also think you are fair game. Whatever you do, don't listen to them if they start in on the innuendos. They'll have us paired up like Romeo and Juliet."

His laugh lines crinkled. "I can handle it."

"Okay, but don't say I didn't warn you. Ready?"

"I want to talk about Thomson first. He was cordial, gracious, even grateful. Not what I expected."

"Trust me—he wasn't that nice on the day I took the boxes, but maybe I insulted him. That's what Mama said."

"A man's pride can get the better of him." He shifted, grasping the door handle with a soft huff. "I don't like him."

Gratified that his intuitive nature had seen what she saw, Carrie nodded. "Me, either. But I like Brody."

"Yeah, he's a good kid. Rough around the edges, but he has potential."

"You're the mentor he needed, Hayden."

"I'm only here for a while. What then?"

"I don't know. He's attached to you."

"I noticed."

He looked too serious for a second, almost troubled, before pushing the door with his shoulder.

They exited the car and walked, side by side, past the other vehicles, through the little latch-gate leading into her parents' yard, tidied up for this occasion. A pair of potted mums colored the front porch with splashes of yellow, and a porch swing rocked back and forth as if someone had this moment leaped out and run inside.

Carrie heard Nikki's laughter and nonstop chatter through the front door. Her sister was there with her boyfriend, the easygoing Rick, whom Nikki refused to marry, though he'd proposed a dozen times. Still, he hung on, besotted of the butterfly sister.

Bailey, the oldest Riley sibling, and her husband, Chad, Mom and Dad and the two grandsons were here, along with Trey. She wondered if her single brother had brought a date. Sometimes he did. Sometimes not.

Carrie tried again to warn Hayden. "Everyone is a couple, so please don't be offended if they assume too much."

"Why would that offend me?"

She refused to get fluttery. "You came for Brody's sake."

Ugh. That sounded pathetic.

He took hold of her hand. "Don't kid yourself."

The flutters started even if she didn't want them.

He was being kind, and she was one of the few people he'd gotten well acquainted with in Honey Ridge. Naturally he'd say something nice.

Nevertheless, she experienced a rush of relief and pleasure. For once, thanks to Hayden's kindness, she'd get through a family gathering without snide remarks about her manless existence. Maybe this time no one would bring up *the incident* and tell her to get over it.

She squeezed his fingers. "Ready to run the gauntlet?"

He lifted her hand and kissed it with a teasing smack. "Just call me Braveheart."

HAYDEN WAS IN the presence of good people, a warm, solid, down-home family whose affection for one another was obvious. Normality.

Surrounded by the average American lifestyle he'd once craved, the friendly, chattering Rileys sucked him in as if he was a friend they'd known forever. The Southern tradition of gracious hospitality was alive and well in Honey Ridge.

He was still examining his gut, trying to determine what kind of relationship he could allow himself to have with Carrie. If she was interested, and he was reasonably confident she was.

Sweet, wholesome Carrie with a dark, jaded soul like him? A man who could give her nothing but the present?

There lay the dilemma he had yet to resolve.

As they entered the kitchen, Mrs. Riley looked up from swirling white frosting onto a chocolate cake. "You must be Carrie's friend Hayden."

"Yes, ma'am." He nodded to the sisters, whom he'd

met at the inn. Both were busy preparing the birthday meal.

"Make yourself at home. We're always happy to have our children and their friends."

He smiled at the idea of any of these dynamic women being children.

"Carrie," Mrs. Riley went on, scratching her cheek with her shoulder, "get the corn ready to grill. Mr. Jacobs had a late crop, and I was lucky to get this fresh from his fall garden."

"Mom, you want me to open these chips?" This from Bailey, her dark hair pulled up in a ponytail, sunglasses perched on top of her head.

"Go ahead and put them on the outside table to munch on. The veggie tray, too. Nikki made her cucumber dip."

"Yum," Carrie said to him. "You have to try her dip. It's awesome."

Unlike the industrial kitchen at Peach Orchard Inn, this room was small so that bodies bumped against each other on trips between the sink and a refrigerator decorated with photos and magnets.

Pathetic that a grown man could wish for a refrigerator loaded with childish drawings and cheerful family snapshots.

When Carrie opened a paper sack of corn, he said, "Tell me what to do, and I'll help."

"You don't have to."

"Your mama said to make myself at home."

In a yellow sundress, Carrie looked as pretty and fresh as a sunflower. She flashed a smile. "Mama's the boss."

"All right, then." He reached for an ear of corn. "Instructions, please."

"Wash it, cut the tops off, rub it with a little oil and Dad sticks it on the grill, shucks and all."

"Got it." Their elbows bumped, and the memory stirred of holding Carrie in his arms. "You still have a scratch on your leg."

They were shoulder to shoulder, her lemony fragrance as light and pleasing as a tall glass of lemonade on a hot day.

With her hair tucked behind one ear, the pearl earring visible and the side of her face looking clear and soft, Hayden was tempted to stroke a knuckle over her skin and watch her pupils dilate with the same desire spreading through him.

She turned her head slightly, bringing them even closer, and words lodged in his throat.

"It's nothing, Hayden. Never was. But thank you for taking care of me."

He cleared his throat. "Happy to."

Their gazes held for long seconds while Hayden wished they were alone. Carrie broke the spell first and, with a self-conscious laugh, turned to the sink.

Glad for something to do with his hands, he reached for another ear of corn.

"Look out for Carrie and corn," a voice behind them said. "She gets mixed up."

Carrie groaned. "Bailey! Do you have to tell that story?"

"If we didn't embarrass you in front of your date, we wouldn't love you."

Carrie glanced at him and mouthed, "I warned you,"

as Bailey launched into a funny retelling of a six-year-old Carrie trying to spell everything on the table.

"When she came to corn, she proudly spelled, '*H-a-y*, corn!'"

Carrie rolled her eyes. Bailey laughed. Mrs. Riley, a spatula full of icing suspended in midair, looked on in amusement and Hayden smiled.

He loved hearing about growing up in a happy family, but family, at least his own, wasn't a bag he wanted to open. He'd felt vulnerable since the moment Carrie had slid into the seat of his Chrysler. Even before that.

His attraction to her conflicted him, called into question every motivation, every erected barrier and the neatly plotted path of his life. To veer from the plot would change the story outcome, a frightening, unconscionable act on his part.

"Don't feel bad," he said, smoothly, easily, hiding his true feelings. "I couldn't spell *cat* when I was six."

He couldn't swim, either.

The intruding memory ached, like a poorly set broken bone. He suffered a momentary flash of gleaming water. Of Blackie Boy.

Carrie bumped him with her side, effectively wiping away the vision. "You're sweet to say that."

"Carrie was a word nerd from the beginning," Nikki said, "even if her spelling was off."

Feeling a kinship, Hayden twitched an eyebrow. "I like that. Word nerd."

"You, too?"

"Always." Words had cost him something, particularly when Dora Lee discovered he read too well to qualify for a disability check, but words had also been his way out. "I read the dictionary for fun."

"Me, too!"

They laughed into each other's eyes. Nikki groaned. "Oh, Lord, two of them."

Trey came inside for the steaks and invited Hayden out to the grill with the men. "Dad's grilling."

"Poor man has to grill his own birthday steak?" Hayden said to Carrie, not really desiring to leave the kitchen and her company.

"The grill is Dad's pride and joy." Carrie glanced toward the backyard, her smile affectionate. "He insisted he wanted a decent steak, and the only way to get one was to grill it himself."

"They've been marinating all day," Mrs. Riley added. "Dad does the steak. We've got the rest."

"But he likes moral support and lots of man talk," Trey said, plate balanced on one hand, "Come on out, Hayden—have a Coke and talk guy stuff. These women will make you wimpy."

"Hey," Carrie said, pretending offense.

Trey patted his shorter sister on the head. "I'm speaking from painful experience, sis. Let the man go."

"Never argue with an officer of the law." Hayden wiped the corn silks from his hands before accompanying the friendly brother outside to a small fenced backyard.

Like Carrie and her sisters, Trey had dark hair and eyes. Athletically muscled and of average height, the good-looking cop probably had women following him around like cats after a stringer of fish. But he'd come stag to the party.

Trey introduced Hayden to the others—his father, Nikki's boyfriend and Chad, a robust man with a ruddy complexion and bright blue eyes. Bailey's husband was an anomaly in the sea of dark hair and eyes.

"Grab a drink from the ice chest and pull up a lawn chair." The birthday dad wore a white chef's apron bearing the words, "Last time I cooked, hardly anyone got sick. How do you like your steak?"

A Jack Russell terrier streaked by in pursuit of a rubber ball. A small, giggling boy, maybe seven or eight, who shared Chad's fair looks, scrambled after him.

Hayden slid his hands into his back pockets. "I'm not particular, but medium rare would be my choice."

"You got it." Sam Riley tossed the well-seasoned T-bones onto the grates. Smoke and a delicious meaty scent circled upward. "Though Carrie won't watch you eat it."

Hayden chuckled, grabbed a Coke from the cooler and joined Trey in the shade of a yellow-leafed maple.

He and Trey discussed mundane things, sports, small-town life, dogs and the art of backyard grilling, which Hayden knew nothing about other than the time his villain blew up the hero's house with propane stolen from the man's own grill.

Hayden always found the sinister in the ordinary. Conditioned response, he supposed.

Brody and his pal Landon streaked past, shooting water guns at each other, squeals high-pitched and energetic.

"Another of Carrie's projects," Trey mused, lifting his soda toward the boys. "Brody, I mean."

"Her projects?"

The stocky brown-and-white terrier lost interest in

the rubber ball and yipped after the water guns, leaping to catch each squirt.

"Haven't you noticed? She drives books to shut-ins. Reads to nursing home residents. Buys kibble for the cat lady. Volunteers at the food pantry." He swigged from the can.

"She buys cat food?"

"Huge bags. And she doesn't own a cat." Trey pointed his drink. "She collects the needy. Brody is the latest."

"A shame he doesn't have a mother to look after him. It bothers him. Do you know anything about her?"

He hadn't forgotten the Sweat twins' accusation, though no one else gave it credence. The Thomson woman had to be somewhere.

Trey trained his gaze on the playing boys. "After Carrie brought him to my attention, I asked around. The Thomsons split up when the boy was around three or four."

"That's what Brody told me. He thinks he might remember her, but the memory is so vague, he's not sure." Hayden shifted in his chair to look at Trey. He understood vague memories of a loving parent. "She doesn't call or visit."

"Sad deal. Everyone assumes that Penny Thomson had enough of Clint's drinking and left him. It happens. Clint's not a bad sort, but he drinks too much. After Carrie asked me about the wife, I ran her through the computer."

"Find anything?"

"Nothing. No social media, nothing on Google search. No DMV records. It's as if she keeps a very low profile or disappeared into thin air."

The hair on the back of Hayden's neck tingled. "Any hint of foul play?"

"Nothing to indicate it. Thomson lives in a small, nosy town. He has neighbors. Someone would have reported if violence went down next door."

"If it happened there."

Trey shot him a sideways glance. "Real life is usually not as interesting as fiction. At least not in Honey Ridge."

"But where is she? Why can't you find her?"

"Maybe she doesn't want Clint Thomson to learn her whereabouts. Maybe she changed her name for exactly that reason. Divorces can be ugly and messy, especially if one party has an alcohol issue."

"Whatever the story is, Brody is the worse for not knowing."

Trey pinched his upper lip. "All the wheels would come off the Riley family without Mama. A kid needs his mom."

Not all mothers were created equal, as both he and Brody could attest. Was a mother who ran away and left her child any better than one that hated you on a daily basis?

A hot feeling swelled against his breastbone. Heartburn? Too much soda?

He slipped the can into the chair's cup holder. "You have a terrific family."

"I didn't know that when I was a teenager. A few years in the big city set me straight and brought me back home."

Home wasn't always the best place to be. Moms didn't always bake birthday cakes.

He waved away a fly and breathed in the afternoon.

Fresh mowed grass and grilled steaks. Laughing kids. Easygoing men. And a dog that never slowed down. An all-American afternoon exactly like the ones he'd never had.

He was glad he'd come.

"My sister likes you."

At Trey's sudden change of topics, Hayden's head whipped to the side.

"I like her, too."

The police officer had his eyes trained on Hayden, assessing. "She's the sensitive sister. I'd do about anything to protect her."

"Are you warning me off?"

Trey lifted a shoulder. "Nah. Just making conversation. I don't want her to get hurt again."

"Understandable. She told me some jerk broke her heart." She hadn't told him the details, but he knew someone other than the college kid had wounded her deeply and left her uncertain.

Trey eyes widened, surprised. "She rarely talks about it, but she hasn't dated much since then, either."

He didn't feel the least remorse at dropping in the little information he had in an effort to gain more. "Being the object of rumors didn't help."

"Not much she could do to stop them. A curse of small-town living. Plenty of people she knew were waiting out the thunderstorm inside the Walmart entry when Simon's wife walked in."

Shock radiated through Hayden. "His wife?"

"She didn't tell you he was married?" Trey pressed back against his lawn chair. "Maybe I should shut up."

Hayden leaned toward him, forearms on his thighs. "Did she know?"

"Carrie? The rule follower?" Trey frowned as he shook his head. "No way. Simon, that was his name, was an out-of-town contractor working on the new bank building next to the library. He set his sights on Carrie, wined and dined her, sent her flowers."

"How long before she learned the truth?"

"About four months. Long enough that the wife grew suspicious and came to Honey Ridge to find out for herself."

"Brutal."

"This wasn't the first time he'd played tomcat with the locals."

"Something else Carrie didn't know."

"Right. But the wife told everyone in listening distance. She said some real cruel things, derided Carrie for thinking a man could fall for a small-town nothing like her."

Hayden's hands fisted. "Was she in love with him?"

"Already talking about the wedding."

A slow-burning anger built inside Hayden. He'd have to kill a contractor in a book soon. A contractor named Simon. "I hope you broke his nose."

A tiny smile tipped Trey's mouth. "Tried."

Hayden lifted his Coke can in a toast. "Thanks."

Trey tapped cans. "For what?"

"Taking care of her."

Trey's dark gaze, so like Carrie's, lingered on Hayden until the four women came out the back door, talking almost simultaneously.

Hayden focused on Carrie, ruminating, filling in the blanks in the painful story. Carrie was gentle and trusting. She'd have believed everything the brainless idiot told her. But to be humiliated in public by his wife took the betrayal to a whole new level of vicious. No wonder she hated thunderstorms.

He wished he could go to her this minute, hold her close and promise that no one would ever hurt her again. Carrie deserved better than she'd gotten.

Better than Simon.

Better than him.

The kids darted past, this time all three boys with the dog yipping and jumping in joyous abandon. Hayden heard Brody's laugh and followed the sound with his eyes as the boy tumbled onto the grass with the hyperactive dog. Rudy licked Brody's face, stub tail wagging faster than a windshield wiper. Brody was happy. Being here with the Riley family was good for him.

Hayden had spent his childhood wondering what a real family was like, envying the boys with clean shirts and no holes in their shoes. The ones with lunch money and backpacks whose mothers kissed them goodbye each morning and hugged them at night. Who didn't smell like body odor and stale cigarettes.

Families like the Rileys.

Trey was protective of his sisters, the way a brother should be.

Carrie would be all right here with the people who would always love her.

A yearning welled up in his throat with enough intensity to make his eyes water.

Family. Home. Love. As foreign as seeing his books for sale in Bangkok.

Carrie looked Hayden's way, smiled and started toward him.

The sensation of falling was so real, he grabbed for the sides of his chair.

In seconds, she was there, along with the rest of her family, surrounding him in striped lawn chairs, asking questions, offering cucumber dip and carrot sticks and more Coke. The folding table was laden with colorful summer foods and centered by a homemade birthday cake topped with a "Dad" candle.

Nikki peppered him with chatty questions, and he settled easily into the conversations. He'd learned to be a chameleon, fitting in anywhere. Involved but only on the surface, a skill he'd developed so long ago, he couldn't remember when he'd first become a watcher.

The Rileys, though, drew him in, made him feel a part. Made him wish he could be.

The grill flamed up, and Mr. Riley yelped. All heads whipped in his direction as a steak flew off the plate to be snatched up by the terrier.

"Rudy! Come back here." Sam Riley chased after the dog, his apron flapping.

In good fun, the three boys whooped and gave chase, as well.

Rudy, convinced they were playing a game, ran in lightning-fast circles around the lawn, steak dangling from his jaws.

The boys were as excited about the game as the dog and ran, yelling, "Rudy! Rudy!" at the top of their lungs. This enticed the dog to run faster, round and round like a cartoon chase.

"The steak is ruined anyway, Sam," Mrs. Riley called. "Don't give yourself a heart attack!"

Sam stopped running, leaned his hands on his knees

to catch his breath. His white apron drooped over his rounded belly. The boys never broke pace.

Rudy changed course and darted toward the ring of lawn chairs, where he leaped onto Bailey's lap.

Bailey squealed and threw her hands up, which knocked her off balance, upsetting her chair so that she tumbled backward. Chad executed an athletic grab, saving the fall, but the dog ran up the woman's body, steak dragging, and vaulted like a champion with jaw-dropping hang time, onto Trey.

The officer had the good sense and great reflexes to wrap his arms around the squirming terrier and hold on.

By now everyone was laughing, Hayden included.

Mrs. Riley caught his eye. "Is your family as crazy as ours?"

He'd been waiting for the family question and was prepared with his practiced answer. Someone invariably asked.

"Almost," he said with a fake smile. Far *crazier*.

"Where are you from, Hayden? I swear I hear the South in that voice, though your book jackets say you live in New York."

"Louisville, originally," he lied, as smoothly as if he told the truth. "I've been in New York a long time, but being in Tennessee must bring back the accent."

He'd worked hard to lose the hills from his diction, hours and hours of repeating videos and imitating the inflections of news commentators. But a little of the South gave credibility to his cover story.

At Mrs. Riley's questioning, he told about his engineer father, now passed away, and the nice schools he'd attended, including the University of Kentucky.

All lies, carefully concocted to sound good, but not so good as to draw suspicion.

"Southern born and Southern bred, we like to say around here." Mary Riley rocked forward, nodding. "Nice to see my daughter with someone from such a good background."

Hayden managed not to wince. Not for the assumption that he was dating Carrie. But he no more had a good background than he could change where he was born.

Carrie rolled her eyes. "Mama…"

"Oh, hush." Her mother flapped a hand, and Hayden grabbed the moment to switch gears, another skill of long standing.

Twisting the truth hurt no one and was absolutely necessary. The fabrication was as much a part of him as Dora Lee—the living, breathing reason he *had* to lie. The story of a strong upper-middle-class background with perfectly normal parents kept him safe from pity, from derision, from Dora Lee.

His creation of Hayden Winters had never bothered him. Never.

Until today.

He liked these people. They weren't reporters pushing for a story angle. They weren't the general populous that didn't really care about him as long as his books enthralled and thrilled.

They mattered. They had welcomed him into their home, accepted him and had even approved him for their amazing daughter.

How did a man receive such open-faced trust when everything about him was a lie?

The warmth and acceptance of the Rileys set his conscience on fire.

Carrie. He looked at her, sitting next to her mother, fresh faced and sweet as the honey on Honey Ridge.

That he cared about her enough to be troubled, when he'd never been one iota bothered by what he saw as a necessity, shook his foundation. A foundation built on survival.

Suddenly, with a clarity strong enough to ruin his appetite for good steak, he understood how much he cared. He, who didn't let himself get close enough to be touched, cared.

He was a liar, a fraud and unworthy to sit in this circle of family.

And he couldn't do a thing to change it.

CHAPTER TWENTY-TWO

LATE THAT NIGHT, after multiple games of charades and later Scrabble, in which Carrie had happily partnered with Hayden to destroy their opponents, the exhausted trio loaded into Hayden's rental and headed home.

"Did you have fun, Brody?" Carrie glanced into the backseat.

"It was awesome." The boy leaned his head on the door and yawned.

"Tired?"

"A little." He yawned again. The boys had played in the porch light until the lightning bugs came out. Then they'd grabbed fruit jars and raced into the darkness.

Brody had insisted on a catch-and-release system, setting the fireflies free almost as soon as they'd been captured.

Huck Finn and his critters.

Her mouth curved. The day had been as perfect as any she could remember.

When they reached the Thomson house, Brody leaped out. "Bye. Thanks."

The dome light illuminated as Hayden pushed open his door and followed. Carrie remained in the car while he walked to the front porch with the boy, his hand on Brody's shoulder.

A light shone inside the house, but no one came to the door. The boy and man stood on the porch, talking.

Hayden had a fatherly side, and she wondered if he even knew it. She also wondered again why he'd never wanted to marry and have kids of his own.

Brody started to go in the house when the porch light came on and Clint Thomson appeared in the doorway, weaving from side to side, a beer in hand. Brody ducked under his arm and disappeared from sight.

The adults exchanged a brief conversation before Hayden returned to the car, his jaw set.

"Is everything okay?"

"Thomson's a bona fide jerk."

"I think we knew that."

"He confirmed it."

"What happened?"

"I asked him about Brody's mother."

"Oh, Hayden."

"He wasn't happy. Told me to mind my own business, though he used some choice words to do so."

"I can imagine. Did he tell you anything at all?"

"Nothing useful." He relaxed his grip on the steering wheel and started the car. "He was drunk."

"I'm not surprised." She could see he was disturbed by the encounter, and, like her, he worried about Brody. "You think Brody will be okay?"

"You want the truth?"

Did she?

She swallowed, the pleasure of the day dissipating.

Hayden put the car in gear, leaning one arm on the steering wheel to gaze across at her. "Even if he doesn't hit Brody, and Brody swears he doesn't, he's angry and cruel. The sad thing is, he does enough good to keep

Brody hoping." He huffed an exasperated gust. "Like when he got drunk and busted a wall in Brody's room."

Carrie gasped. "Did he hurt Brody?"

"No." His nostrils flared in disgust. "He bought him a Nintendo."

"What? I'm confused."

"I'm sure Brody is, too. Don't you get it, Carrie? Thomson behaves like a maniac, and then to assuage his conscience, he sucks Brody in with a gift."

"All of which must keep Brody off balance and insecure."

"The kid never knows what to do or what's coming at him. I'd like to…"

She put a hand on his arm. "Maybe we should call Child Services."

Gray eyes cold and hard as iron, he slowly shook his head. "Brody made me promise not to do that before he'd talk to me. I can't lie to him. I won't."

"Then what do we do?"

"I don't know."

After another sigh, he drove in thoughtful silence the better part of the way to her house.

As he pulled into the driveway, the car's headlights swept over Carrie's lawn. The dandelions had popped up again, though she'd mowed three days ago.

"I hope my family wasn't too overwhelming."

He got out and walked her to the door, his hand at her back. "I enjoyed myself."

"Daddy grills a mean steak." She looked sideways at him.

"The best I've had in a long time. As long as he keeps the dog away."

At the funny, chaotic memory, they exchanged smiles.

The night was warm and humid and smelled strongly of the gardenia blooming beside her small porch. Hundreds of lightning bugs as bright as tiny Christmas bulbs blinked around the evergreen bush. Cicadas pulsed in waves, the rhythm of a Southern night.

"Thank you for coming to the party. I think Brody enjoyed every minute."

"I did, too," he answered, quiet as they stopped at the bottom of the step. "Did you?"

"The best."

His lips curved, and he lifted a finger to touch her face. The tenderness shivered through her.

Her heart started to race, faster than it had that day at the mill.

"Do you want to come inside?" she asked, voice surprisingly husky.

He slipped his hand around the back of her head and stepped close. His warm breath teased her. Softly, he asked, "Do you want me to?"

A lump the size of Chicago formed in her throat. She swallowed past it, aware of what she was asking. It had been a long time. She was not a Goody Two-shoes, as Valery had accused of her being, but she wasn't exactly in Hayden's league, either. A man of the world with his success and money probably had a woman in every state.

Like Simon.

Except Hayden wasn't married.

"I wouldn't ask if I didn't," she whispered.

They started up the steps, and she fumbled in her

purse for the house key. Hayden took it from her and opened the door. She didn't snap on the porch light, afraid the spell would be broken and she'd begin thinking too much.

She started to step inside, to lead the way, but Hayden tugged her back and into his arms. His heart thrummed against hers. He was warm and sturdy, strong and male, the scent of grill smoke and expensive cologne on his skin.

Nervous, she licked her lips, and Hayden followed the motion with his intense gaze.

He touched his mouth to hers, a whisper kiss that made her yearn and ache, a seduction in its sweet simplicity. Then he leaned his forehead against hers and inhaled a long, long breath, letting it out in a sad exhale.

He stepped back, looked at her for another confusing second before whispering, "Good night, Carrie."

Then, he trotted to his rental car and drove away.

TIME AWAY FROM the hills and hollers of Kentucky dimmed the memory of their arresting beauty.

Anxious but resigned to a fate he couldn't seem to escape, Hayden drove through picturesque towns and then out and up onto corkscrew roads deep into the sparsely populated hollows of Magoffin County. There was no place so beautiful, so natural, or as terrible. At least for him.

Visitors came from all across the country to see the stunning beauty, but few traveled these twisty roads, down single lanes through dark-as-coal tunnels beneath the mountains, across rickety bridges to where the least of them hacked out a living from the underbelly of Appalachia. The lucky ones anyway.

Regulations had closed mines and left families without support. Few could find work. Two hours to a good job was near impossible. He knew because he kept tabs and Dora Lee railed at him about his highfalutin lifestyle while she starved on the dole. Thirty-two miles was a long way to travel for a loaf of bread, but not too far to exchange her welfare draw for cases of Pepsi she could trade on the black market for OxyContin. A soda-pop currency.

His vision of Appalachia, he knew, was tainted by a childhood with Dora Lee.

Already missing the soothing company in Honey Ridge, Hayden tugged his blue University of Kentucky ball cap low and sipped the thermos of coffee he'd filled at the one convenience store fifteen miles back.

People here were careful of their friends and deeply suspicious of strangers. He made a point to blend in by thickening his accent, and to remind himself of who he really was, he donned grubby jeans and an old T-shirt topped by plaid flannel. He knew how to blend. He did, after all, belong here.

A hot, hollow sickness had settled in his gut the moment he'd crossed the line from Tennessee into Kentucky. Homesickness, yearning and pure dread.

The Riley gathering, coupled with a guilt he shouldn't have to feel and the latest phone call from Dora Lee, had sent him, quite literally, running for the hills.

He could not start something with Carrie that he'd never be able to finish.

He was a fraud. She was an open book.

At least twice a year, Dora Lee wore him down, guilted him enough that he made the trip deep into the impoverished hills and thick woods of the so-called white ghetto. UPS didn't even deliver this far back in the woods. He knew because he'd tried.

He didn't kid himself about his reasons for being here this time. He was running scared, something he'd stopped doing long ago. He'd run here because of Carrie, to escape temptation and to remind himself once again of all the reasons he couldn't fall in love with Carrie Riley.

She'd invited him in. She'd offered him her heart. Her beautiful, tender heart.

His pulse thumped with a hard, dreadful beat as he rounded the final curve and turned off onto the last stretch of dirt and grass leading to his childhood home, a trailer house exhausted by time and worn down by weather and neglect. Up on blocks and sagging in the middle, the wretched dwelling looked better than its surroundings.

Dora Lee never favored cleaning. Trash went out the front door. Or the back. Or sometimes stayed where it fell.

He swallowed a thick, nasty taste. He'd paid two teenagers to clean this up last summer. Dora Lee had been furious, hounding him to give her the money instead.

Maybe he should have. It would have done about as much good.

The weight of who he was pressed down, as heavy as the hills and as black as the heart of a coal mine. This house did that to him. No matter what his book bio said, he was still the dirty little boy from Appalachia, the boy whose mother would rather see him hungry and cold than to do without her cigarettes or pills.

Just once he wished he could dwell on his father instead of her.

He parked the rental on a patch of overgrown grass, hoping he wouldn't ruin a tire and be trapped here. Thirty miles down the mountain to the nearest service station was a long hike.

As he exited the car, shoulders stooped and steps heavy, the fresh, clean mountain air drenched in the morning's foggy mist wrapped around him.

Drawing it in as if for strength, Hayden maneuvered past a discarded electric heater, a rusted water bucket that made him flinch, a broken plastic chair.

Propped against the gray siding, a filthy mattress bore a large blackened center, an indication that Dora Lee or one of her friends had fallen asleep again with a cigarette. God only knew why she hadn't burned herself to death by now.

How do I help someone who doesn't want to be helped?

He tapped at the door, splintered by time and impatience, before scraping it open an inch. "Dora Lee."

No answer.

"Dora Lee. Are you home?"

The smell wafted out and insulted the mountain air. Stale smoke and food and the earthy odor of humanity.

The sound of movement and then a curse before she yanked the door fully open. For a long moment, she only stared.

Dora Lee must have been pretty once with her baby-blue eyes and golden hair, now as unkempt as the interior of her house. Living on cigarettes and painkillers, she was too thin, her skin sallow and eyes hollow. A purple splotch stained the front of the blue belted robe he'd sent her last Christmas.

She put her weight on one hip, lip curled in distaste. "What are *you* doing here?"

Hayden always swore he wouldn't let her hurt him. She always did.

Like a child caught doing wrong, he shifted from boot to boot. "You called me—remember?"

The phone call had come at a propitious moment as he'd driven away from Carrie's house. Dora Lee had threatened to kill herself, and this time he'd grabbed the excuse to leave Honey Ridge and get his thoughts together.

She didn't look the least bit suicidal. She never did. Not once in the half-dozen times he'd rushed like a wild man to be sure she was all right.

Why couldn't he let her do it?

But he knew. He couldn't live with any more guilt.

"Oh, yeah. I forgot." She sucked a long drag of her cigarette and blew a thread of gray smoke at him. Her hands shook. "'Bout time you showed up."

She turned away, robe dragging open as she shuffled to the sofa and knocked away a pile of clothes.

Without invitation, he followed her inside, sick that his mother lived this way and he could do nothing to help her. Nothing except feed her addiction.

She plopped down, glared at him. "Did you bring me anything?"

No fond hello. No hugs and kisses. No inquiries into his health or his life. Nothing to indicate he was anything other than a stranger.

Once in his life he wanted her to ask about *him*. He

wondered if she still thought he taught high school English.

Yet some perverse and broken part of him needed to please her. "I stopped at the store for groceries."

Cigarette at her side, hand on the couch, she cocked her head, irritated. Smoke curled up from between her fingers and trailed across her face. "I'm out of medicine and you bring food? Stupid."

"Where did you get the cigarettes?"

She hissed through her teeth, though the sound was more of a whistle because of the broken incisor, a parting gift from a long-forgotten boyfriend. Her eyes narrowed in pure hatred.

"Not that it's any of your business, but a friend left them. I got friends, you know, even if you think you're too good to look after the only person in the world who'd put up with you."

Hayden winced. Even though the stab was unfair, it still cut. He hated that she still had that power over him. That's why he stayed away.

"I'll get the groceries." He trotted out to the car for the bags.

When he returned, Dora Lee remained on the couch, the half-smoked cigarette trembling at her lips. She looked as seedy as any back-alley character he'd ever created.

She glared at him, mouth curled in contemplation, the stare that had meant hell to pay when he was a boy.

Darkness closed in, and he remembered in flashes. He felt himself shriveling to nothing, to a small, frightened, lonely nothing. He could hear her voice cursing him over and over again. The reasons varied. He'd eaten the last piece of bread. He spent too much time with his nose in a book. He was underfoot. He snuck off too much.

Why had she hated him?

Someday he'd get the courage to ask.

He turned away from her accusing eyes and began to unload the groceries. Her cupboards, as he'd suspected, were essentially bare.

"You hungry?" he asked with false cheer as he slid cans of soup and premade pasta onto a shelf. "I stopped for Chinese. You like Chinese."

She got up and came to the cluttered table, where he'd scooted aside half-empty coffee cups and overflowing ashtrays.

"What else did you bring?" Like a greedy child, she dug through the bags. When she saw the twelve-pack of soda, she emitted a little sound of glee.

He shouldn't have bought the mountain currency, and yet for that split second before guilt set in, Hayden was happy to have pleased his mother.

He set out the foam box of Chinese and moved to the microwave, dragging guilt and hopelessness with him.

"No electric," she said. "Give it here. I don't care if it's cold."

She sat with a heavy sigh as if she weighed a ton and took the carryout tray. He watched her open the lid and begin to eat, fingers almost too shaky to find her mouth.

"I paid your power bill for six months, Dora Lee. Why is there no electricity?"

"Don't know. They shut me off." She shrugged but didn't meet his eyes. Had she somehow talked someone into refunding her money? Correction—his money.

"Dora Lee, you have to stop doing this. Let me—"

He clamped his lips shut. He hadn't come to fight with her. He didn't know why he kept trying. The definition of insanity was doing the same thing over and over and expecting different results. He must be insane, because the stupid little boy still held out some foolish hope that his mama would welcome him the way Carrie's mother had welcomed her.

God, why did he put himself through this?

"If you're up to it after you finish eating, we'll drive into town and do some shopping. Would you like that?"

"Don't know if I can without my medication." She held up a hand. "I'm awful shaky. My whole body hurts. Please, Hayden, you got to be a good son and help me out."

He didn't answer, and the silence festered like a staph wound.

Lost, uncertain, worthless—feelings he'd run from for more than twenty years—Hayden began to pick up the trash and organize the kitchen. "Is the water on?"

"Water takes electricity." She smirked at him, the meanness back in her glare. His silence had angered her. "What are you, an idiot? Or too uppity these days with your fancy English-teacher job to remember how it is up here with the poor folks."

He raised a hand, weary. "Dora Lee, don't."

"Don't, don't, he says." She mocked him, lo mein quivering on the plastic fork in front of her mouth. "How many times did I hear *that*? When I kept a roof over your head after your daddy died and left me in such a mess." She growled. "Sniveling little suck."

Hayden grabbed a plastic bucket from the clutter and left the house. If he was lucky, she'd calm down while he was gone. He would, too.

He knew where he was going, though he hadn't been there in a long time. He made a point never to go there. He even avoided looking in that direction.

Fifty yards down the inclined backyard, he glimpsed the well. His pulse kicked up, and he couldn't get his breath.

Not from the walk. From panic.

"I should have let you drown."

He veered sharply to the left and trotted down the hillside, through trees and scrubs to the skinny creek below the house. The water might not be as pure here, but it didn't cost him more than he wanted to pay.

Dora Lee was leeching his soul.

He dipped the bucket a few times to clean out the grime before filling it to the rim.

Back at the house, Dora Lee had dressed and smoothed her hair into a ponytail, the Chinese left open and half-eaten.

"I'm ready," she said. "Let's go."

Somewhere between the lo mein and the water bucket, she'd changed her mind about a trip to town, as unpredictably predictable as ever.

Hayden placed the bucket on the counter and followed his mother to the car, driving her the many miles into the community with a handful of businesses, a post office and the school where Mr. Franks had changed his life.

On the way, he tried to make small talk but gave up when Dora Lee stared out the side window, knee bouncing in drug-addicted need, and didn't respond.

"I'll stop at city hall and pay your utility bill, Dora Lee, with the understanding that no one refunds the money for any reason."

She glared mutiny, aware that he knew exactly what she'd done.

"Drop me at Packard's. I want to try on some new shoes." She lifted a foot. "These won't last the winter."

Pleased at her interest in anything except painkillers, he did as she asked, pulling diagonally to the curb outside the town's only clothing and general merchandise store.

Dora Lee exited the car but leaned back in.

"Well?" She stuck out her hand. "I cain't buy shoes on my good looks." She laughed, an ugly sound. "Not like I used to."

Hayden hesitated before handing her a wad of bills. "I'll be back in a few minutes."

"No hurry. I might try on some jeans." She slammed the door and stepped up on the curb.

He was gone less than fifteen minutes, returning with the assurance that her power would stay on throughout the winter. No one seemed to know who had refunded her money. No surprise there nor was he surprised that no one remembered him. Kids from back in the hollers flew below the radar.

Pulling his cap lower, he walked into Packard's in search of his mother. She was nowhere to be seen. He waited another ten minutes, thinking she might be in the dressing room, but when she didn't appear, he knew with certainty he'd fallen for one of her tricks.

She was right. He *was* stupid.

Molars tight, he stalked to the car and called her government-issued cell phone over and over again. She didn't answer. No big surprise.

He sat there like the dummy he was for two hours, waiting for her to return. Dinnertime came. Roaming around town drew attention he didn't want, but hunger drove him to the convenience store, where he filled his car with gas and his belly with deli chicken. Still no Dora Lee.

He tried her cell again, groaning in frustration when she didn't pick up.

When the sun slid behind the mountain, the peach sky reminding him of Peach Orchard Inn and Carrie, he accepted that his mother had taken his money and abandoned him.

Feeling as worthless and empty as a defunct coal mine, he found a motel and gave it up for the night. In his last waking thought, he wondered if the ghosts of Josie and Thad had followed him to Kentucky.

CHAPTER TWENTY-THREE

A millstone and the human heart are driven ever round...

—Henry Wadsworth Longfellow

1867

JOSIE WAS MAD enough to chew nails. The audacity of Jim Swartz to pull such a stunt. Why, she'd never expected such subterfuge from him. The very idea that he'd been one of Tom's dearest friends scalded her. Tom would not have approved of such shenanigans.

Or would he? Would he expect her to defend a friend even if he was wrong? Especially against a Federal and a black man?

While Thad and Abram, both grim faced, discussed the incident and put into place a plan to avoid such confrontations in the future, she went inside for the corncobs. Most for the hogs but some for her sister. Patience made corncob dolls for the church benevolence baskets.

The mill was stifling hot today. She gathered the cobs into a sack and then set about to tidy the downstairs.

When her brother, Edgar, was alive, the mill had served as a local gathering place where farmers chewed tobacco and whittled and shared the news of the day and later of the war. After Charlotte and then Will took over, locals stayed only as long as necessary to drop off their grain. Townsfolk would utilize their services, but they had never embraced the Yankee captain and his British bride.

Josie missed those happier days, missed her brother and the way life had once been.

Now the cane-bottom chairs and a scarred wooden bench lined one wall, empty. The spittoon gathered dust.

She took the broom from the corner and swept the open space. Abram came in. She didn't know where Thaddeus had gotten off to.

"Miss Josie."

She stopped sweeping to look at the man. He held his flat-brimmed hat tight against his chest. A gray kitten had followed him and wound around his ankles.

"I'm obliged for what you done out there."

"Right is right, Abram." Though many would not have done the same, and others would criticize her if they knew.

Not that she cared one whit what any of them thought.

"Yes, ma'am. God bless you, ma'am."

Well. She'd never been blessed by a slave before. Former slave.

Not knowing what to say to such a thing, she went back to sweeping, and Abram went back to his work. There were still cogs to grease and gudgeons to oil before he left for the night.

When she finished sweeping, she put away the odds and ends of a day's work—hand scoops and discarded bags, bits of leather, a punch and an awl. She discovered Thad's white apron tossed to one side and hung it on a peg.

Hot and sweaty but satisfied that she'd done her part as a Portland, she took the water bucket and headed out to the creek.

She filled the pail in preparation for tomorrow and set it in the shade while she removed her hat and shoes and dipped her feet in the cooling stream. How long had it been since she had indulged this way? Perhaps before the war.

Sitting on a rock, legs extended, she tipped her head back and closed her eyes. The hush and hum of insects mingled with the ripple of water. The building groaned above her, settling for the night.

She should go on home before darkness fell. Go home and help with supper.

But she didn't.

When she heard footsteps coming down the brushy, well-trod trail leading downhill from the mill to the creek, she realized she'd been waiting for Thaddeus.

Head tilted back, she opened her eyes and saw him, upside down, his face tired. When he noticed her there, his expression lightened.

"I figured you'd gone to the house."

Josie sat up straight and pulled her feet up on the rock. Her dress bunched, getting the hem damp. "Which means you didn't even notice that I'd cleaned up the first floor."

"I noticed." He lowered himself to his knees and splashed water on his face.

Josie thought of the scars on his arms. Her gaze went there. He did not roll up his sleeves today, but the healed wounds were visible on the tops of his hands.

Her heart squeezed, sorry anew for his loss and curious about the woman he'd tried so desperately to save.

"Was she beautiful?"

His head snapped toward her. "Who?"

"Your wife."

He studied her for a moment as if deciding how much he wanted to say and then, with a sigh, almost of relief, replied, "In her own way, yes, and beautiful on the inside, too."

Josie pulled up her knees and wrapped her arms around them. "Tell me about her. You must have loved her very much."

He settled on a flat gray rock at her side and studied the backs of his hands.

Josie tightened her arms around her upraised knees to keep from touching him. She'd seen dozens of hideous wounds during the weeks and months Captain Will's Federal Army occupied Peach Orchard Farm, but only Thad's wounds had the power to move her beyond anger.

She wondered at the strange emotions he stirred in her breast, but she let them slide away as Thad began to speak.

His voice low and achy, he told of Amelia and their six-year-old daughter, Grace, of the fire he blamed himself for though he'd not been at home when the flames erupted, of the months when he'd hung between life and death, not caring if the burns took him, too.

When he stopped, the painful story shimmered in the humid evening, a ghost of his past, and Josie could bear to hear no more. If she was shallow for her cowardice, she remained unrepentantly so.

"There must have been good times," she said, emotions as fragile as spun glass. "Tell me the best thing you remember."

With a sidelong gaze, he pondered her request.

"The best thing?" He shook his head. "I have trouble recalling anything but the fire. I dream about it."

She dreamed about Tandy lost and alone and about Charlotte locked for weeks inside her blue bedroom. She dreamed of a Federal captain once dead but now alive again and of the guilt she wore like a suit of armor. She understood how dreams could haunt a person.

"Try," was all she said.

He reached for a stick lying on the bank and stirred the shallow waters. Small silvery fish darted away like shadowy ghosts when a lamp was lit.

"We first met at a pie supper," he said, his words softly nostalgic. "Her family was new at church, and no one bid on her pie. My mother nudged me, wanting to make the newcomers feel welcome."

"So you bought her pie, fell madly in love and that was that?"

He chuckled, shaking his head. "It wasn't that simple. I didn't win the pie."

She dropped her hands to her sides and angled toward him. "What happened?"

"As soon as I shouted my first bid, another fellow took interest. He won the pie." He rolled his head in her direction. "But I won the girl."

Josie smiled. And maybe she sighed a little. "That's terribly romantic."

"I didn't think so at the time. However, her mother was so grateful that I had saved her daughter from embarrassment that she insisted Amelia bake another pie for me."

"Did she?"

"She did. I married her six weeks later."

Josie intentionally widened her eyes. "That must have been really good pie."

Her ridiculous statement made him laugh, and the weightiness of their conversation lifted. Josie was glad she'd made him smile. He'd lost too much, a thought that stunned her. She'd never wanted to feel compassion for anyone associated with Northern aggression. But there it was, slick as a mossy rock.

He swiveled the stick round and round in the crystal clear creek, stirring mud until that one spot was murky and dark. How easy in life to poke at one dirty spot and muck up all the surrounding good.

"That's the first time I've laughed when talking about her."

She didn't know what to say to that. Grief, she figured, never fully went away. A man didn't stop caring for his wife and child because they weren't on this earth anymore. But everyone needed to laugh, and if she'd brought him a sliver of joy, even if he was a Yankee, maybe God wouldn't be so mad at her about the other things she'd done.

Behind them, the waterwheel rested for the night and water cascaded over the low falls in a steady, soothing rush. Here, along the shallows dotted by flat rocks, rich, green vines provided a cool respite, and the surrounding woods and natural outcroppings shaded the creek by day and formed a protective glen by night.

Magnolia Creek and the mill were as familiar to her as her home. They were home.

She and Thad sat together in the falling light, saying little. The company and the cooling dusk were enough. Along the horizon, the first star appeared.

"Oh, look." She pointed as she softly quoted a favorite childhood poem. "Star light, star bright, first star I see tonight…"

Her voice trailed off, and she stood, arms crossed against the rush of longing for something she couldn't even name.

"I wish I may, I wish I might, have this wish I wish tonight," Thad finished, standing with her. Standing close enough that her breath caught and the longing grew stronger. "What do you wish for, Josie?"

Her heart banged with a sudden rumble as if thunder rolled over Lookout Mountain and down across the hills and valleys.

"Wishes don't come true."

"Are you sure?" He stepped closer, and in the twilight, his blue eyes were like a beacon to light the way to a place she was afraid to go.

"I wished for many things, Thaddeus. Prayed for them, too, though my prayers, unlike those of the other Portland women, don't seem to matter."

"They matter."

"Do they?" she challenged, fighting against the tide of feelings Thaddeus generated and embracing the guilt that set her apart. "I fear God has no patience with those who commit grievous wrongs against the innocent."

He tilted his noble head and starlight found the paler skin of scars along the side of his face. "For what grievous wrongs do you so harshly judge yourself?"

Insides hot and tight to the point of exploding her

shame like shrapnel over a battlefield, Josie tossed her hair.

She'd never told a soul, but what did it matter if she told him, a Yankee? Darkness covered sins and confessions.

"Lizzy had a son. He was a good boy, Benjamin's dearest friend and constant companion, though Tandy was a few years older." Her voice faded. "Lizzy loved him madly."

"Her only child?" he asked softly.

Josie sighed, guilty, guilty, guilty. "Yes. Her only kin that I know of. Lizzy never named the father, though Tandy's skin and eyes were lighter than hers, and rumors said—" She shook her head. "I should not convey rumors about the dead."

"What happened to him?"

"Edgar sold him to torment Charlotte and punish Lizzy. Because of me." She stared at him defiantly, wanting him to hate her so the boil of feelings between them would cool to frost. "I told Edgar of the secret correspondence between his wife and your cousin."

"Charlotte and Will." His expression remained as mild as milk, and that simply would not do.

"I was the guilty party, not the two of them." She emitted a hard, mirthless laugh. "Charlotte fears God too much to take a lover, though I could not fathom then what a cruel husband Edgar was to her. He was my brother, and I revered him while I despised Charlotte and her calm, pious British ways. She was a traitor, I thought, for cavorting with a Yankee officer and nursing wounded Union soldiers when my Tom was out there somewhere alone."

"We all live with regrets, Josie."

"None so grievous as harming a child."

"Has Lizzy attempted to find him?"

"Charlotte placed ads in the newspapers and wrote letters to plantation owners seeking information. What more can we do?"

"I wish I knew."

She gazed up at the starlight, wondering if Tandy, too, wished on the stars and prayed to find his way home. "He's out there somewhere, missing his home, his mother, his best friend. And I am to blame for whatever has happened to a young, innocent boy."

He touched her shoulder, and she could feel the compassion emitting from him and forgiveness she did not deserve.

To cover the surge of emotion pushing at her chest, Josie twirled away, her skirt hem damp against her bare feet.

Telling the secret shame made it no less burdensome, and she wished she'd kept silent.

Wishes. So foolish.

"When we were children," she managed, though her voice was strained, "Patience and I came to the creek almost every summer day to cool off."

If her change of topics surprised him, Thaddeus took it in stride. She was, after all, known to be unpredictable. When she'd been young and flirty, she'd liked the reputation of driving the men a little mad with her swift mood changes.

"You can swim?" he asked.

She whipped back around, on safer ground now. Her chest wasn't quite as tight and hot, but she kept her arms crossed anyway. "Can't you?"

"Of course I can. It's just—"

"That I am female?"

His eyebrows lifted, and he smiled a quirky little grin. "You are indeed."

Josie didn't know why she did it—perhaps to ease her own strange discombobulation—but when the impulse struck, she didn't resist.

She pushed him into the creek.

Thaddeus stumbled backward, his mouth open in surprise, and landed on his back with a mighty splash. He went under and then surfaced with a sucked-in gasp, eyes wide and hair dripping, dark now instead of light.

Josie snickered and clapped her hands together. "Why, sir, you've been baptized!" Then she laughed outright, feeling immensely better, in control, back on even ground.

Thaddeus stood up out of the water with a good-natured grin and shook like a wet dog. His hat floated toward the bank, and she turned to reel it in, still laughing. She loved a surprise.

The next thing she knew, a pair of very strong arms swept her up. Her hot body touched his cool, wet one and she squealed, flailing her legs. "Put me down this instant!"

"As you wish." His grin was downright wicked as he dropped her into the creek.

The sudden cold against her scalding flesh sucked the breath from her. Her heavy skirt buoyed up around her legs. She slapped down the wet garment with both palms and sat upright.

While she'd like to pretend anger, the water felt divine. Still, she could not allow him to get the better of her in this game.

"You—you—Yankee!" Yankee was the worst insult she could think of.

Hands on his hips, he smirked. "Little red Rebel."

Somehow the words sounded more like an endearment than an insult. She tossed her head. Her hair had tumbled loose and dripped water under her collar and down onto the warm skin beneath. She shivered.

"The least you can do is help me up."

Water splashed as Thad waded toward her. Grinning, he reached out a hand. She did what any self-respecting Confederate girl would do. She jerked him down.

With a magnificent splash that pleased her no end, he landed across her lap and knocked her back into the water. She flailed, grabbing purchase where she could, which happened to be Thaddeus Eriksson's neck.

His was a strong, corded neck with muscles that ran thick across his miller's shoulders. She'd noticed his strong arms when he'd easily lifted her that first day on the street of Honey Ridge. Now, with the frogs beginning to croak along the bank and dusk deepening, she became aware of him all over again.

"I shall drown you," she said lightly, breathlessly, "if given the chance."

She was trapped, her back against the lumpy rock and silt creek bottom with Thaddeus slung carelessly across her, his face mere inches away.

"Don't I know it?" he replied with a half smile on handsome, sculpted lips. "So we have a dilemma. If I relinquish my advantage, I risk death by drowning." His face hovered ever closer, and his voice lowered. "What's a man to do?"

Thunder rumbled over the mountains and into her

chest, though there was not a cloud in the sky. Was Thaddeus threatening to kiss her?

Her breath came faster. My, but his face was handsome, and his eyes, she knew, were the color of a summer morning, a color she'd always admired. He smelled of corn and heat and clear, sweet water. The unfamiliar heaviness and heat of him pressed against her, a different heat than the weather, a troubling heat she rather enjoyed.

His warm, soft breath fanned her face. He blinked, and thick lashes, dark with moisture, fanned his sculpted cheekbones. With his hair pushed back from his face, a small puckered scar appeared beneath his right ear. A burn scar.

She wanted him to kiss her. Desperately wanted it.

And him a Yankee.

"A better question, sir," she said in mock haughtiness, "is this."

In a movement as quick as the darting fish in the creek, she stuck her fingers into his rib cage and tickled. Caught by surprise, he cried out, laughing and wriggling to get away.

As he tumbled onto his side and into the creek, she let go of him to sit up quickly and watch him flail about in the shallows. Satisfied that she'd won the skirmish, both with him and herself, she pushed her hair back in a heavy, wet wad, straightened her skirt and smiled a cat's smile.

He sat up beside her, breathing heavily, expression wryly amused. "Truce."

Josie sniffed. She would have tossed her head, but wet hair was too heavy. "For now."

He chuckled, and when he did, she giggled. Soon

they were laughing, laughing, until tears mingled with the creek water.

Finally, when the mirth subsided, Thad rose and helped her up, this time with the grace of a gentleman. She didn't want him to be a gentleman. His courtesy made her...care. And caring about him was unconscionable.

To cover her discomfort, she found his hat and plopped it on his head. They both dripped, but her long skirts made walking a chore. She lifted the hem and trudged along beside him.

He took her arm, gentleman again, and led the way up the path alongside the waterwheel and down the shadowy, bushy trail leading across the road and into the fields.

"I fear we've missed supper."

"Charlotte will leave something on the stove."

Dusk became nightfall, and the moon rose, full and yellow as an egg yolk.

A thousand thoughts tumbled through her head. She hated Yankees, and Thad was a Yankee. But he was also a good man who made her happy in a way she hadn't been since Tom.

There was the crux of the matter. Tom.

CHAPTER TWENTY-FOUR

Present

Hayden was gone.

It was bad enough he'd left without a word, but to make matters worse, Carrie had to learn about his departure from Lynn at the Miniature Golf Café. Lynn had heard the news from the Sweat twins, who'd heard it from Whitey Farris at the gas station on Bedford Street, which connected directly to the highway leading out of town. Whitey had been on duty when Hayden filled the Chrysler with gas, picked up a bag of trail mix, a bottle of orange juice and one of water and headed north.

Over a chicken salad sandwich, Carrie tried to pretend she was neither surprised nor disappointed, though she was both.

"You didn't know," Nikki said, after Lynn Ringwald slid a Cobb salad in front her and moved away. Carrie's sister, who could read her face before her brain knew what she was thinking, at least had the good grace to lean in close and speak quietly.

With a breezy wave of a paper napkin, Carrie answered, "He was only in Honey Ridge to work on a book. He lives in New York. I suppose it was time for him to move on."

Nikki squinted long-lashed eyes. "But he didn't tell you. And at Dad's party, I gathered that you two were getting close. You've sure spent a lot of time with him."

"I helped with his research." She poked a chip in her mouth and crunched.

"Well, shoot. That's disappointing to hear."

Tell me about it. Disappointing and humiliating. She had invited him in, and he'd left town instead. *Great for a girl's ego.*

"Did you call him?"

"No!" Carrie drew back against the diner chair. "Why would I do that?"

"I'm your sister. Even if you pretend not to care, I saw the way you were with Hayden."

"You keep that to yourself. Hayden has never said one word to lead me on. If I have feelings—and I'm not saying I do—they're on me, not him." After that night and that kiss, the ball was in his court. "If he'd wanted me to know, he would have called me."

The moment when he'd kissed her—she resisted the urge to touch her mouth the way she had a dozen times before falling asleep Sunday night—had been magical. Then he'd backed away and left her bewildered and a little hurt.

And he'd left town without a word.

She didn't invite men into her house every weekend. In a town this small, reputation was everything, a fact she knew too well. She'd taken months, maybe years, to live down the day Simon's wife had called her an ugly, pathetic, old-maid husband stealer—and a lot of other unmentionable things—in front of half the town. The gossips had lapped it up, choosing to believe and embellish every word, even though they had known her all her life.

Gossip burned and scarred like a brand.

She didn't want to do that again, and Hayden was the first man she'd cared about in a very long time. Like, aeons.

He'd only made it as far as the threshold before bolting.

She'd bet a case of books and a Starbucks card that no man had ever walked away from Nikki's invitation.

Nikki picked the purple onion rings from her salad. "You don't think he's married, do you?"

"No."

Nikki leaned forward and put a hand over hers, lowering her voice so that Poker shuffling his cards at the next table wouldn't hear. "How do you know? Some men are lying creeps."

Carrie's appetite went south. She laid aside her fork. "He's a public figure. Someone would know."

"True. I hadn't thought of that." Nikki leaned back in her chair. "Thank goodness, he's not like Simon in that respect."

"Hayden's nothing like Simon. Simon was a sleaze who lied about loving me. Hayden is a friend who's been nothing but a gentleman." He didn't know, couldn't know that she was falling for him. He'd walked away. He'd left her with her pride intact. "Can we change the subject?"

"Any guy who doesn't appreciate my baby sister doesn't deserve her."

Hayden appreciated her. He even found her attractive. But he'd also been honest from the beginning about his plans. Except for the leaving part.

She'd known from the moment they met that he was out of her league. The fact that her heart had cracked a little to discover him gone without so much as a phone call was beside the point. "It isn't me I'm concerned about, Nik. It's Brody."

"They were pals, weren't they?"

"More than pals. I think Hayden felt some kind of kinship with Brody. He was adamant about hanging out with him after school. He took him to a baseball game and fishing."

"I hope he didn't wear those Ferragamos." Nikki pointed her fork and laughed. "Kidding."

"Brody doesn't have much of a family, and Hayden was good to him." She took her sandwich from the thick white plate, contemplating the dill pickle secured to the top with a toothpick. "I wonder if Hayden let him know he was leaving. Brody will be heartsick if he didn't."

"I heard Trey talking to Dad about Brody's missing mother. He's putting out feelers for information. However policemen do that."

Brody's busted wall flashed in her head.

"Clint Thomson's not a nice man. Who could blame his wife for leaving?"

"I wonder why she didn't take her son?"

"That's the question we're all asking. Hayden wonders if the Sweat twins are right and Thomson killed her. The curse of a thriller novelist, I guess. He sees the sinister in everything."

Nikki shivered. "That's creepy. People in Honey Ridge don't kill each other." She grinned. "Well, not physically. We just chop each other to pieces with our tongues."

Carrie laughed. "That's too true to be funny."

"I mean, really, did you notice that tacky window display in Cavandish's Dress Shop? No stylish woman would ever wear those colors together."

"The woman should be forced out of town," Carrie teased.

Nikki was off and running on her rival's poor taste, but Carrie couldn't get Brody out of her mind. Hayden had befriended the boy and made promises.

How could he leave without saying goodbye? Was he planning to return? And wasn't she pitiful for hoping he was?

THERE WAS NO melody so deep and primal as the rhythm of a Southern night. Filled with magic and seductive music, the air thick and heavy and throbbing with secrets.

From the back veranda of Peach Orchard Inn, Hayden lifted his face to the sky, eyes closed, soaking in the sounds of a night sky filled with the distant rumble of a promised storm. The afternoon heat and humidity had waned, leaving behind the gentle tug of heaviness, of perfume on the wind and restlessness in the soul.

But his soul was always restless, more so since returning from Kentucky after the latest battering of his heart and mind.

Three days of Dora Lee had stripped him down to nothing.

The insanity he feared crept in, black and desolate, gnawing at his soul. He carried Dora Lee's ugly DNA, the predisposition to be cruel and wild and self-

possessed. Her mother had been locked away, a danger
to herself. Dora Lee had been a danger to him.

Mental illness flowed in his blood and had him writing of horror and death and man's inhumanity to man.
The line between insanity and creativity, he'd learned,
was a fine one, two sides of the same coin. Take van
Gogh, for instance.

How did a man know when he'd crossed over?

With the dreams coming nearly every night and the
confusion and dark sorrow roiling in his head, he wondered if he, too, was slipping into madness.

He'd gone to Dora Lee's house the day after she'd
ditched him at Packard's. She wasn't home. He'd tried
her cell phone so many times he'd have to give her
money for extra minutes.

The lapse was his fault. He never should have put
cash in her hands.

Inside the trailer, he'd kept busy cleaning, grateful
the power was back on so he didn't have to drag water
from the creek or go anywhere near the well.

He'd considered calling the sheriff. Maybe Dora Lee
hadn't really abandoned him in pursuit of drugs. Perhaps something terrible had happened. Had she OD'd?
Had some other pill addict knocked her in the head,
taken her money or drugs and left her to die?

How many times in his childhood had he lain in the
dark and cold, worrying over those same questions,
both fearing her return and praying for it?

She was his mother, such as she was, and though he
despised himself for caring, he did.

Finally, late that evening she had stumbled in,
singing at the top of her lungs, leaning on a scrawny

bearded dude with black teeth. They were both higher than a Georgia pine.

The memory stung. Of guilt and shame and always, always, the self-blame. He'd done that to her by giving her money.

He simply didn't know how to stop.

In disgust and despair, he'd driven back to the hotel and to his laptop. Since the discussion with Trey, he'd been fueled with a book idea. A missing mother murdered by her husband, but no one suspects a thing until their son reaches the teen years and begins to ask questions.

That night, he'd been dry as Death Valley.

He'd plopped on the motel bed, hands behind his head and insides in a boil.

He had wished he could talk to Carrie, to share all the putrid filth of his life, to vomit it out and be done with it instead of living with the fear that someone, especially her, would find out.

He should have called her before he left. He could have made some excuse about rushing back to New York on business.

Lies. He didn't want to lie to Carrie.

Reaching for his cell, he'd flipped through the contacts and highlighted her name. Carrie. Not Carrie Riley. Just Carrie.

She'd want to know where he was, what he was doing. She'd care that he was exhausted and worried and lonely.

He couldn't tell her where or why.

With a beleaguered sigh, he'd tapped the screen to black and put the phone away.

The next day he'd ordered a new electric heater, a

new mattress and linens along with various other supplies and paid a local for delivery before driving back to the trailer with another load of groceries and more carryout. Perhaps if he made Dora Lee's life better, easier, she would change.

Not that he hadn't tried before.

Dora Lee and her new friend hadn't welcomed him with open arms. His mother had stood in the cluttered yard, smoking a cigarette and giggling while the boyfriend kissed the back of her neck until Hayden needed to vomit.

While Hayden unloaded the grocery bags, the man stared at him with hollow, sneaky eyes, though his hands were all over Dora Lee. Hayden tried not to look. After a while, the man said, "I know you from somewhere. Didn't I see your picture in the paper?"

Hayden's blood ran cold. If Dora Lee's friends discovered his identity, she would, too. His mouth worked, but nothing came out.

Dora Lee guffawed. "Gawd, Jerry, you must be smoking crack," and then she'd burst into hysterical laughter because smoking crack was exactly what they'd been doing. They reeked of it.

Pulse ticking like a time bomb with the fear of discovery, Hayden stepped outside to collect his wits.

Behind him, the door slammed and the lock clicked.

They had what they wanted, and he was a third wheel. He wasn't sorry to be shut out. The need to get far, far away propelled him to the car.

So he'd driven more than five hours back to Honey Ridge, arriving long after dark, too tired and troubled to sleep.

Thank God for a coming storm.

He raised his face to the sky.

The smell of approaching rain was a perfume like no other and could wash away the memory of the previous days. But tonight, the green, clean smell reminded him of boyhood days spent in the deep Appalachian woods inside his hideout when Dora Lee was at her worst. Spurred by stories of Swift's Lost Silver Mines, he'd wandered the mountains in pursuit of hidden treasure and, in the search, had found his own fragile kind of peace.

He thought of Brody and the boy's predilection for camping in the woods with his wounded creatures. He, too, was finding his own kind of peace.

Somewhere nearby, a single bullfrog trilled a long, incessant song, undaunted in his love pursuit by nature's coming fury. The cicadas hummed all the louder, spurred to frenetic action by the heat, humidity and secret cover of darkness.

Miles away lightning flickered above the trees.

Did Carrie hear the approaching thunder? Was she as attuned to the serendipitous moods of nature, though hers in defense instead of pleasure? Was she awake and anxious?

He walked a bit, though the lawn was dark and not a star winked. He had a woodsman's eyesight, and the white angel gleamed luminescent from Michael's garden, hauntingly lovely, a reminder evergreen and poignant of the boy who went to school and disappeared and of the mother who still waited with cookies and open arms.

Most mothers loved their little boys.

Hayden circled the big silent house and headed to his car parked in the graveled lot for guests.

He tried to fool himself into thinking he didn't know where he was going. He was driving with the windows open, feeling the night and the approaching storm, he told himself. Perhaps he'd drive left, up on the ridge and watch the weather roll in. Carrie had taken him to a breathtaking overlook where he could see for miles down into the valley and east to the Smokies.

Carrie. She called to him much as the storm did.

At the end of the long, winding lane leading from house to highway, however, he turned right.

The trip into Honey Ridge was short. He didn't click on the radio or slide in a CD. He let the feel of the night circle and swirl around him like ghosts of the past.

Maybe, as Julia hinted, the inn had them and that's why the dreams kept coming with vivid regularity. Ghosts with a tale to tell had discovered in Hayden Winters a damaged mind and a broken soul that was easily invaded.

He didn't believe in ghosts or houses with messages, but he couldn't deny what was happening.

The admission brought the fear picking at him like a child with a scab.

Main Street was empty, quiet, rolled up for the night. Two blocks down near the park a single convenience store was bright with lights. A handful of cars rolled lazily through a fast-food drive-through.

At the single traffic signal in midtown, he stopped, pondered the police cruiser parked along the curb in front of First Bank. With humor, he mused that no financial institution was ever called Second Bank.

When the light ticked from red to green, he accelerated across the intersection, lifting a hand toward the officer invisible inside the cruiser, wondering if Trey was on duty. How easily he'd fallen into the rhythm of Honey Ridge, had missed it in those scant days away.

In minutes, he idled through a neighborhood of older frame homes and stopped in front of a tidy gray one with maroon shutters and roof. Carrie was home; the blue Volkswagen was parked along the side of the house.

Lights blazed, casting a buttery glow onto the gardenia blooming rapturously beside the porch. He plucked a stem, broke it from the tall spreading bush. The sensual smell wrapped around him as he stepped onto her porch and lifted the brass knocker.

He owed her more than a stolen flower. Yet he didn't dare explain why he'd walked away that night. Her invitation had melted him, and his desire to be with her had almost overshadowed his sense of preservation.

A relationship based on a lie was not what he wanted with Carrie Riley.

The question wasn't what *did* he want, but what could he allow himself to have?

He held the gardenia to his nose and sniffed. A beautiful flower in bloom. Ugly in death.

Facades were built because the outward structure was unacceptable. He was unacceptable. If he told her, he stood to lose everything, including her.

She opened the door, and his breath swooshed away. In loose lounge pants and a fitted camisole, devoid of makeup, she looked sixteen and way too young for the thoughts running through his head, thoughts he'd sequestered since that night on her porch when he'd almost let himself get too close.

Thunder rumbled, a long kettledrum sound, like snatches of Irish music on the wind.

"Hayden?" Backlit in gold by the living room light, Carrie stared at him, arms crossed, her flesh pale against the blue top.

"We're in for another storm. May I come in?"

Something flickered in her expression. She was remembering, like him, the invitation he'd rejected.

She stepped to the side and pushed the door open wider.

"I thought you'd left town for good."

Was that hurt in her voice?

"Not for good." But he'd have to soon, or they'd both be doomed to a heartache he could neither explain nor avoid.

He stepped inside her tidy house, soothed to be in her space. Everything here was clean and in order, like her. The polar opposite of his mother's trailer. "I should have called."

"Brody wondered. He missed you."

He made an effort to smile. He was too heart weary to be here. Fatigue was dangerous. A man needed to be on his best game when he was feeling vulnerable.

"I missed him, too. And you."

"Where were you?" she asked and then waved away the words. "Not my business, sorry."

Thunder boomed closer. Her shoulders jerked. Her ex had humiliated her during a storm.

"You're nervous." He offered the gardenia, glad to avoid the subject of his trip.

She took the blossom, sniffed with her eyes closed. "I'm always nervous when the weather is crazy. I should move to California."

"Then you could worry about wildfires or earthquakes," he teased, voice gentle. "And you wouldn't have gardenias blooming outside your windows."

"My favorite flower."

He knew. He remembered. A husband to bring her gardenias, but a husband he could never be.

He took the blossom from her and tucked the stem into her hair behind one ear. She reached up, touched it, her brown eyes soft and wondering.

He yearned to talk to her. To *tell* her. Sometimes the need to be real with someone was so loud he thought he'd go mad. But how could a woman from a perfect family in a perfectly normal small town even begin to understand or accept where he'd come from? She knew and respected him as Hayden Winters, the author, but would she look down on him, repulsed, to learn of Hayden Briggs, the pillbilly's son?

He couldn't take the risk of her, or anyone, knowing he was nothing but a figment of his own imagination.

With an aching chest, he sighed, bewildered at the struggle inside him. He'd been doing this for years. He'd even become comfortable with the masquerade. Why was lying to Carrie any different?

"Would you like coffee?" she asked, her bare feet padding softly against the area rug as they moved deeper into the living room, a small space with beige furniture and apple-green accessories. The smell of gardenias trailed behind her, as heavy and sweet as the coming rain.

"It's late. Are you sure you don't mind?"

"Are you crazy? I'll be up all night." Lightning flickered, and she cast a worried glance toward the draped windows.

"I thought you might be."

"Is that why you came?"

Was it?

Hayden experienced a sudden hard knock in his chest, an *aha* moment like the ones he experienced in his writing. That moment when everything became clear and he understood the message.

He was falling in love with Carrie Riley, if he understood what love was. He'd never felt it before. Desire, yes. Affection, certainly. But not this shattering need to care for her and have her care in return. To be certain she not only was safe but that she *felt* safe, even in a harmless thunderstorm. The need to pry open his aching soul and pour out everything, trusting that she, of all the women on the earth, would accept and understand.

He was in terrible danger. And so was she. He couldn't do that to her, not to Carrie. Sweet as the honey that named this town, she'd be kind, but his secret would be hers, and secrets revealed destroyed a person.

She took a step toward him, tremulous, and he let his body and mind relax, but only for tonight. For her. She was afraid, her storm phobia running wilder as the storm increased.

Tonight she needed him.

Gently, he drew her into his embrace and held her. She trembled, though he didn't know if it was from fear of the storm or his nearness. He hoped it was the latter and then chided himself for wanting too much.

Her warm breath against his neck sent a shiver through him.

He needed her more.

He brushed his lips over the top of her hair, ever so lightly.

How did he, without sounding like a lunatic, tell her that some part of him had connected to her that day in the gristmill and again at her family gathering, and even now, he instinctively knew his presence made her stronger just as she was a balm to the emotional bruises he'd suffered in Kentucky?

"I don't want you to be afraid. Storms are beautiful."

He stroked a hand over her back, the stretchy camisole fabric shifting beneath his touch. He was careful, respectful, not to slide his hands beneath the shirt. He understood now why he'd walked away that night when he'd desperately wanted to stay. Loving Carrie would be the destruction of Hayden Winters.

CHAPTER TWENTY-FIVE

CARRIE HAD NEVER been so glad to see another person in her life, and she didn't have to examine the reasons to know her feelings were more about seeing Hayden than needing a refuge in the storm.

He'd come back, and suddenly the vague sense of embarrassment that had plagued her all week disappeared like afternoon fog. Hayden had known she'd be anxious in this weather, and he'd come to offer his calm, reassuring support. She didn't know why. She didn't care why.

She was, after all, a romantic fool who read Byron and Keats and sobbed at the end of Nicholas Sparks movies. If her thoughts drifted in the direction of romance, Carrie let them. She was wise enough to know Hayden was in Honey Ridge on business and anything between them would disappear when he left.

For now, she was glad he'd come back.

Long into the noisy, bumpy night, they sipped too much coffee, snacked on pita chips and tried to watch television. When the thunder boomed and rattled the windows, he snuggled with her on the couch, holding her, smoothing his long writer's hand up and down her back until she found herself wishing and waiting for that usually dreaded sound.

When the electricity flickered, kicking off the cable

and threatening total blackness, they'd lit some candles and gotten out the Scrabble board. She'd been so nervous about the thunder, he'd beaten her quickly.

His mind clearly was not in the game, either. Something else troubled him. She'd been so thrilled to see him and so nervous about the thunderstorm that she hadn't noticed at first.

Now she did.

He was distracted. His usual polished charm seemed dulled, and for a man who thrived on stormy nights, he was oddly disinterested in nature's fury. Frequently, while she pondered a new word, he zoned out and stared into space.

Trounced again, she folded the board and began dropping the letter tiles into the velvet bag. "Is everything all right with you?"

Hayden's smoky eyes grew cautious. "Of course. Why?"

"You seem...pensive. Worried. Did something happen on your trip?" She wasn't prying. Not technically. Even if he didn't want to share where he'd gone or why, she cared that he was troubled.

Hayden's expression searched hers. She saw shadows hidden in his eyes, and for a few long seconds that neared the point of awkwardness, he didn't respond.

Maybe she *was* prying.

Leaving the table, he poured another cup of coffee, held the pot aloft until she shook her head, too jittery already. When he returned, Hayden set the cup on the table without drinking and went to the window.

"Come look," he said, and she was disappointed that he hadn't answered her question.

Because of his celebrity, she understood his need for

privacy, at least in theory. She respected it. But they were friends, weren't they? And friends were there for each other, the way he was here for her tonight.

"The storm is passing," he said softly. "You've lived through another."

She didn't know if he teased or was serious.

She went to stand beside him. The windowpane radiated coolness, and drops of water drizzled down like silvery angel tears.

He tucked an arm around her waist. "If you watch when the lightning flickers, you can see the outline of the ridge. It's beautiful."

Protected, safe, she swallowed her fear of lightning and watched the flickers, wanting to share what he loved. She leaned into his side, felt him accept her weight. She wanted to share other things, too, including his heartaches.

"What's wrong, Hayden? You can tell me." And with all her courage, she admitted, "I care."

His breath made disappearing clouds on the glass. Quietly, without looking at her, he said, "Nothing to worry about, Carrie. I went to visit my mother. We had…a disagreement."

"I'm sorry. Are you okay?"

"Tired. That's all."

Fatigue rode his shoulders like boulders, and a kind of mournful sorrow emanated from him. Something she couldn't quite put a finger on. All she understood, and she understood it to her marrow, was that Hayden was sad.

She stroked a hand over the small of his back, offering comfort as he had for her. "Anything I could do to help?"

"No." He sighed in one long, weary huff. "We'll work it out."

There was something false in his solemn words. She waited for an explanation, but when it was not forthcoming Carrie's manners would not allow her to press any further. A man had a right to his thoughts, to his family privacy, to share or not.

A fist of regret squeezed beneath her breastbone.

For him, for his terrible aloneness.

They stood in silence, hands on each other's backs, watching the flickers and flashes and hearing the patter of the soft rain left behind by the tumultuous clouds. Occasionally, a far-off rumble, like a belly laugh, promised the worst had passed.

"I brought you something," he said.

The switch in topics caught her off guard. She tilted her head back to look at his profile. So strong and distant. So haunted.

Hayden was a complicated man who touched a place deep in her heart. She wondered if anyone really knew him.

"Something besides the gardenia?"

"I was going to give it to you later, but—" he turned from the window and started toward the door "—it's in the car."

She regretted the loss of his strong, steady hand against her body. "Don't get struck by lightning."

From the doorway, Carrie watched him dash through the rain to his car, touched that she'd been in his thoughts during his days away.

How long since a man, other than her daddy or brother, surprised her with a gift?

Hayden loped up the step, shook the raindrops from his hair and came inside, holding a small box.

Puzzled and pleased, she reached out, but he shook his head. "This is a sitting-down gift."

She laughed lightly. "Am I going to faint?"

His handsome mouth curved in response "I hope not. We got through the worst of the thunderstorm. I think you'll survive this."

He handed her the square box and Carrie lifted out a silver chain, similar to the one she'd lost at the mill, only this one bore a delicate bird clasp.

She drew in a soft gasp. "Hayden, this is…exquisite."

"Let me."

Kneeling in front of her, he lifted her foot to his upraised knee. A longing stirred deep in her belly. Like Prince Charming and Cinderella, she thought, only Carrie's glass slipper was a dainty ankle bracelet, and her Prince Charming wasn't here to take her away.

But she didn't let her thoughts go there, to the time when he'd be a memory. Now was far too pleasant, too tempting and lovely.

"This is exquisite, Hayden, much nicer than the one I lost. You shouldn't have." Even while she tried not to read too much into the gift, she was wonderfully pleased.

He shrugged away her objections. "My fault you lost yours, so I thought it was only fair I replace it."

"I'm the ninny who fell through the floor."

"My idea to explore the mill. You wouldn't have been there to fall if not for me."

"Silly." But the gift touched her, moved her, heated that place in her heart where he'd taken up residence.

"I would have bought it anyway, Carrie." His warm fingers lingered on her cool skin, his smoky, haunted eyes on hers. "The moment I saw it, I thought of you."

Her pulse skittered, slid and finally caught a rhythm again. She wasn't the kind for glib words, but, oh, her heart was on fire. Did the man have any idea what he was doing?

HAYDEN LOOKED INTO soft brown eyes and wondered what he was doing. He'd promised not to let his thoughts run wild. He should have reserved the bracelet for another time when he was rested and less vulnerable.

Buying the chain had not been, as he'd implied, a casual discovery. He'd searched, stopping at several jewelry stores until he'd seen this one with the small winged bird—a sparrow perhaps, the perfect complement to Carrie's unique natural beauty.

His hand lingered on her ankle a few more seconds until he realized his blood raced and his thoughts headed toward dangerous ground. He wanted more. He wanted her. But an affair would never satisfy the feelings boiling in his chest, and if he was honest, asking that of her seemed shallow and empty, an insult to this thing that stirred between them.

He felt things for Carrie he didn't know how to control, emotions that would get him into trouble.

A man in his situation could not allow emotions to run his life. Only by focusing on the goal could he continue to succeed, and yet, lately, the goal had blurred until he wondered if he was slipping away.

Slowly, he lowered her foot to the multicolored area rug. To torture himself, he caressed her ankle one last time before rising to his feet. "I should head back to the inn."

She rose with him, glancing toward a round wall clock over the sofa. "You must be exhausted."

"I am." That was the only excuse he had for wanting to stay here with Carrie the rest of the night. Admitting he'd been to see Dora Lee had made him feel vulnerable, and yet he fought the wildly insane desire to tell Carrie every ugly detail of his life.

The real Hayden *needed* her and was on the verge of trusting her, a scary proposition. Because he'd inherited his mother's twisted DNA, he was destined to remain at a standoff between what he needed and wanted and what had to be. No kid should have to worry about going crazy and hurting someone he was supposed to love.

"The storm is over," he said softly, wishing it wasn't. Wishing he had an excuse to stay. "Will you be able to sleep now?"

Her voice was subdued as if she too felt the pull. "Thanks to you."

For the life of him, he couldn't muster a witty reply.

"Thank you for the bracelet." She smiled the sweet smile he'd thought of often in Kentucky. Clean and pure and real.

"My pleasure." That much, at least, was honest. He loved the way the chain looked on her ankle, and knowing he'd put it there filled him with some sort of primal, possessive machismo. He'd marked her as his.

He shook his head, ridding his thoughts of the sweet, fulfilling fantasy. Those were the things he'd write in his books. They weren't reality.

She walked him to the door, her hand resting lightly

above the back of his elbow. Hayden battled the foolish part of him that begged to turn into her touch and stay.

Far away on the mountains, lightning flickered. Carrie crossed her arms. Hayden stepped out on the porch and looked up, feeling the wild stir in his blood.

"Come to the inn tomorrow night for dinner. Bring Brody."

"Okay," she said, hand still on his elbow, the warmth of her touch a balm to a troubled soul. "He'll be happy you're home."

Home. Did she realize what she'd said? Or how her words started a jungle drum beating in his vagabond soul?

"Good night, Carrie." They stood with the door open, the rain-washed smell of grass and gardenias sweeping over them.

He leaned close to kiss her. Just once. A friendly, good-night touch of warm lips. But somehow the kiss lingered and deepened until Hayden required all his resolve to trot down the step and drive away, back to Peach Orchard Inn and the dreams that haunted him almost as much as she did.

CHAPTER TWENTY-SIX

*True love knows no boundaries but it crosses
many.*

—Anonymous

1867

HE WAS FALLING in love with her.

Thad walked alongside the spitfire redhead, both
awed and bothered that he could feel something this
profound for Josie Portland. Part of him winced at
being disloyal to Amelia while the other part rejoiced
to feel again. To have his heart beat outside his chest
again.

He'd never expected this. Not with her. A fiercely
loyal Reb with a hankering to draw and quarter anyone from north of the Mason-Dixon Line.

Life was full of surprises.

The woods cast long shadows over the open meadow
between the mill and house, and when Josie tripped on
an exposed root, he caught her elbow. Her head swung
his way, and his chest tightened at her beauty. The
woman he'd dismissed as spoiled and selfish wasn't
shallow at all, though she did her best to hide her tenderness.

He'd told her about Amelia, and if only for a second, he'd forgotten about those final screaming moments when he'd tried to reach his family and failed. Josie helped him recall the good.

He slid his hand lower on Josie's arm, and when she didn't pull away, he laced his rough miller's fingers with hers, surprised to find small calluses on her fingertips.

She sewed. She worked. She cared. He'd been so wrong about her.

"Will said you lost a beau in the war."

She drew in a deep, shuddery breath, and he thought for a moment she'd blast him for prying. But she didn't.

"Tom was my fiancé," she said softly into the gray-black darkness of field and woods. "We were to be married when he came home." Her voice dipped. She sighed. "He never did."

Thad squeezed her fingers. It was all the comfort he had to offer. "What happened?"

Her head turned to look into the black woods as if the answer waited behind the oaks. The moon illuminated the ghostly image of her throat. Thad heard her swallow. "We don't know."

The worst kind of ending for a soldier and his family. Not knowing.

"Any idea where he last served? Or where he'd been?"

"Margaret heard from him last. That's his mama," she clarified. "He was somewhere in Georgia, if I recall."

"And you never heard from him again?"

"Not a word in more than three years now. The army, his superiors, no one seems to know. We keep hoping…"

Thad ached for her. Her fiancé was not the only man unaccounted for after the war. Both Union and Confederate forces had lists of soldiers who'd simply disappeared. Even his cousin Will, sick in a Confederate prison, had been considered dead for months, only to be released after Lee's surrender at Appomattox.

But Union prisons no longer existed, and no living prisoners remained unaccounted for. Josie's fiancé was doubtless dead, buried in an unmarked grave far from these Tennessee hills.

"Since I can remember," Josie said, "Tom Foster was part of my life. No one ever doubted that the two of us would marry except me." She laughed softly, nostalgically. "I gave him a merry chase by flirting with other boys. But as my brother, Edgar, often reminded me, Tom was the only man who could endure my fits of temper and unladylike opinions and still find me charming."

He found her charming and rather admired her unladylike opinions.

"Tom was a lucky man."

She stopped in the meadow with tall grass up to her knees. Moonlight bathed her in gold, and the scent of wild honeysuckle swirled around her, a perfume as sweet as she.

"Because he endured my awful temper?"

"Because you loved him."

"Oh." Her mouth opened in a perfect circle. Even in the shadows, he saw the same confusion in her eyes that struggled beneath his ribs.

Then, whether from pity or selfishness, Thad did something he never expected to do ever again. He kissed a woman.

Softly, gently, he touched his mouth to hers, testing the waters and finding them warm and soft, and if he dared believe, accepting. Inviting even.

His pulse rattled. Blood rushed to his temples. He wanted to crush her to his chest.

She pressed toward him, up on tiptoe.

Thad's stomach leaped. He pulled away, his breath coming more rapidly as if he'd trotted across the field and raced up the stairs with a load of grain on his back.

They stood together beneath the moon, each examining the other with only their eyes.

Josie touched a finger to her bottom lip. Thad's stomach tightened, and the powerful hunger to kiss her again slammed into him.

"I should probably slap you." There was not a speck of animosity in her statement.

"Will you?" he asked, amused and tempted.

"Only if you don't kiss me again."

What could he say? A man didn't want to be slapped when the alternative was so much more pleasant.

He pulled her close this time, arms around her narrow waist, and settled in to savor the strawberry sweetness of her mouth.

JOSIE DIDN'T KNOW what was the matter with her. Perhaps seeing Thad's scars or hearing about the fire had stirred her pity. Perhaps she was touched by the kindness he'd shown to Amelia, the stranger in town. Or maybe it was simply Thaddeus himself that had caused her to do such a thing.

Kissing under the moonlight in an open meadow. Why, the very idea was—was—she closed her eyes and savored the memory—so incredibly romantic.

Long after she'd gone to bed that night, she lay awake thinking of those kisses. Not only the way she felt in his arms but of the man himself. She admired him. There, she'd allowed the shameful thought. She admired a Yankee.

In the darkness with his arms around her and his voice low and gently amused, he didn't *feel* like the enemy.

Her knees shook a little to think such a thing.

Nevertheless, her interest was piqued, and she found more excuses to visit the mill in the following days. A Portland was needed there, and she was nothing if not a good hand with the shelling and bolting and bagging. If she and Thad migrated to the water bucket at the same time or bumped into each other on the stairs or lingered long after dark and walked home together, what harm was there in that?

This particular morning she was in the mercantile, her shoes ringing hollow against the plank floor. There at Charlotte's request, she delivered a load of meal in exchange for store credit to buy sugar and tea and coffee and other items the farm couldn't grow.

Ellen Stockton and her mother came inside the dim confines of Merriman's Mercantile as Josie admired a bolt of the deep blue silk. Whatever was Mr. Merriman thinking to order such an extravagance? Even the banker's wife couldn't afford the luxury in this day and time. But, oh, the cloth was lovely, and her fingers itched to create something beautiful.

"Hello, Josie." Round and dimpled and a bit on the silly side though sweet and sincere, Ellen Stockton belonged to Josie's weekly quilting circle.

"Ellen," she said. "Hello. And to you, as well, Mrs. Stockton. Isn't this silk the prettiest thing?"

"The color would be beautiful on you, Josie," Ellen said and then clapped her dainty hands. "You should buy it and use those nimble fingers of yours to make something swoonworthy. Why, your new beau would find you positively irresistible."

Josie froze. Her nimble fingers, lingering on the silken fabric, grew chilled. "My new beau?"

Ellen's smooth brow wrinkled in worry as if she feared she'd spilled a secret. "I'm sorry. Have I misspoken? I thought—"

"You do not need to apologize, Ellen," Mrs. Stockton said. "Josie surely knows she's the talk of the town. Once again."

"Mama. Don't." Ellen placed a hand on her mother's arm.

"Don't shush me, Ellen. Better to speak to her face than talk behind her back."

A seed of anxiety, as unfamiliar as love, pushed into Josie's throat. Animosity vibrated from her friend's mother. The chance encounter had quickly turned sour. "Tell me what?"

The older woman, her black hair pulled into a bun severe enough to make her eyes slant upward in a near-devilish manner, leaned closer.

"Word is all over town that you are siding with slaves and lollygagging with that new Yankee miller in a most inappropriate manner."

Why, the old gossip. Josie's lips tightened.

"Mama, please. I beg you."

Ellen's mother was not to be deterred. Her slanted eyes narrowed until Josie thought they'd disappear into the folds of fat and never be seen again, and a mercy that would be, she thought.

As a woman who considered herself on the upper shelf of Honey Ridge society, Mamie Stockton was a battering ram who never missed an opportunity to impose her opinions on others.

"Since you never had a mother to teach you right from wrong," Mamie said, "I feel it is my duty as a Christian woman to speak up before you do something regretful and shame us all. Though it certainly wouldn't be the first time."

Josie sucked in a roomful of coffee-scented air, the flare of temper beginning to crawl up the back of her neck. She couldn't cause a scene here. Not in town. Not now. The urge to throw a hissy fit bubbled up in her chest until she feared she'd choke. But choke she would before she'd give this old biddy the pleasure of being proved correct. Nosy Mamie Stockton was fortunate indeed that Josephine Portland was no longer the impetuous girl of old.

With all the dignity her temper would allow, Josie thrust her chin high. Lips tight and flat, she said, "Mrs. Stockton, I am at a loss. Perhaps we should speak of this at another ti—"

"Your lack of understanding proves my point perfectly." Worn lace fanned the air as the harridan shook her handkerchief at Josie. "Just because your family owns the only mill for miles around doesn't make you immune to social conventions or give you a right to mistreat your own kind. First, that—*that man* takes Mr. Pitts's job, and him a loyal employee for many years. And now the Yankee miller is courting Tom Foster's fiancée. Shameful, I say."

Face flaming hot as a blacksmith's forge, Josie shook with the need to strike back.

Temper, Josephine, temper.

"Courting?" She bit off the word in a low, furious voice. If this hateful old woman didn't hush soon, Josie would not be responsible for the consequences.

A well-bred woman practices self-control at all times.

She'd heard the admonishment from grammar school teachers so often she had ultimately lost all control and screamed like a banshee.

Mrs. Stockton probably knew about those little lapses, too. The old biddy.

She and Thad weren't courting. They were simply thrown together by virtue of proximity and the fact that her family owned the gristmill.

And because they'd shared a few meaningless kisses. Kisses she couldn't stop thinking about.

Her fury drained away as quickly as it had come.

Was Mrs. Stockton right? At least in part? Were she and Thad *courting*?

"You'll excuse me," she said stiffly. "This conversation is over."

"Josie, I'm sorry—"

She stayed only long enough to see Mrs. Stockton yank Ellen's arm before she gathered up her purchases; then, head high and cheeks roasting hotter than a rabbit on a spit, she hurried out of the store.

She was *Tom's* fiancée.

But she was falling in love with another man. Tom's enemy. *Her* enemy.

THAD HAD NEVER imagined being happy again. He'd never imagined feeling anything for a woman other than Amelia. He'd never dreamed of wanting another, of longing for another.

Yet in the days following that first moonlight kiss something akin to hope had sprouted under his rib cage like a wild, sweet vine reaching for the sunlight.

Will teased him and Abram noticed his interest in the sassy redhead. Neither judged or chided him, and for that he was grateful. His insides were tangled enough as it was.

That Josie found excuses to be at the mill and linger late for the walk home told him she was interested, too.

Yes, indeed. Something pleasant was astir on the summer air.

His heart tripped pleasantly as he crossed the grass between the rambling farmhouse and the garden out back.

"Penny for your thoughts," he said, coming up behind the woman occupying all of his.

Brown skirt pooled on the dark ground, she bent low over a row of fat dangling green beans. A half-filled basket sat on the bare dirt at her feet.

She straightened and turned to glare at him. Dust stuck to the sweat on her forehead.

"My thoughts, sir, would curdle your blood. I dearly despise picking beans and have less-than-charitable thoughts at the present time. You would, perhaps, do well to give me a wide berth."

Amusement tickled the corners of his lips. Her cheeks were rosy. Green eyes glittered. She was in a snit. A pretty snit. If he said as much to her, she'd hit him with a rake.

He removed his hat and rubbed at the sweat gathered

at his hairline. "Why are you picking alone? Where are the others?"

"They're all busy snapping beans, shelling beans, canning beans." She slapped another handful into the basket. "And the things keep growing. I swear I picked this row this morning."

"You won't complain come winter."

She chucked a bean at him. "Must you always be sensible?"

Chuckling, he yanked a few beans and retaliated. She ducked and made a growling sound, but her mouth quivered and the glitter in her emerald eyes became a twinkle. "Don't make me laugh. I want to be annoyed."

"Laughter doeth good like a medicine." Clapping his hat onto his head, he stepped over the row and began to pick from the opposite side. With long, strong fingers and wide hands, he gathered beans rapidly and tossed them into her basket. She was nearly finished with this row.

"Then you, Mr. Eriksson, have never suffered the insult of castor oil. There is absolutely no good in that particular medicine." She added a double handful of her favorite hated vegetable. Her fingertips, he noted with a hidden smile, were greener than her eyes. "What are you doing here in midday?"

"Day is waning, Josie." He hitched his chin at the western horizon. "The grinding was done, so I left."

She straightened, one hand to her back. She stretched and grimaced. "A behavior uncharacteristic of your overeager work ethic. Is everything all right? Have you taken ill?"

Normally he found plenty of mill work to keep

him busy. Today more pleasant pursuits occupied his thoughts.

"Abram stayed behind to set up for tomorrow. Jenny O'Connor invited me for supper tonight."

Josie prickled. "Jenny did? Are you going?"

Was she jealous? Just a tad?

"Only if you agree to come along. The invitation was for both of us. Angus was at the mill earlier to deliver the message."

"Oh. Well. How thoughtful." She worried her bottom lip as if the invitation troubled her.

"Is something wrong? You dislike the O'Connors?"

The Irish couple with their deep brogues and merry jokes were the first outside the Portland farm to offer friendship. Like Thad, they were not altogether welcome in Honey Ridge, nor anywhere else, for that matter, simply because they were Irish.

He enjoyed their company, but he'd enjoy it more with Josie along.

Josie, however, with her strong prejudices, might not be of the same opinion.

"I like them well enough." She yanked a bunch of beans as if she wanted to strangle them.

"Then you'll come with me?"

"Would you go without me?"

Exasperating woman.

A grasshopper landed on his shoulder. He flicked the bug away, listened to the whirr of wings as it sought a leaf to feed on. "No, I would not."

She perked up. "No?"

"No." He regarded her with a mild look, holding her gaze steady. "This isn't about eating a meal, Josie."

She understood his meaning. He knew because her

breath quickened and a flood of color washed her pink as a peony.

"No, I suppose it isn't." She ripped off a few more beans, and, finally, when he thought she might turn him down, her chin jerked up, her eyes flamed green fire and with almost grim determination, she said, "Yes, I will."

With a whoop, he hoisted her up from the dusty field and spun her in circle until her anger dissipated and she laughed down into his face.

CHAPTER TWENTY-SEVEN

Sometimes the smallest things take up the most room in your heart.

—A. A. Milne

Present

BRODY DIDN'T COME to the library after school. By the time Carrie closed up the building at five o'clock, she was getting worried.

She'd seen him that morning on his way to school and invited him to the inn for dinner with Hayden. As she'd told Hayden by telephone a short time afterward, the boy had grinned until his freckles popped up like measles. He'd been delighted that his hero was back in town and couldn't wait to tell him about the bass he'd pulled out of Seth Westerfeld's pond. A five pounder if it weighed an ounce. He had, of course, put the fish back to catch again someday, but his friend Spence had taken a photo with his cell phone.

Carrie had gone to work cheered and happy, though tired from her late night. For once, a thunderstorm had produced something besides bags under her eyes.

After activating the library's alarm system, though she always wondered who would break in and steal books when they were free to borrow, Carrie locked the door and drove through town, past the school grounds and then to Brody's house.

No one answered the door, and the only visible sign of humanity was a cardboard shoe box crushed on the front porch.

Thinking the boy had been so excited to see Hayden he'd walked to Peach Orchard Inn, Carrie called to check.

"I haven't seen him." Hayden's warm baritone tickled her stomach. "Perhaps he's on his way. Give him another thirty minutes."

"You're probably right." She gnawed her bottom lip and stared at the Thomsons' front porch.

"You sound anxious."

"He said he'd come to the library, and he didn't. That's out of character."

"Maybe he had to stay after school for some reason."

"I never thought of that," she said. "I'll drive by the school again and back to his house."

"If he shows up here, I'll call you. If you see him first, call me."

"Deal."

She hung up and drove around, but after thirty minutes saw no sign of the boy. When her phone rang, her hopes lifted but were soon dashed by Hayden.

"No sign of him?"

"Nothing, and I don't know where else to look."

"I have some ideas," Hayden said. "Maybe he's at the creek or at his campsite."

"I don't know where that is."

"I do. Come out. We'll look together."

She started to ring off, but his voice drew her back. "Carrie?"

"Yes?"

"Stop worrying."

"Right." But the bad feeling in her gut wouldn't go away.

THEY WALKED THE woods and searched inside the gristmill, climbed the waterfall and called his name.

Hayden pressed deeper into the woods where the trees still dripped last night's rain.

"Why would he be this far away from town?" Carrie asked.

"Just a hunch I have. He built a hideout where he camps sometimes."

Carrie's gaze flew up to his. "On the bad days?"

He nodded. *The bad days.* Those were Brody's words when Hayden asked about the rabbit.

Hayden had understood more than he could say.

"Not too much farther." Hayden led through a bramble of blackberry vines and underbrush a quarter of a mile down the creek and back into the woods.

Hayden lifted a hand, and both of them paused to listen.

The soft murmur of Brody's voice came from deep in the trees.

"Sounds like his buddy is with him," Hayden said softly.

Hidden from the boy's view by brush and trees, Carrie shook her head and whispered, "Hayden, I think he's crying."

She started forward, but Hayden put an arm in front of her. "Wait."

The trees eavesdropped, too, their leaves whispering overhead as sun dappled the still-wet earth. Something skittered through the underbrush, but it was the boy's words that grabbed Hayden's attention.

"You didn't do nothing wrong," Brody said, words shaky and broken. "You're the best friend I ever had. I'm so sorry for what he done. I love you, Max."

Suddenly the boy's voice ruptured into sobs, long and deep and wounded.

Hayden exchanged glances with Carrie. She had tears in her eyes that matched those in his soul.

"What's happened?" she mouthed.

He reached for Carrie's hand, aware that he was chilled through his bones in a way that had nothing to do with the cooler day.

Life was hell for some kids.

Teeth tight, he nodded toward the sound. "Come on."

Dodging limbs and briars, they swiftly reached the crying boy. Brody huddled on the ground outside his brush lean-to, holding something in his hands.

Hearing their approach, he glanced up, his face streaked with dirty tears.

"Max is dead." He held out a hand. The small lizard lay motionless on his palm.

Stomach churning with dread, Hayden crouched at his side. "What happened?"

Brody looked down at the lizard, tears falling, but said nothing.

"You can tell us, buddy. We're your friends. We liked Max, too." Hayden touched the boy's shoulder, letting his hand rest there in much the same way Mr. Franks had done for him. A connection, human to human, that said he mattered.

Brody drew in a shuddering breath. "I'm real careful to keep him in the box at home. The old man never even knew."

"Your father did this."

Brody nodded. "I should have released Max sooner. Back to the wild. Before the old man found him."

"This wasn't your fault, Brody."

"Max was a good lizard. He never bothered anything. He was my best friend." Tears welled up. "He stomped Max. Stomped him with his steel-toed boots."

Carrie crouched beside them, horror in her eyes that said she couldn't comprehend a parent who would do such things.

A terrible sense of déjà vu roiled through Hayden like a consuming tidal wave eager to suck him beneath the cold, ugly, black water. The stray dog. Dora Lee. She could be so vicious.

Sickness rose in his throat. He only committed murder in his books, but right now, he wanted to put his hands around Clint Thomson's neck and squeeze until his bloodshot eyes bulged and he begged for mercy.

"I hate him, Hayden," Brody said, mouth trembling and tears flowing. "I hate him."

"I know. But you love him, too."

"I guess."

"Sometimes adults get messed up and do things they don't mean."

"He meant it."

"Was he drinking?"

"Yeah." Brody looked at the dead lizard again. "I hate him so much."

Hayden's chest throbbed. He draped an arm around Brody. "Living with an unpredictable parent can make you hate sometimes, but he's still your father."

"I wish he wasn't. I wish my mama had taken me with her when she left."

How many times had he wished he'd died with his father?

"I know, buddy. I know." With a long exhale, he shifted, finding a comfortable position next to the boy so they could talk. Left unattended, this incident would fester into a lifelong sore that never, ever healed.

Aware Carrie hovered nearby, listening, he was careful. "I knew a boy once when I was in school. He was a lot like you."

"Yeah? His dad drank, too?"

"Something like that. Only it was his mother. His daddy…left, same as your mother did."

The dead lizard cradled against his neck, Brody listened with interest. "Was she mean?"

"Sometimes. Like your dad, she was unpredictable. The boy never knew if she would be happy or sad, mean or kind. He had hiding places in the woods. He was a friend of mine, so I went there with him sometimes."

"Like me."

"Yes, like you. He had a pet once, too, like you. Only his pet was just a stray dog, slick and skinny, but as loyal as daybreak." *Blackie Boy. Best dog ever.*

Brody sniffed. "What happened?"

Memories flashed, cruel and rapid. The dog. His mother's anger. The well.

Hayden's pulse beat in his throat, heavy and painful. She'd promised as long as he was no trouble, the dog could stay. Then, in a rage, furious at Hayden for something he couldn't even remember, she'd drowned the only thing that loved him. And she'd made him watch.

Trembling with grief and hatred, Hayden had buried Blackie Boy deep in the woods and prayed that all dogs really did go to heaven.

"His mother killed him just like your dad killed Max. It was mean and awful and the boy hated her for a long, long time until he grew up and learned that she was broken and he didn't want to be broken, too." He shifted to look into Brody's face. "Do you understand what I'm saying, Brody? You can't let this break you. You can't let your father define who you are and who you will become."

Brody drew a sleeve across his soggy face, saying nothing, eyes downcast and shoulders stooped.

"Hayden's right, Brody." Carrie smoothed Brody's cowlick. "You are a good person with a gentle heart. Don't let your dad's actions change you. Go on being kind and sweet and caring."

"I don't want to be like him."

"You can't change who your father is, but you don't have to be like him," she added. "And you don't have to be embarrassed or ashamed when he drinks or acts terrible. That's his fault, not yours, and you're not responsible for his actions. You're not him, Brody."

Hayden telegraphed his gratitude.

Brody sniffed and gently lifted the lizard from his neck. "I gotta take care of Max now."

Carrie's heart ached until she thought her chest would crack open. People didn't do things like this to their children. Not in her world.

And yet they did.

She knelt on the wet ground, not caring that last night's rain soaked through to her knees as she listened to Hayden speak.

She hoped the tale was a figment of his fertile imagination to cheer Brody and not reality for some poor child he'd really known. Judging by the stark grief in Hayden's face when he'd spoken, Carrie was very afraid the story was true.

She gazed at him with fresh eyes, wondering anew about his background, his family. He'd told her plenty about New York, about his writing life and many travels but nothing of his childhood other than an upper-middle-class background. Perhaps his boyhood had not been as rosy as he let on.

"Max has been a good pet," she said to the shattered little boy. "Would you like for us to help you bury him?"

Brody's mouth turned down as if he might start crying again. He nodded.

Gently, Hayden took the crushed lizard from the boy's hand and stroked a finger over the slick reptilian back. "Do you have anything in your fort we could wrap him in?"

Brody shook his head. "Maybe."

He crawled inside and returned with a strip of white cloth. "The bunny's leg is nearly well. He won't need this."

So with sad and solemn respect, Hayden and Brody burrowed a long, narrow hole while Carrie wrapped the lizard and gathered a handful of wildflowers for the grave.

It was only a lizard. A slimy, yucky lizard like the kind she'd normally avoid, but to Brody, Max was a friend. What mattered more and cut deeper than the loss of the pet was his father's heartless betrayal.

"Ready?" Hayden asked.

Brody's blond head dipped. Kneeling, he placed Max into the ground, scooped and patted the dirt and then tilted back on his heels. Carrie handed him the white daisy-looking flowers, which he solemnly placed on the tiny grave.

"You were a good boy, Max," he said, patting the damp earth. "I hope God has lots of crickets for you up in heaven."

Then he squeezed his eyes closed and began to murmur the Lord's Prayer.

Carrie exchanged glances with Hayden. He reached for her hand and gently squeezed.

Tears seeped from the corners of Carrie's eyelids. For the boy and his lost pet but also for the man who told stories that broke her heart.

CHAPTER TWENTY-EIGHT

THAT NIGHT, HAYDEN murdered two people.

The fictional deaths relieved some of the rage brewing under his skull like a witch's poison, but the relief left him vaguely ashamed.

If that wasn't enough to disturb his rest, when he'd finally settled into the Mulberry Room, he'd had the dream again. Thaddeus and Josie.

At 3:00 a.m. he'd flung the story onto his laptop and then called himself an idiot.

He squeezed the bridge of his nose and rubbed his eye sockets, worn and irritated.

Maybe dreaming of a time past reflected his own psychological condition and his need to work through a boyhood he'd yet to reconcile, a past much like Brody's. It made more sense than a message-sending house or ghosts.

Skipping breakfast, he drove to Brody's house. Thomson was likely still in bed, working off a hangover. He hoped the jerk had a raging headache.

With grim satisfaction, Hayden pounded his fist on the door.

Thomson appeared, blurry eyed and unshaven. Scowling, he said, "What do you want?"

"Do you have any idea where your son is?"

The man straightened. "What's he done?"

"You're the one who's done something."

Thomson squinted, hackles raised. "What are you talking about?"

"I'm talking about your worst nightmare. Me. I came by to give you a warning. Don't do anything to hurt Brody again."

"I never— Did he say I hit him?" Thomson gritted his teeth and pulled his shoulders back, defiant. "The lying, sniveling little—"

Hayden sliced a hand through the air, cutting him off. "You killed his pet."

"That boy's got no pet. I don't allow animals in the house."

"Max may not have been a pet to you, but he was to Brody. He loved that lizard." Hayden's fists tightened at his sides. "And you stomped him to death. In front of Brody. While you were getting drunk, your devastated son was alone, burying Max in the woods."

"Whining little wuss. Always sniffling about some poor little animal. Doesn't have the gumption to kill a bug. Just like his worthless mama."

Hayden itched with the need for release. He was a peaceable man and certainly didn't want the negative publicity, but Thomson released a monster in his soul.

"Do you have any idea how much you hurt your boy? His own father, the person he's supposed to trust and depend on?"

"It was a filthy lizard! How was I to know the kid kept it as a pet?"

"The box should have been a clue, Einstein, and the fact that Brody tried to keep him hidden under the bed. Away from you. Or are you stupid as well as a drunk?"

Thomson's face worked with emotions, fury, confusion, guilt. Through tight, flat lips, he said, "You need to mind your own business, Mr. Big Shot."

Hayden realized he was breathing hard, as if he'd run the distance from Peach Orchard Inn to this little house on the west of Honey Ridge. His heart hammered, pumping hot fury through his veins. "You've had your warning, Thomson. Do anything to hurt that boy again, and you answer to me."

"What I do in my own house is up to me. You come here again, and I'll call the cops on you."

Hayden froze, calculating, smiling a little, though his smile was anything but friendly. "You do that, Thomson, and while they're here, tell them what happened to your wife."

Thomson drew back. "I don't know what you're talking about."

"Sure you do. Penny Thomson disappeared from this town, and no one has ever heard from her again. There's no driver's license in her name, no record of her anywhere. I find that more than a little suspicious."

"You accusing me of something, mister?"

"No accusation. Only the facts." He turned to leave but spun back. "Remember what I said about Brody. I'm watching."

"THE MAN SHOULD be horsewhipped." Carrie's mother, Mary Riley, stood at the back door of Bailey's modern brick home watching her grandsons and Brody play catch. "Poor little boy."

"I'll gladly provide the whip." Carrie dipped a celery stick into a puddle of ranch dressing and gnawed the end, doing more thinking than eating as she discussed yesterday's incident with her mom and sisters.

As often as possible, the Riley women gathered for lunch on Saturday after Carrie closed the library at noon. Today, they were shocked and angered by the treatment of one little boy.

"He's a nice child," Mary said. "His father has no business mistreating him that way."

Nikki's face was a mask of concern, furious as well as fashionable. "Do you think he's physically abusive?"

Carrie waved the celery stick. "Hayden and I have both looked for bruises and found none. Brody insists his father doesn't hit him, and he talks to Hayden a lot. More than to me."

"It's still not right," Bailey said. "Trey should go over there and give that man a talking-to."

"I think Hayden beat him to it."

Nikki's head swiveled toward Carrie. "Really? He went to Thomson's house?"

She nodded. "Surprised me, too, but he and Brody have a strong connection, and Hayden was quite upset over what happened."

"Speaking of our rather attractive author-in-residence, Clara Stanfield said Hayden was at your house really late the other night." Nikki pointed a carrot stick. "The wayward one returns. So, what's the little midnight rendezvous all about?"

Clara, Carrie's next-door neighbor, never missed anything that went on in the neighborhood. "You know how I hate storms."

"Apparently, Hayden does, too, because he needed your comfort." Nikki grinned at her own cleverness. "Then dinner at Julia's last night. He must have missed you something fierce when he went off to…" A furrow appeared in her forehead. "Where did he go?"

"To visit his mother."

"Oh." Nikki slumped in disappointment. "I expected something more exciting from a famous author. A movie premiere or something. Ooh, wouldn't it be great if he invited you to one of those? You could hobnob with the likes of Reese Witherspoon!"

Carrie groaned. "Nikki, stop. You're having an out-of-mind experience."

"You mean out of body."

"No. I meant out of your mind."

The four women chuckled as Bailey dragged a chair away from the table, sat and leaned her chin on the heel of her hand. "So, back to you and Hayden. Spill the goods. What's going on?"

I love him. But she didn't say that.

"Hayden likes thunderstorms. I hate them. He knew I'd be nervous, so he came over to hang out."

"That's so sweet!" Bailey pitter-patted a hand over her heart.

"And he talked you down from the ledge," Nikki said.

Bailey snickered. "More like out from under the bed. Remember, Carrie, how you used to drag your Elmo doll under there and have him talk to you to drown out the storm noise?"

Hayden's company had been far more effective than dear old Elmo. She'd been so focused on him and the bracelet that she'd almost stopped jumping at every thunderclap.

"Hayden is no Elmo doll, Bailey." Nikki twitched an eyebrow. "And if she's dragging him anywhere, I hope it's not *under* the bed."

"We played Scrabble, people!" *And snuggled on the couch and held each other and kissed.*

"If that's true, you're pathetic. I've never seen you like this with a guy. Not since—" At Carrie's warning glare, Nikki finished, "The unmentionable one."

Carrie raised her hands in surrender. "Don't bring that up."

"Girls," Mary admonished softly. "Stop teasing your sister. She can't help her phobias any more than Nikki can help her lust for expensive clothes." She nailed Nikki with the mother eye. "Hayden and Carrie have things in common, and I think he's a fine young man."

Carrie shot her mom a grateful look. "Mama's right. Hayden's a wonderful man, and we both love books. Right now, we're both concerned about Brody."

Bailey's voice softened, losing its teasing edge. "And you like him a lot."

Carrie pressed her lips together and sighed, deep and long. She needed to discuss him with someone, and who better than her sisters? They teased, but they loved her.

"I don't think I've ever felt quite like this about anyone. But we all have to remember, especially me, Hayden is only here in Honey Ridge for a limited time. We can't get any crazy ideas." Like the ones already flowing through her own head.

"Since when did that matter?"

"It matters to me. He'll go back to New York and his busy life. As you well know, I'm not going anywhere. Not that he's inviting. We all know who he is." And who she wasn't. "When this is all over, I'd like to remain friends and maybe talk now and then."

"Well, he is certainly not too good for my daughter!"

"Hayden would be the last to claim that, Mama, but we're from different worlds. I'm smart enough to know that."

Mama stroked a hand over the top of Carrie's head. "I don't want you hurt again, honey."

Carrie reached up and caressed her mother's hand. "I know."

Sometimes the heart had a mind of its own.

"How close is he to finishing his book?"

"He doesn't have to be in Honey Ridge to write, Bailey. Once he has the information he needs, he'll go home." She grabbed a broccoli spear and munched. At least she was getting a healthy load of greens during this interrogation.

Her mother pulled out a chair. "I still think it's odd that a man without intentions would buy you jewelry."

"Mom! I told you the story behind that. It's not a big deal." But the ankle bracelet had felt like a big deal the night of Hayden's return from Kentucky. She'd gone to sleep with his kiss on her lips, his silver chain on her ankle and his name on her mind.

"Jewelry is always a good sign." Nikki slid a plate of chicken quesadillas on the table. "I think he's smitten. A man with his taste in clothes is a man to grab on to. New York is not that far away. I'd be glad to keep you company while we hang out with the rich and famous crowd."

Carrie laughed. "Nik, I'd say you're hopeless except you love Rick and he's an ordinary guy who couldn't be hog-tied and mailed to New York City."

"He's worse than ordinary. He bought his last pair of jeans at a yard sale." She shrugged and forked a bite of quesadilla, lofting it to study the melting cheese. "However, I would love a brother-in-law with excellent taste."

Carrie rolled her eyes and was saved from coming up with a reply when a knock sounded on the door and a male voice called, "Hey, Mama, got any food for your baby boy?"

"We're in the kitchen!" Mary called. "Come on in."

Bailey pulled another plate from the cabinet as Trey entered the room. "Something smells good."

"You always know when lunch is ready."

"You trained me well, my sweet mama." He leaned over and kissed his mother on the cheek. "Hey, sisters times three," he greeted. "I'm on duty, so I can't stay long."

"Even policemen get a lunch break, Trey."

"I'll tell the captain my mama said so."

She pointed a finger at him. "You do that. Charlie Wright's a good boy. He'll do right by you."

The siblings exchanged grins. Captain Charlie Wright was a former marine, six foot five and tough as boot leather.

Trey helped himself to the food and the family settled in to eat quesadillas, sip sweet tea and catch up on the week's news.

Her mother revisited the topic of Brody for Trey. When she finished relating the incident, she asked, "Isn't there anything the police can do?"

Trey chewed, swallowed and dabbed his mouth with a napkin. "Mama, unless the man breaks a law, our hands are tied. When Carrie first came to me about him, I checked around, talked to Child Services, but they're in the same boat. Killing a lizard isn't against the law."

"What about the way Brody is left alone so much of the time?"

"Latchkey kid. If we yanked every child whose parents have to work, we'd be talking about more than half the families in town. Brody's eleven, old enough to be alone. Thomson may not be the father of the year, but he's not committed a crime."

"That we know of," Carrie said.

"About that," Trey said, pushing the grilled tortilla and cheese around with his fork. "Something interesting came over the chatter yesterday. It may turn out to be of no interest in this specific situation, but I'm watching it."

"What?" All four women leaned in.

"State troopers were testing new sonar equipment at Long's Lake and discovered a submerged car, a 2004 Ford Focus." He leaned back in his chair. "Containing skeletal remains."

A collective gasp sucked the air off the table.

"Trey, that's terrible."

He nodded his agreement. "They're pulling the car up today."

"Why would Honey Ridge police be interested in something that happened over there? Long's Lake is miles from here."

"Because Penny Thomson left Honey Ridge in a 2004 Focus."

"Oh, my gravy." Carrie's fingers touched her mouth. "Do you think it's her?"

His uniformed shoulders twitched. "We'll have our answer to that question when the state medical examiner compares DNA."

"Which means you'll need DNA from Brody?"

"As the only known blood kin to Penny, it's likely. But that's not my area of expertise."

"You let the state police know, didn't you, that we have a missing woman who drove a car like that?"

Trey's smile was patient. "Carrie, I've been a cop for a long time. Of course I did."

She offered a sheepish grimace.

"I don't know whether to pray it is Penny or pray it isn't," her mother said.

"I feel the same way. Brody longs for his mother, and if she's been dead all this time…" Carrie shook her head, staring at her nearly empty plate. "So sad for him."

"Finding her would bring closure, sis," Trey said.

Which was better? Carrie wondered. To know your mother was gone forever? Or to hold on to the hope that she might come home again?

HAYDEN FOUND CARRIE on her knees beside the front porch, viciously jabbing a trowel into the soft ground.

"Need any help burying the bodies?" he asked, amused, as he exited his car and crossed the small lawn to where she worked.

She sat back on her haunches and smiled. "We divided Mom's daffodils this afternoon."

"The way you're wielding that trowel, I thought you might be hiding evidence."

"Spoken like a true writer of crime." Carrie grinned up at him, flashing a dimple. Her cheeks were rosy from exertion, and her eyes glistened a deep, dark, luscious chocolate. He wanted to go to his knees and kiss her right there in the dirt. "But you've also reminded me of something I want to share with you when I get finished here."

"You found a body? Killed someone? Discovered the grave of Jimmy Hoffa?"

She laughed. "You're in a good mood."

"I am eternally buoyed by the evil that lurks in the hearts of men and my innate ability to cash in on that voyeuristic predilection."

"You also have an impressive vocabulary."

He laughed. "Spoken like a true librarian. The latest royalty check was deposited to my account today."

She looked up at him, wiping the back of a glove across her cheek. "Must have been a good one."

"No complaints. Want to go to dinner with me? Somewhere nice. Celebrate?"

She looked up at him and smiled. "I'd love to celebrate with you."

She poked the remaining bulbs into the prepared hole and covered them. "That should do it. The extent of my gardening skills. Stick a bulb in the ground and forget it. All three of us girls are on our knees this afternoon."

He arched an eyebrow. "Praying for anything in particular?"

"Absolutely." She pointed a gloved finger toward the freshly planted ground. "I'm praying Mama doesn't give me any more bulbs."

Lighthearted and laughing, enjoying her company, he offered a hand. She whipped off the dirty glove and accepted the quick tug to her feet.

She didn't ask what he was doing at her house, and he didn't offer an excuse. He just wanted to see her.

Wanted to be with her. To relax in her company and be as real as Hayden Winters could ever be.

The visit to Dora Lee had depressed him, but the confrontation with Thomson had snapped him out of it. The only thing better than seeing the fear in Thomson's eyes was being here with Carrie.

Feelings for her had crept up slowly, a honeysuckle vine of sweetness. Carrie was about as real as he could get.

"Come on inside, and I'll make some tea."

"Water's fine."

"Oh, loosen up." She tapped a finger on his chest. "Get in touch with your Southern roots and have some syrupy sweet tea."

His Southern roots? That way spelled insanity, but he acquiesced and followed her jean-clad behind up the steps.

"You have some dirt on your—ah—backside."

Carrie arched her back, dusted her bottom and went on inside the house. Hayden was glad she couldn't see the admiring grin on his face.

While she made the tea, he entertained her with stories from the good ol' boys down at the café and shared in depth the encounter with Clint Thomson, which made her brown eyes darken to black.

When the tea was poured, he took a glass and they settled on the couch.

"Trey came to Mama's house for lunch with us girls today."

"Yeah?"

"He had some interesting news." She told him about the submerged car. "Trey thinks it might belong to Penny Thomson."

The bottom dropped out of his stomach. "No kidding? How could that have happened?"

"Long's is a huge, deep lake, a reservoir really, with lots of remote, narrow roads and sharp curves. Wildlife, too. If she got lost in the dark in a strange area, she could have missed a turn or dodged a deer and lost control on the curve."

He rubbed a hand over his jawline, stunned. "I imagined a number of possible scenarios but not this one." He'd even started a book with the wife-killer premise. "Do you really think it could be her?"

"We'll find out soon enough. Sometimes truth is stranger than fiction."

"Has anyone told Thomson?"

"Not yet. They'll have to soon if they want to retrieve DNA from Brody."

"That won't be hard. A saliva test, a hair from his head."

"But what if it really is his mother, Hayden? How will Brody feel? I keep asking myself if it would be better to go on believing your mother abandoned you and *might* possibly return or to discover she's dead and all hope is lost."

"Easy answer. Abandonment is far worse."

"You think so?"

Carrie, in her ivory tower, had no comprehension of a child left alone to fend for himself, worried his parent wouldn't return but every bit afraid she would. Certainty was always preferable.

"Sure I do. I'm a writer. We know stuff," he said lightly. He sat back and sipped his tea.

"Speaking of which, how's the book going?" She curled her legs beneath her, bare feet touching the couch. The bracelet, he noticed, was in place and her toenails freshly painted.

"There's not much to tell." He pushed a hand over his hair with a rueful laugh. "Starts and stops. I murder a few people and then lose interest. The wife-killer premise may eventually go somewhere."

"Anything I can do to help? Other than shoot someone."

His mouth twitched. He set his tea on the end table. "Not really. If I could stop having the crazy dreams—"

He caught himself. Carrie, with her easy manner, made him forget to keep his guard up. And if there was anyone on earth he trusted with the dreams, it was her.

Hayden turned the thought over in his head. He'd been moving toward this, trusting her, wanting to confide, believing that Carrie had some magic he could believe in. He couldn't decide if he should run or give in.

"What kind of dreams?"

She ran her fingers down the moist outside of the tea glass, interested but not overly so, unaware she'd stepped into the realm of his most secret fear.

"Do you believe in ghosts?" As soon as he asked the question, he wanted to suck it back inside.

A tiny frown tweaked her eyebrows.

"Ghosts?" She shook her head. "I don't think so. Lots of people in Honey Ridge do. The Southern thing, you know. Do you?"

"No. I don't know, but something decidedly unusual is happening in my dreams." The need to talk through the bizarre occurrences with Carrie was as thick as the sugar in her tea. "Have you noticed the display of artifacts in Julia's entry hall at Peach Orchard Inn?"

"The old things they found during the renovation? Sure. They're fascinating."

Hayden fiddled with his glass, contemplated only long enough to take a sip.

"I dream about them and about the people who owned them. Over and over." He breathed deeply through his nose, holding in the air, holding in the worry. "The scenes change each time I have the dream, like a chapter-by-chapter retelling."

She leaned toward him, interested and puzzled but not calling him crazy. "As in a book?"

"Exactly." He shared a synopsis of the dreams, ending with the latest. "This sounds crazy. Don't think I'm crazy, Carrie."

"You're the least crazy person I know." Her lips curved. "Except for the lightning fetish."

A bit of his anxiety edged away.

"It's as if a book I didn't write is being read to me in my sleep," he said. "As if I'm privy to a real-life movie that took place more than a hundred fifty years ago." Spoken aloud, the thing sounded even more insane. He rammed damp fingers through his hair. "How could I know those things?"

"Don't laugh, but there are rumors about the inn having an…angel…or something."

"Julia hinted at that."

"You should listen to her. Julia isn't one to chase goblins."

"I found an antique marble." He reached in his pocket and pulled out the clay ball.

Carrie touched the marble with her fingertip. "I've heard about these. Valery says they appear when the house is trying to help someone. I've never noticed anything weird when I was there, but some say they've heard music or a boy's laughter."

"But I had the dream when I was out of town, too."

"Maybe the dreams are trying to tell you something."

"You mean like a message from my subconscious?"

"Or whatever."

"That's what Julia said about the house."

"There you go, then," she said.

"I thought you weren't a ghost believer."

"I'm not, but the Bible tells of men who dreamed prophetic dreams. Even if it's not that, and you don't want to believe in angels or spirits or what have you, you have a powerful sense of fantasy, Hayden. You're a novelist who thinks in scenes and chapters. Being in the inn, seeing those cool old antiques and visiting the mill stirred something inside your psyche."

"Maybe." In fact, he was certain those things played a part. But how did he explain the rest? That the dreams began the very first night they'd met before he'd been to the mill or noticed the display? Before he'd found the marble or learned of the inn's reputation?

"You're seriously worried about this, aren't you?"

He forced a laugh. "Sometimes I think I'm losing it."

She set the glass down and touched his arm, her tone gentle. "It's only a dream, Hayden."

Was it? Or was it, as she'd suggested, some kind of message from the past creeping into a weakened mind? Or worse, a sign that he was losing it?

CHAPTER TWENTY-NINE

1867

TOM'S MOTHER MET Josie at the door and drew her into a loving embrace. Margaret Foster was a comely woman in her late forties with Tom's golden hair, though hers had faded to white at the temples from the years of war and worry. Shorter and rounder than Josie, she was still an attractive woman, and Josie thought it such a shame that there were so few eligible men left to appreciate her. With the young women vying for every remaining male in Tennessee, women of an age stood little chance. Even the old men married the younger women.

But if Margaret longed for another husband, she'd never said as much. A widow for fifteen years, her missing son was the only male in her conversations.

"There you are, my dear. I've missed your visits."

Guilt sent a flush of heat up Josie's neck and over her ears. Time with Thaddeus took time away from Margaret. She'd not been here in days.

Supper at the O'Connor farm had been lighthearted fun, something sorely missing in Josie's life since the war. She and Thad had stayed late into the night, talking and playing parlor games until long after the O'Connor children fell asleep on the floor.

Some, like Mrs. Stockton, would be scandalized to

know Josie had set foot in the home of an Irishman. But Josie found the O'Connors cheerful and kind, and Mr. O'Connor played a lively, toe-tapping fiddle.

The O'Connor children jigged and high-stepped while she'd laughed for joy. Laughter, as Thaddeus had once told her, was good medicine.

When she and Thad had arrived home to the squawk of the hateful old gander, she'd helped Thad put away the wagon and horse. Then he'd walked her into the house and kissed her good-night at the bottom of the stairs.

Mrs. Stockton would be scandalized if she knew about that, too, and frankly, Josie didn't care. Margaret, however, was another matter. After Tom had marched away with the army, she and Tom's mother had come together in mutual love for their soldier boy.

"I've been working at the mill more," she said, aware that the rehearsed words fell from her lips in a nervous burst of explanation. "And the harvest is coming in. Beans and beets and corn and okra. You know how a farm is, Margaret, especially without the slaves. Work is never done."

Though the excuse was honest, a nagging sense of disquiet grew in Josie's chest.

To hide her worry, Josie hurried to the worn horsehair settee. Seeing the threadbare couch, she exclaimed, "Oh, I forgot to bring the coverlet Patience knitted for you!"

Tom had been his mother's soul provider, and now with him gone, Margaret eked out a living from her large garden and chickens. She had no money for coverlets or doilies.

Margaret waved her off. "Never you mind about that. We've other important things to discuss."

Josie slithered onto the sofa, her mouth going as dry as cotton. She squeezed both hands into her cotton skirt. "What things would that be, Margaret?"

Margaret's brown eyes rested on Josie with such curiosity that Josie squirmed.

Something was amiss? Did Tom's mother know about Thad? About the late-night kisses?

No, no, it wasn't possible.

But Mamie Stockton knew, and she was the biggest gossip in Honey Ridge.

The worry hammered against Josie's temples until her head began to ache.

"Would you like me to make tea, Margaret? I'd be happy to do so." Josie hopped up, eager to do something besides squirm beneath the weight of her own guilt.

Margaret pointed at the sofa. "Sit down, Josephine. I'm quite capable of pouring tea."

Stung at the tight, sharp tone, Josie slid back into place. Her pulse began a hard, steady thrum.

Had Margaret gotten wind of Mamie Stockton's tirade at the mercantile? Was she angry? Hurt?

Guilty as Judas, Josie watched her dear friend fidget with two glasses.

"I brought the quilt top I promised, Margaret, to get your opinion on the backing." She patted the folded top lying next to her.

"That's very kind." The reply was stiff, not the usual happy repartee she and Margaret enjoyed.

She knows. She knows. Be sure your sins will find you out.

Was it a sin to enjoy Thad's company? Was it a sin to take supper with the Irish O'Connors?

Jumpy, nervous, she sought for anything to say and rattled the first news that entered her mind.

"Priscilla Duncan is marrying Franklin Wellburg. Patience has been asked to play a special piece she wrote, though the wedding is to be small and held at the Duncan home."

Thinking about the wedding only made her remember Tom and the wedding she would never have. She should have kept her nervous mouth shut, and the thought intensified when Margaret seemed preoccupied and didn't reply.

Was her guilty conscious at work, or was the atmosphere growing increasingly stiff and uncomfortable?

By the time Margaret returned with two glasses of blackberry tea, Josie's hands were sweating and she wished she'd not come to visit.

Josie sipped. Like most other households in Honey Ridge, Margaret created her own teas out of whatever was available. "Delicious, Margaret, and wonderfully refreshing on a warm day. Thank you."

Margaret set her glass on the table between them, and then went to a small desk in one corner, where she removed a worn envelope and held it against her stomach.

Josie's stomach tightened. Tom's last letter home. "Where was he when he wrote that letter, Margaret?"

"Somewhere in Georgia." She took a step closer, brown eyes intent. "He could still come home, Josie."

Josie licked lips gone dry even while the taste of blackberry tea lingered. "I pray every night for his return."

"Do you?"

She gasped, stunned that Margaret would ask such a thing. "Yes, of course I do!"

Margaret's shoulders drooped. She heaved a sigh that bespoke of heartache and loss and resignation. "There is a nasty rumor afloat, Josie. I must know if there is any truth in it."

Hot with guilt, Josie reached out a hand. She'd never wanted to hurt this woman who'd already suffered far too much sorrow. "I love Tom, and I always will, but he's been gone a long time."

Margaret's fingers tightened on the envelope. Her white bodice bunched at the waist. "So it's true? You're courting the Northern miller?"

"I—I don't know."

With a quiet swish of gray cotton skirts, Margaret sat down, her fingers tight on Josie's arm.

"You can't give up, Josie. Tom is coming home. I know he will. Soon. Very soon."

The feverish declaration was spoken with bright, unshed tears.

Josie's pulse leaped. "Have you heard something?"

The woman deflated. "No. No. Dear heaven, how I wish." Her head dipped, and she stared at her fingers in her lap, wringing them lifeless. "Don't do this, Josie. I beg you. Don't betray Tom. Don't betray what he fought for."

Josie was frozen, caught between the past and the present and the terrible unknown. "I don't want to betray anyone."

"A Yankee, Josie? After you promised to wait."

She had. She'd made that promise, confident her

Tom would march triumphantly home waving the banner of a victorious Confederacy. Neither had occurred.

In a raspy, agonized whisper, she asked, "What if he never returns?"

Margaret's tormented face beseeched her. Lines of worry around her eyes and mouth, haunted eyes and a desperate plea ripped the scab from Josie's own wounds.

"Another year or two. That's all I ask."

"Margaret," she started, aware with deep, throbbing regret that she no longer believed in Tom's return. Her bonny golden-haired beau with the lanky limbs and serious brown eyes was never coming home. He'd never march or ride or even crawl back into their lives. Her beloved fiancé was gone forever.

She had a terrible choice to make.

"Margaret, please. You and I both know Tom is never—"

Hard fingers dug into her arm. "I know you're lonely, my dear, and you are still very beautiful, but if you cannot keep your promise, if you cannot wait, then do not defame my son's memory with the Northern miller."

Oh, would the woman ever stop jabbing at her conscience?

"Thaddeus is a fine man."

Margaret shot up from the settee, two bright circles on her cheekbones. Shaking with angry, she spat, "He's a Yankee, Josie! He may be the very man who took Tom away from us. Did you ever think of that when you're with him? Did you ever wonder if he is the man who *killed* your fiancé?"

As if the spew of fury rent her in half, Margaret bent

forward, face in her hands, and sobbed. Long, shuddering, harsh sounds emitted from the depths of her soul.

Sick and shaking and guilty as sin, Josie put her arms around Tom's mother and held her while they both cried.

THAD SAW HER there on the second-floor balcony long before he reached the house.

She hadn't come to the mill today.

For the best, he'd told himself. She distracted him from the work, but he'd missed her, and Abram had noticed, teasing when he'd been grumpy.

Worried that she'd taken ill, he'd sent for word of her health. Abram, by way of Lizzy, said she'd gone into town to visit her fiancé's mother.

Fiancé.

Josie was engaged. He'd wrestled with that some, and perhaps the nagging worry that he loved another's betrothed had added to his cranky mood. Upon sharing his concerns with Will, his wise cousin agreed with the painful truth Josie had yet to accept. Tom Foster, like so many soldiers, was long freed from the bonds of this earth.

Josie was engaged to a memory and none other.

Weariness from a long day of labor rode his shoulders, but seeing Josie in the moonlight, a poet's inspiration, his flagging energy spiked.

Once inside the house, he bypassed the parlor with little more than a lifted hand when Charlotte called that his supper was on the stove. He didn't want food.

On the floor of the parlor, Benjamin knuckled marbles against the wall to the sound of a Scottish air expertly played by Patience, the ethereal blonde beauty.

Will and Charlotte sat with heads together in quiet conversation, a sight that begged envy. Thad was helpless not to feel it.

He wanted that kind of loving contentment again.

His boots thudded softly on the staircase that rose from the entry to the second-floor hallway. At the top of the stairs, he circled around toward a corridor that split the upper floor into two sides lined with rooms. Directly in front of the staircase landing a double door opened out onto the veranda, which wrapped around the bedrooms on either side.

He rarely invaded this private sanctuary of the family, but tonight he was bold as he stepped through the opened doorway.

"I saw you walking across the meadow," she said without turning around.

The memory of moonlight kisses quivered on the night air. He longed to go to her, to take her in his arms and kiss her again and again.

All the way from the meadow, the pocket watch had bounced against his rib cage, as if to remind him of the family he'd lost. Amelia had loved him truly and faithfully. She'd always wanted the best for him. He could not help believing she'd want him to be happy again.

But was tempestuous Josie Portland the answer to his loneliness?

"You look beautiful." He hadn't meant to blurt the obvious even though he'd thought of little else since spotting her here, a copper-and-gold goddess bathed in starlight.

Josie turned from the railing, one hand on one of the pillars that supported the upper balcony and the slanting attic roof. Her flowing, curly hair hung loose in a way he'd never seen it before. In a way he'd imagined.

"'She walks in beauty, like the night of cloudless climes and starry skies, and all that's best of dark and bright meet in her aspect and her eyes.'"

The smallest of smiles graced her perfect lips. "You would quote Byron to me?"

"I haven't thought of that poem since the schoolroom."

She watched him, expression gentle and wistful, a rarity for this spitfire female.

He fell a little bit more in love.

"Indeed, the stars you so eloquently address are brighter from here," she murmured. "I can hear the whip-poor-wills and smell the river."

"I missed seeing you today." The throb in his throat revealed too much.

"I…was busy." The tender gaze flickered. She dropped her head to stare at the blue-painted planks of the veranda. In a voice that throbbed with conflict, she said, "You really should go."

The demand took him aback. They were sharing poetry. He'd told her she was beautiful.

"Go?" He stepped toward her. She shrank back. "Have I done something to offend you?"

She crossed her arms tight against her body and turned her back to stare out across the black woods and shadowy hills.

"No," she whispered. "No."

He stepped alongside her, grateful when she didn't slide away again. Her hand gripped the railing, and he rested his fingers on hers. "What's wrong?"

She pulled her hand away. "Us. We're wrong. I can't do this, Thaddeus."

He shook his head, fear boiling up. "Do what?"

"Continue to see you." She tilted her head, and for a fleeting second the sassy spark of Josie returned. "You are courting me, aren't you?"

"I'm trying my best. If Byron doesn't do the trick, I'm in trouble."

Her beautiful, succulent mouth curved, and Thad fought the desperate need to remind her of how much she liked his kisses.

"You can't court me."

"You don't care for me, then?" he asked, reeling, hurt but not at all convinced.

"I didn't say that."

"What *are* you saying, Josie?" He raked a hand through his hair in exasperation. "Speak plainly. I'm lost."

"I cannot allow myself to care for you. I cannot allow your court." She pressed a dainty hand to the ruffles on her blouse. "I am a betrothed woman, Thaddeus. I should never have led you on."

Cold as an Ohio winter, cold clear to his bones, Thad shook his head in denial. "Tom is dead, Josie."

"Perhaps." Her shoulders twitched without the usual sass and spirit. Resignation. "But one thing will never change."

"What's that?"

"I'm a Reb. Tom was a Reb." She lifted a hand, let it drop to the rail. Emotion flickered across her perfect features. Sorrow, pain, anger. "And you are a bloody Yankee."

Thaddeus sucked in a long draft of fragrant air and

released it as slowly as he could, gathering his thoughts and emotions. He loved her, but he would not apologize for who he was and what he believed.

Softly, wistfully, he murmured, "I can't change that, Josie. I had no power over my birthplace any more than you did. I wouldn't be me if I'd been born elsewhere."

"Would you? If you could?"

He knew what she wanted him to say, but he was a man of integrity. To lie only to please her would hurt them both in the long run.

"I cannot change who I am or the values that I hold to be true."

She nodded, her bottom lip quivering the slightest bit, enough that he wanted to put his lips there to soothe her.

"Then, sir," she said in stiff formality as if they hadn't splashed in the creek or kissed with wild abandonment, "I shall bid you good-night...and farewell. I do not wish to be courted by anyone of your ilk."

CHAPTER THIRTY

Hope is the thing with feathers
That perches in the soul
And sings the tune without the words
And never stops at all.

—Emily Dickinson

Present

BRODY HAD NEVER seen his father cry. He'd seen him drunk and mad, stumbling and passed out, but he'd never seen him cry.

Scared and uncertain about what to do, Brody sat in his living room with his shoulders hunched and blood pounding in his ears while, across the room, his father sobbed, face in his hands, shoulders shaking.

Mama was dead. She'd died a long time ago in a lake too far away for him to even know where it was. The police knew for sure the woman was his mama because they'd had him spit on a big Q-tip and matched his DNA to the woman found in the car.

"I thought she ran off, Brody," his daddy sobbed. "I thought she'd left us."

Brody had thought the same, probably because the old man had hammered it into his head for as long as he could remember. Penny was no good. Brody was no good. Nothing was good but a bottle of whiskey or a can of beer.

"I should have looked for her. I should have gone after her. But, no, what did I do? I got drunker. What kind of man does that, Brody? What kind of man doesn't search for his wife?" He broke into more long sobs that made Brody's stomach ache. "She was too good for me. You see that, don't you?"

Brody didn't know what to answer, so he remained silent. Like in the cop shows. He had a right to remain silent. Anything he said could be used against him.

"I asked you a question, boy!"

Brody jumped. "Yes, sir."

He wasn't sure what he was agreeing to, but the reply satisfied his father.

"I told her to not go." Clint laughed harshly. "And then I *ordered* her to leave, like some cocky drill sergeant who thinks he controls the world. We had an awful fight that night. You know what she said to me?"

"No, sir." His father never talked about his mama. Never. That he was talking about her now both scared and thrilled Brody. His hands were shaking along with his guts.

"She said I loved whiskey more than her. And you know what I said?"

Brody stared down at his hands. "No, sir."

"I told her she was right. No woman was going to tell me what to do. If she thought for one minute I'd give up the only relaxation a man got after a hard day's work, she could find some mama's boy to pay her bills. That's what I told her. And you know what she did?"

"No, sir." He could feel the tears welling. His chest hurt so bad with the news about his mother, he could hardly breathe. He wanted to run to the inn and talk to Hayden. He wanted to call Miss Carrie. She'd touch his hair, feed him cookies and tell him everything would be all right.

First Max and now Mama.

He wanted to be anywhere except here with his crying, talking father.

"You were asleep. She started toward your room. I blocked her way, cussing and ranting like a maniac. 'You're not leaving,' I told her. But she said she was only going out for a drive while I calmed down. That's what she claimed, but I knew she was leaving for good. If she took you, she was gone forever.

"'The boy stays,' I said, thinking she'd come back if you were here. She was crazy for you. Rarely let you out of her sight.

"She fought me then, like a tiger. She pushed and shoved, trying to get into that room where you slept, but she was a little woman, no match for me. I laughed in her face and dragged her to the front door and shoved her outside."

He hung his head, wagging it back and forth. "Stupid. Stupid. I told her to get out. I made her leave. She was crying. Begging. Asking to stay. Because of you."

He raised his face, stricken. "Her last words to me were 'You can't keep me away from my baby.'"

A tight place loosened in Brody's chest. "She wanted to take me?"

But his father didn't answer. He kept on talking, talking.

"Every time I looked at you, I'd think she *has* to come back. She'll come for him. After a couple of days, I vowed to quit drinking, to go to church or take her on a cruise, whatever she wanted. If she'd only come home." He put his head in his hands again. "But she never did. She couldn't."

His mother had loved him. Brody's mind throbbed with the news. She'd loved him and fought for him.

His father looked up with red-rimmed eyes. "All this time I hated her for leaving, and I blamed you because she didn't come back. Doesn't make a lick of sense now, does it? Not a lick."

Brody rose from the chair and started slowly and cautiously toward his father. He pretended the sad-looking man on the couch was a bird with a damaged wing or a dog growling out of fear because he'd been hit by a car. A broken creature.

When he reached the sofa, he stood inches away. Slowly, stiffly, he lifted his hand and rested it on his father's shoulder.

"I'm sorry, Daddy." He didn't know what he was sorry for except that his mother was dead and his father was sad, but saying the words freed something inside him.

With a groan, Clint pulled Brody into his arms and hugged him close, rocking, crying and muttering unintelligible promises. And as sad as Brody was, he didn't feel so lost anymore.

A MEMORIAL FOR Penny Thomson was held on a cloudy, humid Thursday. Taking the afternoon off work, Carrie attended the service along with Hayden and Bailey and her son. As moral support, the group sat directly behind Brody. The little boy looked bewildered. His father looked worse.

Only a handful of people attended the small service, mostly Brody's schoolteachers, Clint's coworkers from Big Wave and a few others. Clint's brother drove down from Memphis but left right after the service, and if there were other family members anywhere, they hadn't bothered to come.

Carrie found the situation immeasurably sad. Her own life was filled with family and extended family, but Brody and his father were basically alone. Hayden, who bore no sympathy whatsoever for Clint Thomson, claimed the man's behavior had estranged him from anyone who'd tried to care, including his own wife and son.

Hayden's reaction was harsh and swift, and she wondered anew if there was more behind his anger than concern for Brody.

After the short service, Carrie drove to Brody's home with a plate of her mother's fried chicken and another of homemade peanut butter cookies, Brody's favorite. She'd invited Hayden to come along, but he'd declined. He wasn't Clint Thomson's favorite visitor, but he sent a written message for Brody that made the boy's sorrowful face light up.

He'd also invited Carrie to spend the remainder of the afternoon with him at the inn.

Bailey, tall and stunning in a black sheath dress belted in red, had overheard the invitation and muttered, "He's hot for you, baby sis. Unbutton those top two blouse buttons."

Her sisters were hopeless romantics. So was Carrie, but mostly she was practical.

And she practically adored Hayden Winters. Every single minute in his smart, insightful, charming company.

After dropping off books to three patrons, including

the cat lady, she aimed her blue Beetle toward Peach Orchard Inn.

When she arrived, Hayden sat on the veranda, feet propped on the railing, his laptop open on a round table. A glass of Miss Julia's peach tea waited, half-gone, at his elbow. Bingo, Julia's Australian shepherd, sprawled in the shade beneath the eaves behind him.

As she exited the car, Hayden glanced up and smiled, and her heart turned over.

"You look like a fine Southern gentleman surveying his plantation," she said, coming toward him across the grass, glad she still wore the navy pencil skirt she'd worn to the memorial. She looked nice. Even Nikki had said so, mostly because the crepe skirt and white top had come from her boutique. Carrie would not, however, unbutton the top two buttons on her blouse.

"Ah, if only it was so. I like it here." Hayden dropped his feet to the wooden porch with a thud and stood. "Think Julia will sell?"

"Not a chance."

As she stepped up next to him, he kissed her lightly. "You look…beautiful. You and that sexy ankle bracelet. A good choice, even if I do say so myself."

Carrie never knew what to do with compliments. "Silly."

"You're beautiful, Carrie, and you distract me. Like this inn and that orchard and these peaceful surroundings." He smoothed the back of his index finger down her cheek. "So, did you deliver the cookies and chicken?"

She suppressed a delicious shiver. Even if his words weren't true, they fed her confidence. He made her feel special. "I did."

"How was Brody doing?" He pulled out a chair for her, and she sat across from him.

"Surprisingly well. I gave him your message, and he seemed thrilled. What was that all about?"

Hayden hiked one eyebrow. "You didn't read the note?"

"I wouldn't do that. It wasn't mine to read."

He appeared genuinely surprised. "I would have. But since your curiosity is not quite as overpowering as mine, or perhaps you simply have better manners, I'll tell you. I offered to take him to a riding stable in Shelbyville on Sunday afternoon."

"Hayden, that's a wonderful idea. An outing will help get his mind off—" she waved her hand vaguely "—this tragedy."

"My thinking, too. He told me he's always wanted to ride a horse."

And you're making it happen for him. So thoughtful. So kind. No wonder she'd fallen hard.

"He talks to you about a lot of things—doesn't he? And I have a feeling you talk to him, too."

"Sure." His shrug was casual, but his eyes were shuttered. "Guy stuff."

"Do you ride?"

He scoffed. "Not a bit, but I'm always in the market for new experiences. Book fodder. Want to join us?"

Carrie laughed, but the joke was on her. "Horses are big and scary."

"The place I contacted promises the gentlest animals in a controlled environment. We can do this. For Brody."

"Oh, you don't play fair, mister."

"Never said I did. When I want something, I find a way. And I want to spend Sunday afternoon with you."

"And Brody."

He grinned. "Uh-huh."

"This may sound odd, but he seems happier since he learned about his mother, and he and his dad— I'm not sure how to describe it other than they seem to be relating. I even saw Mr. Thomson pat him gently on the back, and Brody stood close, as if he was…supporting his father."

Hayden's nostrils flared. "Surprising indeed."

"I think things may be improving."

"You're an optimist."

"Maybe, but people can change, Hayden. There were several people coming and going while I was there, offering condolences, dropping off casseroles. The mood was somber but cordial. Thomson was sober and polite, and Brody, bless his heart, is hopeful."

"Why?" Hayden's expression remained dubious.

"A preacher and a man from Thomson's work were there. The man said he'd been an alcoholic, too, with anger issues like Clint's." Heat rushed up her neck. "I don't usually eavesdrop, but I overheard. They invited Brody's dad to an AA meeting at the Baptist Church and promised to help him."

"AA meetings? At a church?" Hayden almost laughed. "Seeing Clint Thomson in a church would require more than optimism. That would take a miracle."

"He said he would go. He seemed sincere, almost eager, as if grasping a lifeline. Maybe the death of his wife shook him up enough to change his ways."

Hayden made a face. "I wouldn't count on it."

"Oh, ye of little faith."

"Brody's had enough disappointments. Don't get his hopes up."

"'Hope is the thing with feathers,'" she quoted. "Brody won't ever stop hoping that his father will be the man he needs him to be."

Hayden sighed and glanced toward the orchard, where leaves slowly faded toward yellow. A peach-scented wind drifted from the house.

"Most likely true. Let's hope, along with your feathery Dickinson poem, that he follows through with the AA meetings and gets sober for Brody's sake."

"That's exactly what I hope."

"But I'm still keeping an eye on him."

For now. But what about after he left?

That was a path she didn't want to follow today, so she motioned toward the laptop. "Any progress?"

"I took your advice about putting the dreams down. I'd already written the first ones but decided to purge them all. Maybe once I do, I can let go of them and focus on the paying job."

"What about your research? Do you need more? Want me to show you more nooks and crannies and places to hide the body?" She was pathetic, searching for reasons to keep him in Honey Ridge.

"I'm thinking the gristmill is the perfect place. Maybe I'll crank up the waterwheel and grind someone—"

"Hayden!" She clapped her hands over her ears.

He laughed. "No grinding today. I'll wait until I get back to New York to do the evil deed."

Back to New York. Soon. Carrie tried to keep smiling.

Hayden closed the laptop and stood. "Today a

charming woman is distracting me, and I'd rather spend time with her than work."

"Ooh, smooth talker," she teased, trying not to take his words seriously, but her heart fluttered anyway.

A cell phone buzzed, and Hayden fished a smartphone from his back pocket, frowned at the screen and said, "I should take this. Will you excuse me?"

He moved away, walking out toward the orchard. Bingo rose, shook himself and trotted along with him, his dog tags jingling.

The cadence of Hayden's voice drifted back to the porch, though Carrie couldn't make out the conversation. Eavesdropping once today was more than enough.

Watching a handsome man, on the other hand, was not bad manners.

She admired the easy grace of his movements and the manly stretch of his shoulders. She thought of his tenderness when he held her and the way his kiss, light and gentle, could make her whole being sing for joy. She considered the silver bracelet sliding against her skin, a constant reminder of him, the man she'd fallen in love with.

Love was a funny thing. She hadn't wanted or expected to fall in love, certainly not with someone so out of her league, but Hayden wasn't like that. He was natural and easy to be with, as if *she* was the special one.

He stopped talking and stared down at the phone in his hand. The sun peeked from behind a cloud and glinted off the screen. He didn't turn around, didn't even move for long enough that worry tingled at the back of her neck.

"Hayden?" She stepped off the porch and started across the dying grass.

He turned her way. Lines of concern creased his forehead.

"What's wrong? Bad news?"

He inhaled deeply, releasing the breath in a gust. "Yes."

"What is it? How can I help?"

"It was… My mother's in the hospital." His expression was pinched and anxious, as if he didn't want to share such news but felt he must because she was there and asking.

The realization stung a little. He'd rarely confided, except about the dreams. And those seemed to worry him, as if he thought she'd think less of him because of an interesting dream.

A sick mother, however, was too important to keep inside.

"What happened? She'll be okay, won't she?"

He shook his head, rammed a hand through his hair, blew out another breath. "She's very ill. I'll have to go to Louisville."

Hayden, usually so smooth and together, was frazzled.

Carrie moved close and slid her arms around his waist. She laid her head on his chest and held him, offering her librarian calm.

His arms embraced her in a crush. She felt his anxiety, the slight tremor in his body, a manly body that smelled of Hugo Boss cologne and sun-warmed skin.

"You're worried about the disagreement the two of you had."

She heard him swallow, his heart thudding mightily beneath her ear. He hurt, the love for his mother apparent in his strong reaction to the disturbing news.

"She's your mom, Hayden. She loves you. She'll understand you still love her even if the two of you disagreed. Mamas always forgive you. It's the way they are." She stroked his back in small circles, wishing she knew more about his family, longing to know the woman who'd given birth to this wonderful man, and sorry that she lay in a hospital far away.

For several minutes they stood in each other's embrace, with the sun playing peekaboo with the clouds above and the moist, decaying coolness of early autumn sneaking in from the woods.

"I should pack," he said. "Make a plane reservation. I dread this."

The insight touched Carrie. "She'll be okay, Hayden. Don't worry so much, not until you know more."

"You're right. You're right." He loosened his hold, retreated a few inches but didn't step away. His anguish moved her to action.

"Would you like me to go with you?" The thought had come from deep inside, the place that loved him, the place that wanted to be there for him. As much as she hated airplanes, she gulped down the dread for Hayden's sake. "Sometimes having a friend along makes things easier to handle."

Her offer appeared to startle him. He took another step backward, already shaking his head. "No. No."

She followed, grabbed his hands to say, "Are you sure, Hayden? You're very upset. You need someone… who cares about you."

He seemed to compose himself then, and the sophisticated Hayden regained control. He pulled her close, kissed her softly. And though she tasted his worry, he said, "I'll be fine. Don't concern yourself. I'll call you when I know more." He kissed her again and whispered, "I love you for caring."

Then he walked quickly toward the inn, leaving her alone to wonder if he'd refused out of consideration for her, or because he hadn't wanted her with him.

I love you for caring.

Perhaps she'd been too forward, too obvious.

At the front door, Hayden paused and turned back. He looked so alone.

He stretched a hand toward her. "Help me pack?"

A cord of tension released in Carrie's neck. She followed him into the house.

CHAPTER THIRTY-ONE

HAYDEN DEBATED BETWEEN driving and flying. When all was said and done, he flew, needing the time to shut out the world with his headphones on and his eyes closed to collect his thoughts.

Carrie had shaken him with her offer to come along. He'd longed to say yes, and that had shaken him more.

He'd come so close to breaking his own vow.

I love you for caring, he'd said when he'd really meant, "I love you. I need you. Come with me."

She would have.

Carrie loved him. Or rather, she loved who she thought he was.

With dark humor he mocked his thoughts. If she came with him to Kentucky, she'd learn the ugly truth. She'd know who he really was. How would she feel about him then?

Better to keep the facade in place, protect her from the seed of insanity, the roots of addiction, the man behind the mask.

Upon arriving in Louisville, he'd gone straight to the hospital. He didn't know how his mother had ended up in this city or this hospital and didn't ask. Nothing about Dora Lee ever surprised him.

Overdosed and malnourished, she suffered from a host of complications caused by her addiction. The doctor, a thin, graying woman whose glasses were bigger than her face, had asked if Hayden knew his mother was an addict. He'd been too angry and humiliated to laugh. He'd stood with his head down and arms limp at his side like a scolded boy, helpless and guilt-ridden.

Later, after consulting with the physicians, he'd stood at Dora Lee's bedside, staring down into her pale, emaciated, unconscious face while machines whooshed and beeped around her greasy blond head. He'd wondered if he'd ever outgrow the need to rescue her or the need for his mother to care one iota about him the way he did about her.

Love and hate, like creativity and insanity, two sides of the same coin.

He remained at Dora Lee's bedside through the night while she slept on, oblivious to her son's presence or his deep concern.

By the time he reached the hotel late the next morning after meeting again with the doctors, he fell across the bed, too exhausted and tormented to undress.

Sometime later his cell phone awakened him. He jerked upright, grabbed for it, fearing the worst. Without even reading the caller ID, he choked out, "Hello."

"Hayden? Are you all right?"

Blinking sleep-glazed eyes, he fell back against the standard-issue pillows, heart rattling in its cage. "Carrie."

"Yes, it's me. I'm worried about you. You sound… Are you okay?"

Her voice was the sweetest music, a soothing melody that he desperately needed right now. "Long night. I was asleep."

"I'm so sorry. I'll hang up so you can rest."

"No, no. I'm glad you called." He found the hotel alarm clock and checked the time. "I need to get back to the hospital soon."

"How is she?"

"Unconscious."

A stunned pause before she asked, "What happened, Hayden?"

She partied herself into oblivion. She's a pillbilly.

He didn't, of course, admit that. Carrie couldn't begin to relate to a mother like Dora Lee. She'd proved as much when she'd tried to comfort him with promises that his mother loved him and would forgive their disagreement. Not all mothers were like Mary Riley.

She didn't know, could never know the degradation and rage he'd lived with for sixteen years and run from all his life.

"Kidney and liver issues. They're running tests." That much, at least, was true. The overdose had damaged both. "University is a good hospital. If anyone can help her, they can."

"I wish there was something I could do to help."

"Hearing your voice helps. Talk to me, Carrie." He propped the phone between his shoulder and ear and rested his head against the headboard.

"Have you eaten anything?"

He blinked at a pastoral painting on the wall of racing Thoroughbreds, trying to remember. "Yesterday, when I landed in Louisville."

"No food, but I bet you've had gallons of coffee, probably from a machine."

"The nursing staff shared theirs, but it wasn't as good as yours." Still, they'd keep him plied with coffee so he could maintain his bedside vigil, and for that he was grateful, especially since not one of them knew he was Hayden Winters, author. People saw what they expected, a pillbilly's frazzled son in grungy jeans and a beat-up ball cap.

"How much sleep did you get?"

"Enough."

"Hayden, you sound exhausted. You have to take care of yourself. Do you have other relatives who can come and help you through the crisis?"

"Not a soul." Having Carrie fuss over him even if she was prying into things better left uncovered filled a dark place inside him. He wished *she* could be here. He needed her. Wanted her.

But the thought of fresh and innocent Carrie discovering the truth about his drug-addicted wretch of a mother, a woman he was too crazy to stop loving, created an earthquake in his brain that shook him to the soul. Not that Carrie would spread the word and sell him out to tabloids. She wouldn't do that. Not Carrie.

But she'd *know*, and knowing would change everything good between them. Better that he left her believing the best thing about him, the facade that was Hayden Winters.

"How's Brody?" he asked, intentionally switching the subject. "Have you seen him today? Did he go to school?"

"No school. But he was here at the library for a short time, long enough for me to tell him about your emergency."

"I'll call him tonight if his old man will let me talk to him."

"I think he will. He came to the library with Brody. First time ever."

"Shocker. Can the cretin read?"

She laughed softly. "Hayden."

"I'll never be a fan." He thought of his own mother, lying in the hospital, and made the easy comparison. Parents who hurt their kids deserved no concession.

He hated being in Kentucky because it made him remember, made him feel out of balance. The moment he touched Kentucky soil, he started to shake inside the way he'd done that day when Dora Lee had proved how much she hated him.

The emotion oppressed him in dark, heavy waves, pressing in until he couldn't breathe. Like going under the water too many times.

Carrie's voice called him into focus and recentered him, though his heart thundered still, scared, helpless, drowning. "But you like his son."

He put a hand to his throat, swallowed and blinked away the dark memory.

"Brody," he managed, "is one sweet apple that fell far, far away from the rotten tree." The way Hayden hoped *he* had. Please God, don't ever let him be anything like Dora Lee. "Make sure he knows I'll reschedule the horseback riding when I get back."

"He would understand if you didn't."

"No, he wouldn't. He's a kid, and he's had enough disappointments. I'll make it happen." He buried a yawn.

"You sound so tired and worried."

"I am." Too tired to create a flippant reply or to pretend everything was peachy. Or to be anything but honest. "I miss you."

He missed her freshness and her soft, clear eyes, the way she looked at the world through clean lenses. He missed the way she made him feel more whole than he'd ever been.

He really should hang up before he blurted out something more damaging.

"I miss you, too," she murmured. "I wish you didn't have to go through this alone."

"It meant a lot that you offered to come with me. I don't take that lightly, Carrie."

"I want to be there to support you."

"I know." Then he said again as if he couldn't help himself, "I love you for caring."

He swallowed the longing he heard in his own voice and wished he hadn't used the word *love* again. It hovered like a butterfly, eager for escape. He couldn't do that to her. Offering empty words out of his own need would sully what he felt for her, would be unfair, unkind. Carrie was too good for that kind of treatment.

A silence ensued, and then with a sweetness that melted him, she said, "I care very much, Hayden."

His eyes fell shut.

He knew. He knew. Everything she did and said broadcast her feelings and heaped guilt on his head. He didn't want anything to hurt her, and yet he probably would. It was wired into his DNA.

They talked awhile longer, mostly about Brody and a little about the innkeeper's upcoming wedding, a conversation that made him long to be back in the clean, comfortable Mulberry Room and among the most sincere people he'd met in a long time.

Carrie asked him about the dreams, and he realized he hadn't dreamed at all last night. Then she made him smile with a tale of the Sweat twins and their parrot, Binky, and he teased her about the thunderstorm phobia, wishing he could always be there to hold her when the rains came.

He couldn't even calm his own storms.

Before they disconnected, Carrie admonished him to eat, to rest, to take care of himself. He'd soaked it up, filling his mind with her voice. Pathetic that a grown man craved nurturing.

"Promise?" she demanded, sounding bossy, but bossy with a spoon of sugar.

"Promise," he said and fought like a mad bull to keep from blurting out the truth and begging her to come to Kentucky.

THE REST OF the day Carrie fretted about Hayden. Knowing he was upset and worried hurt her, but she had no idea how to help.

After work, literacy class and an hour of distributing bags of potatoes for Interfaith, she drove out to Peach Orchard Inn with her sisters to meet with Julia about the upcoming wedding. Part of her dreaded a repeat confrontation with Valery, but this evening the vivacious sister was on her best behavior and greeted Carrie as if the harsh words had never been spoken.

Carrie breathed a sigh of relief.

"Tea or coffee?" With perfect hostess skills Valery ushered the sisters into the entry, where a mahogany credenza held pamphlets advertising raft rentals, horseback riding and a host of other outdoor and historical activities for guests.

"Coffee for me," Carrie said. "I need the caffeine boost."

Behind the glass doors of the credenza as well as

in a shadow box above, the artifacts of Peach Orchard Inn's past reminded Carrie of Hayden's dreams.

Was he okay? Was his mother?

"Julia made peach cobbler scones for y'all," Valery said.

Carrie hummed in approval. She'd not had a bite to eat since noon when Tawny left early for a doctor's appointment, and lunch had been a quick cup of microwave noodles.

Had Hayden eaten anything at all?

"Sorry, I'm watching my carbs." Nikki's shoulders slumped. "And I do mean I'm sorry. Julia makes the best peach cobbler scones in the world."

"Oh, Nikki, you're already perfect," Carrie said. "Why do you worry?"

"So I can *stay* perfect," Nikki said, and then laughed at her own conceit.

"Well, I'm having one. Maybe two. With coffee. What about you, Bailey?"

"Absolutely. Bring on the carbs. We'll make Nikki green with envy."

The four of them traipsed down the hall to the kitchen, where Julia was sliding the golden scones out of the oven. The smell of cinnamon and peaches filled the air.

The scent brought guests down the stairs, and even the dog and his boy, the quietly pleasant Alex, appeared in the doorway.

Julia handed her soon-to-be son a glass of milk and a scone. "I'm ruining your dinner, Alex."

He grinned up at her with a missing tooth. "I won't tell."

Julia, looking happier than Carrie could ever remember, kissed him on the head with a loud smack. "My coconspirator. I think Daddy will notice when you don't eat your peas."

Alex stuck out his tongue in a grimace. "Scones are better."

After availing themselves of refreshments, the women reconvened in the family parlor at the back of the lower floor. Carrie, thankfully, had been asked to attend the guest book. She could handle that, and addressing invitations in her tidy hand was no problem at all.

She'd polished off her first scone and started on the second when Valery said, "Have you heard from Hayden?"

Uncertain of what he'd told Valery and Julia about his abrupt departure, she said, "I talked to him this morning."

Julia rested her hands on the book of samples in her lap. "How is his mother?"

"He told you about her illness?"

"Valery pried it out of him."

Valery shrugged. "I wanted to be sure he was coming back. Couldn't have him running out on us." She smiled a cat's smile. "Or should I say on you?"

Carrie sidestepped the comment. Her nerves were already raw with worry.

"His mother is not doing well. He thinks her kidneys are failing. You can imagine how frightening that is." She picked a crumb from the corner of the still-warm scone, remembering the strain and fatigue in his voice. Even when they'd discussed other topics, the anxiety was there. "Hayden's very worried."

"So are you." The innkeeper's blue eyes studied her.

"Is it concern for Hayden or for his mother that put the frown between your eyes?"

She picked another crumb. "He's alone. I hate that he's going through this without anyone else's support."

"No family?"

"None. No siblings, and his father died when he was small." Other than his assistant and agent, he'd never mentioned anyone close. If he had close friends or someone special, he'd never told her. There was always that wall around him. A nice wall, polite and charming, but a wall nonetheless.

"Sad." Valery sipped at her tea. "Why didn't you go with him? Unless my radar's off, the two of you have a good thing going."

Nikki laughed. "Your radar is right on, although baby sister is afraid to believe a guy like Hayden could have a thing for her."

"If he's any kind of man at all, he sees my sister's value," Bailey said with a sniff, and Carrie adored her for it. "Val's right, Carrie. You should go to Kentucky."

Hadn't she asked him to take her? And he'd refused. "I'm not sure he wants me there."

"Are you nuts? Of course he does. He just doesn't want to inconvenience you."

"Nikki's right, Carrie," Julia said. "Hayden doesn't like to impose. He even makes his own bed here at the inn, no matter how many times I've told him I would do it."

Was that Hayden's reasoning? Had he refused to let her come along out of concern for her? Not because he didn't want her there?

"Do you really think he believed I wouldn't want

to be there for him? That going was too much trouble to ask of me?"

Nikki stretched her manicure out in front of her and studied her pumpkin-colored nails. "Julia, if you and Valery haven't figured it out yet, our girl Carrie is in love with Mr. Book Writer."

"Nikki!" Heat rushed up Carrie's face. "Don't."

"Well, you are, even if you're too scared to admit it. And I think Hayden feels the same."

"Don't be silly. He's a famous writer."

"Like that makes him immune to human feelings? Although when I think about the graphic stuff he writes, I wonder."

"Hayden is the kindest, most generous man," Carrie said. "Did you know he drove to the cat lady's house with a signed book and an order of Cambodian pork and spent an afternoon talking to her? Nobody does that. Not to mention the fact that he paid to have Penny Thomson's remains returned to Honey Ridge."

All four women looked at her with wide eyes. "He did?"

Carrie clapped a hand over her mouth. "I wasn't supposed to know that. Mr. B. let it slip."

Julia leaned toward her, eyes narrowed. "How much did he donate to the library?"

Carrie groaned. "Too much. Please don't let him know I told you. He's very private."

"And alone. We're back to that." Bailey pinched off a crumb of scone. "A man who does good things shouldn't face his mother's critical illness without the support of family or friends or someone—" she gave Carrie a knowing look "—who loves him."

"Look," Nikki said, her expression serious. "I'm not

the best person to give out sage advice. That's Mom's area, but I see something potentially awesome happening here."

Her pulse fluttered in her neck. "Meaning?"

Nikki bit her lip. "Ever since the *other thing* happened, you've been running scared, but you know the old saying, when one door closes—"

Bailey leaned forward and pointed. "Another opens."

"Another door is opening, little sis. Don't be afraid to walk through it. What's on the other side may be your knight in shining armor."

Valery hoisted her teacup. "That would be Hayden."

Nikki whipped out her cell phone. "Let's make a reservation right now and get you on a plane first thing in the morning."

"I couldn't."

"Do you want to?"

She wrung her hands in her lap. Get on an airplane? Fly to Kentucky by herself? Did Hayden really want her there and was too caring to ask?

Was he worth the risk?

The answer came easier then. Like Nikki said, sometimes a person had to take a chance. If she loved him, she'd step outside her comfort zone and be the woman he needed.

In a squeak, insides quaking but sure, Carrie took a leap of faith. "Yes."

CHAPTER THIRTY-TWO

The probability that we may fail in the struggle ought not to deter us from the support of a cause we believe to be just.

—A. Lincoln

1867

THAD HAD THOUGHT he couldn't hurt any worse. He'd suffered a war, a fire that left him fearful and scarred and the loss of his wife and daughter. He'd thought the pain was behind him.

But Josie's rejection of everything he stood for, of the man he was, of the honor he'd fought for, cut through him like a dull bayonet.

"Mr. Thad, sir."

Abram appeared at the entrance of the mill's basement, an area adjacent to the waterwheel that housed the cogs and pulleys and tools needed to keep the mill in operation.

Thad brushed an exhausted hand over his damp forehead. "What is it, Abram?"

The lantern, hanging from a post, flickered as the hired man approached his boss.

"Time to go, sir. You's working too hard."

"Machinery don't repair itself."

If the sharp tone bothered Abram, he didn't let on. "Yes, sir, but you been working too hard and too late for the past three days. Something wrong?"

Thad stretched his neck to the right and then to the left. A hard knot had settled between his shoulder blades. "Nothing."

Abram studied his face as if he could read the heartache, but he kept his thoughts to himself. Even though Thad was not a harsh manager, Abram's slave days were too deeply ingrained to refute Thad's claim or to pry deeper.

"Go on home, Abram. I'll be along directly."

"Yes, sir." Abram turned and started out, but at the stairway, he turned back. "Mr. Thad, I ain't seen Miss Josie around here lately."

His fingers convulsed. "You won't, either."

"She having herself a woman fit? Miss Josie, she good at that."

Thad chuckled. A woman fit sounded about right for Josie. He missed the flare of her temper and her contrition after it had taken control. He missed the times she'd threatened to disembowel him and leave him for buzzards and then the way she'd kiss him or bring him spring-cold lemonade to give the lie to her threats.

"Apparently, I'm not the right man for her. Now, you go on home like I said and get some rest. I'll see you tomorrow."

Abram nodded and left Thad to his thoughts and chores. He greased the cogs and examined the pulleys while shadows gathered and the old mill settled around him. Every squeak and groan had become dear and familiar. He was a good miller and an honest one. He was needed here.

Perhaps he should go back to Ohio, back to where the word *Yankee* was not considered profane. But he'd promised Will a year, and he was not a man to break a promise.

He'd lived with a broken heart before. He could do it again.

With his thoughts spinning, he barely heard the sounds coming from outside the mill. Hoofbeats. Voices.

He put down the oilcan and cocked his head to listen. No customer would come this late. Was there trouble at the farm? Was something wrong? Had someone come to fetch him?

He trotted up the steps, and as he reached the second floor, he heard voices. Not a one belonged to the Portland farm.

"I seen a light, Jim." The voice, young and thin, sounded nervous. "I know I did. Someone's in here."

Heavy, thudding footsteps, like boots and brogans, sounded on the floorboards. Light, brighter than any lantern, cast long, flickering shadows across the upper floor.

"Stop being a coward and git on in there and do what we come to do."

"You know how they treated Oscar and me." The voice sounded familiar. "We don't cotton to Yankees and their lot running our town."

Thad mentally sorted through his customers' voices and landed on Jim Swartz, Josie's friend. What was he doing here?

The younger voice rose to a shout. "Let's teach them a lesson they won't ever forget."

Hair stood on the back of Thad's neck. There were

at least four of them. He didn't know what they were up to, but clearly no good was afoot.

He could hear the men moving through the mill and saw the flicker of their lights, torches from what he could tell.

Sliding sideways along the wall, he worked his way toward the office and his rifle. God knew he'd never wanted to raise arms against another man, but the mill was his responsibility.

In the darkness, he fumbled for the weapon, running his hands along the wall.

A shout prickled the skin on his arms.

"Run, boys. She's set!"

Footsteps thundered through the mill. Men shouted. "Go. Go! Get out of here!"

"Jim, Jim!" The young, thin voice rose in a near scream.

Thad rushed to the mill entrance, rifle raised, his eyes adjusting to the darkness, though he could only make out shadows.

Thad fired his rifle into the night, but he was too late. Heads covered in white sacks, three mounted horsemen raced into the night, fiery torches aloft.

A bloodcurdling scream yanked Thaddeus around.

Flames shot from the lower floor, where stacks and stacks of unprocessed grain, corn shucks, cobs and empty bags awaited the miller's hand.

A room now glowing in the dark.

Thad's blood turned to water. He went to his knees. *Not fire. Not a fire.*

His mind flashed to that night more than a year ago and to his daughter's screams.

"Daddy! Daddy!"

"Gracie," he whispered. "Dear God, no. Not again."

Another terrified scream ripped the night air. "Help. Somebody help! Please help me!"

Sweating now but shivering, too, Thad staggered to his feet and ran for the mill exit. Once outside in the sweet air, the smell and vision of smoke dissipated. He wiped a shaky hand over his eyes.

He had to get help. The farm. He'd head there.

Another scream, this one of fear mixed with pain, spun him around.

Someone who'd intended harm to the mill and to him remained inside the burning building.

Thad clamped down on his back teeth. He couldn't go in there. He couldn't.

The man inside deserved whatever happened to him. He'd been up to no good. If he died, the fault was his own. Let his suffering be a lesson to the others.

The scars on Thad's body throbbed, a reminder of the pain and agony of fire eating through flesh.

The flames grew brighter, the screams more desperate.

Thad's whole body quaked.

"God help me," he whispered.

With the visions of Grace and Amelia in his mind and the memory of his own excruciating burns, Thad did the only thing his conscience would allow.

He rushed back into the mill.

CHAPTER THIRTY-THREE

Love seeketh not itself to please
Nor for itself hath any care
But for another gives its ease
And builds a Heaven in Hell's despair.

— William Blake

Present

"MR. BRIGGS. MR. BRIGGS." A voice intruded on Hayden's dream.

Who was Mr. Briggs?

He was.

Hayden's eyes flew open. He straightened, his neck aching and tense. His heart pounded, and his brain was flooded with images of fire.

A scrubs-clad nurse stood next to his chair.

He wasn't at the burning mill with Thaddeus. He was in Kentucky, where he'd fallen asleep in the stiff vinyl waiting room chair. He sat up and glanced at his watch.

"I'm sorry to bother you, sir, but I thought you'd be relieved to know your mother's level of consciousness is improving."

He scrubbed his hands over his face, reorienting himself. "She's waking up?"

"Slowly."

"Thank you."

The nurse offered a professional smile and hurried away. Lights over patients' rooms flared and beeped. Gurneys, both empty and loaded, rumbled down the tile hallway. A television on the wall entertained no one.

Hayden cataloged the overload of sensory input, along with the smell of antiseptic struggling to over-shadow the odor of sick humanity. It was useless, like dressing a pillbilly's son in Armani. It changed noth-ing. It only hid the truth.

He rarely let those things bother him, but lately his upbringing haunted him like the dreams did. Josie's hatred of all things Yankee kept her from appreciating the good in Thaddeus, and only she could change it.

Hayden rubbed a hand over his face, felt the scratchy beard. He'd tried to change who he was. The only per-son he hadn't fooled was himself.

His cell phone buzzed. A glance at caller ID bright-ened his outlook.

"Hi."

"Hayden?" Carrie's soft-as-rainwater voice took the edge off his fatigue. "How is she?"

He pushed out of the chair and started walking. "I'm heading down to the room now. The nurse says she's better."

A sigh. She was relieved for him. "I'm so glad." He felt her hesitate. "Hayden?"

He slowed his steps, frowning. "Is something wrong?"

"I hope not. I was worried about you. I thought you

might need someone." In a rush, she said, "I caught a plane. I'm here."

Breath froze in his lungs. "You're here? In Kentucky?"

"Yes." She sounded nervous and uncertain. He didn't want that any more than he wanted her in this hospital.

His heart rattled against his rib cage. "Stay there. I'll come to you."

"I'm already in a cab on my way to the hospital."

Though he'd written plenty of hospital scenes in his books, none played out quite as dramatically as this one.

She'd find out. His brain whirled, grabbing at excuses and solutions.

"What room?"

He tuned back in. "Excuse me?"

"The room number, Hayden."

"Fourth floor. ICU. You can't go in." He didn't know if that was true, but he was grabbing for lifelines.

"That's all right. I came to see you, Hayden. To be with you."

"Right." He started walking again, faster this time until his steps brought him to Dora Lee's unit. A nurse exited, cast a friendly nod in his direction.

"I'm hanging up now, Hayden. The cab just pulled up in front."

He tapped the end icon and pressed the phone against his thudding chest.

His breath came in short bursts. She was here.

HE LOOKED HAGGARD.

That was Carrie's first thought when Hayden

stepped off the elevator and strode toward her across the hospital lobby.

The uncertainty she'd battled in the cab disappeared. She went to him, confident now that she'd done the right thing by coming. He shouldn't go through this alone, not without someone who cared. She walked into his open arms.

"I was so worried about you."

His embrace tightened. "I'm okay."

"No, you're not. You're trembling with exhaustion."

He didn't deny her claim. "You hate airplanes."

She smiled against his shoulder. "You'd be proud. I didn't even throw up."

She didn't mention the white-knuckle grip or the sweaty imprints she'd left on the seat arms.

"Proud indeed." He kissed her ear. Now she was the one trembling. "You shouldn't have come."

Her heart stuttered. "You don't want me?"

He sighed. "Oh, I want you, all right. More than I can say."

She sighed, too, relieved and happy. He needed her. This man who kept himself aloof and shielded his heart needed her.

No man, not even Hayden Winters, was an island unto himself.

"I'm here for you. Whatever you need." She rubbed a hand up and down his back. "You're very tense."

"You have no idea." He huffed softly and eased back from her but didn't let her go. His gaze searched her face. "You're the most beautiful sight I've seen in days."

"But you said I shouldn't have come."

His beloved mouth ticked up at the corners, though

there were shadows in his eyes. He rocked her side to side. "Did I say that?"

Her anxiety dissipated completely. Here with Hayden in his time of difficulty was where she belonged, and here she would stay as he long as he wanted her.

"Shouldn't you be with your mother?"

The shadows deepened, his concern evident. He glanced toward the elevator and back to Carrie. His throat worked.

"I came out of her room right before you arrived. She's mostly out of it, heavily medicated, and the doctor said to let her rest."

"Did he say the same to you? You look as if you belong in a hospital bed yourself."

"I could use some food and sleep." He glanced at the roller bag at her side. "Have you checked into a hotel yet?"

She shook her head. "Not yet. I wanted to see about you and your mother first."

"The hotel has a good restaurant. I was about to head back there." He laced his fingers with hers. "Join me? Make me feel better for a while?"

Her smile bloomed. That's exactly why she'd come.

HAYDEN MANAGED TO get Carrie out of the hospital without learning about Dora Lee's real diagnosis. For now.

He knew that wasn't enough. She couldn't return to the hospital with him. He had to get her out of Kentucky.

But he didn't want to hurt her, either. Truth was he didn't want Carrie to leave. He wanted her with him all the time. He was better, happier, cleaner and more worthwhile when she was with him. Sweet, pure Carrie was a refuge he sorely needed.

He was tiptoeing on broken glass, and any minute he'd slip and slice an artery.

A waitress clad in standard black and white slid a pair of menus onto the table. "I'm Annie. I'll be your server."

Then she dashed off to get their water.

"This isn't exactly the celebration I'd had in mind when I asked you out to dinner," he said. "A causal bar and grill inside a hotel."

"That seems long ago instead of only a couple of days."

"I've been planning to take you somewhere special." To wine and dine her properly and show her how important she'd become to him.

"This *is* special, Hayden." She captured his eyes with her soft brown ones and melted him. A woman like her deserved better than lies and evasions. But the truth would break her heart.

He glanced at the colorful menu, hiding his culpability. "Anything look appealing?"

"Everything. I was too nervous to eat before I went to the airport, and I sure couldn't eat on the plane." She flipped the single-leaf menu to the back and studied the desserts and drinks.

Getting on an airplane was the last thing he'd expected Carrie to do. Yet she'd done it for him.

The knife of guilt plunged a little deeper.

"What are you ordering?"

He pushed the menu aside. "Grilled lemon chicken and portobellos, maybe?"

"Works for me." She stacked her menu on his.

While awaiting their order, she caught him up on Julia's wedding plans and told him that Brody's dad had actually gone to the AA meeting. He still didn't believe it would last, and he was still going to keep his eye on Clint Thomson. Somehow.

He urged her to talk, letting the pleasant lilt of her Tennessee voice soothe him.

When the food arrived, she turned the topic to Louisville, land of the Kentucky Derby.

"Have you ever been?" she asked.

"Once." It was a good memory. Not too long after his second book was tapped for a major motion picture. He'd been living the dream, thinking he could. "The Derby is quite a spectacle. Have you been?"

She shook her head. "No. I always feel sorry for the horses."

"You sound like Brody. But Thoroughbreds are born to run. They love it. It's in their blood."

"I suppose you're right. It's in their breeding. If the mother and father are runners, they have no choice but to be runners, too."

The chicken lost its flavor.

DNA won every time.

AFTER DINNER, THEY stopped at the front desk, where Carrie secured a room down the hall from Hayden's. He offered his credit card, but she batted his hand away. She didn't want the desk clerk thinking...*that*, even if she'd had a funny flutter when he'd instructed the clerk to put her on his floor.

She was glad if a bit uncertain. Being alone in a hotel was creepy. Always before she'd had her sisters or a friend along.

Hayden carried her tiny bag up the elevator and used her key to open the room. After checking behind every door and glancing out the window, he gave his nod of approval. "Looks safe enough."

She giggled. "You act as if you expected a bellman to be hiding under the bed with a hatchet."

His grin was suitably sheepish. "It's a curse."

"And a wonderful gift."

"There is that." He perched a hand on each hip. "You want to freshen up a bit or go for a walk, maybe a swim? The pool is heated."

"I didn't bring a swimsuit, but a short walk sounds good after I freshen up a little. Unless you'd rather get some obviously needed rest."

"Too keyed up. The exercise will help me relax." He went to the door. "First, I want to call the hospital."

"We should go back. Your mother might need you."

His expression tightened. "I'll call. I'm in 4106 when you're ready."

Fifteen minutes later, she tapped on his door and they headed out onto the sidewalk. The city, like most metropolitan areas, hummed and zipped around them.

"How's your mother?" she asked.

"Her lab results tonight are better. She's more awake."

"If we need to go there—"

"Not tonight." His curt tone surprised her. When she looked at him, he took her hand and said, "Sorry. The strain is taking a toll."

"I hope you can sleep better tonight."

"No worries." He ignored the flashing light at the corner and tugged her across the street. "The river area is a couple of blocks from here. Want to walk down there away from the traffic? It's nice."

"Sure. Wherever you say. This is your hometown. I'd be lost on my own."

They walked past several high-rise hotels before coming out to a paved courtyard overlooking the Ohio River.

"The bridges are stunning, especially that one." She pointed to a magnificent arching structure of steel and concrete stretched far, far across the water. "It's almost elegant."

"Big Four Bridge." He sounded pleased, a change from the earlier grumpy tone. "Used to be an old railroad trestle, but now it's a pedestrian attraction."

Carrie suffered a pang of guilt for keeping him away from the hospital with his mother, but the decision was his. She was there to support in whatever way he required. As he said, he needed a distraction, and she was happy to provide it.

"You should see the bridges during Derby week. They present an air show and fireworks along the river. It's impressive."

"Do you ever miss living here?" she asked.

"No." He started walking again, eyes straight ahead as if she'd said something wrong. Again she wondered about his childhood and about the woman lying a short distance away in the ICU.

Gray clouds scudded overhead, drawing a chill from the nearby Ohio. Carrie shivered, and Hayden slipped an arm around her, tugging her close to his very warm, sturdy side.

How right it was to be a woman with a man. How

perfect the fit of her body next to his, feeling protected and cherished.

Out on the water, a riverboat drifted past, and a smaller, faster boat created a noisy wake.

Hands clasped, they walked to the center of Big Four Bridge, where they exclaimed over the views of the Louisville skyline and, on the opposite end, southern Indiana.

The breeze picked up, cooler now. The sun descended behind a fluffy bank of gray clouds, creating a yellow horizon that reflected on the water.

Carrie gazed up at the man who'd stolen her heart and said, "This is lovely, Hayden." Lovely like the emotions ripe between them.

His gaze was tender as he lowered his face and kissed her. "Glad you like it."

"I'm sorry the timing is so awful," she said, "but I'm not sorry to be here with you."

His handsome face pensive, he squeezed her fingers and said no more but stared out at the fading golden glow.

Night fell, and when the bridge became a multitude of ever-changing colored lights, she tugged his hand. "Ready to go back? You need sleep."

He nodded. "I think I can now. You're good medicine."

The words were balm to Carrie, her reason for taking the risk to come to Kentucky. Whatever ultimately happened with this relationship, she would never be sorry for loving this good man.

LATER, WHEN HE'D retired to his hotel room and she to hers, Carrie phoned her mother. If Mary Riley disapproved of Carrie's sudden, uncharacteristic rush to Kentucky, she kept her thoughts to herself, reminding her only to "be careful."

When Nikki called, full of bubbly romantic notions, Carrie told her about the river walk and shared her concerns about Hayden and his very ill mother.

After a bit of conversation, she cast an anxious glance at the hotel window. "I think it's going to rain. Do you think storms follow me? I don't want to be here in a strange place in a storm."

Nikki, for once, didn't chide her about her silly phobias. "Close the curtains and you won't even know."

"Okay." With the phone cradled beneath her chin, Carrie drew the drapes as lightning flickered over the brightly lit skyline.

After ending the call, she went to bed. Lying in the darkness, she revisited the day. Hayden's tired eyes, his worry-tightened mouth, his tenderness toward her.

A thunderbolt rattled the windows. At least she thought the glass had rattled. Her pulse pounded in rhythm with the hard-pounding rain.

She was four floors up. What if a tornado struck the hotel?

She clicked on the bedside radio and found a strong music channel to drown out the noise and pulled the covers over her head.

The radio crackled with interference, a reminder rather than a distraction. She reached for her smartphone and fumbled for the music icon.

As she leaned to turn off the radio, a thunderstorm warning beeped across the airwaves.

She had no idea what she'd do if a tornado warning was next.

Shivering now and breathing hard, she sat up. She would not bother Hayden. He was exhausted and desperate for sleep, not for some rain-phobic female to keep him awake all night.

She clicked off the radio and huddled beneath the covers. She was a grown woman. She could be alone in a strange hotel in a strange city during a rainstorm.

A thunderbolt sat her straight up in bed.

HAYDEN ROUSED FROM a deep sleep. Flashes of light patterned across his bed, coming through the drapes he'd failed to close.

Rain.

He got up and closed the drapes and then fell back onto the bed. His eyes had barely closed when his mind regained clarity.

To Carrie, a simple rainstorm was a hurricane.

She would be nervous, more so because she was alone in a hotel in a strange city.

He turned on his side and thumped the pillow. He couldn't be with her. Not this time. Too dangerous.

She'd be scared, shaking.

He tossed to his other side, grinding his back teeth. *Don't be stupid.*

She was safer with him here in his own room. His control was already thin just knowing she was down the hall, maybe in her cupcake pajamas.

With the lightning flashes, she wouldn't get a moment of sleep.

He sat up, scraped a hand over his face.

She'd flown in an airplane, coming all the way to Kentucky because she'd known instinctively that he needed her.

Now she needed him.

He sucked in a deep breath, blew it out.

Dressed in a T-shirt and the gray sweats he'd loaned to Brody, he got up and took his phone from the charger.

Carrie answered on the first ring.

"Hayden?" She sounded breathless, shaken.

"You okay?"

"Sure." Her voice was tremulous. She was not sure at all.

"I'm here." And here was where he needed to stay.

"You're awake."

"Thinking about you." He shouldn't have said that. "I knew you'd be anxious."

"I'm fine. Go back to bed." She was not a convincing actress.

"It's only rain, Carrie. No tornadoes. No danger."

"Okay. Go back to sleep."

"You sure you're all right?"

"Yes. Good night." She clicked off.

He held the phone against his chest, holding Carrie there, too.

Her bravado was for his benefit. She knew he was tired.

With a sigh, he left the room and padded barefoot down the quiet lighted hall. Thunder rumbled, and lightning flared.

Either that or his heart was on fire. A storm brewed beneath his rib cage.

At her door, he tapped softly. She yanked it open without even asking who knocked, her eyes wide and skin pale.

"Hayden?" she squeaked.

He stepped inside the dimly lit room and drew her to his chest. "It's okay. Everything will be okay."

"I wouldn't have bothered you," she murmured, trembling against him.

"You couldn't bother me, Carrie." He smiled, aching.

He'd known he would end up in her arms, finding solace in his gentle, lovely sparrow even as she drew from him.

She tilted her face and kissed his jaw. "Thank you."

In return, he kissed her nose, her forehead and finally the lips he'd thought of for hours tonight. "I'm here."

He always wanted to be here for her, a fantasy he could only manufacture in a book.

He couldn't write love stories any more than he could live them.

There could be no happy-ever-after for Hayden Winters.

Her small hands stroked his back, and she clung to him as thunder rolled.

"I wouldn't want to be with anyone else," she said. "You make me safe."

His last thread of control splintered and cracked like lightning. He made her safe.

Carrie owned him, tortured him with her exquisite goodness. He closed his eyes and battled against his raging heart.

He swallowed the knot of near painful tenderness. "I never want you to be afraid. You're too…important to me."

A beat passed as rain pattered the windows, and Hayden fought to be the man Carrie deserved.

"Truly?" Her words were breathy and hesitant and full of longing.

He cupped her precious face in his hands and drowned in eyes of espresso brown, knowing he was lost.

"Very special," he murmured.

"I love you," she whispered, killing him.

This could only end badly.

"I know," he murmured as he pulled her even closer, hating himself. Loving her. "I know."

It would take all the strength he had to be the man she needed, the man he wanted to be…because of her.

CHAPTER THIRTY-FOUR

*Where mercy, love, and pity dwell
There God is dwelling too.*

—William Blake

HAYDEN WAS GONE. Again.

Carrie read the note he'd slipped under her door and wanted to cry. Instead of the flowery phrases her heart longed for the note was short and efficient.

> My mother is much better this morning. The crisis is past. I've settled your hotel bill already. No need to concern yourself. Go home to Honey Ridge, and I'll be there soon.

And he'd signed it *H*.

She didn't even know when he'd left her room last night. But as the night's events played through her head, she vacillated between happiness and despair.

He hadn't said he loved her, but she thought he did. Everything in his caring, in his kisses and in the tender way he'd held her through the storm and talked until she'd fallen asleep said he loved her.

But now he was gone, leaving her out of his life, pushing her away after she'd bared her soul to him. She'd told him about Simon, about the stormy evening when Simon's wife had accosted her in public and shattered her illusions of love.

Love meant Hayden.

Hayden hadn't seemed the least bit shocked that she'd consorted with a married man, had loved him and been humiliated in return. Hayden had simply held her and whispered assurances and made remarks about the brainless idiot who hadn't seen her worth. He'd even made her laugh when he promised to dispatch Simon in a future book.

She'd told him she loved him. Not once but twice.

Now he was gone, and last night's whispered words seemed cold. Had she humiliated herself yet again?

She'd been the bold one, following him to Kentucky. She'd thrown herself into his arms and pledged her love.

"Thanks a lot, Nikki." Maybe taking a chance wasn't such a good thing after all.

She battled her insecurities, wishing Hayden had awakened her, wishing he would text or call and reassure her that all was well. That she wasn't the biggest fool in the world.

Maybe she was. Maybe she should go home, and if Hayden followed her, she'd know he returned her feelings.

Throat tight and heart hurting, she packed her bags and called a cab. As she leaned forward to ask the cabbie to take her to the airport, a fierce energy gripped her.

She was tired of being Carrie, the easily frightened sparrow, the mouse who squeaked, the scaredy-cat who shivered and hid beneath the covers.

She squared her shoulders, took a deep breath and said, "University Hospital, please."

DORA LEE WAS not only awake; she was in full screaming, fighting, cursing mode.

Hayden stood at her bedside, trying to break the news. Maybe he should have waited for another time when he was less vulnerable, when his heart and thoughts weren't torn in two directions.

But the hospital team thought now was the time to make the move and that he should be the one to break the news.

"It will go down easier coming from someone she cares about," the social worker had said.

Hayden hadn't known what to say to such a gross misstatement.

Dora Lee was outraged, as he'd known she'd be, but he'd signed the paperwork for her to be committed to a private rehabilitation center for addicts. The move would cost him dearly in more ways than one. She'd hate him for this.

Dora Lee had always hated him anyway.

"You can't stick me in a nuthouse," she said, her voice rising. "I'm not crazy. I just need my medicine."

She looked wild today, her blond hair sticking out in every direction and her eyes hollow from illness, hollow and furious. A heart monitor kept rhythm with her anger while IV fluids dripped into her dehydrated veins.

His own heart beat with anxiety.

"Rosewood isn't a nuthouse. It's a recovery center where you can receive treatment for your addictions."

"I don't want any treatment. I won't go, and no one

can force me." She shot a hateful glare at Hayden. "Not even you. It's illegal."

"No, it isn't," he said tiredly, knowing the explosion of hatred was about to spew all over this room.

Her eyes narrowed in her pale, yellowed face. "What are you talking about? What have you done behind my back?"

"Because of the overdose, you aren't considered competent to make your own decisions. You're a drug addict, Dora Lee. You need help."

Not that he believed for one second that a rehab program would fix Dora Lee, but the psychiatric care couldn't hurt. He had to do *something*.

She pointed a shaky finger. "You're having me locked away? You?"

"It's in your best interest."

She turned on him then, in all the fury she'd used against the boy he'd once been. He fought not to cower as he'd done then.

Hayden tried to tune out the filth and vitriol as she cursed him, demeaned him, hated him with words he wouldn't even write in his books.

He stuck to the mantra he'd practiced since making the decisions with the medical team. "You need help, Dora Lee."

"You have no idea what you're talking about. You and your high-living lifestyle, sneering at me because of the pills."

"And the meth," he said quietly, wanting all the cards on the table. "You've been an addict as long as I can remember. It makes you mean and cruel."

"Oh, and now that you're a big shot, this is payback. Is that it? You're getting back at me."

He sighed, pinching the bridge of his nose. "I only want to help."

"Then get out of my life. Get out of my business."

He stepped closer but not close enough for her to hit him. He was done with that.

He didn't know why he couldn't let it go. Only a miracle would change Dora Lee, and she didn't want one.

"I wish I could, but you're my mother."

Dora Lee's laugh was bitter and ugly, rising into delirium. "You stupid, stupid fool. You're as stupid as *her*, as stupid as your father was for thinking I'd ever love his bastard child."

Hayden's blood chilled. "What did you say?"

"That's right, Mr. Important. You're nothing but a filthy bastard. Your daddy thought he was so smart, sneaking around with that Townsend girl, and when she died in childbirth, he brought her squalling brat to me, the wife he should have been faithful to."

Hayden's ears buzzed. He stared at the woman with the nasty mouth and drug-ravished body. She wasn't his mother?

"I'm not your son?" Numbness crept over him. "Then why—"

She laughed again, harsher, more bitter and angry. "Because he had to be punished. Every single day, he paid penance for what he did behind my back. He bought my pills, doted on my headaches, anything as long as I took care of his kid."

Like a prizefighter staggering from the final blow, Hayden wagged his head back and forth. His mouth had gone dry as sand. "But you didn't."

She wasn't his mother?

"I was always nice when he was home, wasn't I?"

Her eyes were conniving and evil. "He loved me once, you know. Promised to build me a house and take me to wonderful places if I'd marry him."

He couldn't believe this. It had to be another crazy, convoluted dream.

"Did you ever...care about him all?"

"He had a good job. That was enough." Her mouth twisted. "Then he up and died and all I had left was his slut's kid."

"You had lovers. You always had lovers even when he was alive." Her betrayal of his hardworking father had wounded and embarrassed him, but he'd never told a soul. Especially his daddy.

Dora Lee sneered, voice malevolent, her body shaking from weakness and the need for drugs. "A woman gets lonely when a man works all the time. After what he did, I had a right."

The shock went on and on, reverberating through him in waves that nearly staggered him. In his wildest dreams, he'd never imagined she wasn't his mother.

"You hated me. Why didn't you give me up when he died?" Foster care couldn't have been worse than Dora Lee.

She made a derisive noise. "Are you that much of a fool? You were worth money. If I dumped you, I lost my meal ticket."

And her drug money.

"Daddy's Social Security check." He stepped closer, seeing her for what she was, a heartless, selfish woman. She'd used and abused him as a boy and even as a man. And he'd let her out of some primal need for a mother's love. Love that didn't reside inside a woman like Dora Lee.

"You always hated me, didn't you?"

Her eyes narrowed to slits. "Hated you then. Hate you now."

She wasn't his mother.

A strange kind of freedom unfurled deep in his midsection, rising like a flag on a war-torn island. She was not his mother. He was not her son. He was battle scarred and weary, but now he was free.

Free to choose. For himself. For her.

"Hate me all you want, Dora Lee, but you're still going to rehab."

She screeched obscenities, lunging to rake at him with her fingernails.

He jerked back but not before she'd drawn blood.

He stared down at the red droplets. The bedside pitcher struck him in the chest. Water sluiced over his shirt, chilling him, though not nearly as much as her vile hatred.

"Get out. You worthless scum. You're nothing to me. Nothing, you hear! I never want to see your face again."

With all the dignity he could muster and jaw tight, Hayden quietly said, "I think that can be arranged."

Blood racing in his head until he thought he might pass out, Hayden moved to the door. Vile words pummeled him as she polluted the air with her screams and curses and threats.

His mind whirled with the revelation and with the relief running through his veins. He was not her son. He didn't know who he was, but he didn't carry Dora Lee's heartless, addictive, demented genetic code.

Perhaps he could put the past behind him now and pretend it had never existed. Dora Lee would be out of his life. He wasn't her son.

Maybe he could become the man Carrie thought he was after all.

Stunned but relieved and hopeful, he stepped out into the hallway…and bumped into Carrie.

From the horrified expression on her pale face, she'd heard every crude, repulsive word. Could hear them still.

The world tumbled in on him.

She knew the truth about him, about his ugly past, about Dora Lee. There could be no starting over. He saw it in her shocked eyes. She knew he'd lied. She knew and was both stunned and disgusted.

What was left of his battered heart shattered into a million pieces, crushed like pavement glass after a car accident.

He'd lost her. And in her, he'd lost everything good he'd ever wished for.

Whether he was Dora Lee's blood kin or not, the vile woman in that hospital bed had raised him, and the son of a pillbilly would never be good enough for clean and wholesome Carrie.

She'd trusted him with her heart, with her words of love, and he'd lied to her. She'd believed in him, had faced her terror of flying to be with him in his time of need, and he'd given her this in return.

"You heard."

"Yes." Her fingers touched her lips, soft, soft lips he'd kissed many times and longed to kiss again, to promise that all of this was a nightmare. "Oh, Hayden—"

Harshly, he cut her off. "Go home. I never wanted you to know." Then, as shame coursed through his body, he said more gently, "I don't expect you to be able to deal with this. God knows I barely can."

Her eyes searched his, and he read the shock, the hurt, the questions and finally the resolve.

She hated him now. The cold set of jaw, the anger that flared in her eyes.

"Carrie," he started, aware he could never explain away Dora Lee or the past five minutes.

Carrie wasn't listening anyway. She turned away from him. His heart cracked.

"Excuse me a moment," she said, back as stiff as her tone.

Then she shoved open the door to Dora Lee's room and marched inside.

CARRIE SHOOK ALL over and prayed her knees wouldn't give way.

She had never been so angry in her life.

"You have no right," she said, marching up to the scrawny blonde woman lying in the bed.

The woman's lip curled. "Who are you?"

"I'm the woman who loves your…" Carrie faltered. This washed-out, drug-addicted woman was not Hayden's mother even though he'd believed she was. "Hayden," she finished. "You have no business speaking to him in such a tone."

"Get out of my room."

"I'm not leaving until I have my say. Hayden is one of the finest men I've ever known. When he learned of your illness, he rushed to your side. He's been distraught with concern. Then you dump something like this on him. And you scream horrible, nasty cruelties."

"You don't know anything."

"Maybe not, but I won't allow you to hurt him. Never again." She leaned close enough to point a determined, though shaky, finger. "Do you hear me? Never!"

The woman slapped at her, eyes shooting daggers. Satisfied she'd made her point, Carrie whirled and marched out into the hall and right up to Hayden.

"And now you." She poked her finger into his chest. "Why didn't you tell me?"

"I thought—"

"You thought I'd turn away, that I'd judge you by something you can't help?"

He blew out a breath. "In a nutshell, yes."

"I wouldn't have."

He was already shaking his head, denying her claim.

"I'm a fake, Carrie. I'm not Hayden Winters, the suave bestseller from a classy upbringing." He touched his chest, mocking himself. "My college degree? A fabrication like the rest of my history. I was raised in the worst kind of poverty and neglect by an abusive, addicted woman who hated me." He huffed. "You heard the rest."

Carrie's tone gentled. The pointed finger became a tender hand flattened against his heaving chest, stroking, consoling.

"She's not your mother, and you are no more a fake than I am. You're a dear and caring man who befriended a hurting boy, a man who is determined to do the right thing for that awful woman in there even though she's mistreated you so terribly. That's the man I love."

Hayden wrapped his hand over hers. "You can't be serious. I have no right to believe—"

"You have every right."

"What you said in there to Dora Lee, I'm— I don't know what to say. You're incredible, brave, beautiful."

She cupped his jaw with one hand, no longer the frightened sparrow spooked by the slightest wind. "A woman who doesn't stand up for those she loves is not much of a woman."

"Then you're some kind of woman, Carrie Riley, and I'm a very fortunate man."

She stepped into his chest and wrapped her slender arms around him, holding him while he digested the past few minutes that had changed his life.

"I'm so sorry for what you've been through," she whispered. "I can't imagine."

No, she couldn't.

"If you ever want to tell me—" She left the offer hanging. So like Carrie not to push, not to pry, which made her bold confrontation with Dora Lee so much more meaningful.

She loved him. Real love. The kind that stood up for what was right and didn't back down.

He was awed, humbled…and determined to silence his childhood once and for all. He would tell her. He would trust her. Carrie deserved no less than all of him.

Dora Lee had held him captive since infancy, and he had one more thing to do before he was fully free.

"There's somewhere I have to go," he said softly, though dread laced the determination racing through him. "Will you go with me? I want you to know all of it."

"I'll go anywhere with you, Hayden. Anytime."

Hayden hoped he could prepare her as well as himself for what was to come. Like Thaddeus, he was about to run into the fire. He hoped they both survived.

CHAPTER THIRTY-FIVE

Being deeply loved by someone gives you strength, while loving someone deeply gives you courage.

—Lao Tzu

1867

THE HOUSE STIFLED her tonight. Sitting in the parlor while Charlotte and Will made eyes at each other annoyed her. Not even sweet Benjamin's offer to play chess had improved her mood, so Josie had retired to her bedroom to sulk.

She'd made her decision. Her conscience was happier and Margaret would be, too. A loyal Confederate did not lollygag with a Federal soldier, no matter how handsome he might be and how much poetry he quoted with such lovely eloquence. The words clung to her heart like honey to a spoon.

Josie took the scrimshaw hairbrush that had once belonged to her mother and wandered out on the veranda to brush her hair the requisite hundred strokes.

Thad's eyes had gleamed when he'd seen her hair hanging down her back.

Closing her eyes to remember that last wonderful moment before she'd tossed him out like yesterday's dishwater, she filled her lungs with the honeysuck-led night.

Her eyes snapped open. She didn't smell honey-suckle. She smelled smoke!

On the horizon, a terrifying glow lit the sky over the gristmill.

Her heart stopped. "Thad."

She raced down the stairs, screaming like a banshee. "Fire! The mill's on fire!"

Before the shocked faces in the parlor could react, she bolted out the door, jerked her skirts thigh high and dashed like a jackrabbit through the field.

The closer she got to the mill, the brighter the light glowed against the black horizon.

With every thought she alternately prayed and chanted his name.

Thad. Thad. Thad.

Flying over the weeds, heedless of the sticks and stumps and brambles tearing at her clothes and skin, she made the mill road in time to see a figure dart in-side the burning mill.

"Thad!" she screamed, breath short, gasping for air. "No. No! Thaddeus!"

But her cries came too late. He was gone.

Her beloved Thaddeus who feared nothing on this earth except fire was inside a living inferno.

Terror sliced her heart open like a bayonet.

She sprinted toward the creek and waded in, ripping off her petticoats as she soaked herself head to toe. She tore the garment into two strips, wrapped one around her face and head and shoved the other for Thad into her bodice.

Dripping wet, she raced back up the incline…and into the mill.

Smoke and heat slammed her backward. She gasped, stumbled.

No one could survive in there for long.

She removed the cloth. Smoke gagged her. She coughed raggedly and screamed, "Thad!" and then slapped the petticoat against her mouth again.

Except for the flames shooting from the back, a deeper darkness than anything she'd ever seen enveloped her. She followed the flares, praying, pleading, mind chanting her love as if love alone was strong enough to douse a fire.

Halfway to the storeroom, she saw him. He stumbled, nearly fell atop a sack he dragged. No sack of corn was that valuable.

She pressed closer. Heat seared through the wet dress as she saw with a terrible knowing.

He didn't drag a corn sack. He dragged a human.

Thad stumbled to one knee and coughed, weaving as if he'd collapse.

Josie rushed to him and yanked the wet petticoat from her bodice and wrapped it around his face. He nodded his gratitude and pointed toward the inert figure on the floor.

With a nod of comprehension, she ripped away her face protection and quickly wrapped it around the man's face.

Thad grabbed her hand, tried to stop her. She pushed him away and reached for the fallen man's wrist. "Help me."

Smoke choked her immediately. She sucked in tiny draughts of air, fighting the cough, eyes streaming.

Thad struggled to his feet and took the other wrist. Together they dragged the limp body over the bumpy boards, across the threshold and out into the fresh air.

Shouts and lanterns circled the mill and filled the night. Men and woman, a dozen of them, formed two bucket brigades from the creek to the burning edifice.

Thad and Josie collapsed on the grass. Unfamiliar hands pressed water on them and took over care of the fallen man.

In the lamplight, Josie recognized the unconscious figure and gasped. "Freddy Stockton."

They went to the same church. She'd known him all her life. And yet he'd done this to her family's mill?

Beside her Thad struggled to stand, face soot covered and grim, eyes running. Hands pushed at him to stay down, and Will's dear Yankee face appeared. "Rest now, cousin. We'll take care of the mill."

But the stubborn miller stumbled toward the bucket brigade, and Josie pushed wearily upward to follow. If a man covered in burn scars and exhausted from a smoky rescue could battle her family's fire, so could she.

More people arrived, farmers and townsfolk, and in a short time, the flames were beaten down and the sheriff, at a word from Thad, hauled away the young fire starter with a promise to find Jim Swartz and learn the names of the other hooded figures.

"I heard about their sort," Sheriff Williams said. "They're burning out folks and stirring trouble over Pulaski way. We don't tolerate that behavior in Honey Ridge."

For a while, folks stood around talking, exclaiming shock over the event and relief that no one was killed. Finally, the weary group began to scatter.

Josie stood beside Thaddeus. She reeked of smoke, and so did he. She didn't care. He was alive. Her prayers had been answered, this time with a yes.

"You coulda let that boy burn to a crisp and been in your rights," a man said to Thad.

Thad shook his head. "No, Slim, I could not."

"Then you're a better man than most."

"Pitts always was a liar." Slim rested a hand on Thad's shoulder. "Maybe we were wrong about you, Eriksson."

Voices muttered, some like Slim with a cautious new respect for the Yankee, while others simply drifted away.

They'd all been wrong, especially her. The realization cramped Josie's belly.

She'd rejected a good and honorable man who would risk his life for another while she'd considered Jim Swartz a friend, a Southerner like her...and he'd set fire to her livelihood.

She turned her head and coughed, the taste of humility stronger than the smoke.

The scattered words of some long-ago sermon tumbled through her thoughts. Or maybe Charlotte had read it to her and only now did the words make sense. There is neither Jew nor Gentile, slave nor free, male nor female: for ye are all one.

North nor South, she added. Yankee nor Reb.

A man's character wasn't determined by the circumstances of his birth.

Oh, Thad. I was so very wrong.

The weary crowd slowly dissipated until only Thad and Josie remained beneath the stars to stare at the yawning black hole in the rear of the mill.

"At least we didn't lose everything," Thad said.

Even if the mill was a total loss, *her* everything had survived.

Gritty-eyed and smelling of smoke so strong she'd never be able to sleep, she collapsed in exhaustion on the creek bank. Thad tumbled down beside her.

Weary beyond words, they lay on the cool, wet grass for long moments. Josie listened to him breathe, grateful beyond reason that he still could.

The old mill snapped and something fell. Neither turned to look.

"I was wrong, Thaddeus," she murmured into the smoky night above. "Tom is dead. I am not."

Margaret might never forgive her, and Josie would mourn their friendship, but tonight had changed her forever. She could not deny the truth any more than she could deny her love for Thaddeus.

He remained still, and she thought he might have fallen asleep until at last he spoke. "You hate Yankees."

There is no Jew or Gentile...

"You can no more change where you were born or who you are than I can."

"I think I've heard that somewhere." Tired amusement laced his words.

He'd said those very words to her, hadn't he? "I'm eating humble pie. Will you make me choke on it?"

"No. No." Thad's voice deepened, serious now. His hand found hers in the darkness. "You saved my life."

She'd nearly lost him. Because of men she'd trusted more than the man she loved. She couldn't bear to speak of it.

"You'd have managed fine and dandy without me," she said. "We did, however, spare that *stupid* boy, for which he and his gossipy mother should be eternally grateful."

Would Mamie Stockton change her sanctimonious views? Not likely, but perhaps others would see what the old gossip could not.

Thad rolled his head toward her and, smile tired, voice husky from smoke, murmured, "A team like us should stick together. I love you, Josephine."

A giggle, completely inappropriate considering the night's events, rose up in her chest. A giggle of relief, of joy.

In a single move, she rolled on top of him. Her riotous curls, wet and stinky, dripped onto his soot-covered face, and she kissed him.

The only part of him that moved was his lips. Hot and soft and smoky.

Teasing and so tender inside she wanted to cry, Josie asked, "Was that a proposal?"

His arms wrapped around her, heavy in their fatigue, but loving, too. His blue eyes, so tired and red, twinkled. "If it was, will you accept…or cut out my tongue?"

With a mischievous bounce of eyebrows, she trailed a finger across his lips. "I can think of better uses for that tongue of yours."

"Is that a fact? Why, Miss Portland, you shock me."

The ornery fire that had gotten her into all kinds of trouble flared up. She leaned closer, voice lowered.

"Then, my beloved Mr. Eriksson, allow me to shock you further." She touched her mouth to his, whispering, "I love you, too."

There on the banks of Magnolia Creek with the stars occluded by smoke, Josie let go of hatred and anger and prejudice. She didn't care if Thaddeus was Yank or Reb. His heart was good, and he was hers.

Life as they'd both known it was gone forever, but men and women like them would build a new South.

It was time to put aside the past, to forget what came before and to let the future begin.

CHAPTER THIRTY-SIX

It's no use going back to yesterday because I was a different person then.

—Lewis Carroll

Present

THE DRIVE FROM Louisville took less than three hours, but the place where Hayden grew up might as well have been on another planet.

Carrie was struck by miles and miles of little except nature's beauty. They passed through tiny towns with only a post office or a gas station and past empty, leaning houses and rusted school buses not far from lovely homes and modern schools—a contrast in lifestyles she'd not seen before.

As the rental, a Jeep this time, took the hairpin curves and sharp inclines up into the far reaches of the Appalachians, Hayden's hands tightened on the wheel and he grew less and less inclined for conversation.

She felt his anxiety, though he still hadn't told her why he needed to return to the place of his childhood. Not that the reason mattered. He'd asked her to come. He needed her support.

"The countryside is breathtaking, Hayden," Carrie said from the passenger seat. "Look at the leaves and the colors."

Fog the color of Hayden's eyes hung over the mountains, a stunning frame for the autumn spectacle.

"I forget about this sometimes, about how beautiful it can be and what a wonderful place it is for some." He rubbed at his chin, pensive. "Not all of Appalachia shared my experiences. I understand that on an intellectual level. There's good here as well as the ugly and evil."

"As there is everywhere."

"But the bad sticks in my head. In my heart."

It was the most revealing thing she'd heard him say, and she understood, at least a little. Her betrayal by a man she hadn't known was married had clouded her view of relationships and had stuck in her heart, as Dora Lee's abuse had stuck in his.

He hadn't told her everything, but enough that she knew his childhood had been a nightmare and he'd used his storytelling gift to escape.

Thank God he'd had that.

They parked in front of a badly rusted and listing trailer with plastic over the windows and trash littering the yard.

They got out of the car and crossed the obstacle course of clutter and stepped up on a porch so rickety she worried about falling through.

Hayden pushed open the door, and they went inside.

Unwashed dishes and pans and carryout cartons piled the table, the sink, the stove. Ashtrays filled with cigarette butts sent up a stench that mingled with the disturbing smell of rotted food and mouse droppings. Trash and clothes spilled out everywhere, and bits and pieces of broken furniture crowded the tiny space. There was hardly a walkway from the door to the inside.

"Home sweet home."

The bottom fell out of her stomach. Hayden had lived here?

"This was my life, Carrie. This is who I am." Shame filled his eyes. "You deserve to know who I really am."

She shook her head. "Do you think this matters to me? You were a helpless child, Hayden. You couldn't help what happened to you any more than Brody could."

"There's something else I want to show you. Something I have to reconcile once and for all."

She tilted her head, saw the dread and something else in his face. Hayden was afraid.

Reaching for his hand, she offered her most confident and loving smile. "Together."

LITTLE BY LITTLE, Carrie was setting him free.

Hayden was still stunned and thrilled that she hadn't walked out on him at the hospital. No matter how many times he apologized for leaving her at the hotel and for the lies, he knew he'd failed.

He didn't want to fail her anymore.

If they were to have any chance for a relationship, she deserved the whole truth. He loved her enough to give her the one thing he'd never given anyone else. Himself.

But to live in truth for the future, he had to resolve his past. All of it.

Hand in hand, with his belly trembling but his head determined, they walked behind the trailer and down the steep grassy incline toward the place of his torture. When the well came into sight, he paused to calm his thrumming pulse and catch his breath.

How many times had he stood here so terrified that he couldn't breathe?

The well had held him captive for far too long.

"What a picturesque old well," she said. "Did your family use this for water?"

Picturesque? He tried to see the round rock structure through her eyes. Tried and failed. "I hate this place."

"Why?"

He drew in a strengthening breath and started down the incline. When he came to the well, it seemed a harmless hole of water rocked up the sides with an overhead crossbar where once hung a rusted old bucket and a well rope.

He refused to let it frighten him ever again.

"Dora Lee…drowned things here. Things that annoyed her."

Carrie gasped, hand to her mouth. "She did *what*?"

"I think she enjoyed playing her sick game of omnipotence. A mouse. A bird. A rabbit. She'd hold me by the arms and make me watch them swim and claw and struggle until they died, all the while threatening to drown me, too."

"Hayden! That's heinous."

"Isn't it?"

He turned to her then, wanting to pull her close and forget this odyssey into his childhood but knowing he must purge the past to ever be completely free.

"That's not the worst of it."

"You don't have to talk about this unless you want to."

"I don't want to. I *need* to." He sucked an audible breath through his teeth. "It isn't pretty."

She touched his arm, soft brown eyes full of compassion. "Then tell me, Hayden. What happened here that hurt you so terribly? Let me help you carry it."

He'd carried his past and the memories of Dora Lee's abuse like a weight that grew heavier with each passing year. At Carrie's quiet offer, the burden seemed to ease. That was the magic of Carrie's love. He could tell her. He knew intuitively that he could trust her with everything. Even with Hayden Briggs.

No wonder he'd fallen in love with her.

He sighed, the sound mingling with the sigh of the breeze blowing through the red-and-yellow leaves. It was indeed beautiful here with fall flowers coloring the grass and birds singing in the trees. Nothing here could harm him anymore.

"She drowned my dog here, too," he said, throat tight with memory. "I fought her that day, and when Blackie Boy could swim no more and went under for the last agonizing time…" He hesitated, still seeing the last desperate bubbles rise and fade. "She shoved me into the well with him. I was nine."

"Oh, dear Lord. That's despicable. How did you survive?"

"She finally threw down a rope, but not before I'd gone under enough times to satisfy her fury. After that, I knew she hated me enough to let me die."

"But you thrived instead."

He gazed at her. With wonder in his tone, he admitted what he'd never considered before, what she made him see. "I guess I did."

"You survived. You overcame and you thrived. You became the good and decent, amazing, gifted, successful man you are today in spite of enduring her unspeakable evil. She scarred you, but she didn't ruin you."

"I never looked at it that way. I thought—"

"You thought people would judge you by her."

"Yes." He saw now, through Carrie's eyes and wisdom, how wrong he'd been. Some might have looked down on him, but those that mattered wouldn't have. He would never shout his past from the rooftops, but he didn't have to be a slave to it, either.

A warm sun broke through the misty fog as the clouds of the past lifted from his life.

Words from his dreams came back to him. He could no more change where he was born, who raised him or what had happened to him here than Thaddeus could change his Yankee roots. Like Thad and Josie, he had risen above his roots, and if he was the man he wanted to be, the man Carrie believed he was, he would stick around to help Brody do the same.

So that's what the dreams had been trying to tell him.

The past, his roots, did not define him. Nor did they control his future.

A bird fluttered to a landing on top of the well's crossbar and lifted her head in song.

He watched the small warbler, letting the breeze cleanse him, letting go of the pain. The scars, like Thad's, would remain, but he would use them as stepping-stones instead of stumbling blocks.

"Are you all right?" Carrie asked gently, her eyes

searching his, concerned and full of a love that humbled him.

"More than all right." He gazed tenderly at the woman who'd changed him, who'd given him the courage to be himself, who loved him anyway.

Her mouth curved, and he bent to kiss it. Sweet and soft and giving like her. "I love you, Carrie."

The words he'd never said to anyone else in his life were the final catharsis.

With an arm draped over Carrie's shoulders, he turned to stare at the well and imagined he saw the sad, frightened boy he'd once been standing there, waiting for him. Whether in his spirit or his mind, he didn't know, but he beckoned to the child, watched the tattered, battered Hayden break away from the well and walk toward him.

When the child stood before him, Hayden smiled a welcome, and Hayden Briggs, the hurting boy, melded into Hayden Winters, the damaged man.

And he was no longer a figment of his own imagination.

EPILOGUE

BRODY THOMSON HEARD his father come inside the house. It was Friday. He'd always hated Fridays.

"Brody!"

Brody ran the comb through his hair once more and then slapped at the cowlick before giving up and going to greet his father. Things were different since they'd learned about Mama. Daddy was going to AA and anger management, and he hadn't been drunk in a long time. Miss Carrie told him to give the old man a chance.

Still, out of long habit, he paused in the doorway, gauging his father's mood.

His dad stood in the center of the living room, clear-eyed and steady in his blue work shirt.

"You're home from work early," Brody said. What he meant was that his father hadn't gone to the bar on Second Street, and his daddy knew it.

"I don't do that anymore, son."

Brody nodded once in acknowledgment.

His father shifted on his work boots, nervous-like and kind of awkward. The way Brody felt when he had to give an oral report in front of the whole class.

"I been thinking, Brody. I talked to that counselor and learned some stuff." He huffed a short laugh, like something was funny but it wasn't. "I made a lot of mistakes in my time. Treated you bad. Treated your mama bad. I did wrong."

Brody swallowed, unsure of what to say.

"That lizard you had—"

"Max."

"Yeah. Max. I shouldn't have done that." He cleared his throat. "So, what I'm trying to say is, if you'd be wanting to get another lizard or maybe a pup or something, I'd be okay with it."

Hope rising faster than a hot air balloon on a windy day, Brody said, "You mean it? A puppy? Could he sleep in my room?"

His dad rubbed his whiskers and made a scrapey sound. "I guess that would be fine. If you train him and take care of him."

"I will. I promise." He was breathless with excitement so that he felt as if his heart was going to jump right out of his chest. *A puppy. A real puppy.*

"How about tomorrow? We could go down to the shelter and take a look."

The tension left Brody's shoulders. This was real. Really real. "You're not ever going to drink again— are you, Daddy?"

His father licked his lips, but his eyes remained steady. "Two months without a drop. I won't stop now. I promise you, son. You and me, we're a family. We had fun on that fishing trip, didn't we?"

A grin snuck up on Brody's mouth. They'd rented a boat, and Daddy brought pop instead of beer. And they'd caught a mess of catfish for supper. "Yes, sir."

"You're just like your sweet mama. Good to the bone. I got some pictures of her and you put up. That preacher down at the church said it was time I dealt with it. I know he's right. Want to see them?"

Brody's throat thickened with tears. "Yes, sir. I sure do."

"All right, then. Let's order a pizza for supper." His father draped an arm around him and tugged him close. "And I'll tell you about the finest woman I ever knew."

Brody sighed against his father. Fridays weren't so bad after all.

ON A MILD December Saturday, with the antebellum parlor of Peach Orchard Inn draped in tulle, bedazzled with white lights and candles and filled with family and close friends, the beautiful innkeeper Julia Presley pledged her troth to a resplendent Eli Donovan.

In a pink-peach gown accented with gold and white, she'd floated down the staircase, seeing only one person in the room of many. Eli gazed up at her, love in his eyes strong enough to weather anything. Beside him stood Alex, his son, in a matching black tux, the ring box in his hand.

It was a beautiful ceremony full of joy.

Hayden sat on the bride's side of the double row of white chairs next to Carrie, feeling more at home here among these new acquaintances than anywhere he'd ever been. He glanced at Carrie's profile, crediting her. Home was wherever she was.

She turned her head, smiling, and his chest swelled to know this beautiful, smart woman loved both Hayden Briggs and Hayden Winters. He'd always wondered how loving and being loved would feel.

It felt better than he'd imagined.

She filled the emptiness inside him, lit the dark

places and completed him in ways he hadn't known were possible.

He took her hand and tugged it to his thigh, holding her there, needing to be close, as he alternated between watching Carrie and observing the tender exchange of vows.

When Julia and Eli kissed to seal their love and then bent to kiss Alex on opposite cheeks, applause sounded. Tears streamed down Julia's face, and Alex hugged her before Eli pulled her up to wipe away her tears and kiss her again. Tenderly, sweetly, and with the passion of a man grateful for the love of his woman. A sigh ran through the crowd.

Hayden understood that kind of gratitude.

Afterward, as the wedding party made their way outside to the reception tent near Michael's garden, Hayden and Carrie followed.

"Beautiful, wasn't it?" Her eyelashes glimmered with happy tears.

"Love does that," he said.

"Makes everything beautiful?"

"Heals the hurt that's gone before." He paused on the back veranda. Soft inside from the romantic ceremony, he needed a moment just for the two of them. "You did that for me."

"I never want anything to hurt you again." Her fingertips caressed his face and sent a shiver of pleasure through him. "I love you too much."

He covered her hand with his, loving her touch. "Words aren't big enough, Carrie. Even *love* doesn't seem strong enough for what I feel for you."

"A writer without words." She smiled into his eyes. "Did you finish the book?"

"Emailed to my editor this morning. Maybe Josie and Thaddeus will leave me alone now."

"Your dad would be pleased."

"I think so, too. Maybe a little embarrassed. He was a quiet, humble man, but I'm proud to be his son. I want to honor him."

He'd worried about changing genres and destroying his suspense career, but Carrie had encouraged him to write the historical book under his father's name and continue writing his thrillers as Hayden Winters. His agent and editor loved the idea, though both had been surprised that the very private author would take such a step of revelation.

He wouldn't have without Carrie. Seeing her reaction to Dora Lee, feeling her love wrap around him in that crucial moment gave him strength to do what he thought he couldn't.

"It may not sell more than a dozen copies." Sales mattered, but they weren't everything. Not this time. He was doing this for his dad. And the dream people.

She laughed gently, lovingly mocking his uncertainty. "It's marvelous. Of course it will sell."

"I'm grateful to them. Josie and Thad." He gave her a glance, knowing she'd understand. "If not for them…"

"I like that they came to you to tell their story. Not that I understand how it happened."

"You don't think I'm a little left of center because I somehow connected to a couple that lived more than a hundred years ago?" This time he teased. He was no longer worried about losing his sanity, not with Carrie to balance him.

"If not for the dreams, you might have been stuck in

your past forever. Alone. And I would have lost you."
She draped her arms around his neck. "You needed
their message, Hayden. You needed to accept yourself
and let go of the past, just as Josie had to accept Thaddeus and let go of hers."

"I needed them, and they needed me to share their
story, as bizarre as that sounds."

"Will you write the missing-wife thriller now?"

"That's the plan, and with a twist you won't see
coming."

She tilted her head. "Like what?"

"You'll have to buy the book to find out."

"Hayden!" She laughed and pulled away. "I can't
wait that long."

He caught her hand and tugged her back. "I'm going
to New York next week on business. If you come with
me, I'll tell you."

"Bribery. I like it."

"So you will?"

"You know I hate airplanes."

"Me, too. Let's hate them together." He rocked her
back and forth in his arms to the slow melody float-
ing out of the reception tent. "The city is beautiful all
dressed up for Christmas. I want to show it to you."

"We could see the Rockettes?"

"Anything you want."

"You," she breathed. "All I want is you."

"You have me. Body and soul and warped mind."
He touched his nose to hers and smiled tenderly. "I'll
buy you gardenias and chase away the storms and never
let anything scare you."

Her lips curved, igniting that one dimple. "I learned

something from Josie and Thad, too, you know. I refuse to be afraid of life anymore."

"Is that a yes?"

She gave one short nod. "New York, here we come."

"Then back home for Christmas with your family. Can't miss that."

Home. At last. A writer could work anywhere, and Hayden knew deep in his soul, he'd found his place right here in Tennessee with Carrie.

Full of wonder and gratitude and manifest joy, he pulled her close enough to feel the rhythm of her heart and kissed her, deep and long and with all the pent-up love she'd released in him.

Time stood still. The music faded. And he noticed neither cold weather nor people moving around. His whole world centered on one woman.

When the kiss ended, he held her with his eyes. No words were needed. All the loneliness, the lies and fear were gone.

Carrie's love had made him real and set him free.

* * * * *

 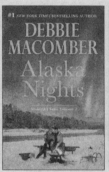 

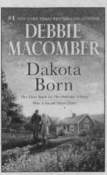  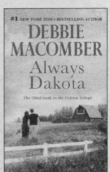